LADY OF THE REALM

LADY OF THE REALM

STRANGER MAGICS, BOOK NINE

ASH FITZSIMMONS

Print Edition ISBN: 978-1-949861-21-1

Cover design by BespokeBookCovers.com.

www.ashfitzsimmons.com

CHAPTER 1

When I was a kid, I kept a running mental list of all the things I wanted to do before I was too old to have fun—say, thirty. Convincing my parents to let me take Georgie out for a solo flight was at the top of that list, but although the dragon seemed perfectly willing, Mom wasn't so easy to persuade. Once I learned where the merrow congregated, I wanted to perfect the spell that would let me dive without a tank—the wizard's version of scuba—but Toula, my theory tutor, was leery about letting me go for a test swim and seeing how well my craft held up against the pressure. Someday, I wanted to slip back to the mortal realm and see the sights, the big cities and bright lights that I'd only read about. Then I wanted to come home, learn to sail, point my boat toward the western horizon, and see if Faerie had a firm border or simply went on into infinity.

Dropping out of high school had never made my list. Yet there I sat in Dr. Stowe's office on the Monday morning after the end of term, watching him fidget with a retractable ballpoint pen—a steel-free model, naturally—as he told me that I shouldn't return in the fall.

I hadn't flunked out. As long as I'd lived with my parents, they'd stressed the importance of a solid education in matters mundane and magical alike, and with a bit of occasional help, I'd made good grades for the last four years. I wasn't at the top of the class—that spot belonged to Fergus Go, who'd been studying entrance exams for half a dozen countries since the seventh grade—

but I brought home respectable marks, and I kept my nose clean. Ninth grade had been my best year yet: Mr. Galloway had given my sculpture second prize at the spring art show, I'd made it through the semester without burning down the chemistry lab, I could write geometry proofs in my sleep, and I'd managed to return almost all of my library books in a timely fashion. Even Dr. Stowe had given me an A on my final history paper, and he was notoriously tough, a college professor who'd never quite acclimated to high school writers.

But as of that morning, my successes over the last months were for naught.

"It's nothing Ros has done," said Dr. Stowe, pen in hand. *Click.* "I don't have to tell you she's a good kid," he added, sweeping his glance to my left and right to look at my silent parents. *Click-click.* "But under the circumstances…it would be better if she switched into independent tutoring next fall." *Click.*

At least he had the decency to look pained as he pronounced my fate.

"She has it under control," said Mom, leaning toward Dr. Stowe's book-covered desk. Our principal did many things well, but I'd yet to see his office in any state approaching tidy. "Has Ros *ever* had an accident in school?"

"No," he admitted. *Click, click, click.* "As I said, this isn't about anything she's done. No one's trying to punish her—"

"But you are," Dad interrupted. He'd folded his arms at the beginning of our meeting, and the only indication of his growing agitation was the increasing tempo of his index finger as it drummed against his bicep. "Come on, Rufus, what's she supposed to do, sit in her room for the next three years? Talk to the walls? If you want to hear about how much fun self-study is, by all means, give Aid a call. I dare you."

With a long, frustrated sigh, Dr. Stowe dropped his pen

and massaged his forehead. "I know it's not ideal, and it's not fair, but guys, I've got to consider the rest of the student body. The parents are scared."

"Our daughter is not a *threat*!" Mom protested. "If she'd hurt someone, I'd understand, but—"

"She *could*," he countered, "and that's the problem."

Mom's lips pressed into a thin white line as she chose her words. "More than half my class was mundane, and I never attacked any of them. None of us did."

"And I don't doubt that, but how many of those mundane parents would have been comfortable in the knowledge that there were wizards in their children's school, do you suppose? Especially one of your caliber, Helen? Don't you think there would have been pushback?"

"All I'm saying is that my classmates made it out with all their limbs intact. Ros's have nothing to worry about."

Dr. Stowe continued to rub his head as if that would make this situation smooth itself out. "I hear you, I really do, and I'm sympathetic. But her track record's no secret. I've had parents complaining since the day she started, and they've only become more insistent." He paused his scalp massage, then opened his desk drawer and slowly slid a piece of paper toward us across the detritus of books and notepads. "They circulated a petition last month."

Mom snatched it up before I could get a good look, but I glimpsed it long enough to see the columns of blanks at the end, each of which was filled with a signature in blue or black ink. She scowled as she read it, then passed it behind me to Dad, whose expression quickly shifted to match hers. "'Endangering our children'?" he snapped, looking back at Dr. Stowe. "You said yourself she's a good kid—"

"In a room of duds, near-duds, and a few who are fae only if you squint and use your imagination," he replied, falling into the patient tone he'd always pulled out when we didn't understand the reading. "The other parents are concerned, Joey. I can't say they're crazy."

Dad didn't buckle. "And yet, they're thrilled to leave their little darlings with you all day."

"I wouldn't say *thrilled*," said Dr. Stowe, taking up his pen again, "but they know I have a long history of not murdering students."

"You're stronger than she is."

"I'm also not a teenager, with all the hormonal delights that entails." *Click. Click-click.* "What I propose is setting up a system of tutors for Ros, someone other than the two of you who can make sure she's getting the material. I wouldn't mind meeting with her, and I know there are a few other faculty members who could be convinced to step in. Might even ask Ellie—she misses teaching, whether she admits it or not." *Click.* "Give me a couple of months to make the arrangements, and this fall, we can start private instruction."

Dr. Stowe's eyes kept darting away from mine when I tried to meet his gaze, but then again, I was the subject of the whole uncomfortable situation.

My parents were far from placated by his offer. "How's she supposed to socialize, then?" asked Mom. "She can't just hang out with her parents."

Click-click. "What about the Powell girl? They're still friendly, right?"

"Texting and the occasional video chat isn't the same as interacting with her peers on a daily basis. You know that."

His face shifted as he mentally tested responses, and then he settled on, "I'm sorry. It's the best I can do. I've got to consider the community here, and...I mean, don't get me wrong, I love having your daughter in class," he added in a rush, "but it would be best if we pursued other educational options for her."

Dad put the petition back on the desk face-down. "And what about Malcolm?" he said softly. "What are you going to do when they're collecting signatures about *your* kid, huh?"

"I don't know," he murmured, shaking his head. "But Mal's just five, and he can't enchant his way out of a wet paper bag. Maybe we'll cross that bridge in a few years, but…you know, with time, feelings could change…"

"I don't remember anyone being opposed to Ros when she took on Mulligan," said Mom, staring at Dr. Stowe until he was forced to look her way. "At the *very* least, the Fringe owes her an education."

"And she will have one," he replied. "Just through private instruction. It's best for everyone involved."

Click.

By the age of fifteen, I'd acquired something I'd never had growing up in the Arcanum silo in Montana: a support network. My parents almost always had my back—truth be told, I probably could have come home covered in blood, and their first question would have been what the other guy did to deserve it. If I wanted to talk through my problems, my uncle Aiden was good for a sympathetic ear. Gran and Pop *always* had cookies, which cured many ills, and for more difficult situations, Gran's grandmother, Liza, had an almond frosting recipe to die for.

But sometimes, a girl just needed to punch something, and when that was the case, I knew to seek out Val.

Once she was satisfied that I'd mastered the basics of shooting and shielding, Toula had pushed my magical education in more technical and esoteric directions, showing me the ever-more-complicated sides of spellcraft. But while she focused on my theory and technique, her older brother had become, more or less, my sensei, meeting me in Coileán's practice rooms during his off-hours and teaching me to spar. I didn't worry about wandering into the king's palace uninvited—through a quirk of the gnarled fae family trees, Coileán was half brother both to Aiden and to Liza's father, and in spite of my initial shyness, he'd made it clear that I was family. As a consequence, Coileán didn't protest when I showed up and pestered the captain of his guard into putting me through my paces, and Val was usually happy to oblige.

In general, young wizards are encouraged to practice sparring with well-matched opponents. Having taken up residence in the heart of Faerie, however, I had no such luxury, and so I'd gone to the other extreme. Val and I were keenly aware that he could throw me into a wall with a flick of his finger, and even my strongest shield would eventually crumble before him. But as he'd spent better than two millennia being trained and training others, he knew how to temper his blows to give me a fighting chance, an old wolf indulging the nips and growls of a rambunctious pup.

That afternoon, he worked me for two hours until I was bruised and dripping with sweat, then pulled a towel from thin air, pointed to the bench, and asked what was on my mind. He knew already, of course—I'd felt the quick flutter of his mental intrusion when I'd stormed into his cramped office—but with my anger and outrage tempered by exhaustion, he finally gave me leave to complain. Mopping my face dry, I presented the condensed version of my meeting with Dr. Stowe, then looked to him for sympathy. But to my chagrin, Val merely shrugged.

"It's the safest course," he said, passing me a water bottle. "Were I in your peers' place, I would not want you around."

"It's not *fair*," I protested.

His eyebrow quirked. "Who promised you fairness, little girl? Life is full of moments like this—make the best of them and put them behind you. And here, before your mother complains..." He waved a healing enchantment into existence over the fresh cut on my cheek.

I'd grown so accustomed to the soft tingling of my flesh knitting together that I hardly gave the enchantment a second thought. "They didn't have to sign a stupid petition," I muttered.

Val let me sulk for a moment, then said, "I have acquaintances in town, you know. Given his druthers, Coileán would probably spend every evening in Slim's bar, and Eleanor's spoken well of the restaurants. Still, we don't often go."

I frowned at him, trying to slot the non sequitur into the conversation.

"The Fringe knows what we're capable of," he continued. "The only half-bloods who spend any time in that place are the Stowes. We make the Fringers uncomfortable."

"No one here has ever attacked the Fringe—"

"It doesn't matter. Everything comes down to potential, Ros. They can rationalize their feelings all they like, but they know they're defenseless, and it frightens them. You, now—you may follow the rules, but you will always be the wizard in their midst, and on some level, they will always fear you."

"But—"

"Remember who made them refugees. They lost more than half of their number to wizards."

"To *Mulligan.*"

"A wizard," he said calmly. "Think of how many of the hostages have yet to fully recover their faculties."

"That isn't *my* fault!"

"No, but they know you have talent enough to harm them. And now they live here at the pleasure of the king and queen, defenseless against the rest of us, an enclave protected only by edict and the occasional Stowe. Not the most reassuring situation, is it?"

Val held my stare, and I fought the urge to glance away. Like all half fae, he seemed to be in his twenties unless you looked too carefully at his eyes, which were dark brown, soft, and far too old for his face. The mismatch was disquieting if you knew what you were seeing, and something within me cautioned that it was unwise to draw the attention of eyes like those. The feeling was irrational—Val had never hurt me outside of a practice room—but it was hardwired deep in my brain, a self-preservation instinct.

I caught the flicker of a small smile as he registered my discomfort. "Do you realize how easy it would be for me to destroy their town?" he asked, lowering his voice. "Most of them are little better than mundane—they couldn't fight me. The Stowe boys would have difficulty. So bear in mind, then, that the only thing protecting the Fringe from annihilation is the fact that those of us who could eradicate them choose instead to allow them to live." A second water bottle appeared on the bench beside him, and he took a long swig. "Now, granted, you're not capable of destruction on that scale—not yet. But your presence among them is a reminder of how tenuous their position is. You can insist to them that you present no threat until the end of time, but they will never fully believe you, and that's a fact you must accept."

"So what am I supposed to do?" I mumbled.

"Well, if you don't have a set time to be in class going forward, I could probably work out my schedule to accommodate a dawn training regimen...I'm kidding," he said, chuckling, before I could voice my dismay. "Enjoy your break, take time to breathe, and remember that this is not the end of the world. Come back tomorrow," he added, and went to his feet. "We'll play with swords again."

I followed his lead, draping my towel around my neck. "We still aren't telling Mom and Dad about that, right?"

"We are not. But if I teach you properly now, I won't have to undo your father's bad habits again." He opened a gate to my front yard and motioned me through. "Go home, rest. We'll resume in the—"

"Hey!" Dad yelled, running toward the gate. "Ros, Val, hurry over, you need to see this!"

Frowning, Val stepped through behind me and closed

the rift. "What's happened?"

"Nothing bad," said Dad, leaning over while he caught his breath. "Remember when Georgie went off to have a little alone time last month?"

"Yes…"

He grinned at us both. "Looks like she wasn't so alone after all. She just laid her first clutch."

Val's eyes widened. "How many—"

"Six." Dad beamed, then glanced over his shoulder at the house and its hangar-sized appendage. "We're going to need a bigger barn."

Georgie's clutch was small but typical of a first-time mother, according to the only information we had on hand. About twelve hundred years before, a madman named Tyrel had embarked on a decades-long program of dragon breeding, the only attempt of its kind in Faerie's history. Though Tyrel had been eaten in the end—he'd tired of the project and tried to send his dragons to a farm upstate—he'd left copious notes, a hundred-foot dragonhide scroll that had ended up in a box in Coileán's library. Dad pored over the scroll all evening, then did what he could to make the barn more comfortable for Georgie, adding plenty of hay and heating the floor so that she could wander out to the sheep pen and eat without worrying about the eggs.

Watching her lumber around the barn, I wondered how she managed not to break them. By egg standards, hers were huge, about five feet long and quite fat. But Georgie was two hundred feet from snout to tail tip and weighed at least a hundred tons, yet she practically tiptoed around the nest she'd made in the hay, curled her long neck to protect the eggs, and spread one wing over them at all times as a warming blanket.

Tyrel had noted that a dragon clutch took about sixty days to hatch—extremely fast by lizard standards, but considering how rapidly dragons grew once they were out, their quick development wasn't surprising. Dad marked the clutch's due date in the first week of August, then stepped back and gave Georgie her space, and warned me to do likewise. Georgie and Dad loved each other, but he didn't think that would matter if her instincts deemed him a threat.

Still, I couldn't stay away from the barn. With no homework to keep me locked in my room, I had hours of free time to kill and a nest of dragon eggs tantalizingly close at hand, and the only thing occupying my schedule was my daily session with Val. And so, when I wasn't getting pummeled and sliced, I slipped through the retractable kitchen wall and into the barn, popped onto a hay bale, and tried to keep Georgie company. She seemed to appreciate it—instinct or no, she was more or less trapped and bored—and I alternated between reading aloud and projecting my computer's screen onto the wall to let her watch movies.

I kept my distance, but one afternoon, near the end of June, she rose to grab a late lunch and nudged the eggs into a tight pile. *They're moving in there*, she thought, glancing my way. *If you press against the shells, you'll feel them.*

It was the closest she'd come to an invitation, and I climbed through the straw to see for myself while Georgie picked off the sheep. The eggs were harder than typical reptile eggs, almost like the giant, cream-colored version of the eggs I'd cracked for breakfast, and quite warm. I crouched on the edge of the nest and placed my palm against the nearest, and after a few seconds, I felt something inside knock against the shell. I was making my way around the nest when Georgie returned, and I smiled up at her. "They're kicking, aren't they?"

Perhaps. I can't tell what they're doing, but they're alive, she replied, and waited until I'd cleared the area before coiling herself around the eggs again. *Can you hear them?*

"Barely." The proto-dragons had just begun to

broadcast in the last week, and their faint telepathic murmurings felt like television static to me. "Can they hear you?"

I talk to them. Whether they understand me is another matter, but they're young yet. She snorted as she made herself comfortable. *I remember hearing my mother, but only vaguely now. My clutchmates, too.*

Georgie's siblings were seldom of interest to her. Dad said she'd been a late hatch, and by the time she'd emerged, her mother and the rest of the clutch had been gone, leaving nothing but trampled grass and dry shells. If she wondered about them, she never shared her musings with me, and she'd never gone questing after her kin. As far as Georgie was concerned, Dad was her family, and that was all she needed.

Once they're out, someone will need to give them an understanding of spoken language, she continued, slowly blinking. *Well, at least one of your languages. This would all be so much easier if you could communicate properly.*

"Excuse me for not being a mind reader," I retorted, which earned a flash of teeth—Georgie's form of a quick smile, terrifying to those not acquainted with her. "Have you thought about names?"

She snorted again and adjusted one wing. *I should probably name them, shouldn't I? That would make things simpler for everyone, I suppose...suggestions?*

I had no idea what to name a baby dragon, but I *did* have Internet access—something Aiden had worked up and the rest of us took for granted, much like the enchantment that made our phones operate without cell towers. A quick search returned dozens of sites full of nothing but names. Selecting a promising page, I asked Georgie, "Boy, girl, or both?"

Whatever is convenient.

"Guess we're starting with the As, then," I muttered, and took a sip of pop. "Okay, I'll read these, and you tell me if you hear something you like."

Are there many?

I scrolled down the page without reaching the first B. "Let's just say you have options."

Dad's predicted hatching date was almost on the nose. On the first Monday of August, I woke at dawn to hear my parents' excited voices in the hallway, then rolled over when Dad knocked and opened my bedroom door. "They're out! Come see!" he announced. I slid out of bed and threw on shorts, emerging just in time to catch Dad hurrying down the stairs in his bathrobe and bare feet, excited as a little kid on Christmas morning.

By the time we made it out the front door, Georgie had led the hatchlings into the sheep pen and was busily slaughtering breakfast for her brood, which moved like Shetland ponies trying to find their sea legs. The hatchlings flapped their little wings and growled at each other, bumped into the oblivious enchanted sheep, and stumbled over themselves in their rush to stay underfoot. Unable yet to control their telepathy, the dragonets broadcast every thought to anyone in a hundred-foot radius—mostly variations on the dual themes of *food* and *Mama.*

Georgie lifted her head at our approach and bared her jagged, wool-flecked teeth in a proud draconic smile. *They're so strong!* she thought, gazing down at her young as they squabbled over an ewe. *They move like drunks still, but they're getting more coordinated. Here, now, there's plenty,* she added to the hatchlings, nudging two away from the carcass before they could snap at each other. *Be patient, Mama will get you another. Joey, could you—*

"On it," said Dad, climbing the fence. The hatchlings looked up inquisitively as he wandered into the enclosure, and one of the sheep fighters, who was red and slightly bigger than the others, began to charge him with its teeth flashing. Before it could close on him, Georgie roared, and the little dragon fell to its belly, then turned to her and plaintively announced, *Hungry*.

He's not food, Georgie insisted, and shook her head. *Sorry, Joey. Are you all right?*

"Never better. Morning cardio is great," he replied, clutching at his chest in mock terror. "Okay, I make no guarantees that this will be as smooth as it was when Coileán did it for you, but I'll do my best. Let's start with you," he said, heading for his would-be assailant. "Who's this little...guy?"

Male, Georgie confirmed as Dad took the hatchling's head between his hands and gently massaged his brow ridge. *That's Horus.*

"Horus," he repeated, and smiled down at him. "All right, buddy, let's see how this goes..."

The hatchling stiffened and squeaked, then looked at his mother in alarm. "Horus? Hey, Horus," sad Dad, and snapped to draw his attention. "Sorry about that. Did it hurt?"

He cocked his head and stared at Dad—it had to be strange for him that sounds suddenly made sense—then thought, *No. Surprise.*

"Good." Dad gave him a last quick rub as Horus leaned his head against him like an overgrown, scaly cat, then patted his neck and sent him back to his mother. "Who's next?"

One by one, he put Fae in their heads—blue Obelia, green Zafira, black Rego, and purple Neve, two males and three females in total. After the fifth, he frowned up at Georgie and pointed to the barn. "Number six hasn't hatched?"

No, she replied, but sounded unconcerned. *Aren't they beautiful?*

By midmorning, the overwhelmed flock had shrunk past its equilibrium point—the sheep couldn't bud quickly enough to keep up with the demands of the hatchlings. Coileán stopped by to make the necessary adjustments to the sheep's reproductive tempo and see the new arrivals, but while he and my parents discussed the logistics of feeding and housing half a dozen dragons, I wandered into the barn and headed for the nest.

The sixth egg sat alone in the middle of the trampled straw and shell fragments, exposed but still warmed by the enchantment in the floor. I put my hand against it and waited until I felt the dragonet inside move. It was alive, then, and surely getting close, but I couldn't rush it. "Hey in there," I said, pressing close to the egg. "Everyone else came out this morning. You're missing some good mutton." When that news didn't lead to immediate hatching, I gave the egg a pat and started to pile more straw around its base. "Okay, then, take your time, but I bet all the best sleeping spots will be gone soon if you don't hurry."

And then I heard it, a soft voice in my head, tinged with panic: *Mama?*

I stopped and stared at the abandoned egg as I realized what its occupant must be feeling. For the last month, the developing dragonets had heard each other's voices and the comforting voice of their mother—and now, without warning, the last egg was sitting alone in a silent barn. "It's okay," I said, running my hand over the warm egg. "She's just outside. They're all here, waiting. No one's forgotten you."

Mama?

The dragon probably couldn't hear me, I decided, and even if it could, without a linguistic fix, it couldn't understand me. But still, I stayed with it until Georgie led the rest of the clutch back into the barn for a nap. The satiated dragonets collapsed in the straw, and their mother curled around them, leaving the remaining egg to fend for itself. "What about this one?" I asked Georgie, pointing to the egg.

If it hatches, it hatches, she replied, closing her eyes. *I can't worry about it with these five to feed.*

It might have sounded cruel, but Georgie had a point.

The hatchlings had voracious appetites, and when they weren't eating, they were either following her like clumsy ducklings or picking fights with each other. Horus and his smaller brother, Rego, were usually the culprits, but Zafira was known to throw herself into the middle of their skirmishes while their other sisters focused on more important things like food. As the hatchlings gained coordination, their fights became more serious—they'd emerged with teeth and claws, though at least they wouldn't be airborne for another month—and Georgie had her hands full keeping them from bloodying each other for the fun of it.

Though the bumbling dragonets were adorable in their way, I couldn't forget about the sixth egg. Its psychic distress calls intensified when Georgie and the rest of the brood were out of the barn, which was more and more frequently as the hatchlings tried out their legs, and I hated to leave the pitiful straggler by itself. I couldn't talk back to it, but I hoped it could feel me as I settled in on a nearby bale with my comics. True, I wasn't Georgie, but at least the little thing wasn't alone.

The hatchlings grew rapidly over their first few days, and by the time they were a week old, Georgie deemed them ready for an excursion. *We're just going into the woods*, she told Dad, who'd come out to assess the sheep population. *They need to practice hunting, and there's more manageable prey out there. Back by night.*

I watched from the barn door as she led the five dragonets off into the trees. "Didn't want to go along, huh?" I asked Dad.

"She doesn't need me slowing her down," he replied, ruffling my hair. "I'll be with Aid until dinner—he's updating the mapping software, and someone needs to check his work. Lucky me," he muttered, and rolled his eyes. "Mom's with Toula if you need her. Try not to burn the place down, okay?"

Soon enough, the house was quiet, and I retreated to the barn as usual to keep the egg company. "Morning," I told it, settling in with a cup of tea and a book. "They'll be back in a bit. How're we doing today?"

I listened, but the egg had gone oddly quiet.

"Awake in there?" I asked, sitting up as my stomach began to knot. "You all right, little one?"

I held my breath, hoping to hear a psychic peep from the egg and fearing the worst. Instead, after a long moment of silence, I heard the distinct cracking of breaking eggshell.

I might have squealed a bit as I climbed through the trampled nest to watch. A small hole had appeared near the top of the egg, the center of a jagged fissure. Through the hole, I thought I saw a flash of movement, and then a tiny forked tongue flicked out, tasting the air.

"Hey, baby," I cooed, and held the egg steady as the hatchling widened the hole. When it paused in its efforts, I slipped my fingers through the gap and gave the top of the shell a good yank. It ripped off in my hands, and suddenly, I was staring down into the blinking red eyes of a cramped white dragonet. "Hang on, you're okay," I breathed, pulling another chunk of the shell away, "here you go, just a little more, and you'll be free…"

But by then, the hatchling's eyes had focused enough to follow me as I worked. As I broke its shell open, it slid out into the straw, took two faltering steps, stretched its little wings, then looked up at me and joyfully cried, *Mama!*

"Oh…oh, no, I'm not Mama," I told it, backing off a step. "Mama's coming home soon, I'm just the babysitter—"

Mama, it insisted, stumbling closer, then headbutted my stomach and growled with happiness. I rubbed its brow ridge and horn buds, hoping the dragonet wasn't picking up on my panicked internal monologue, which primarily consisted of, *Shit, I'm dead.*

Dad and Georgie had always been upfront about how they ended up together: Georgie was an abandoned late hatch, Dad was the first sentient being she saw, and she'd bonded to him as if he'd been her mother. He'd tried to make it clear to her that he wasn't actually her missing mom, but Georgie didn't care. Still, even though he'd done well on the dragon-rearing front, Dad had breathed a sigh of relief when Georgie's clutch hatched with only her around. "I'd have felt awful if one of the little guys got confused about me when Georgie's sitting right there," he'd said with a laugh that night. "Wouldn't that have been awkward?"

Awkward didn't begin to describe it. I sank onto my bale, and the dragonet put its head in my lap, gazing up at me with a reptilian look of love. *Mama*, it thought, then flicked its tongue again. *Hungry*.

I couldn't let it starve, so I stood and walked out of the barn, the hatchling on my heels, and headed for the sheep pen. One of the nearer ewes bleated and split in two, and the hatchling's mental excitement intensified. I stopped at the fence and held up my palms to the hatchling, told it to wait, then climbed the fence into the pen. Since the hatchling couldn't understand a word I was saying, however, it scrambled after me and tumbled over the top rail with an undignified squawk.

Well, I thought, helping it roll over, at least I now knew it was male.

He shook himself off, folded his wings, then scurried after me as I chose a victim. "Sorry," I muttered, holding out my hand to the unlucky sheep, then channeled a bolt of power through its head. The sheep dropped dead, and I narrowed my focus to cut open its belly. "Um…dig in," I told the dragonet, and barely stepped aside in time to avoid the splash of blood and viscera as he shoved his snout into the warm carcass.

For only being a few minutes old, the hatchling had an enormous appetite, and I sat in the grass in his line of sight while he worked his way through the sheep. When he'd had his fill, he stepped back, licked the blood from his face, and plopped down beside me. *Mama*, he thought, then laid his sticky head on my legs, closed his eyes, and gave a contented snort before he fell asleep.

He proved to be a good napper. Twice that day, he woke hungry and complained until I prepared a fresh sheep for him, but I was able to coax him back into the barn afterward to continue his rest in the hay. He snuffled and twitched in his sleep, and I stretched out beside him, keeping my hand where he could smell it and watching the lengthening shadows with unease.

Too soon, I heard a gate open and my parents' laughter echo across the field. "Ros?" Mom called. "Honey, are you still in the barn? Need a li—*oh*," she whispered, catching sight of the hatchling, who woke at the commotion and crawled next to me. "Wow, is that—"

"The late one," said Dad, and hurried to my side. "When did it hatch?"

"Little after you left," I told him, rubbing the worried dragonet's face. "And I told him Georgie's coming back, but he doesn't understand me, and…um…"

"And he bonded." Dad squatted beside the dragonet and smiled. "Don't worry, buddy, this doesn't hurt," he murmured, then transmitted Fae into his head.

The dragonet blinked rapidly and looked to me, broadcasting confusion. "It's all right," I assured him, "you're fine. Your mama will be home soon."

His head cocked. *Mama.*

"No, I'm Ros. Mama is with your brothers and sisters. They'll be back any minute."

Mama, he insisted, wiggling further into my lap.

"Ros. I'm Ros."

He considered my expression, then snorted and repeated, *Ros.*

I thought I was out of the woods for a few seconds until he quietly added, *Mama.*

"What do I do?" I asked Dad. "Georgie's going to have a cow when she gets here."

He patted my shoulder and stood. "Leave Georgie to me. You stay here with him, okay? Keep him calm. I'll go wait for her and the brood."

Half an hour later, as the first stars came out, I felt Georgie's heavy footsteps shake the ground and heard the psychic chatter of the hatchlings as they returned from their outing. They stopped by the sheep pen, and Dad called to Georgie. I couldn't make out what he was saying, but after a few minutes, she walked into the barn and found her youngest scrunched up against me. "I tried to tell him—" I began.

He's alive and fed. You've done well. She went to her belly and looked at the hatchling, who climbed to his feet but stayed close to me while he regarded her.

"This is Mama," I told him, pointing to Georgie. "See, I told you she'd come back."

But the hatchling was shy, and Georgie didn't force herself upon him. *He's much smaller than the others*, she told me as she stood. *A week behind. They could hurt him if we put them together now.*

"Georgie, I swear, I didn't mean to—"

He didn't hatch alone. Thank you. To my surprise, she didn't sound angry, merely weary from the day spent with her other five children. *I could use the help, if you'd be willing to watch out for him.*

The hatchling was headbutting my side again, and I resumed his interrupted massage. "Doesn't look like I have a choice, does it?"

Her response was tinged with amusement: *I think he's made his wishes clear.*

"Think you're right." I looked down at the dragonet—*my* dragonet—then back at his mother. "So, uh…what's his name?"

Georgie studied the little white hatchling for a moment, then nodded. *Frank. That one's Frank.* She turned at the sound of the other dragonets stomping into the barn, then looked back at me and offered a brief glimpse of teeth. *He's not going to let you out of his sight tonight. You might want to find a cot.*

CHAPTER 2

Georgie was absolutely right. For the first three days, Frank was my shadow unless I slipped into the house to use the bathroom, and then he complained vociferously from the edge of the kitchen. I didn't shower, woke every time one of the exploring dragonets got too close to us, and remembered to eat only when my parents brought me food. Mom seemed worried about my predicament, but Dad was calm and sympathetic. "Give him a chance, and he'll settle down," he assured me as he handed me a ham sandwich. "Once he understands that you aren't about to abandon him, he'll let you sleep in the house again."

I tore into the sandwich, my stomach reminding me that hand-rearing a dragonet was hungry work. "How long until he *willingly* lets me sleep in the house?"

It may be a few months, Georgie interrupted, and Dad nodded. *Sorry, Joey*, she added, sounding slightly embarrassed.

"We'll fix you up a better cot," he offered, and left me to my quick lunch—if I dawdled, Frank or one of his siblings would sidle close and try to steal my food.

With Frank as my new focus, I forgot about my tutoring regimen, which was due to begin at the end of the month. Life had shrunk to keeping my rapidly growing charge from starving or getting into a fight with his bigger clutchmates, and I saw no visitors until Val shook me awake on Frank's fifth morning and pressed a thermos of coffee into my hands. "Drink this, then breakfast," he ordered, leaning against the barn wall while I sat up and tried to work the cot kinks out of my back. "We'll train here today."

"Here?" I mumbled. "But the babies—"

"Georgie will keep them out of the way. Go on, Ros, drink it."

I only made it through a few sips before Frank was awake and bumping against me. *Hungry, Ros*, he thought, cutting his eyes to the barn door as if the sheep might have disappeared overnight. *Up. Hungry.*

"Stay there," Val told me, then stood over Frank until the hatchling looked up at him. "She has to eat, too," he said to Frank, "and you can find your own breakfast."

"Not yet, he can't," I said, wiping coffee off my lips with the back of my grimy hand. "The rest of them can take down the sheep, but he's still too little."

Val grunted, then marched toward the barn doors. "Frank! With me!"

Frank looked at me uncertainly, but I nodded and motioned him on. "Follow Val. He's going to the food," I told him, which was all it took for Frank to lumber out into the dawn.

I finished my coffee while the smell of roasted mutton wafted in on the breeze, then peeked outside to find Frank happily devouring a well-charred sheep. "Thought he might like it cooked," Val said with a shrug. "Georgie always did. Now, for you…" He gestured, and a table and chair materialized in the trampled yard beside me, upon which appeared a platter of eggs, meats, and bread. "Eat."

He didn't have to tell me twice—the smell of bacon was ambrosial—and I dug in. "Going to join me?" I mumbled with my mouth full.

"I've eaten," he replied, shaking his head. "That's all yours."

I paused, considering the massive load of protein and carbohydrates spread before me. "This is a ton of food."

"You'll need it. Eat, girl."

To my surprise, my appetite didn't flag while I wolfed

down my meal, and Val smiled knowingly as I mopped up the last of the bacon grease. "I remember when your father did this," he explained, refilling my coffee thermos. "Didn't eat unless someone brought him food, slept poorly, and then he shoveled out the barn the hard way. Looks like he's learned from that mistake," he added, glancing behind me at the clean straw. "Better?"

I tried and failed to stifle a belch. "Much. Thanks."

"Don't thank me yet." He smirked and produced a pair of wooden practice swords. "Frank!"

The dragonet raised his head from his sheep. *Yes?*

"Ros and I need to work," said Val, tossing me one of the swords. "Stay out of the way, and don't try to help her. She'll probably fall and hurt herself, and I'm sure I'll hit her—repeatedly," he muttered, sotto voce—"but she needs this. Understood?"

No.

"Just keep eating," he said, and took up his stance. "Okay, Ros, let's see if you remember anything before we add shields to this. Come at me."

By his third week, Frank had accepted that Val throwing me around was a part of life, that there would always be sheep available, and that the other, slightly larger dragonets running about the yard were the rest of his clutch. He perked at their mental chatter—though they were learning not to broadcast, they forgot in their excitement, and so I was often privy to the dragonets' conversations, or at least the little I could comprehend. When Georgie communicated with me, her thoughts were almost like hearing speech in my head, fluid and familiar, but when the energetic hatchlings quarreled with each other, their thoughts were faster and less intelligible, more akin to flashes of desire or emotion in a murmuring mental fugue. Frank, still quite undersized in comparison to his siblings, often hung back and watched them, but as he gained confidence, he began to chase after the others, snapping at the bits of sheep they tossed around like gristly footballs and fleeing to the safety of my orbit whenever Horus and Rego chased him off. Georgie watched their interactions with quiet satisfaction, and she almost knocked me onto my face one afternoon when she gave me an affectionate nuzzle from behind.

And then, all too soon, the dragonets discovered their wings.

Obelia, eldest and largest of the girls, was the first off the ground. When a bird swooped too low at breakfast, she noticed and jumped for it, then flapped as she began to fall and managed to glide to her feet. Perplexed at what had transpired, she looked back at her wings, gave them an experimental shake, then took off at a gallop for the end of the yard and leapt. That time, she spread her wings quickly enough to gain altitude, and in seconds, she was banking above the yard, squawking for attention. Georgie jumped and joined her, a massive black shadow to the blue dragonet, and stayed beneath her until Obelia, exhausted, landed on her mother's back. When Georgie touched down, Obelia tumbled off with a grunt, and Georgie reached around to right her, rumbling with pleasure.

By the end of the day, all five of them had been airborne—even Neve, who would have been content to crack sheep bones all day if her mother hadn't nudged her toward the sky. While they experimented, Frank lay by my side, watching with undisguised jealousy as they executed ungainly takeoffs and landings. Though he had tried to follow his siblings, his wings were still too weak to carry him, and the little guy was distressed to be left out once again. "Just a bit longer," I promised him, rubbing his neck—already, he'd grown large enough that I had to stand to reach the top of his head. "You'll be up there soon."

Tomorrow?

"Probably not tomorrow," I said, feeling his

disappointment. "We'll try next week, okay?"

That didn't appease him, but there was nothing I could do to speed the process along. All week, Frank watched as his siblings gained skill and confidence, until finally, Georgie decided to take them on a short group flight. She called for Dad, who, having been grounded for three months, ran out to join them in his leather duster and helmet. "Won't be long," he told me, then scrambled up Georgie's side, perched at the sweet spot at the base of her neck, and gave her a pat. She leapt, followed in short order by her brood, who jockeyed for place around her.

Frank snorted as they disappeared over the trees. *It's not fair.*

"I know, buddy," I told him. "But they won't be out all day. Come on, there's bound to be a sheep with your name on it."

But for the first time, he refused the lure of food. Instead, as I watched from the fence, Frank ran up and down the yard, jumping and flapping, gaining a few feet before crashing in the dirt. Over and over, he trampled the grass with determination, stopping only when I called him aside to wash the mud from a gash in his neck. Once bandaged, he went straight back to his work until, with a squawk of surprise, he managed to coordinate his wings. Mentally crowing in triumph, he circled the house three times, then adjusted his wings as he'd seen his siblings do and came in for a stumbling landing.

"That was fantastic!" I said, running to hug him. "I don't think even Horus stayed up that long the first time."

He didn't, he thought with smug satisfaction, then turned around and looked at me over his shoulder. *Come on, let's catch them.*

"Frank, sweetie, they've got two hours on you…"

I'm not tired. Come on, Ros.

"Absolutely not. I'm too heavy to carry."

To my surprise, Frank didn't argue that he was just as strong as the others. Instead, I got a psychic flash of fear—he yearned to go after them, but he was terrified to do it alone. The rest of the clutch had Georgie, and Frank wanted me with him.

Please? he asked, giving me what passed for puppy eyes among the draconic set.

I sighed and considered his back. Frank had gained height in the last days, and if I straddled him when he stood, my feet would no longer touch the ground. He was still scrawny next to his siblings, but I had to admit that he'd put on weight. The little hatchling I'd seen into the world had grown to the size of a draft horse in under a month.

"Okay," I said, trying to sound more confident than I felt about the idea of going skyward with a first-time flier. "Lay down, let me get up there." Frank obliged, and I locked my ankles around his neck—I wanted the saddle Dad had always used when taking me up with Georgie, but that wasn't an option. "How's that feel?"

He stood and spread his wings. *Not bad. You're not heavy.*

"Are you sure about—"

That was as far as I made it before Frank took off at a run. I leaned forward, clinging to his neck, and squinted into the wind—and then, with a stomach-churning jolt, we were up, climbing over the trees and banking toward the north, where the others had flown.

I had always felt insignificant atop Georgie, a small barnacle clinging to her and barely above her notice. Her powerful wingbeats snapped like a loose sail before a storm, but there was hardly any turbulence in the middle of her body—well, until she dropped into a quick dive. But Frank was a crop duster next to Georgie's jumbo jet, and one with an inexperienced pilot to boot. I felt every twitch of his muscles as he tested his wings, and though the wind in my eyes stung, I was grateful not to have a helmet in case I needed to be sick. Frank rose and fell as he tried to stabilize himself, and I prayed his strength would hold long enough to get us home. Too late, I mulled over all the many ways this had been a *stupid* idea.

It seemed there was a merciful deity in the neighborhood that day, as we hadn't been up more than fifteen gut-wrenching minutes before I spotted a familiar black shape on the horizon. "It's them!" I yelled into the wind. "They're heading right for us!"

Frank called at the pack, and a moment later, Georgie roared in response. Her voice echoed in my head in the next instant: *Joey wants to know what the hell you think you're doing.*

"Frank?" I said. "Can you talk to your mom?"

Yes.

My legs tightened as he hit an updraft and bobbed. "Tell her we're okay, will you?"

After a few seconds, I heard Georgie again. *He isn't buying it, and Frank's weaving all over the place. Hold your course, we're coming.*

Georgie dove, picking up speed and leaving the other dragonets to follow in her wake. She sped our way, and soon enough, she passed beneath us and called out to Frank. He awkwardly banked and turned, and Georgie aligned herself so that when she rose, Frank landed perpendicularly across her neck, then slid down toward the saddle. Dad braced himself for impact, but Georgie's neck undulated just enough to prevent the collision, and as Frank's flight came to an undignified end, I looked back at Dad and tried to smile at his helmet. "He was feeling good about it!" I said, raising my voice against the rush of Georgie's wings.

Dad tapped the side of the helmet, and the visor retracted to reveal his incredulous face. "He's barely stable! You were one stiff breeze away from a fall!"

Relax, thought Georgie, banking in a slow circle to give the rest of the clutch time to catch up. *I took you up pretty early, as I recall.*

"That was different!" he protested, his voice still amplified by the helmet's microphone and speaker.

How?

"I knew how to ride, for starters!"

Georgie's thoughts were colored by amusement. *What do you think we've been teaching Ros all this time? Maybe she doesn't get any style points for that ride, but she stayed on. That's the goal, yes?*

Dad huffed his frustration, then shook his head and stared at me. "We do *not* tell your mom about this, got it?"

I flashed my thumb in reply. "Wasn't planning on it. I want to live to see sixteen, you know?"

He lowered the visor and gave me a curt nod. "That's my girl."

Of course, Mom found out eventually—she always did, much to Dad's chagrin—but by then, Frank was competent in the air, and Dad had put together an adjustable saddle for me. I hadn't pushed the issue with Frank, but as he'd seen Dad and Georgie together and realized there was a way to keep me close on his experimental flights, he insisted that I come along, at first for reassurance, and later for company.

As much as he craved the air, though, we never got in more than a couple of hours per day. Dragon-rearing duties aside, there was still the matter of my education to consider, and my tutors began coming by in September: Dr. Stowe for most of my academic subjects, Toula for magic, and Mr. Galloway for art. Val continued to show up, often at ungodly hours, to teach me combat. Aside from weekly programming lessons with Aiden, which took place in his shielded server room, my tutors were willing to work on my front porch, which meant that Frank could keep an eye on me. Though I encouraged him to play with his siblings, he insisted on sticking close, and he lay in the yard during my lessons, either dozing in the sun or listening. On occasion, he'd volunteer an answer, much to Dr. Stowe's delight.

I was glad that Val had explained the facts of life to Frank early on, as my physical training only got more brutal that year. Frank glowered and growled whenever Val threw me particularly hard, but he never tried to attack. Granted, Val could have defended himself if Frank had come to my aid, but it reassured me to know that the threat of my combat coach being jumped by an angry dragonet the size of a Cessna was minimal.

And Frank grew exponentially, lengthening and packing on muscle from his high-protein diet. By his first spring, though he was still the smallest of the males in the clutch, he had surpassed his sisters in size and weight, and he could fly for hours at a time. As he learned to go higher and faster, I took my parents' advice and put together a proper flying kit for myself: a long coat and gloves against the cold, as Dad recommended, and a ballistic vest, as Mom insisted—not in case of ground impact, but to protect against high-speed debris. Aiden even made me a helmet like Dad's, which obviated the need for goggles, amplified my voice—a necessity for communication as Frank's neck stretched—and gave me access to the mapping software.

GPS systems didn't work in Faerie, for obvious reasons, but the helmet was the next best thing. The onboard cameras constantly recorded what I was seeing and sent it back to a dedicated system in Aiden's apartment in the palace, which analyzed the data, pinpointed my location, and sent the information back in real time. Dad had made me promise not to try to push beyond the mapped areas without him, but by then, he had done so much mapping that Frank and I never ran out of known terrain to explore. As the spring days lengthened toward summer, we flew farther and stayed out longer, often going west to sea and chasing the sunset so that Frank could enjoy the breeze and eat sea birds on the wing.

And therein lay the problem.

Long ago, to preserve order in the realm, all faeries had joined one of three courts: Mab's, Oberon's, and Titania's. By the time I came along, the original Three were dead, and Coileán and Eleanor ruled as absolute monarchs in place of Titania and Oberon, with whatever little remained of Mab's court either locked in Coileán's prison cells or in the wind, presumably hiding in the mortal realm. Inter-court conflicts were rare, primarily because the two sides had been ordered to leave each other in peace or face their rulers' combined wrath, but *intra*-court conflicts were another matter. Since even a matter as trivial as fence color—let alone placement—could spark a deadly feud between full-blooded faeries, all such grievances could be brought to court for resolution, and the king or queen's decision was law.

Dad had equal blood ties to both courts, but he'd chosen Coileán. The choice had come as no surprise to anyone who knew them; they'd grown from unexpected comrades into friends, especially once Dad took Aiden under his wing, and I often came home after a long trip with Frank to find the three of them on the porch with beers. Mom, as a wizard, claimed no court allegiance, but it was understood that she could go to Coileán if she needed assistance—there was mutual respect there, and besides, Aiden was half brother to both of them, making Mom quasi-family, as far as Coileán was concerned.

As for me, I hadn't given the matter much thought until I got my first summons to court and realized I couldn't very well feign the flu.

My parents made me go alone. I was only sixteen, but I was at fault, and we all knew it. Walking into the cathedral-like throne room, I told myself that I was being responsible and mature by not trying to hide behind my parents' legs, but that message didn't make it all the way to my stomach, which threatened to revolt with nerves. I hugged the wall, fidgeting with the hem of my blouse, then paused between two stained glass windows and surveyed the room, desperate to find a reassuring face. Some around me I knew by sight, but I spotted no one who would be particularly bothered by my anxiety. And then, as I began to choose a lonely row of chairs in which to wait for my fate to be decided, I spotted the boy.

He looked out of place, a scared teenager maybe a year older than me plucked from a church pew or job interview and dropped alone into the heart of Faerie. The black suit he wore seemed too tight across his broad shoulders and too short at the wrists, and the knot in his dark green necktie was too perfect to have been the result of a first attempt. His hair, auburn and slightly wavy, appeared to have been recently trimmed. As I watched, his knee began to bounce. He slapped his palms on his thighs to stop the motion and resumed casting cautious glances at the vaulted ceiling, but soon enough, his leg was jittering again, and his hands were along for the ride.

Curious, I slid into his row and sat two chairs down from him. "What are you in for?" I whispered.

He jumped, then turned to me, his hazel eyes large and startled in his suntanned face. "Uh...um...I mean," he stuttered, "I do not think I have done anything...yet..."

His Fae was halting, his twang unmistakable. "Someone just gave you the head treatment, huh?" I asked in English, tapping my temple.

The boy's face melted in relief. "Oh, thank God," he said, switching languages. "You speak—"

"I'm from Montana. Ros," I said, offering my hand.

He clasped it with a firm, callused grip. "Sam. Nice to meet you." Releasing me, he leaned closer and murmured, "So what'd *you* do?"

I pointed to a row of chairs far ahead of us, where a woman sat stiff-backed in a poofy lilac confection of silk and tulle. "Accidentally wrecked her garden party."

"Dang," he replied, and flashed a crooked grin. "Gate crashing gets you hauled in around here?"

"It was slightly more than that. What about you?

Where'd you come from?"

"Wide patch called Red Plank, about three hours from Dallas and Houston. Don't guess you've heard of it, huh?"

"Can't say that I have."

"Nothing really to hear about. My mama's people have been ranching there forever, but unless you like farmland, there's not a lot going on."

"Got it," I said, smiling back at him. "So, what brings you all the way out here?"

His expression wavered, and he turned to point to a pretty brunette in a pink dress standing across the room, deep in conversation with Toula. "My neighbor brought me. She said it was time I got introduced."

"You're...half?" I guessed.

Sam shrugged. "Miss Bonnie thinks so. Said they'd be able to figure me out here." He paused, and his knee began to jiggle again. "My mama...she isn't doing so good, and she thought I...you know...might still have a dad out there somewhere."

"Is she sick?"

He nodded. "Cystic fibrosis. She gets pneumonia all the time now..."

His voice trailed off, and I murmured, "I'm really sorry."

"Thanks."

In the silence that followed, something hit me. "Wait, your mom's a rancher?"

"Yeah. We run a couple hundred head of Black Angus."

"Not to be rude, but if you're half fae..."

Sam grimaced. "Bingo. I'm pretty useless around the place. The herd won't let me get near them—I can't tell you how many times one of the bulls has charged me. Used to be okay with mechanical stuff, but of late, if I get worked up when I'm around anything delicate—"

"You fry it?"

He chuckled. "You too, huh?"

"Not exactly," I admitted, "but I've heard about it happening before. Someone here will sort you out." I hesitated, then added, "You, uh…were you going to stick around for a bit? Need a place to crash? We've got a guestroom, and my parents probably wouldn't mind."

"Thanks, but no. As soon as this is over, I'm going home—Mama needs me. Least I can still grill for us." He shifted in his seat, angling himself further toward me. "Okay, now, how'd you get here from Montana?"

"Long story," was all I had time to get out before one of Coileán's aides tapped my shoulder.

"Lady Roslyn?" he whispered. "He's ready for you."

Sam's eyebrows rose. "*Lady* Roslyn?"

"Technicality. Nice knowing you," I mumbled, and rose to face my fate.

As I followed the aide down the side aisle toward the dais, I took mental snapshots of my surroundings. There, too far away to be helpful, was Toula, who had folded her arms and was whispering to Sam's neighbor. I saw backs of heads, some plain, some adorned with fantastic jeweled updos. Bored faces turned at the sound of our footsteps on the stone, the flesh colored by the light falling through the rainbow-hued windows. At the front stood the aggrieved, Carille, in her purple gown…and there, enthroned atop the dais, was Coileán, looking underdressed in chinos and a white button-down. He crooked his finger toward me, and as I neared, I noticed Val standing just behind him, watching the proceedings with an unreadable expression. Willing my jelly legs to cooperate, I took my place at the foot of the dais and waited, swallowing hard.

"My lord," Carille began with a flounce of skirt, "this—"

He held up a hand to stop her, then absently brushed his dark, tousled hair aside, leaned on his armrest, and looked down at me. "I've read the petition thoroughly," he said, cutting his eyes to Carille, who reddened as if holding back her spiel was causing her physical strain. "What happened, Ros?"

After a deep breath, I managed a rapid, "It's my fault. I told Frank to head for the lights, and he—"

"Whoa, back up, slow down. You were out with Frank?"

I nodded. "Yes, sir. And…" I paused, assembling the pieces into a coherent account. "Aiden took the system offline that evening for a major update, but I didn't know he had one scheduled, and he didn't know anyone was going to be out that late. I wasn't planning to be out after dark, but there's this island, you know, the one with all the feral pigs…"

Coileán nodded.

"Frank wanted to hunt, and we thought that'd be a good place. But he was *really* hungry by the time we got there, so it took a while for him to eat his fill, and then, when we went up again, there was this really nice breeze, and—"

"You lost track of time?" he offered.

"Yes, sir. We started back around twilight, and we were still a long way out when my helmet went dead. I didn't bring my phone, so I couldn't call Aiden to see what was wrong. We were flying blind, and it was dark."

"Why didn't you open a gate home? Could have flown Frank right through."

"I panicked," I mumbled.

"Mm. All right, so you're out over water without any navigational aid…"

"We talked it over, and Frank thought we'd have a tailwind if we headed for shore, so that's how he steered us for a while. And then I saw lights on the horizon, and I thought that if we aimed for those, we'd definitely find the coast, and we could follow it home."

"Fair enough," he said, resting his head on his fist. "And the lights you saw were Carille's garden party, I assume?"

My accuser was still fuming. "I didn't know until we were on top of it," I replied.

"What happened?"

"Fireworks," I muttered, pushing the unpleasant memory down. "*Tons* of them, all at once."

"I spent weeks designing that display," Carille interrupted. "Perfectly coordinated with my concert, and that *thing*—"

"It spooked him," I protested. "We didn't know it was coming, and suddenly, there were explosions all around us, and Frank freaked out, and…"

I paused and looked up at the throne, expecting the worst, but surprisingly, I noticed that my uncle—well, technically, my third great-granduncle—was trying and failing to hide a smile. "Go on," he urged.

As I sought the politest way to conclude my explanation, Val caught my eye and winked. Obviously, both of them knew what was coming, and I got the sneaking feeling that they just wanted to watch me squirm through the retelling. "Like I said, he'd eaten a lot of pigs that afternoon, and the fireworks…um…well," I said in a mumbled rush, "they scared the crap out of him. Literally."

"All over my lawn!" said Carille, unable to restrain herself any longer. "A downpour of *dung* in the middle of my party…I cannot describe how *foul* it was," she added, glaring at me. "It splashed onto the bushes, the benches, the bocce court—"

"Was anyone hurt?" Coileán interrupted.

"No, but my concert was ruined! No one could pay attention with the memory of that…that…"

"*Memory*?" he repeated. "You cleaned it up quickly, I imagine?"

She gave him a queer look, her expression simultaneously confused, disgusted, and uncertain, as if he'd asked whether she bothered to dress before leaving the house. "Of course, my lord. The stench was horrid."

"How long did cleanup take?"

Her confusion deepened. "Seconds, I suppose. But my concert—"

"Carille," he said slowly, staring down at her, "you have no injuries and no lasting damage, the child was lost, and she ended up in the middle of a barrage of fireworks. What sort of recompense are you asking for?"

She straightened and held his gaze. "I want the beast's head. It'll make a lovely addition to my trophy room wall."

My stomach dropped, and I fought the urge to run up the dais. "He didn't mean to, he was scared!" I interjected. "It's my fault, I should have been more careful, don't punish him—"

"No one is punishing Frank," Coileán murmured, keeping his eyes on Carille. "The dragon's not even a year old, and you want to kill him for dumping at the wrong time?" he asked incredulously. "Little harsh, don't you think?"

"They ruined my party," she said with a sulky glare.

"Be that as it may, I'm not executing either of them." He turned his attention to me for a long, silent moment, and when Carille was distracted by a wrinkle in her skirt, he quickly rolled his eyes. "All right, kid, you screwed up. You've apologized?"

"I sent her a letter," I mumbled.

"Good. I want you on the ground by sunset for the next month, understood?"

"Yes, sir."

"And in the future, stay away from Carille's place, and, uh…tell Frank to get it out of his system before he starts flying over inhabited areas, yes?"

"Will do," I said, not believing my good luck.

"Very well. You're dismissed."

As I turned to go, I heard Val's voice whisper in my thoughts, *You really thought he was going to punish you?*

I didn't have his mental skill, so I formulated a reply and held it while he was peeking into my mind: *It was bad.*

He read the petition, cackled like a madman, then made me read it. It's been passed around the guards. Carille has a rather florid touch with a pen. He paused, and I could feel the smirk in his thoughts. *She tried to convey a picture of the evening in verse form.*

She writes her own songs, doesn't she?

Perhaps she should stick to singing others' words.

I smiled to myself as I took my vacated seat and turned to Sam. "Whew," I said, wiping my brow, "that could have been a disaster."

He leaned closer, wide-eyed. "Was I hearing things, or did y'all say something about a dragon?"

"Frank." I nodded. "He's my bud. Only about ten months old, so he's still kind of small, but—"

"You have a *dragon*?"

In response, I pulled my phone from my pocket and began scrolling through my photos. "Here he was as a hatchling…and that's two months, he was all wings and feet for a bit…and that's me in the saddle, Mom said we needed a group shot…oh, those two are his brothers…"

"Ros?" whispered a woman's voice behind me, and I turned to see Eleanor standing at the end of our row, casually dressed in gray leggings and a flowing blue tunic, her red hair pinned back in a soft chignon. "Was your thing with Carille today?"

"Yes, ma'am," I whispered back. "You heard about that?"

"Heard about it? *He* was supposed to call me!" she replied, jutting one finger toward Coileán. "Did she have any more poetry for the occasion, at least?"

"No," said Sam, "but from the looks of it, she is…" He paused, sorting through the unfamiliar words, then settled for English. "She's in a snit."

"Undoubtedly," said Eleanor, following his linguistic lead, and took the chair beside me. "I haven't had the pleasure, but from everything I hear, she's a stuck-up twit." Giving him a second glance, she asked, "You're Samuel?"

"Yessum." He reached across me to offer his hand.

"Sam Rockwell."

"Ellie," she replied, and smiled as she clasped it. "Been waiting long?"

"Eh, a little bit." He pointed to his neighbor, who was still chatting with Toula across the room. "Miss Bonnie said this could take a while."

"Well, yes, but I'm not averse to a little queue jumping." Standing, she cupped her hands around her mouth and called, "Forgetting something, Coileán?"

He jerked, pulled from listening to the latest complaint, and smacked his forehead when he saw her. "Damn it. Sorry."

"You'd better be. And this poor child is about to be sick with worry," she added, cocking her head toward Sam, "so since we're all here…"

"Sure. Come on down," he said, and Sam, giving me a last nervous glance, followed the queen toward the dais. I slid out behind them and claimed a chair near the front, partly as moral support but largely to satisfy my own curiosity about the half-fae would-be cattle rancher.

Coileán descended as Eleanor neared, and Toula escorted Bonnie up the aisle to join them. "Okay," he said as their huddle coalesced, "Bonnie, was it?"

She dipped her chin. "My lord."

I saw him cut his eyes to Toula, and something unspoken passed between them. "Be welcome," he told the stranger. "I understand if you don't plan to stay, but for now…well, no one's going to jump you."

Bonnie's lips moved into a slight smile. "My thanks. I had hoped to avoid joining the rest of my fellows who've returned to this realm."

"You come invited. That makes a difference."

Confused, I looked to Val, who stood on the outskirts of the group, keeping a watchful eye on the room. *She's one of Mab's,* he explained. *Not her blood, but her court. And since every other representative of that court currently in Faerie is still being held in the cells…* His eyebrow arched, and I nodded in comprehension.

"Badger said you're thinking half fae," Coileán continued. "You've been training the boy?"

"As well as I can," she said, nodding, and put her arm around Sam, who watched in awkward silence. "He has the talent and all the side effects. I know his mother's hoping there's a father still in the picture, but all things considered…"

"Might be easier if there weren't," Eleanor finished. "Still, he has a right to know where he comes from." She gestured toward a chair in the front row. "Have a seat, Sam. This won't hurt, but it might feel odd."

He did as he was told, looking to Bonnie for reassurance as Toula moved into position in front of him. "Aural examination," Toula explained, holding out one hand. "Sit tight, kid."

As Sam clutched the sides of the chair, she whispered the spell into being, and a glowing orb developed over her open palm. The lattice of the orb was an equal mixture of blue and red, and she squinted as she held it closer to her face. "Well, you're definitely half fae," she announced. "Let's see if I have your father on file."

She flicked two fingers, and the orb split into its component colors and flattened. "Blue's your mom," she explained to Sam as that portion vanished. "This one's your dad's signature, and if we run a search…" She tapped the quartz ring that functioned as a repository for all of the aural lattices she'd collected over the years—to my knowledge, everyone in Faerie had been required to give Toula a sample, fae and Fringer alike—and a series of red lattices began flashing in the air beside of Sam's. In less than thirty seconds, she had a match, and she peered at the label data floating just above her ring. "It's a boy."

"And?" Eleanor prompted.

"And it's Hugo."

"*Hugo?* Moon and stars." She sighed and shook her head. "I haven't let him out of this realm since I called him in. How old are you, Sam?"

The boy, who was looking slightly green, mumbled, "Sixteen, ma'am. I, uh…I'll be seventeen in August."

"Then you're probably his youngest. He has twenty others I know of, but that's no guarantee of a comprehensive list…" Seeing his jaw drop, she patted his shoulder. "Your father's better than five hundred years old, and he's not exactly *chaste*. He's also one of my brothers. We're, ehm…a substantial family, you might say. If you forget a name or ten, you can hardly be blamed."

He looked around the huddle, still perplexed. "Miss Bonnie mentioned the courts…" Eleanor and Coileán nodded, and he relaxed a degree. "Do I…fit in one, I guess?"

Eleanor blinked, taken aback, then covered her mouth as she chuckled. "Mine, dear. I suppose I didn't introduce myself properly, did I?"

Bonnie bent closer to Sam and murmured, "Lady Eleanor."

"Or Aunt Ellie, as the case may be," she said. "It doesn't bother me. So, now," she continued, taking the chair beside Sam, "we need to talk about your education. If you'll stay, I'll find a tutor for you, get you sorted." She hesitated, then said, "If you absolutely *must* meet your father, I'll arrange it, but I wouldn't expect a Hollywood ending, were I you."

Finding himself at the center of a ring of waiting adults, Sam seemed to shrink into his seat and had to clear his throat before he answered the queen. "Thank you, but…um…my mama…"

"He's not ready to move out," Bonnie offered. "His mother's quite ill."

Eleanor's face softened. "No, of course," she said, squeezing Sam's hand, "you should be with her. She could come here…"

But Bonnie shook her head. "I've tried, but Audra won't leave. That ranch is in her blood."

I couldn't quite read Eleanor's expression, but for a brief moment, the queen's mind seemed to be elsewhere. "Tell her the offer remains open," she finally said. "And Sam, when you're ready...come see me."

She stood to quietly conference with Coileán, and Sam wandered back to join me, still in a daze. "What just happened?" he mumbled, taking a seat.

"From where I was sitting, it looks like you're now a nephew of the queen of Faerie, so, you know, could have been worse." I snickered. "Lord Sam."

"Huh?"

"Your grandfather was a king, your father's a high lord, and you, my friend, get the title."

Sam shook his head and stared into space. "Unbe-friggin-lievable," he muttered. "And you...you're a niece or—"

"My dad's great-great-grandfather was half brother to both of them," I said, pointing to the king and queen. "Honestly, I'm more wizard than anything else."

"So, like, you've got a wand and stuff? *And* a pet dragon?"

"He's not a pet, and yeah, I've got a wand, but I don't need it. Like Toula, the woman who did your orb."

"Huh. Still, that was definitely a picture of you on top of a dragon."

"Only because he lets me." As Bonnie headed toward us, I pulled my phone out again. "What's your number? I'll send you mine, and if you have any questions, shoot them my way."

We quickly exchanged contact information, and Sam stood to join his chaperone. "Hey," he said, quickly turning back to me, "are we, like, cousins or something?"

I made a face and tried to visualize the tree. "We're half first cousins...four times removed? I think? Family relationships get a little weird around here."

"You can work it out later," said Bonnie, opening a gate. I could see a grassy field on the other side, and in the distance, a herd of black cows. "Come on, Sam, your mama's waiting."

He moved to follow her, but before he stepped through, he patted the pocket holding his phone.

I bunked in the barn that night. Frank felt terrible for putting me in front of Coileán, and since I'd been grounded from night flights, he stayed down out of solidarity. My hatchling had grown to nearly a hundred feet long, and he'd taken to wrapping himself in a circle around my cot, the better to protect me from his restless siblings as they flopped in their sleep.

We'd just made ourselves comfortable when my phone buzzed. *Who's that?* Frank asked, cracking one eye open.

The message was brief: *Nice to meet you. How's Frank?*

"It's Sam," I said, and aimed the camera toward him. "Give me your best 'I'm grumpy because you woke me with a text message' face." He slitted his eyes and bared his fangs, and I snapped the picture for Sam. *Hey, you,* I wrote, sending the image off to Texas. *What's on your mind?*

Mama's had a rough night. She just got to sleep. I'm wide awake.

For a moment, I listened to the rumbling of half a dozen snoring dragons, then smiled and typed a reply: *Me, too. Talk to me.*

CHAPTER 3

Sometimes, I tapped into my phone, *I get the impression that I'm failing at this adulthood thing.*

I lay on my bed—its linens now a mature navy and white instead of lilac, but still very much my comfortable childhood bed—and stared up at the star-covered ceiling. The phone's screen glowed in my hand, then went black, and I'd almost given up and put it on the nightstand when I heard the message chime and opened Sam's response.

How so?

Tracing my own constellations with my eyes, I tried to sort through my jumbled thoughts. Mom and Dad hadn't said anything—not in so many words, at least—but both of them were college graduates. Dad had even started seminary before Coileán wandered into his life with all the subtlety of a hurricane. As for me, I'd finished high school under private tutelage, received good marks from my teachers, and then...nothing.

Nothing had changed. Toula kept tutoring me to improve my spellcraft. Val left me cut and bruised on a regular basis. Frank and I explored by air, pushing into the undefined areas of Dad and Aiden's map to see if there truly were monsters in the margins. Life went on.

And now I was twenty, gaining on twenty-one, an adult by the Arcanum's reckoning and close to it by everyone else's, and still living in my parents' house. Bee sent me regular updates from Edinburgh, where she was studying medicine, full of photos and stories about the city, her classmates, her weirder professors, and her dodgy neighbors. She'd even met someone: Daisy Hornby, a new-blooded wizard from London who'd only been discovered when she was fifteen and had been taught the basics of magic remotely. As a wizard, Daisy couldn't hold a candle to Bee, but she was a pretty, freckle-faced girl with wavy chestnut hair and a broad smile, and my old friend had fallen hard. They'd gotten a flat together the previous fall, which suited them nicely. Bee needed peace and quiet to study, and Daisy, a linguistics major who pulled far fewer all-nighters, was tidy, considerate, and happy cooking for the both of them.

Bee had fledged. So what was I still doing sleeping down the hall from my parents?

I should get a job or something, I wrote.

Sam's reply was quicker that time: *Doing what? Aerial excursions? Dragon petting zoo?*

Ha.

But he wasn't finished. *Ooh—glass-bottom boat mermaid-watching tours. Perfect!*

Someday, you're gonna see a merrow, and then you'll know why that's a bad idea.

In response, he sent me a picture of a purple-tailed, bare-chested mermaid curled demurely on a rock and flashing bedroom eyes at the viewer. I was about to troll the Internet in search of an appropriately unsexy reply in kind when my phone began to ring. Tapping the line open without bothering to check the ID, I said, "Listen, cowboy, you start with that shit around the merrow, and they're liable to eat your face."

There was a brief pause, and then a voice that most definitely wasn't Sam's asked, "Do I want to know?"

Startled, I looked at the screen and grimaced. "Uh…hi, sorry, I thought you were—"

"It's all right," said Coileán, chuckling. "Sounds like you're having a better evening than mine."

"I don't know about that. Looking for Dad?"

"Called you, didn't I?"

I heard the clink of ice against glass on the other end and held my peace. The king was known to indulge, though I'd never seen him drunk. Then again, given how long he'd been cultivating a tolerance, the amount of alcohol it would take to intoxicate him would have been staggering.

"We've got a proposition for you, Ros," he said after a sip. "Ellie and me, I mean. Could you come by in the morning? Say, nine-ish?"

That wasn't a request, and we both knew it. "Yes, sir," I replied, sitting up in bed. "Have I, uh…am I in trouble?"

"No, no," he assured me, and drank again. "Just a favor we'd like to ask of you. Talk about it in the morning. Good night."

I stared at the suddenly silent phone, then flopped onto my back and sighed. The king and queen wanted a favor from *me*? How the heck was I supposed to sleep with *that* hanging over my head? And it wasn't as if I could, in good conscience, keep Sam chatting all night. There had been no follow-up message to the mermaid, and so, reluctantly, I put the phone away and tried to will myself to sleep.

Before I could so much as doze, however, there came a soft tapping at my window.

My parents' house was the kind of architectural monstrosity one only found in Faerie, a mishmash of styles reconfigured on a whim and barely paying lip service to the concepts of structural engineering and physics in general. At its core, it was a gray, two-story colonial with a wide porch and white trim, but one of its walls butted up against the dragon barn, a vaguely coordinating building that could have housed ten 747s. My bedroom was another weird blip in the house's style, an upstairs corner room with two walls made entirely of glass. Dad had only designed the walls as windows, but a bonus balcony had sprouted around my corner one night, and a door had spontaneously appeared in one wall to allow egress. He and Mom had asked how I'd managed to tack that on—I'd been a gifted ten-year-old, but ten all the same—and I could only shrug and blame Faerie.

The realm's consciousness—its soul, more or less—was ancient, all-seeing, and fond of me. Having tried and failed to tweak me into a younger version of Toula, she'd still managed to make a strong talent out of me, and she followed my progress. Every so often, when I least expected it, she'd pop by for a moment to chat, occasionally answer my questions, and warn me not to go so far over open water on a dragon who was still growing.

That night, I looked out the window to find her standing on the balcony, a petite blonde in a gauzy, pearl-colored gown who glowed against the black sky. She lifted a hand in greeting, and I hurried out of bed to meet her.

"Hey, Kura," I said, slipping through the glass door in my T-shirt and plaid pants, and noticed she wasn't smiling. "This wouldn't have anything to do with Coileán, would it?"

"Perceptive." She leaned against the railing and folded her bare arms.

"You're upset," I ventured, trying to read her expression. Kura could be emotive when she chose, but she'd cultivated a remarkable poker face over the millennia.

"Concerned," she replied. "Unsettled. It may be nothing, but—"

"If *you're* worried, it's probably not nothing."

That earned a flicker of a smile. "Your aunt and uncle would disagree. I...have been known to be somewhat cautious about whose presence I tolerate in this realm, and they seldom appreciate my warnings." Sobering again, she continued, "Something feels wrong. There's a...a current, I suppose, that shouldn't exist. A calm foretelling storms. A sound in the distance, too low yet to name but growing closer." She paused, frowning. "Does any of that make sense?"

"Maybe?"

"More plainly, then. I fear an attack, but I cannot pinpoint the source, and it's driving me mad." Pursing her lips in thought, she tried, "An itch, I suppose. But in the middle of my brain, becoming more aggravating, and unscratchable."

"That sounds miserable," I replied, joining her at the railing.

"It is." She sighed. "I haven't told Coileán and Eleanor yet, as I have no guidance to offer them. How can I show them the threat to defend against when I have no knowledge of it myself? But..." Kura hesitated, studying my face in the glow of her physical form, then murmured, "I fear that whatever is causing this disturbance has its source in the mortal realm. And if I am correct..."

"Arcanum," I finished. "Most likely."

She nodded. "Arnold Lowe has chosen his successor. The new grand magus has held office for two weeks, and to his credit, he's attempted to establish communication with the courts."

"Probably a smart move. Do you know anything about him?"

Kura ran one hand over her arm as if trying to warm it, but I suspected she didn't feel the night chill. "He is called Bertram Wold. English. Two years your senior. Arnold gave him time to finish his studies before stepping aside."

The mention of *studies* only reminded me of my growing disquietude toward my own situation, but I tried not to show it. "Got a degree?"

"No—his tutors have been working on his spellcraft since he was identified as the likely candidate. He seems skilled enough."

For a wizard was the unspoken end of that sentence.

"So...we're going to be on decent terms with him?" I asked.

"He sent Arnold across the border to suggest diplomatic relations. An emissary from the courts living in Glastonbury, someone to whom he can turn in time of crisis or if certain individuals take liberties with the mundanes. Toula served in that role in the past, albeit in the other direction—a representative from the Arcanum who came freely to Coileán when there was a message to be conveyed."

I thought of my tutor, who, though she was discreet about it, was known to be on more than friendly terms with the king. "Don't suppose Coileán would want to send her to Arc 2."

Kura maintained her unreadable expression, but I imagined I saw a hint of a smirk. "Unlikely. They wish to send you."

"*Me*?"

She shrugged. "Why not? You know the Arcanum as well as anyone here, excepting your mother. You've been taught to defend yourself and use your talents, and you will not age past your prime for several years. You're the logical candidate for this task."

I stared out at the night-dark hills and listened to the sheep bleat as they multiplied. "This is what they're going to ask me about tomorrow?"

"Yes. I thought you would prefer foreknowledge."

There was no point in trying to disguise my unease. Sure, I'd wanted to venture back to the mortal realm, but as a tourist—maybe a few days with Bee in Scotland, a week backpacking in the Alps, a Jeep safari across the Masai Mara, all trips I could do before, like Mom, I would need to relocate to Faerie permanently to avoid aging out of my twenties. The idea of going back to an Arcanum installation nauseated me. I'd barely escaped one, after all, and I was in no hurry to jump into the morass of wizard politics.

Kura's hand landed on my shoulder, and I turned to look down at her drawn face. "I know this is unpleasant for you," she murmured, "but think about it. I would feel better if I knew someone there had an ear to the ground."

Before I could mount a protest, she vanished, leaving

me alone on the balcony with my thoughts. I shivered in the breeze, hugged my goosefleshed arms, then returned to my bed and burrowed as if I could hide from the morning.

I had planned to play dumb—there was no need to let the powers that be know that the realm had spoiled their surprise—but seeing the queen and king struggle to actually present the offer, I showed my hand. "Kura ran it by me last night," I said, cradling my untouched tea to give my fidgety fingers something to do. "You want me to do a stint in Arc 2?"

They seemed relieved to not have to break the news. "If you're willing," said Coileán.

"But *only* if you're willing," Eleanor added, leaning across Coileán's coffee table. "If you want nothing more to do with them, that's completely understandable, and you won't upset us."

"We wouldn't ask if there were anyone else with your qualifications," Coileán continued, "but under the circumstances..."

He left the thought unfinished, and Eleanor picked up the thread. "Toula is confident that you can hold your own against this Bertram fellow. *We* are confident that you would be able to leave in a hurry if trouble arose. You do have a track record, dear." She took a sip of tea and watched me worry my lip. "And you would be going for the both of us, at least at first. I'd prefer to have an independent representative if we're to establish relations, but for the time being, as Coileán and I aren't working at cross-purposes—that I know of," she said, cutting her eyes to him.

He shook his head and drank his coffee.

"Then you could fill this role for us both," she concluded.

"Not for long," said Coileán. "Maybe a year or two, see how things shake out. And you wouldn't have to stay in

Glastonbury around the clock—do a bit of traveling, see the sights, whatever you like. You know money isn't an obstacle."

"And you would be doing us a favor," Eleanor murmured.

Independence, travel, unlimited funds, and the goodwill of the heads of Faerie—the offer had undeniable perks. There was just the *tiny* matter of having to relocate onto Arcanum turf, the thought of which made my guts roil. Ten years on, I still woke from the occasional silo-related nightmare—something vicious in the darkness, Grandpa's sharp scissors, or the old standby, running down an endless gray corridor with Mulligan, the murderous usurper, always ten steps behind.

"Do Mom and Dad know?" I asked, stalling.

"Not yet," said Eleanor.

"You're of age," Coileán explained. "It's your decision. I can tell you right now that they won't be thrilled—"

"Probably as thrilled as Aiden will be," Eleanor added.

He grimaced in quick acknowledgement. "But it's up to you, Ros."

I stared into my tea for a long moment, as if the answer might lie somewhere just beneath the milky brown surface, then finally asked, "How long until I would need to be there?"

"Would a week suffice?" asked Coileán. "Enough time to pack?"

They looked hopeful, and despite my misgivings, kin or not, I thought it would be unwise to disappoint them. "I…could give it a try."

My parents and my uncle reacted as we'd anticipated: surprise, a little horror, and then heated words with Coileán about sending me into hellholes without running his cockeyed plans past them first. But though they didn't like the notion, I tried to sound positive about it—I'd be in

England, not Montana, playing tourist and keeping tabs on the new grand magus, and only for a couple of years. Mom was the strongest holdout—no surprise there, considering how her own stint as grand magus had gone—but I promised to call at least every other day, and she grudgingly stood down.

My much larger and more vehement source of pushback was Frank.

While Dad and Georgie were out and the rest of the pack were lunching on the uncaring flock of sheep, I took Frank into the barn and explained what I'd agreed to do. He seemed amenable to the idea at first, even asking about the climate and accommodations in Glastonbury, but once he realized that I intended to go alone, he began to panic.

You're going to leave me? he protested. *Why?*

Those who suggest it's difficult to read a dragon's expressions simply haven't spent enough time with one. Even without the emotional coloring of his thoughts, I could tell Frank was distressed—his eyes flickered around the barn, and his mouth twitched as if the problem could be solved with the judicious application of teeth. On top of that, the mental impression he gave me was enough to make me cringe with guilt: a mixture of fear, disbelief, and heartbreak.

"Buddy," I said, rubbing his snout, "it's just for a little while. I'll come home on visits, I promise."

Let me come, too!

"You'd hate it. You'd be stuck outside the castle, there's no barn, no sheep, you couldn't even fly around without putting yourself at risk of being shot—"

I don't care. I want to go with you.

I sighed and tried to reason against instinct. Frank was almost five years old, fully grown, and judging by the stories I'd recently heard concerning his brothers' pursuit of females on their forays away from home, mature. The hatchling bond he'd had with me as his caregiver should have lessened—after all, the rest of his siblings no longer had to be in constant contact with Georgie. But then I had to consider Georgie, who remained fiercely protective of Dad long after she'd had children of her own. Frank wasn't just my hatchling—he'd been my friend and my partner in crime all his life, and now, without warning, I was walking out on him.

"They need me to do this," I told him. "As much as I'd love to have you with me, there's just no place for a dragon in Glastonbury."

I'd coaxed him outside to eat—distraught or not, dragons still have massive appetites—and I'd gone inside to begin sorting through my things, fairly confident that Frank would accept the inevitable. But when I came downstairs that afternoon to check on him before dinner, I saw only a flattened patch in the straw where he usually slept, and Obelia, curled up nearby, thought, *He flew off.*

"Did he say where he was going?" I asked with growing unease. "When he'd be back?"

No, nothing. He went alone. She lifted her massive head and snorted. *Seemed upset.*

I assumed he'd gone for a long flight to let off steam. As night fell and the moon rose without a sign of him, however, I paced my balcony and scanned the horizon, hoping to see a dark blot against the stars. But for the first time, Frank didn't come home.

The next day, Dad reminded me that Frank's siblings went off on their own from time to time, and his behavior was perfectly normal for a dragon his age.

The following morning, Val assured me that Frank was, at most, sulking, and threw me against a wall when I let my missing partner distract me.

By the third day, Mom suggested I ask Kura where he might be, but she refused to show herself.

None of the other dragons had seen or heard him, but they seemed unconcerned about the situation. *Maybe he's found a female*, Rego suggested while I wandered through the barn, looking around as if Frank might have secreted himself in the rafters. *Mating can take a few days if there's competition.*

And he'd have better luck without us around, Horus added, working a tuft of wool out of his fangs.

They had a point—Frank remained the smallest of the boys, though all three of them had surpassed their mother and sisters. And the other two had gone off in search of mating opportunities, I reminded myself. Maybe Frank finally decided to scratch the itch. God knew he didn't need me supervising *that*.

But as the week passed without a trace of Frank, I couldn't help but worry. Was he hurt? Lost? Or was he so angry about my impending departure that he wouldn't even let me say goodbye? I'd already made the rest of my rounds—coffee at one of the settlement's cafés with Toula, a trip to Dr. Stowe's office, dinner with Mr. Galloway in the pub down the block from his studio—and the thought of heading off without even taking a last morning flight with Frank killed me.

Mom and Dad had given me peace on the afternoon before my scheduled departure, slipping off to the town's theater for a matinee date while I double-checked my packing list. Satisfied that I'd crammed everything I could conceivably need into my suitcase and overnight duffel, I sat on the edge of my bed and messaged Sam: *Heading to England tomorrow. If you're in the neighborhood, say hi, okay?*

Ha, he replied after a moment. *Sure, I'll pop over for tea.*

You could, you know. Gates aren't hard.

I'll think about it. Gotta go, vet's here. Safe travels.

I sighed and put the phone down. Faerie lord or not, Sam was reluctant to use his talents around his mother, and Bonnie, his neighbor and mentor, had left town shortly after she'd brought him into the realm for the first time. She'd gotten too old and needed to build a new identity elsewhere, Sam had explained, but from the wistful way he spoke of her, I knew he felt the loss. Without Bonnie to spot him, he seldom experimented, fearful of creating an enchantment more powerful than he could control. But at least he'd stayed in touch. Either Faerie hadn't scared him that badly or he was lonely on the ranch with his sick mom, the busy hired hands, and the hundreds of cows who wanted nothing to do with him.

I was mulling over mailing him a care package from Glastonbury—tea, exotic cookies, something kitschy and printed with the Union Jack—when the doorbell chime pulled me from my thoughts. We hadn't been expecting company, as far as I knew, and so, curious, I hurried downstairs and yelled, "Coming!" Skidding into the foyer in my socks, I opened the door, expecting to find one of Coileán's aides on the porch.

Instead, I found myself staring at the well-muscled chest of the stranger standing on the doormat. Sure, said chest was covered with a black T-shirt, but the shirt was tight enough to leave no doubt as to what was underneath, and it showed off the stranger's strong arms nicely. His jeans weren't nearly as clinging, but the effect was aesthetically pleasant all the same. The surprise came when my eyes traveled up. The stranger was pale—even his lips seemed drained of color—and his close-cropped hair was white. He sported a large pair of round, frameless black sunglasses, which gave his face an almost skull-like appearance—not frightening, but striking. It was a face I'd have remembered, but I couldn't recall having seen him before. He seemed to be about my age, perhaps a hair older, but then again, this was Faerie, and appearances seldom reflected reality.

"Uh…hello," I said, moving into the gap left by the open door. "Can I help you?"

He said nothing, but he removed his glasses, giving me a peek at the vibrant red of his irises. No true albino had eyes like his, and I assumed I was seeing a creative glamour.

"Are you looking for my parents?" I asked, still trying to place him. "They've gone to the settlement. Should be back by dinner."

He retreated a step from the door and held my gaze...and then, quite unexpectedly, I heard a familiar voice in my mind murmur, *Can I go with you now?*

"*Frank?*" I cried, clinging to the doorframe in my shock.

His mouth opened quickly, revealing a flash of teeth— a draconic attempt at a smile, oddly transposed onto human features. *Is it good enough? Do I pass?*

"What the hell did you *do?*"

I heard the shade of amusement in his reply. *Mom told us once that when she was young, she had to hide in the other realm for a time, and Toula transformed her. So I went to Toula. She claims she's worked out the kinks, but...well.* He paused, then moved his shoulders up and down, a carefully considered shrug. *Convincing?*

My mouth opened and closed a few times, but it took a moment before I recovered my voice. "How...how are you even walking, that—"

She's a good teacher. Demanding, but effective. I'm sure she didn't cover everything, but—

"Can you speak?"

Vocally? His lip curled in a frustrated snarl. *Not yet. Making sounds is one thing, but putting them together...it's a lot,* he admitted. *But if you'll let me come with you, I'll keep trying. Please let me come, Ros,* he thought, the words flashing more quickly through my head as I felt the edges of his desperation. *Please. I'll stay out of the way, I won't be trouble, just...don't leave me behind...*

I caught him off guard when I sprung from the doorway and wrapped him in a rib-cracking hug, and after an uncertain moment, he gave my back an awkward pat. *This...means yes?*

"You big goober, I can't believe you," I mumbled into his shirt.

So yes?

"And you had me worried sick all week!" I said, looking up at his new face. "Moon and stars, Frank, I thought you might have been dead in a ravine somewhere!"

I didn't disguise my feelings, and Frank's eyes lowered. *Sorry. Can I still go?*

Studying his porcelain skin, I could just make out the traces of the transformation bind, buried deep within his natural aura. Sure, he looked a little unusual, but perhaps that would protect him—after all, who would be rude enough to stare at a potential albino long enough to notice the delicate spellcraft flowing around him? He couldn't talk, but at least he was upright, and with time...

Frank stood stiffly in my embrace, and I realized he had no idea how he was supposed to be reacting. "Of course you can come," I told him, and leaned my cheek against his shirt again. "Put your arms around me and *gently* pull me closer."

Like this?

His arms felt like warm stone, and I imagined he'd excel at the caber toss. "Good start."

How long do we do this?

I patted his back and released him, and he followed suit. "Depends. Did Toula send you with any luggage?"

Frank nodded to the black backpack on the steps behind him. *Basics, she said.*

"Let's see. Come on in, my stuff's upstairs."

I stepped back, and Frank, having retrieved his few belongings, tentatively crossed the threshold and looked around with naked curiosity. He'd never been in the house—he hadn't been able to fit inside for most of his life—and he stared at the blinds and the lamps as if he were trying to divine their purpose.

"This way," I said, taking his hand. "My room's up a floor and down the hall."

Slowly, he followed me up the staircase, holding his

pack by one strap. When we reached the landing, he asked, *Could you do something for me?*

"What's that?" I said, leading him toward my bedroom.

Toula gave me a bunch of bottles of stuff. I'm still not sure what goes where. You have a weird fixation with getting wet and rubbing gel all over yourselves, you know.

I smiled back at him over my shoulder. "Welcome to the human race, bud. It only gets weirder from here."

My parents had been surprised to find me home alone with a boy, then floored when Frank greeted them. By then, I'd already called Toula and protested that she'd let me worry all week when she knew *exactly* where Frank had been hiding, but she'd been unrepentant. "He thought there was less chance of you saying no if he got the basics down first," she told me. "And Georgie and the others knew what was going on in case of a real emergency."

It wasn't a satisfying explanation, but I'd taken it. "Anything I need to be aware of?"

Toula had paused and sucked her teeth. "I mean, I wouldn't take him anywhere with multiple forks yet. He's probably going to need wardrobe assistance for a while, and don't expect calligraphy. But if he keeps his thoughts to himself and his head down, he should get by all right."

As Dad made dinner, Frank started to leave the house, but Mom caught him by the arm and asked where he was going. He pointed to the sheep pen, where the rest of his family was dining, and Mom looked at him quizzically. "Just how did you expect to take down a sheep? Rip it apart with your bare hands?"

Frank considered the question, absently running his tongue over his flattened teeth. *Maybe Mom would disembowel one for me.*

"Or maybe a few hamburgers would suffice," Dad called from the kitchen.

He perked at that. *I didn't know—*

"You thought we weren't going to feed you?" Mom asked incredulously. "Sit down, Frank, there's plenty."

It became evident that my ensorcelled companion had been shown the rudiments of proper table behavior, but he seemed relieved to learn that burgers were finger food. After tasting a few toppings—and making some fantastically disgusted faces—he settled for plain patties and a lake of dipping ketchup, eschewing the buns, beans, and even the steak fries.

"I mean, he *is* a carnivore," said Dad, pushing the burger platter closer to Frank, who by then had downed three and was well on his way through a fourth. "No spell can change that. How's your stomach feeling, Frank?"

Getting full. He swallowed a bite and belched. *This isn't sheep, then?*

"Cows. Beef," Mom explained. "Ground up and cooked. Tastes okay?"

Great. And this? he asked, pointing to the ketchup.

"It's tomato-based. That's a plant, but—"

I like it. He dipped his patty straight into the pool of sauce like a meaty cookie into a glass of milk and grunted appreciatively while he chewed.

With dinner and my last-minute packing out of the way, I decided to turn in ahead of the next morning's early start. I showed Frank to the guestroom, pointed out which of his supplies was toothpaste and why he should use it, and burrowed under my covers. Lying in the darkness under my reproduced sky, I listened to Frank's restless footsteps across the hall, and then, as I was drifting off, there came a knock at my door. "Yeah?" I mumbled, uncovering just enough of my face to be heard.

The door opened, and Frank popped his head inside. *It's too quiet. Can I sleep with you?*

For someone who'd grown up falling asleep to a chorus of snoring dragons, the house had to be jarring in its evening silence. "Sure," I replied, closing my eyes, and scooted closer to the edge of the bed to make room. But when the door latched and Frank's shuffling ceased, I had yet to feel his weight on the mattress, and I looked around to see where he'd landed.

Eschewing the bed, Frank had curled up on the rug beside me with one arm crooked under his head. I leaned over the edge and whispered, "There's room up here, you know."

Hard to get comfortable. This works better.

"Want a pillow or a blanket or something?"

Nope.

"Okay. Let me know if you change your mind," I told him, and tried to lose consciousness. Before long, I heard movement against the rug, then checked again to see Frank's hands and feet twitching. Leaving him to run in his dreams in peace, I slept.

My extended family gathered at breakfast to see us off, including Aiden, my grandparents, and Liza. By the time Coileán and Eleanor arrived for last-minute instructions, the rest of my kin had almost acclimated to Frank's new look, and they wisely let him finish the bacon. As I was running through my final checklist with the king and queen, Toula showed up, with Val only a few seconds behind her. In a quiet moment, the two of them took me aside into the living room and closed the door. "Be *careful*," Toula murmured, holding my chin. "Remember your training. Whatever this kid can do, you can probably do it more effectively."

"I'll be fine," I insisted, ignoring the nagging butterflies.

"I'm sure you will be, but if something does go wrong, don't be a hero. Get yourself out of there, and we'll regroup. Got it?" She paused to study my face, then reached into her pocket and extracted a folded piece of notebook paper. "And here, a little something to keep you occupied," she said, handing it to me. "Coileán doesn't have copies of these books, and *I* sure as hell don't, but if memory serves, they're in the Arcanum library or stashed somewhere in the Archives."

"Homework?" I sighed, only half in jest.

"*Yes*, homework, and stop whining. Keep up your studies, kiddo—it's good for you."

When Toula released me, Val clasped my shoulder and stepped closer. "I have every confidence in you. With that said, should I be mistaken, there is help to be had."

I nodded, and they led me out to collect my luggage.

Finally, having made my goodbyes, promised to call, and slipped a gallon-sized bag of Gran's cookies into my suitcase, I was ready to take my leave. At the appointed time, a gate opened on our front lawn, and Arnold Lowe, sporting a formal black robe over a green polo and khakis, passed through. The former grand magus seemed to be taking his return to mere magus status well, I mused, glancing at his boat shoes. He greeted everyone, joked with Mom that she'd had the right idea in stepping down when she did, had a quick word with Coileán about who the big fellow acting like my second shadow might be, then smiled at me and swept his arm toward the gate. "Ready?"

"Ready," I said, and started through into Arnold's office. Frank hesitated on the threshold, and I reached back to take his hand. "Doesn't hurt," I assured him, and, screwing up his face, he crossed between the realms.

As Arnold closed the gate, he gave us both a once-over, then studied Frank more carefully. "Keep the glasses on for now, and none of *this*," he said quietly, then tapped his forehead and arched an eyebrow. "Yeah?"

Frank's head bobbed.

"There's plenty to eat in the canteen, so don't worry about trying to find a butcher. I'll have a flat set up for the two of you while you and Bert get acquainted. We were only expecting one," he added, sloughing off his robe, and dropped it over the back of a leather-clad chair. "But not to worry, we'll find space—and I don't think Bert's going to protest if the envoy *he* requested brought a friend along.

Come on, I'll make the introductions."

"How is he?" I asked, following Arnold into the stone-walled corridor.

"Young," he replied without elaboration, and led the way toward a spiral stone staircase. "Stay close, now. You'll have the grand tour in a bit, but it's easy to get lost in here. The floorplan isn't nearly as regular as the silo's," he added, chuckling.

Just the mention of Arc 1 made me tense, but I tried not to let on. "How big is this place?" I asked as we climbed.

"Well," said Arnold, taking the stairs in stride, "the original castle wasn't particularly large—four eight-story towers and the connecting bits around a central courtyard. We've had to expand over the years, you see."

"You made the towers taller?"

"We added more. Twenty-four towers altogether now, including storage space." Glancing back, he saw my dismay and smiled. "There's a map. You'll be fine."

We puffed to the top of the tower, and Arnold escorted us down a rug-lined hallway into one of the connective buildings. As we traveled its length, I looked at the many paintings on the walls—the official painting of every magus for the last two centuries, I assumed, given their abundance. There was, I noticed, a distinct time gap near the most recent of the bunch, the usual number of portraits from the first half of the twentieth century, then only a handful until the post-Mulligan crop of magi appeared.

Catching the direction of my stare, Arnold murmured, "I put the Mulligan-era ones in storage. They're part of our history, but I didn't want to stare at those smug bastards all day." Giving my shoulder a light squeeze, he paused outside an unassuming door, then rapped twice before poking his head inside. "Bert? Got a minute?"

"Come in," said a voice from inside—English, definitely, a low tenor with a touch of fry—and Frank and

I followed Arnold through the doorway.

The new grand magus looked barely older than me, certainly not out of his early twenties. He stood behind an antique, monolithic mahogany desk, a thin man of average height wearing a French blue dress shirt and black trousers beneath a simple black robe and his golden chain of office. His light brown hair was just long enough to show its tight curl, which did nothing to help whatever air of gravitas he was hoping to cultivate. He sported a pair of half-moon glasses on the end of his upturned nose—the reading glasses of a much older person, I thought, until he turned his head enough to show me how thick they were. Beyond the desk, which seemed to be a decent piece of furniture, his office was a disaster of half-filled shelves, open cardboard boxes, and stacks of crumbling leather books.

"Hello," he said, hurrying around his desk and almost kicking over a leaning stack of manuscripts in the process. "Bertram Wold. And you are—"

"Ros Bolin," I replied, clasping his outstretched hand. "Ros."

"Bert." His palm was warm and slightly moist, and the smile that accompanied it revealed his trepidation. "And, ehm…"—his eyes rose toward Frank's dark glasses—"who might you be, then?"

"This is Frank," I interjected, releasing Bert's hand. "My guard."

Frank nodded and folded his arms, which did wonders for his pecs.

"Oh. Ehm. Well, that…that's all right," Bert stammered, taking a step out of Frank's strike zone. "Suppose that's fair enough. I assume you'll want to stay near Ms. Bolin, Mr., ehm…"

"White," I improvised. "And he doesn't speak, so don't take it personally."

Bert's brows knit. "He's mute?"

Again, Frank nodded, and I added, "But not deaf. He and I get along."

"Of course, ehm…sorry," he mumbled, looking up at Frank again. "I could have asked you directly, hmm? Yes or no, twenty questions, all that?"

Frank's head cocked, and I stepped in before he could be tempted to talk to Bert. "Yes, he's a smart guy." My companion showed me a pleased flash of teeth, and I patted his bicep. "Arnold said he'd give us the tour, and I don't want to keep you…"

Bert looked grateful. "I'm sorry, you can see what a mess I have to sort. Moving's never simple. But, ehm…listen, I'd love to talk with you properly," he said in a rush. "Maybe…dinner? Would that work?"

"Sure," I told him, then looked at Arnold and grinned. "Couldn't even leave this place tidy, huh?"

"Oh, I haven't moved," Arnold replied. "Bert wanted a different office, and this one's been empty for a while. Half of this crap is Council storage," he explained, pointing to the cardboard boxes.

"*Ah*. Old place wasn't up to grand magus standards?" I teased Bert.

He began to flush. "Bit cramped. And…well…" He turned and gestured toward the pair of large windows behind his desk. "I preferred the view in here."

I glanced past him and saw gray stone towers rising on the other side of the glass. Far in the distance was the edge of the bubble of spellcraft hiding the castle from view and from exploring mundanes. "Didn't want windows on the other side? Look out over Glastonbury?"

"Glastonbury isn't my concern," said Bert, returning to his desk. "My charge is to protect the Arcanum, and that's where my focus should be. Always."

"Uh…sure, okay," I said, and edged toward the door. "Well, nice meeting you—"

"Seven?" he asked.

"Yeah, that's fine. Uh—"

"I'll send one of my assistants."

He took his seat and picked up a notepad, and I

assumed my interview was over.

Arnold closed the door behind us, then motioned us down the hall and into the next tower. "*Slightly* tight-wound," he murmured. "If you could work on that Ros, I think we'd all be grateful." With that, he pulled out his phone and tapped a button. "Yes, hi, Gemma, change of plans on that flat setup…"

CHAPTER 4

As I wandered through the corridors and up and down the castle stairs behind Arnold that morning, praying for landmarks, I began to worry about Frank. He seemed to be keeping his balance and appeared interested in his surroundings, but I caught his hand straying to his midsection and lingering. "Hungry again?" I asked when the three of us started down an empty hall. "The time here is ahead of home right now, so they'll serve lunch soon."

Not hungry, came the quiet thought. *My stomach feels weird.*

"Queasy?"

He considered the possibility, then thought, *No. Just...odd. Is it warm in here to you?*

"Not really." I frowned, hoping we hadn't inadvertently discovered a dragon-loving pathogen in our first hour in the realm. "Do you want to take a nap?"

I'll be fine, he replied, and showed his teeth.

"We've got to work on that smile of yours," I said, linking my arm around his. "It's not quite right, bud."

His response was colored with bemusement. *It's just a brief display of teeth, yes? What's wrong with it?*

"We'll talk," I assured him, and tugged him along as Arnold began the lengthy circuit to our new apartment.

He apologized, but we'd been assigned to a flat on the fourth floor of one of the less desirable towers, which tended to be drafty and housed a colony of rats that had, so far, evaded every magical means of evicting them. It wasn't Arnold's fault—Arc 2 was the most popular of the seven Arcanum installations, and even with the additions over the years, ideal living space in the castle was sometimes hard to come by.

When Arnold took the reins after the messy end of the Mulligan regime, one of his first acts as grand magus had been to lift the rule requiring wizards to live in one of the installations. I'd heard that the resulting exodus had been pronounced in certain communities—most Australians fled the Outback for the comforts of Sydney and Melbourne, Arc 4 lost three-quarters of its population as they beat a retreat from Mongolia, and quite a few North American wizards decided that there were better places to make a life than the middle of nowhere, Montana—but Glastonbury's diaspora had been mild. True, a significant chunk of Arc 2's inhabitants headed straight for London or home to the far-flung corners of Scotland, but as the center of Arcanum governance moved into the installation, an influx of newly minted magi, their assistants, and the research and archival staff almost made up for the loss. Even the Archives, long my grandfather's responsibility, had been removed from Arc 1. The castle had plenty of room for offices and storage areas, but when it came to housing, the new arrivals had been confronted by small flats, stone walls, and an abundance of fireplaces. The ones who had come from Arc 3, a massive Alpine fortress with ski access, had complained most vociferously about the accommodations, but as I heard it, the Arc 1 crew, freed from their converted missile silo, were just thrilled to have windows.

Frank and I had been assigned to 2042—tower twenty, fourth floor, flat two, as Arnold explained, showing us around the place. Though clean, it had been sparsely furnished. The outer door opened into a den equipped with a television, sofa, and coffee table. To the right were a dining nook and galley kitchen, and to the left, a pair of identical bedrooms and tiny baths. "We'll redecorate," I quietly assured Frank, and Arnold ordered lunch delivery—one of the perks of his job—while we moved in.

Frank, who had little to do, sprawled facedown on my bed and closed his eyes while I hung clothing and sorted my possessions into drawers. "Still feeling weird?" I asked him.

Yeah. This place smells weird, too.

"You're probably smelling mold. It's a castle—things get damp in here."

Maybe. He sounded doubtful. *There's something else, but I can't name it. You don't smell it?*

"No." In truth, I was too busy working through the kinks of my bathroom remodel to worry about strange odors. Having spent the last decade in Faerie, I'd grown accustomed to the higher concentration of raw magic there. Back in the mortal realm, I had to be more judicious with my spellcraft, and I silently thanked Toula for nagging me into precision casting. I colored the walls pale blue, replaced the old bathroom tile, and cleared away the stubborn mildew in the shower grout, and I'd just turned to the question of lighting when Arnold announced that lunch was served.

I wasn't starving by any means, but I figured it couldn't hurt to acclimate to the local schedule and helped myself to the soup and sandwiches he'd had brought up. At my suggestion, he'd ordered a plate of naked sausages and a bottle of ketchup for Frank, who ate with gusto. As I mopped up the last drops of my bisque, Frank leaned back in his chair and let out a contented sigh. *Those were good. What were—*

Suddenly, he burped, and a jet of flame shot skyward with the expulsion of gas. He yelped in surprise and clamped one hand over his mouth, and Arnold and I jumped from our seats to get out of the way. I looked at the plastered ceiling, which now bore a blackened oblong from the fire, then at Frank, who stared at us in wide-eyed confusion. *What was that? What happened?* he asked, turning from me to Arnold and back in search of answers. *How did you do—*

A second burp tried to rise, but he kept his mouth tightly shut.

I slapped my forehead and groaned at my oversight. "Dark magic, that's what you're smelling. Dragons don't see magic, they *smell* it—"

I can't use magic, Frank protested.

"No, but dark magic starts the fire up. Shit, I should have thought of that…"

What fire? he asked, beginning to panic.

Arnold regarded him quizzically. "You've never heard the phrase 'fire-breathing dragon'?"

No…

"Surprise, then," he muttered. "As I understand it, your species is native to the Gray Lands, and there's enough dark magic in this realm to trigger your full abilities. Ehm…how gassy are we feeling right now?"

While Frank mulled it over, he stifled a little belch, and twin curls of smoke rose from his nostrils. *How do I stop it? What do I do?*

Arnold sat back down and rubbed his chin. "Well, now, I suppose we could try to treat your burping. Maybe an antacid, something to calm the stomach…"

"Or we do the smart thing and call Dad," I interrupted, already scrolling through my phonebook.

Two rings later, he picked up. "Miss us already?" he teased. "How's the food?"

"Food's just dandy, but Frank's discovered fire."

"*Ah.* Hang on."

I heard the squeak of the couch springs, then the tap of Dad's boots against the wooden floor, which muted when he stepped out of the kitchen and into the straw-covered barn. A moment later, he said, "Okay, I'm here with Georgie. Is Frank nearby?"

I put my phone on speaker. "He's listening."

"She says not to worry about it. He'll figure it out on his own in a day or two."

Frank snorted and leaned closer to the phone. *And if I*

set this place on fire first?

"He's not convinced," I told Dad.

After a pause, he said, "Frank, your mom says you need to trust her and stop overthinking this. Just be mindful of it until you work it out. Okay?"

I can't turn it off?

"No," I told him, "I don't think you can stop it."

"Big no on that," Dad chimed in. "Not around dark magic. But hey, look at it like this: you're walking around with a flamethrower now. No one's going to mug you in a dark alley."

He rested his head on his arms and frowned, and I said goodbye to Dad. "Hey, Frank?" he added before signing off. "Georgie says she loves you, be careful, and don't try to eat any cats."

"They're pets here," I quietly explained, and held the phone closer. "Did Georgie ever—"

"Stu had half a dozen once. She was tempted. Behave yourselves," he said, and let me go.

I tucked my phone back into my pocket and looked at my companions. Frank seemed morose, and Arnold had put a slight distance between the two of them. "Right," I said, putting my lunch dishes on the delivery tray. "Guess we wait it out and pray Frank doesn't get the hiccups."

When Arnold left us, I finished unpacking, and then, deciding I didn't feel like getting lost in the castle quite yet, I laid down for a nap. I listened as Frank flopped onto the floor in his room next door, and then I heard an odd, muffled snuffling. Concerned, I got up and peeked around his door, and he raised his head, revealing watery eyes and a runny nose. *And I'm leaking now, too,* he thought. *What else is going to go wrong today?*

I stretched out beside him and did my best to curl around his much longer body—I hadn't measured, but Frank had to be better than six and a half feet tall. His torso was as warm as a heating pad, and when I draped my arm over his side, he clasped my hand. "It's going to be okay," I murmured. "I'm here. Don't be scared."

What if I forget and hurt you?

"You're not going to hurt me." I felt his chest hitch and suspected he was trying to suppress the unfamiliar physical reaction to his distress. "If you want to go home, just tell me. I'll understand."

His grip on my hand tightened, which was all the response I needed.

Even with a thick rug, the stone floor wasn't exactly comfortable, but Frank didn't need to be sleeping alone. We dozed there together through the long afternoon—as warm as he was, I didn't want for a blanket. Several times, when I was barely awake, I felt his mind probe for mine, making sure I was still there. He hadn't checked for me so frequently since he was a hatchling, but then again, he'd just stumbled into an unfamiliar world with a body he couldn't quite control for a second time. Frank might have been grown, but if he wanted me there for reassurance, I wasn't going to leave him.

I'd asked him once, when he was three, why he'd bonded with me instead of waiting for Georgie to come home. "You knew her voice, right?" I'd pressed as we flew in after a long day of exploration. "You all talked to each other before hatching—even *I* heard that. Once she came back that night, you had to know she was your mother."

Frank had considered the question for a long time in silence, and I'd begun to fear I'd offended him when he'd thought, *Yes, I recognized her. But she'd been gone for a while by then, and so had the others. When I couldn't hear them anymore, I could still hear you. You were the only one who didn't leave me.* His head had turned toward my seat at the base of his neck, giving me a side view of his enormous red eye, covered by its translucent inner eyelid against the wind. *Why wouldn't I have bonded with you?*

"I mean, it's pretty obvious I'm not a dragon."

So? You waited for me. Mom didn't.

I'd hesitated then, almost afraid to ask my follow-up question, but my mind-reading partner was seldom shy about conducting his own investigation.

No, I don't wish things were different.

"You could be off with the guys. They've been gone for a week, and that sounded like it might be a fun—"

They don't have you, he'd replied, ending the discussion.

As the shadows lengthened, I pushed myself off the rug, and Frank sat up beside me with a quizzical look. "Dinner with the grand magus," I reminded him. "I should probably brush my hair."

Are you going alone?

I felt his concern and patted his shoulder. "For tonight. Better mind my manners. Come on," I said, standing, then offered him a hand off the floor. "I think I remember my way to the dining hall. Let's see if they do takeout."

The grand magus's apartment was far neater than his office, albeit spartanly furnished. The couch in his living room was nice enough, a brown leather number decorated with brass studs and red throw pillows, but the accompanying end tables were devoid of knickknacks, and the walls were bare stone but for a single antique tapestry. The only sign of clutter was his book collection—his shelves strained beneath the weight of the accumulated volumes, which had spilled over into three piles on the rug. As for dining, he'd pushed a little table below a window overlooking the courtyard, and we sat together in the waning summer evening light, eating delivered food on his plain white china and making awkward conversation.

After a discussion of English weather patterns, the local attractions, and Arsenal's previous season, Bert put down his fork, took a sip of wine, and watched me work through my chicken Kiev. "So," he said, "I'm trying to decide whether the decision to send you was a friendly gesture or a power play."

I swallowed and laid my utensils aside. "Come again?"

"Why you? There's a message here, obviously, but exactly what it might be is—"

"They asked me to go because, one, I was raised Arcanum, so the culture shock is minimal," I interrupted, counting off on my fingers, "and two, I'm a decent wizard and can look after myself."

Bert blinked behind his thick glasses. "But you're not, are you?"

"Not what?"

"A wizard. You're witch-blooded."

The fact that I had mixed magical heritage didn't usually bother me, but Bert's tone made my hackles rise. "If you don't think I can cast, Grand Magus, then I'll be happy to meet you in a practice room and prove you wrong."

He leaned back in his chair, looking alarmed, then raised his hands and shook them as if to keep my irritation at bay. "No, no, you misunderstand," he hastily replied, "I'm not questioning your skill, I just..." He paused, then sighed in frustration and rubbed a spot above one of his thick eyebrows. "Sometimes," he muttered, "I say things, and they come across as insensitive or inappropriate. I, ehm...I'm not particularly gifted at conversation. Doesn't come naturally, you see. I can make myself clear on paper, but in the spur of the moment, sometimes I seem...well, rude. Or so I'm told." He studied his plate, then looked up at me over his lenses. "I've never had to spend much time with people until now, and it appears there are areas in which my education has been somewhat lacking. I asked you because I'd been told about your parentage, and I thought I might have been misinformed. That's all."

His look of contrition made my indignation fizzle. "You heard correctly," I said, resuming my meal. "Let me guess, private tutors?"

"Since I was seven," he replied, stabbing at his carrots.

"I showed promise when I was quite young, and Magus Jenner allowed me to begin my education early. Once she was...ehm..."

"Removed?" I offered. *Convicted of conspiracy to commit kidnapping and murder* seemed like a mood-killer.

"Yes, removed from office. Grand Magus Lowe was informed of my performance, and he permitted me to switch into private instruction. My parents homeschooled me, but they shifted my focus away from mundane subjects when I was thirteen, so most of my education has been individual study with magi. I suppose I didn't get the usual school experience, but I can't say it's been detrimental to my career," he added, smiling to himself.

"Wait—you've done nothing but study magic since you were *thirteen?*"

"Primarily, plus Arcanum history and some political science." He paused to peer at my face, then frowned. "You seem disturbed."

"I mean, yeah, I've studied magic, but my parents insisted that I learn the mundane stuff, too. The thought over there is to prep for college if you want to go—"

He chuckled. "What, faeries at university?"

"Fringers. There's quite a few kids now, and maybe half so far have come over here after high school." Bert still looked at me with amused incredulity, and I focused on my dinner to keep my temper in check. "The principal of the school in the settlement is a former history professor, and he's gung-ho for continued education. It's not hard to put together a transcript sufficient to get someone into college, and I know of a few kids who've transferred to better schools after a year or two. A girl in the class above mine actually ended up at Cornell. They go back, by and large, but the point is to get them into this realm, let them see it for themselves, and give them the option to make a life here if they want."

Bert broke a roll in half and reached for the butter. "Actually, I was hoping we might discuss the Fringe situation. I have a proposal for the courts, and I'd appreciate your cooperation."

"Yeah?" I speared a forkful of green beans and watched him doctor his bread. "What sort of proposal? I'll tell you what, if you wanted to invite some of the more talented witch kids here for formal instruction, it might be a nice gesture. I doubt you'd get many takers," I admitted, "but if you have someone willing to do remedial teaching, I could run it through the school and see if anyone would be interested."

"That wasn't exactly what I had in mind," he replied between bites. "Correct me if I'm wrong, but the majority of the Fringe are currently in Faerie, yes?"

"As far as I know. There's been a little repatriation, and not everyone evacuated during the Mulligan years, but yeah, most are over there now."

"Mm. I suppose Grand Magus Mulligan might have soured their—"

"Don't insult me by calling that murderer a grand magus," I snapped.

Bert started, again surprised by my reaction. "He *did* hold the office."

"He stole it from my mother, kidnapped her, kidnapped a chunk of the Fringe, tried to kill the rest—"

"Yes, I sat through the trial."

"Then maybe you understand why I'd be thrilled if his name were blotted out of every record book in the damn Archives."

My dinner companion watched me cautiously, a chess player contemplating a rogue on the other side of the board. "He did some terrible things, granted," he finally said, "but you have to admit that he also managed to—"

"*Don't.* Just don't." I put my utensils across my plate and wadded up my cloth napkin as I stood, watching the world as through a red film. "Sorry, indigestion. Thanks for dinner."

"Ros, wait," Bert called, hastily rising as I marched

toward the door. "I just…can we discuss this? Rationally? I'm not saying he was great, or even particularly good, but when you consider what he accomplished—"

"You have *no* idea," I spat, turning to glare at him, and was surprised to find my arms shaking with rage. "I had to live in that fucking hole, worrying that if I put one toe out of line, Mulligan would figure out what I was up to and kill my mother. I was *ten*! And you know what else?" I said, stomping toward him as Bert backed into the table. "I went to school with some of the Fringers. I've heard the stories. Do you have any idea how many orphans there are? How many people rescued from the silo who are *still* catatonic? How many who lost their minds?" I grabbed his shirt and stared into his glasses. "And even among the ones with problems magic could fix, the nightmares come back. They *always* come back. So don't sit there and tell me to be rational about Mulligan."

I released him and stepped away, not bothering to camouflage my disgust. "Maybe you should have gone to Arnold for tutoring," I said, and left without another word.

I was in a foul mood when I returned to my new apartment, but seeing Frank's awkward smile from the couch began to calm the storm. *Want to watch?* he asked, pointing to the television. *This old woman's dead. I think her mate did it, but it might be her daughter. Stabbed and left in a ditch. And everyone's clothing is weird*, he added, brows furrowing.

I'd discovered police procedurals as a teenager, and I'd inadvertently given Frank the bug by sitting out in the barn with my computer, explaining the plots and characters. We'd spent the previous summer systematically going through *Law & Order* together. "British cops," I explained, glancing at the screen. "They have different uniforms."

Ah. How was dinner?

I grunted and flopped onto the couch beside him.

That bad? May I?

Nodding, I closed my eyes and felt him rummage through my superficial thoughts. The contact lasted no more than a few seconds, but Frank was a pro at extraction, and I opened my eyes again to see him glaring at the door. "What?"

Can I fight him?

"Moon and stars, Frank, *no*! He's the grand magus!"

But he upset you.

"Yeah, well, I'm guessing he's a pretty decent caster, and since you're *slightly* smaller than usual…"

Frank turned to me, gave me a deliberate stare, then snorted smoke while I watched.

"No crisping Bert," I told him, but patted his knee. "Thanks anyway, bud."

Let me know if you change your mind, he replied, then stiffened and reached for my phone, which I'd left on the coffee table. *Forgot. This started ringing.*

I flipped through the call log, saw Bee's number, and called her back. She picked up on the third ring, sounding almost effervescent. "*Finally!*" she said by way of greeting. "Where are you?"

"Sorry, I had a dinner thing," I replied. "I'm in Glastonbury."

"Well, yes, but *where*? What's the flat number? I'm not going to search this bloody castle all night."

"You're here?"

"With Daisy, and she's dying to meet you. So where do I pick you up?"

"2042," I told her, beginning to smile again. Bee's enthusiasm was contagious, and in truth, it had been far too long since we'd seen each other. "Come on over, I don't have any plans."

"Perfect. We're taking you to a proper pub. Be round in five, ta."

Bee had always been the punctual sort. I barely had time to put on fresh lipstick and coax Frank back into his shoes when I heard her knock, and I ran across the apartment to let her in. "Hello, gorgeous!" she exclaimed, then threw her arms around me and squealed.

I didn't get a good look at her until she broke away and allowed me to breathe again. Bee had capped out at an inch shorter than me, but her abundant red curls more than made up the difference. She was boyish as ever in her figure, thin and mostly flat, but she'd finally gotten contacts and retired her much-loved cat-eye glasses. Her green eyes practically sparkled, though that might have been due to the glittery shadow she'd selected. She'd chosen a floral sundress with gray leggings and a matching shrug that night, an ensemble fit for the cautiously bohemian woman about town. I looked downright sensible beside her in my black pants and blue silk blouse.

"Come in, check it out," I said, stepping back from the door. "It's *so* good to see you again, Bee, I had no idea you were coming down this soon—"

"Wait, wait," she interrupted, pausing on the threshold, and pointed playfully at Frank. "Did we meet someone and forget to mention it?" Before I could explain, she hurried inside and jutted her hand toward Frank, who leaned against the back of the couch, watching the proceedings. "Hel-*lo*. Bee Powell, and *you're* a tall drink of water. Who might you be, now?"

His mouth curled as he met her handshake. *You mean you don't recognize me, Bee?*

Her jaw dropped, and she stared up at him, wide-eyed and gawking. "Oh, my God, *Frank*? What the hell did you do?"

That's the same reaction Ros had, he replied, and looked at the other visitor—Daisy, who lingered in the doorway with her hands in the pockets of her red shorts, puzzling over Bee's reaction.

Bee had sent me pictures of her girlfriend, but they didn't do her justice. Daisy was shorter than Bee and curvy, her dark hair shoulder-length and manageable, her eyes large and mahogany-hued. Her mother was Lebanese, and Daisy had inherited her coloration—all but her freckles, a gift from her English father. Meeting my glance, she dimpled as she smiled. "You must be Ros. I've heard so much about you."

"Lovely to finally meet you," I told her, giving her a quick hug. "Bee only tells me good things."

"Selective, that one," she replied, her smile widening. "And this is your partner, then?" she asked, turning to Frank.

A look of horrified surprise crossed his face, and he shook his head vehemently. *No, nothing like that, I—*

"You've got *telepathy*?" She laughed. "That's amazing! How did you learn—"

"He didn't," Bee interjected. "Daisy, Frank. Frank, this is my girlfriend, so be nice."

"Frank?" she repeated, cocking her head. "Sorry, I thought Frank was—"

Ensorcelled. You're right.

"Whoa." Daisy took two steps closer and peered at him. "Oh, wow, *there's* the bind…that's nice work. Ros, did you do that?"

"No, my teacher," I admitted, deciding that I liked Daisy. Anyone whose first reaction to "that's a dragon" was to get in his personal space and hunt for traces of spellcraft was my kind of reckless.

"Toula does a good job," said Bee, examining Frank at a distance with folded arms and a smirk. "*Very* good."

I caught her drift and chuckled. "Since when do you fancy men?"

"Hey, just because I don't want to jump into bed with him doesn't mean I can't appreciate the aesthetics," she shot back. "The albinism thing is rather striking, but overall…can't say I disapprove. Bet he looks *fantastic* in black."

Frank sent me a blip of wordless bemusement, and I grinned up at him. "Objectively speaking, you're cute."

"Better than that," Bee muttered.

His eyes darted back and forth, trying to make sense of the three of us. *Cute?*

"You're good looking, for a guy," she offered. "Colored contacts might help, but even without..."

Though stuck against the couch, Frank still leaned back in alarm. *You don't think anyone will get the wrong idea, do you?*

"What idea?" asked Daisy.

That...if I... He paused, flustered, then glared at me in exasperation as I bit my lip to hold back my laughter. *You know what I mean!*

I took a deep breath to keep my mirth contained. "It's...entirely possible that someone might flirt with you. Roll with it."

The notion that his disguise might be too good was a new, disquieting idea for Frank, who sat on the back of the couch and mulled it over. The tip of his tongue darted in and out of his mouth as he thought, though whether he was just cogitating or trying to smell something in the room, I couldn't say. Finally, flummoxed, he turned to me and frowned. *I don't know your mating signals. What should I not do? I don't...* He hesitated, then thought, *No offense intended, but the idea of...mating...*

"Frank! Are you calling us ugly?" Bee teased. "That almost hurts."

No, but...

"Stop torturing him," I said, and headed for the door. "Come on, Frank, we're going out. The answer to your question is best demonstrated with visual aids."

In the centuries since the castle was first begun, Glastonbury had grown up and diversified, and the former heath and fields that separated the two had slowly turned to farms, then to modest neighborhoods and light manufacturing. To save people the long walk to the shops and restaurants, a quasi-permanent gate had been constructed in the castle's central courtyard, linked to a locked closet outside a public toilet by a car park. It took a bit of spellcraft to open the closet—plus sense enough not to open it when mundanes were about—which prevented the younger kids of Arc 2 from running wild in town. Bee went first, waited until the coast was clear, then pulled together a slight camouflaging spell until the rest of us had popped through.

The pub that she and Daisy had chosen was better than the dark hole in the wall I'd imagined. True, the inside was decorated with wood paneling and antique fixtures, but the attached garden was filled with picnic tables and strung over with a canopy of twinkling white lights, and anyone under forty was drinking al fresco. We parked at a quiet corner table, then began the long trial-and-error process of figuring out what Frank would drink. Bee's beer made him grimace, and a sip of Daisy's vodka tonic sent him into a coughing fit—which, considering his newfound fire breathing and the proximity of alcohol, could have ended in disaster. My prosecco was similarly rejected, as Frank had almost no sweet tooth. Finally, Bee returned to the table with a Bloody Mary and a straw, and Frank declared it tolerable. *Is this ketchup?* he asked, turning the glass back and forth. *It's thinner than before.*

I explained the concepts of tomato juice and Worcestershire sauce, then stole Frank's spear of garnishes, as the obligate carnivore at the table had no need of a baby gherkin.

The conversation came easily—Bee and I had always been able to slot back into each other's flow on her occasional visits to Faerie, and soon enough, Daisy was relaxed and laughing, offering stories about Edinburgh and their neighbors. "You must visit, both of you," said Bee. "It's not a palace by any means, but it's big enough for a small crowd over a long weekend. We'll play tourist! I never get to do that anymore."

"Because you're not a tourist after three years in a place," Daisy reminded her.

"Details." She sipped her Heineken and surreptitiously pointed to the group two tables over, a mixed half-dozen men and women. "Okay, Frank, lesson time."

For the next hour, we offered running commentary about our fellow patrons, hypothesizing about which were in relationships and which were trying to start them. Frank drank and asked clarifying questions, trying to pinpoint the exact cues to avoid, but despite his best efforts, he was mortified when we told him at the end of the evening that he'd been getting intrigued looks from several of the people around us.

The night was pleasant, and Bee thought it best to show us the long way home. As we approached the castle—which, thanks to the protective spellcraft around it, looked like a boring field and some trees, and gave mundanes who came too close a deep, primal warning to go elsewhere—Daisy sidled up to Frank and said, "I want to ask you something out of professional curiosity."

Huh? he replied, glancing down at her.

"So, my course is linguistics, but I'm planning to do postgrad work in speech therapy. My mum's a speech therapist," she explained. "Grew up around it, I suppose. What I was wondering is whether you can phonate, or is it all a bit limited in there?" she asked, rubbing her throat.

I can make sounds like yours, but putting them in order...quickly... Frank offered an exaggerated shrug.

"Well, I'm here with Bee for a few weeks, and since I'm not busy...could I work with you? See if we can get you on your way to vocal? Only if you want," she added hastily. "If that's not on your agenda, then—"

I'm interested. He cut his eyes to me, and I nodded. *Yes. When—*

"Great!" Daisy smiled and linked her arm around his. "I'll see you after breakfast, then. This'll be fun...for me, at least."

I lay awake in my unfamiliar bed that night, staring at the ceiling and missing my glowing stars. Though Frank had started the evening in his room, he'd migrated into mine after half an hour alone, and he'd soon managed to fall asleep on the floor—still wearing his jeans, I saw, and made a mental note to talk to him about pajamas in the morning. But sleep was slow in coming for me, even as I tossed and turned, looking for the sweet spot on the mattress.

I'd just begun to doze off when my phone rang. Groaning, I rolled over to the nightstand and glanced at the screen, expecting Sam. Instead, to my surprise, the caller was Amy Levey, Sam's witch-blooded Fringer cousin. I tapped the line open but kept my voice low so as not to wake Frank. "Hi, Amy. What's up?"

I couldn't help but be anxious. Amy, a talented crafter of wands and other magical tools, ran a computer store in a seaside Virginia town that served as cover for Fringe HQ in that realm. For the better part of twenty years, she'd shared quarters with her husband, Kip, a Gray Lands native, and Badger and Seamus, a couple of retired British detectives—well, that, and a wizard Fringe coordinator and Val and Toula's half-fae nephew, respectively. Still, her time with them had done nothing to temper her South Carolina drawl.

"Hey, Ros," she replied, sounding tense. "How's England?"

"You heard, huh?"

"Word's gotten around. Seamus was warned in case of emergency."

I smiled to myself in the darkness. I'd met Seamus a handful of times when he came across to train with Val, and the poor guy always left with a heavy healing enchantment on him. "Can't imagine who would have told him," I joked. "So, what's up?"

The tension didn't leave Amy's voice. "Something. Not quite sure what, yet, but it's something. Badger doesn't want to worry you," she murmured, "but since you're back in this realm, I thought you shouldn't be kept in the dark."

"About what?" I asked, suddenly queasy.

Amy sighed. "Two members of the Minor Arcanum have been found murdered in the last two weeks."

"*Shit.*"

"I know."

As wizard confederations went, the Minor Arcanum was quite a bit smaller than the Arcanum, but its members were no less talented. They'd jumped in when the Fringe was in jeopardy, and I'd been told that the Fringe community in the mortal realm still kept close ties to the Minor Arcanum, partly for safety. If someone was killing wizards...well, the pool of likely assailants was limited.

"How did they die?" I asked.

"Bolt to the head. Temple shot at close range—death would have been instantaneous. Other than that, we've got nothing."

"No suspects?"

"Nope. The only signature tying the murders together is the victims' wands."

"What about them? Broken?"

"Missing," she explained. "No sign of them on the bodies or among their possessions, which seems pretty odd to me." She cleared her throat. "Anyway, Badger and Seamus are looking into it, but I thought you needed to be aware. Be on your guard, okay?"

"I will. You, too," I told her, and hesitantly asked, "You don't think it's an Arcanum job, do you?"

"Right now, we're not ruling anything out," she muttered. "Watch your back, hon."

Amy let me go, and I lay awake in the oppressive darkness, missing my family and trying not to think of wizards with holes magically blasted through their skulls.

CHAPTER 5

Given my druthers, I'd have spent at least the next day locked up in my apartment with Frank, junk food, and the worst that British television had to offer. I was in no hurry to run into Bert again after our aborted dinner, and I hoped he wouldn't send Arnold by to check on me. Storming out on the grand magus in a huff wasn't exactly the best way to begin this liaison gig, and I didn't need to be reminded that I'd perhaps been a *little* touchy. Amy's phone call also weighed on my mind, and the best remedy at that moment appeared to be ignoring the problem with couch time. It didn't hurt that Frank radiated heat like an electric blanket—a plus in the old castle.

But I'd barely cleaned up from breakfast when Daisy knocked and asked for Frank. He seemed excited about the notion of serving as her linguistic guinea pig, and so I let him go without protest. Morning television proved to be disappointing, I didn't want to go back to bed, and with Frank away, the apartment was far too quiet, the kind of silence that let me hear the blood rushing in my ears and the rats in the walls. Finally, having paced the length of the den enough times to memorize its dimensions, I changed out of my pajamas, grabbed my computer, and set off to find my way to the library.

I wasn't thrilled with the notion of plunging into Toula's reading list, but I needed a distraction, and parsing handwritten Latin seemed as good a task as any. Having scanned my homework sheet, I had to assume that most of the books weren't just out on the shelves for sticky fingers to discover. Once, when Grandpa had been in one of his infrequent good moods with me, he'd bragged that the Arcanum's collection rivaled those of the finest rare-books libraries in the world—and none of the others had a fraction of the magical tomes and scrolls that the Arcanum had squirreled away for protection in the Archives. Fortunately for me, the Archives had been transferred to Glastonbury when Arnold moved his base of operations out of Montana, so I had hope that at least the majority of the books I sought were somewhere on the premises. I also hoped I might find a friendly librarian who wouldn't hear my name and try to hex me—that is, if I could remember where in the massive castle they'd hidden the damn library. Arnold had walked us by the open doors, and with a passing glance, I'd noted the soaring ceiling, rows of old wooden tables, and side doors that had to lead into the stacks, but retracing my footsteps proved to be a challenge. Finally, I conceded defeat, unfolded the copy of the map he'd provided, and wound my way through the towers, feeling every inch the tourist.

Tuesday midmornings in June were obviously not the library's peak time. The pale light of the gathering storm outside fell through the high windows and onto the largely empty reading room. An old man sat at one of the tables, doing a crossword by lamplight, and a pair of girls giggled over the computer they shared several tables away, but otherwise, I had the place to myself. Glancing at the girls as I passed, I saw a pouting, blandly handsome teenage boy on the screen and smiled. Sure, British schools might still be in session, but if those two were cutting class for the day, I wouldn't rat them out.

A thick green runner over the stone floor muffled my footsteps—too well, apparently, as I had to cough for attention before the blond behind the circulation desk raised his head.

"Sorry to bother you," I whispered, catching a glimpse of a Sudoku book before he shoved it aside. I slid Toula's list across the polished wood and tried for a nonthreatening tone. "Looking for a little light reading. Don't suppose you could help me? Or is there a computer with Libsearch handy?"

But the librarian ignored the wrinkled paper. Instead, he stared at me, his pale blue eyes wide and his mouth slightly ajar, until he snapped out of his moment of frozen surprise and whispered, "Oh, my *God*."

His accent was American, and I fought the sudden urge to put up a shield. "Uh...hi, have we—"

"Ros Carver?" he asked, eyebrows raised.

"It's Bolin," I muttered testily.

My reaction didn't seem to dampen his sudden enthusiasm, however. "Antony Copeland," he replied— and, to my astonishment, he *smiled*. "Remember me? We were in the same year until...you know?"

"Yeah, I...I remember," I mumbled, kicking myself for thinking this library expedition was a good idea. Of course I remembered Antony—he might have been the weakest of the trio of boys who had done their best to make my life a living hell throughout elementary school, but he'd shot his share of spitballs. The man he'd grown into was leaner than the boy had been, more polished in a green-striped dress shirt and matching tie, and nothing in his clean-cut appearance gave any hint of the hellion he had been when I knew him.

"Wow," he whispered, grinning, "never thought I'd see *you* again. What're you doing here?"

"Work," I said lamely, still too shocked to give a better answer.

"Ah." He scanned my reading list and made a face. "Yeah, no one would check these out for fun. Come into my office, let's see what I can do," he offered, and pointed to a door behind the circulation desk.

I didn't want to follow him—the part of me that was still ten years old and paranoid suspected that the rest of Antony's crew were biding their time in there—but manners won out, and I slipped around the desk and through the wooden door, which led to a narrow hallway lined with modest offices. Antony headed for the last one on the left, a book-cluttered cubbyhole with a computer and a pair of chairs, and beckoned for me to come in. "Sorry about the mess," he said, dropping my list on top of a musty-smelling Greek dictionary, then pulled out his chair and started typing. "I can tell you offhand that most of what you want is going to come from the Archives, which means I need to do a bit of digging in—"

"Arcview?"

He stopped typing and looked at me quizzically. "How do you know about Arcview?"

"Used it to go through Mulligan's files." I cleared off a chair, sat, and folded my arms, daring him to object.

But Antony wasn't spoiling for a fight. "Huh," he said as he bent back to his work. "How'd you get access? Your granddad's machine?"

"They gave me an old Council laptop for Christmas and didn't format the hard drive. My uncle found—"

"The backup copy," he finished, and rolled his eyes. "Our security is *amazing*, isn't it?"

"Not the word I'd use."

Antony chuckled and pulled my list into his lap. "Amazingly bad, then. The grand magus—the old grand magus," he amended—"let us tighten up some of the loopholes on the tech side, but most of what we do is way over his head, and he took things slowly. I don't think the new guy's much better in terms of network security. Have you met him yet? Grand Magus Wold?"

"Yeah," I muttered.

He looked up from his work again and smirked. "What's the local term, 'wanker'?"

I raised an eyebrow.

"Come on, he's a self-satisfied little prick," said Antony. "Practically grew up in the library, has no idea how to talk to folks, probably gets off on giving speeches about our glorious heritage and whatnot."

"Gee, how do you really feel about him?"

He snorted. "Last summer, when I'd been working here long enough for him to realize that I wasn't actually part of the furniture, he put two and two together, asked about Aunt Billie, then asked me how I came to be disabled. *Disabled*," he repeated, drawing the word out as he gave me a long look around his monitor. "I'd have told him to go shove his wand where the sun don't shine if my boss hadn't been working at the other end of the desk."

I frowned in confusion. "No one bound *you*, did they? Your parents weren't even magi back—"

"They still aren't, and no, I'm not bound." He resumed typing. "Officially, I'm a wizard, but only by the skin of my teeth. Never could use anything better than an oak wand."

The tone of his voice told me that *I'm sorry* wouldn't be an appreciated response.

"But I got this gig after high school," Antony continued, "and I've been doing college online, too, so things worked out. It's a good job. Don't need much in the way of talent to shelve books, you know?" he joked. "And since I managed to avoid a mundane job, my folks don't give me grief about it. Okay...yes, I've got the first one, but it's back in the restricted stacks, so I'll have to go hunting tonight. You're not going to be able to take it out of the library—is that okay? I'm sorry, there's a lot that hasn't been digitized yet."

"That's fine," I said, making myself as comfortable as I could. Unless Arcview had been radically overhauled in the last decade—unlikely, considering the general wizard disdain for technology—I was in for a long wait.

"Gotcha. Can I be nosy and ask what you want with Marangi? Gertrude Holtz built on a lot of his stuff, and she's more accessible."

"But not all, and since the only copy I've had on hand is damaged and a bad French translation, my tutor suggested I pull the original."

"It's in Latin, you know," he cautioned.

"Learned that from a native speaker. My Latin's better than my French, at least."

Antony seemed poised to ask another question, then paused, perhaps remembering where I'd been, and let it drop. After a few minutes of typing, frowning at the screen, and making notes of locations on my list, he quietly said, "I never thanked you, Ros."

I'd been playing with my phone and almost missed it, his voice was so low. "Sorry—what for?"

"When Russell Mulligan came after me...thanks for stepping in. I was black and blue for two days. Saw the hole you left in the wall, and I heard someone had to help him out of that closet," he added, faintly smiling. "That's got to sting, getting taken down by a fifth grader."

"It was Bee, too."

"Yeah, but...well, thank you. My skull appreciates it."

"You're welcome," I said, glancing at my phone. "Just because I hated you guys didn't mean I wanted to see your head smashed in."

Antony gave no response for a long moment, then cleared his throat and pushed away from his computer, the better to look me in the face. "We were pretty shitty to you, weren't we?"

I nodded and put the phone aside. "Yeah."

"I'm sorry. Back then...you know, not my proudest memories."

He said it simply, and even without Val's talent for quick mental examination, I knew from his tone and demeanor that the apology was sincere. "People grow up," I offered, shrugging.

"That doesn't excuse everything. Anyway, thanks for taking up for me."

As he resumed his work, I tried to make polite conversation. "So, uh...how are Lyle and Silas these days?"

Antony didn't look away from the monitor. "Couldn't

really tell you. We don't stay in touch."

"Oh?"

"No. When the people you thought were your best friends stand back and laugh while you're used as a human piñata, it kind of sours your relationships. This one's actually in the public stacks, so I'll pull it after I finish here."

"I'm sorry about them."

"I'm not." He looked up just long enough to meet my stare. "After the trial, once Silas's dad and Lyle's mom were bound and the guys had to stop wearing those stupid gold necklaces, they were jerks to everyone. I mean, yeah, anyone in our class who wasn't related to a magus shunned them for a while, but they lashed out a lot. Got detention for fighting at least a few times a year, all the way through high school." His lips twitched into a fleeting smile. "The other silo kids didn't want anything to do with me, either—I had that great combo of Aunt Billie and my general assholery to work past—but once the mundanes realized that I was through with Lyle and Silas, a few of the guys reached out. Ended up joining the computer club—our app took third place in a state contest senior year."

"Congrats."

"Thanks. Nice to find something you're actually decent at, right? I mean, I think we all knew from fifth grade that I wasn't destined to be a magus."

"Fair enough," I replied. "So, what happened to those two, anyway? Still in the silo?"

Antony shrugged. "Last I heard, they were going off to Florida for college, but really, we don't keep in touch. They never saw much use for me after Russell called me out as a near-witch, and I never saw much use for them after they turned on me. Anyway." He stood and picked up my list, now covered with his neat notations. "Think I've got a handle on these, or at least leads. Come on, I'll show you where the public ones are, and I'll at least give you an update on the rest tomorrow."

I followed him out of the office, down another pair of hallways, and into the library's main stacks. "Hey, Antony?" I said as he guided us through the long aisles of bookcases.

"Mm?"

"I'm going to be around for a while, and, uh…if you ever wanted to grab lunch and *not* talk about Montana…"

He looked back at me and grinned. "Might have to take you up on that."

While Antony was happy to pull books for me, he couldn't let me leave the premises with them, seeing as I had exactly zero borrowing permissions in the Arcanum system. As a workaround, he set me up in a quiet little reading room, a small, tapestry-lined chamber with a pair of overstuffed sofas, a scuffed rosewood table between them, and a window overlooking Glastonbury. For the next three days, while Frank holed up with Daisy, I kept myself busy and mildly entertained, or at least distracted.

On Friday afternoon, however, there came a quick rap at the reading room door, and Antony popped his head inside. "Hey," he muttered, "got a visitor."

I barely had time to put my bookmark in place before Antony stood aside to let Bert slip into the room. Giving me a last eye roll behind the grand magus's back, Antony closed the door and departed, leaving me trapped with Bert and afflicted by a sudden touch of claustrophobia.

"Hello, Ros," he began, standing near the door with his hands clasped. "I think we should talk."

I concentrated on straightening my sprawl of reading materials so as to avoid meeting his stare. "About what?"

"I…believe we could have got off to a better start," he replied stiffly. "May I?"

Though I still wanted nothing to do with him, manners dictated that I should at least hear him out. I gestured toward the opposite couch while I tidied, and he sat with a swirl of his deep blue robe.

"After our, ehm…dinner, I spoke with Grand Magus Lowe," he began, settling into the cushion. "He reminded me that you probably approach the Mulligan administration from an emotional position, and I could have been more sensitive. I didn't consider that."

"You didn't live with him," I said. "I did. I know a lot of people who lost *everything* because of him."

"Which I don't dispute." Bert pulled off his glasses and began buffing the smudges with a fold of his robe. "Most of my tutors were magi, you understand."

"What does that have to do with—"

"The majority of the current Council were aides before their elevation. During the Mulligan years, you see. They have an insider's perspective on that period, and I suppose it's shaped some of my thinking as to my predecessor," he explained, offering a wry smile.

But something in his quasi-apology caught my attention. "You're telling me Arnold pulled the new Council from the old one's gofers?"

His brow furrowed. "An aide is so much more than a *gofer*—"

"That's not the point. The current magi—they were part of the old magi's staff? The magi who were convicted and bound?"

Bert seemed perplexed by my incredulity. "They were the most qualified. Aides are selected from among the highly talented, and in theory, magi should be the most skilled among us. Plus, Grand Magus Lowe needed people who knew how this organization had been run while he was away." He paused to slip his glasses back into place, then added, "He was an aide once himself, you understand. He knew what he was doing in selecting the Council."

"Did he? Because if I were trying to clean house, the last thing I'd do would be to choose new magi from the pool of Council staffers."

He said nothing for a moment as he considered my response, then murmured, "You're concerned about their loyalty?"

"You aren't?"

"No, they've never given me cause. Quite honestly," he added, crossing his legs, "Grand Magus Lowe needed insiders in his camp. His credibility was almost nil when he took office."

It was my turn to regard my companion as if his mental gears were slipping. "What the heck are you talking about? He was the *only* member of the Council to do anything about Mulligan."

"Yes," Bert replied dryly, "and in so doing, he abandoned his office, joined up with a lawless band of rogue wizards, and swept back into the Arcanum in the vanguard of a faerie invasion. Not exactly an auspicious career path."

"The Minor Arcanum isn't lawless," I protested, focusing on the one charge I could fight. "They just don't give a damn about what the Arcanum thinks."

"They shouldn't exist. Unschooled, undisciplined, unsupervised—"

"Effective," I countered.

"*Dangerous*. The Arcanum is meant to be a solitary institution. That my predecessor tolerated the so-called Minor Arcanum did not go unnoticed, and his wasn't a popular decision." Before I could argue, he leaned toward me and said, "Rules keep us safe. The structures and strictures of this organization have protected our kind for the last millennium, and part of that has always been subduing those who would splinter off. The Minor Arcanum exists without oversight, and as such, it's putting us all at greater risk."

"From *what*? If I've got the story straight, they're the ones who were willing to fight Nath while the Arcanum twiddled its thumbs."

"I'm not talking about the Gray Lands," he replied,

cool in the face of my mounting irritation. "What sort of protocols do they have for dealing with mundanes? For emergencies? Can you name them?" I said nothing, and he settled back against the couch with a little sigh. "It's reckless to leave them to govern themselves. I intend to begin negotiations to integrate them within the year."

"Good luck with that," I muttered.

Bert seemed oblivious, purposefully or not, to my sarcasm. "Thank you. And then there's the matter of the Fringe to sort—which I was going to discuss with you before your sudden stomach upset."

To be honest, my stomach wasn't feeling any better at the moment, but I pushed my discomfort aside. "What's there to sort out? Did you want to try to repatriate them or something?"

"On the contrary. I want to negotiate with the courts to patriate *all* of them. Convince the ones remaining in this realm to join their peers in Faerie."

My face screwed up as I puzzled through his proposal. "I don't think anyone would have a problem with moving more Fringers into the settlement, but what's wrong with having a few here? Most of the ones in this realm are native—this is home."

"But not all." He ran a hand through his brown curls as he thought, and when he spoke again, he sounded weary. "Witches and lesser fae running about, using whatever magic they can without any sort of restrictions…it's a miracle they haven't outed us yet."

"You're forgetting about the coordinators. But that's why I suggested that you invite the kids in for formal training, help them learn to really control their talent. I mean, they wouldn't join the Arcanum. Mom made overtures in that direction, and she got shot down—and that was before the Arcanum tortured and murdered half the Fringe. But offering classes would be a nice goodwill gesture."

"I'm not concerned with goodwill. The last thing we

need is to be responsible for the castoffs."

"*Excuse* me?"

He twitched at the edge to my tone. "How else would you describe them? We've no use for witches, and I doubt the courts have much to do with the lesser bloods. And then there's…ehm…"

He fell silent as a fireball appeared in my palm. "You were saying?" I murmured.

"You're the exception among witch-bloods, I suppose," he resumed after a long, cautious pause. "Think about the others." Leaning deeper into the cushion, he pressed the heels of his hands against his eyebrows and began to give himself a massage. "Assuming the courts are amenable to my plan, I'd like to move the remaining Fringe into Faerie. Get them out of this realm once and for all."

"So, what happens the next time a witch is born, huh? Or a dud?"

"Give them a choice, I suppose. Either move to Faerie or be bound and integrate into mundane society."

I extinguished my fireball, though at the moment, I wanted nothing more than to lob it at him and watch his robe go up in flames. "What, wait until they're twenty, then just round up anyone with an oak wand or worse, and if they won't leave—"

"Bind them, yes," he finished, and groaned as his hands worked a sore spot. "Keep them from misusing magic, first and foremost. There would need to be false memories as well—something that would stop them from remembering the Arcanum or the fact that they're bound."

"That's *horrible.*"

Bert opened his eyes and cocked his head. "How so? It would be a kindness."

From the pounding at my temples, it seemed Bert's headache was contagious. "You're talking about stripping people of their childhoods, their families—"

"What families?" he countered. "There aren't any

witches—well, *official* witches," he amended—"in the Arcanum. They leave when they're of age. Why not erase their past, all those years of failure and disappointment, and give them a fresh start in the wider world? Eliminate that constant reminder that magic will always be out of reach for them?" He pointed to the reading room door and said, "Take the chap on the circulation desk, for example. Have you met him?"

"Who, Antony?"

"Yes, exactly. His aunt's Wilhelmina Tamworth. *Fantastically* talented magus before she was bound. His parents are respectable wizards, as are his siblings—he has a brother who's an aide in Montana, I believe. And then there's Antony, barely competent with a wand. Don't you think he'd be happier if he weren't an object of pity?"

"Well, I don't know," I snapped. "Have you tried asking him?"

Bert chuckled as he shook his head. "Oh, I'm certain he'd object, but it's our responsibility to look out for the least among us. Either send them off to join the others in Faerie or send them to university with new memories and let them succeed on their own."

I sat back and folded my arms. "Badger Parsons."

"I beg your pardon?"

"Let's just say Harrison had tried your stupid idea," I told him. "Arnold's uncle was a witch. Under your plan, he's bound, sent to parts unknown, and then has Badger. She's as talented as any magus. What would you do in a situation like that?"

"I'm well aware of the Parsons case," he said, mirroring my pose. "To answer your question, exceptions could be made. Binds can always be broken, after all. But as for Ms. Parsons…" He shook his head and pursed his lips. "A bloody mess is what that is."

"Really? Last I checked, she was the finger in the dike against the Gray Lands."

"And unnecessary. We can protect our own borders

without a rogue wizard running about." He turned to stare out the window at the puffy summer clouds. "Grand Magus Lowe says he isn't bothered, but I do feel badly for the rest of the family. That's quite an embarrassment."

Even sitting in a library, it was becoming increasingly difficult for me to keep from shouting sense into Bert. "You know, one of my best friends is a Parsons cousin. She has nothing but nice things to say about Badger."

"Is that so?" He sounded surprised. "Perhaps it's different for the younger cousins. The elder Parsons have been thoroughly humiliated."

"Why? Because Badger called her grandparents out for giving her a shadow alder wand?"

"That...was unfortunate," he allowed, "but honestly, it would have been far kinder if she and her father had been bound. Instead, she declared for the Fringe, she consorts with the Minor Arcanum, and then there's her partner, whom she doesn't even pretend to hide." Bert picked up speed as his indignation blossomed. "I mean, it's bad enough that she blatantly flouts the Arcanum's authority— even her own cousin!—but to knowingly take up with a *faerie*..."

Finally, as hard as I'd tried to be civil, I reached my limit. "And what, pray tell," I said, going to my feet, "is wrong with *that*?"

Looking up at me as I loomed over him, Bert appeared to remember his audience and tried to backpedal. "You must understand, within the Arcanum—"

"*Fuck* your Arcanum," I spat, and stormed out, slamming the door behind me.

As I marched past the circulation desk, Antony cocked an eyebrow and muttered, "That sounded like it went well."

"He can kiss my ass," I told him, then recalled why I'd been in the reading room in the first place. "Sorry, I left my books—"

"I'll clean up. And there's a decent running route if you

want to head toward town. Just in case you need to blow off steam."

"Speaking from experience?"

Antony leaned over the desk and gave me a tiny smile. "Let's just say that I'm an excellent jogger, okay?"

I didn't want to run—I *needed* to vent. But with Bee out in town on a girls' afternoon with her mother and Frank holed up with Daisy elsewhere in the castle, I was at a loss for a sympathetic ear. The notion of calling my parents to complain offended my burgeoning adult sensibilities, and even as I sulked on my apartment couch, I could hear the lecture Toula or Val would give me for letting Bert get under my skin. My mood only soured as the afternoon went on, however, and finally, as the sun started to dip and the dinner hour approached, I found myself knocking on Arnold's office door.

He seemed unsurprised to find me in the corridor. "Let's talk," he said by way of greeting, shepherding me inside with an arm around my shoulders. "Make yourself comfortable. Tea?"

While he locked the door behind us, I took the liberty of casting his teapot full of hot water and added leaves from the tin on the tray. He sat behind his desk and let me work without interruption, and he smiled after a test sip. "That's nice. Biscuit?" he offered, producing a half-eaten pack of digestives from his desk.

I took one, dipped it into my tea, and watched the crumbs break off and float just below the surface. "Have you spoken to Bert lately?"

"I have," Arnold replied, nibbling his cookie.

"Guess he told you I've walked out in a huff twice now, huh?"

"And more." He took another sip of tea. "You're thinking of throwing in the towel, I take it?"

"Maybe," I allowed, sending another volley of cookie

crumbs to their watery end. "He was telling me all about his plans to memory-wipe witches and—"

"I'm well aware of Bert's...notions," Arnold replied with pursed-lip distaste. "Which is why I pushed him into asking for a liaison."

I stopped playing with my food and squinted at the magus. "Come again?"

"You thought bringing one here was purely his idea?" he asked, then snorted. "If Bert had his way, we'd treat every faerie incursion into this realm as a declaration of war. An attack on our sovereignty, as it were." One eyebrow rose as he drank his tea. "The boy's a talented wizard, I'll give him that, but his head's so far up his arse that he could give himself a colonoscopy. I'm trying to save the Arcanum, Ros," he murmured, staring at me from across his desk. "And to do that, I need to get through to Bert."

"What, he won't listen to you?"

Arnold sighed and pulled another cookie from the sleeve. "When I took over for your mum, I had to make some difficult choices. Filling out the Council was an exercise in compromise. There are some magi whom I'd trust with my life, and there are others who would just as soon toss me into a volcano, but that was the best solution—a balance between magi who saw Mulligan and his policies for what they were and magi who think he might have had a few decent ideas. It's all to do with politics," he explained before I could interject. "One does not simply ignore the more prominent of the old-blood families, especially if one more or less took power in a coup." Arnold paused for a bite of cookie. "Now, would you like to guess which of my magi were primarily responsible for Bert's education?"

"Why didn't you step in?" I asked.

"Because, my dear, I had the entire Arcanum to run, and I couldn't be bothered to make little Bertie's lesson plans on top of the rest. And it's not as though anyone was blatantly indoctrinating him—it was subtle. I started to notice it once I brought him on as my aide, and then I realized how...well, *rigid*...he could be in his thinking. Once Bert takes a decision, he's not likely to stop and reevaluate. So, I coaxed him into bringing a liaison here in hopes of confronting him with a different perspective," he concluded. "A little pushback to some of his grander schemes, you see. He doesn't fully trust me because his tutors have been whispering in his ear, and so I need someone else to shake him up."

Arnold passed the digestives, and I helped myself to another. "We aren't getting along," I told him between bites. "I...*guess* I've been short with him..."

"You're challenging him," said Arnold, shaking his head, "and he hates it. He doesn't do well with an unsettled mind, and you're pushing him in unconsidered directions, sad to say. But I can tell he's intrigued. You're a puzzle to him."

"The only puzzle is figuring out how I'm supposed to keep from killing him," I muttered.

"Eh, you're clever enough, you'll think of something. Give it another week, what do you say? For me?"

I drained my teacup to its crummy dregs, then looked back at Arnold's hopeful smile and scowled. "Not promising miracles, here."

"Believe me," he said, working another cookie free of its wrapper, "I'd settle for plain old progress."

As I walked back to my apartment, I mulled over the information Arnold had presented me. I was supposed to be a liaison between the Arcanum and the courts, not the nascent grand magus's newest tutor. Something told me that Arnold hadn't been entirely forthcoming with Coileán and Eleanor when he arranged this gig—I could only imagine how quickly they'd object if I informed them of Bert's proposals concerning the Fringe.

But Kura wanted me here, watching, listening. Could Bert be the coming storm she feared?

Lost in thought, I jumped when I opened the apartment door and found Frank and Daisy waiting for me in the den. "Hi!" I said, clutching my chest, and leaned against the wall. "Sorry, wasn't expecting you yet—"

"Bee's meeting us in half an hour," said Daisy, beaming as she rose from her chair. "We're going out to celebrate."

"Celebrate?" I echoed.

She turned to Frank, who shot me a flash of teeth over the back of the couch. "The work has been slow," she said, "but the building blocks are there. We were going to keep going about it the hard way, but my partner, brilliant as she is, worked up a spell to help scaffold everything until it's automatic. Put it together this morning, and I *think* you'll be impressed."

"You, uh...you put a spell atop the transformation bind?" I asked, my mind's eye showing me a preview of the disastrous results of that spell breaking prematurely.

"Bee did," said Daisy. "It's literally atop it—there's no interaction between the two, so the bind's integrity isn't affected. And she got your Toula's blessing before doing it, so everything's square."

I folded my arms and glanced at Frank. "Going to give me a demonstration, bud?"

He thought for a moment, and then, in a voice as deep and rich as a swimming pool of molten dark chocolate, haltingly said, "It...not perfect...but...with practice..."

I stared at him, bug-eyed, and Daisy cackled. "I know, right?" she said. "Isn't it great?"

"Not smooth...yet," Frank protested. "Not great."

"She's not talking about your speed," I explained, and took a seat beside him on the couch while he watched me in bemusement. "Um...how to put this...it's a nice voice. Did Toula—"

"She says it's natural," Daisy interrupted. "I called her back and let her listen, and she says she didn't augment it—the spell took what was there and put it in direct translation, so to speak. That's all Frank."

He looked back and forth between us, still trying to decipher our conversation. "Go ahead," I told him, tapping my temple. "Less awkward if I don't actually have to spit it out."

His mental probe was swift and painless, and I knew he'd found what he was after when his eyes flew open wide. *I don't…but I'm not…*

"It's a *really* nice voice."

"Magical. The kind that makes knickers disappear," said Daisy, giving him a playful smile. "Once you're up to speed…"

Frank rested his face in his hands and groaned.

CHAPTER 6

I'd been planning to sleep in on Saturday morning. The four of us had made a late night of it, and near the end, we'd concocted a game of sending Frank to various bartenders and seeing how many free drinks he could score without actually flirting. He brought back a surprising number, and as it would have been bad manners to let that much booze go to waste, we'd all done our part—well, all but Frank, who couldn't see the point of doing shots. Daisy had tried to explain the pleasure of the tingly burn all the way down, but that did little to impress the member of our party who could belch fire.

Unfortunately for me, my plans for a nice, long morning of sleeping off Friday night were curtailed by an insistent rapping at the door. Dragging myself from bed in my ratty T-shirt and shorts, I stepped over Frank, who was still passed out on the rug, and shuffled through the apartment to see who might be disturbing me at the ungodly hour of nine. I unlocked the door and cracked it open, then immediately wished I'd feigned sleep.

"Ros," said Bert, giving my pajamas a once-over. "Good morning?"

"Hi," I croaked, then stepped back and opened the door a few inches wider, wishing I'd thought to put on a bathrobe. Bert's robe of the day was forest green and fell perfectly to the top of his wingtips, a complement to his wrinkle-free black shirt and trousers. "Need something?"

"Well, I'd hoped we might have lunch and try to put some of yesterday's, ehm…*unpleasantness* behind us, but if that would be inconvenient…"

Much as I wanted to tell him to go perform anatomically impossible feats, I remembered what Arnold had confided and forced myself to say, "Coffee does wonders. Noon?"

And so, against my best judgment, I soon found myself on one of the grand magus's office couches with the Arcanum's version of room service quiche and salad, a fuzzy feeling on my tongue, and an unusually quiet host. We spoke of little beyond the quality of the cuisine as we ate, which suited me just fine—I knew it was possible to cure a hangover with magic, but I hadn't quite gotten the knack of it, and my aspirin were still kicking in. Only once we'd cleared our dishes and stacked them back on the delivery tray did Bert get down to business.

"I took the liberty of discussing our situation with Grand Magus Lowe," he said, pushing the tray to the far end of the coffee table. "Hope you don't mind."

I brushed a crumb of crust off my skirt. "What situation would that be?"

"Well, obviously, this isn't working out," he replied, twitching a finger back and forth between us. I started to make a conciliatory remark, a vague admission that I could have been less testy with him, but before I could do more than open my mouth, Bert said, "I've never been despised before. It's not the most pleasant of feelings, you know."

"I don't *despise* you," I protested.

"Could have fooled me," he muttered into his tea.

Part of me felt like I should say something to make him feel better—awkward or not, he was upset—but I pushed down the urge to comfort him. "I don't know you well enough yet to make up my mind about you. Now, your grand plans are, at best, stupid, and you're so ignorant of anything outside this damn castle that you don't even know how insulting you are, but…" I shrugged. "Maybe you're not as awful as you seem."

Bert's shoulders slumped. "You really think I'm

awful?"

"You haven't done much to convince me otherwise."

"*Why*? All I'm trying to do is protect us—"

"By force. At least by edict. And how dare you suggest binding witches who've done nothing wrong?" I pressed, my voice rising. "Against their will? What gives you the right?"

"It's the kindest thing—"

"You don't get to make that call," I snapped. "And before you start in on getting rid of the Minor Arcanum and the Fringe to protect the Arcanum, maybe think about the fact that they were there to protect this realm when the Arcanum wouldn't." I leaned toward him across the table, pinning him to his seat with my stare. "You think your tutors had an insider's view? I learned from my uncle and my parents and Toula and the Fringers. I mean, do you even realize that the only thing keeping Nath out of this realm is her agreement with Badger? When Nath put out a challenge, Badger walked into the Gray Lands to treat with her. *Alone*. So before you go criticizing rogue wizards, think about what they've done for us all."

I'd braced myself for an immediate, angry rebuttal, but none came. Instead, Bert glanced at a spot over my left shoulder and scraped his bottom lip with his teeth as he thought. After a moment, he met my eyes again and calmly said, "I hear you, Ros. But if I'm to consider your position, then it's only fair you give equal consideration to mine."

I sat back and crossed my arms. "Okay, I'm listening."

Bert softly sighed. "I am responsible for the lives and well-being of every—*nearly* every—wizard in the world," he murmured. "Protecting ourselves is an issue of paramount importance. So when I look around and see wizards using magic without any oversight or restrictions, or witches without proper training or mastery trying to cast close to mundanes, or faeries running amok, I have to think first about my responsibility to my people and to this organization. That means neutralizing threats—even when they aren't yet threats," he said before I could interject. "Do you understand?"

"I think so," I replied. "But what I'm suggesting is that you have to balance that goal against, you know, the Fringe's right to exist."

"The Fringe isn't my responsibility."

"But you can't just push it out or eradicate it because it displeases you!"

"All right, let's change the scenario, then: what do you suppose your bosses would do if a bunch of faeries broke off, said they were forming their own organization, and to hell with the courts?"

"That's completely different."

"*How*? That's no different than our position here with the Minor Arcanum and the Fringe! And don't get me started on the Dark Company…"

I began to argue with him, but I knew another fight wasn't going to help the situation. "You know, maybe we should talk about Arsenal again," I mumbled.

He relaxed into a slight smile. "You don't really follow them, do you?"

"Just trying to make conversation."

"Appreciated." He rose and took the lunch tray into the hall, then left it on the runner for the kitchen staff. "I was thinking," he said, slipping back into the room, "that you've not had a proper tour of Glastonbury, have you?"

"I've seen a bit," I told him. "Pubs, mostly."

"That's not exactly welcoming." He stuffed his hands into his pockets and slunk close to the wall. "This might sound forward, but my mum makes the best Sunday roast in town, if not Somerset, and…I suppose it might get old eating with your guard every meal, and my parents' house is a nice walk from the castle, and—"

"You're inviting me to Sunday dinner?" I asked in disbelief.

"Lunch," he clarified. "If you'd like. Just, ehm, a way to see a bit of town. I do step outside the castle, you know," he joked. "From time to time. Mum gets cross when I don't come round."

"Tell me about it," I muttered, thinking of my phone's queue of unanswered texts from home.

"You'll come, then?"

I had to stifle my upwelling incredulous laughter. "What, after all the lovely talks we've had?"

Bert smiled weakly. "Give me a chance to prove I'm not awful, eh? And if nothing else, Mum's Yorkshire puddings are very nice."

If I was going to get anywhere with him, I realized, I needed to at least accept the proffered olive branch. "Sure," I said, and forced a quick grin. "Lunch with your folks sounds...pleasant."

Frank disagreed—all afternoon.

"I go with you," he said as I brushed my teeth that night. "Safer."

I spat and rinsed my mouth. "*I'll* go with you."

He snorted his impatience with my nitpicking. "Close."

"The answer's still no. Most of the meal is probably going to be carbs, anyway. You wouldn't like it."

Frank started to protest, then gave in and thought at me. *You don't know these people. You don't especially care for Bert. If I go along, at least you'll have backup.*

"Against three wizards?" I asked, splashing water on my face.

Hard to cast if your hair's on fire.

I refused to be swayed, however, and soon, he curled up on my rug and drifted off. I had just finished my toilette and was giving my phone one last check for the night when a message came through from Amy: *Another body. No wand. No update.*

Like last time? I texted back, leaning against the bathroom door.

Her response came quickly: *B&S say it's the same MO.*

You hearing anything?

Nope.

Be careful, she wrote.

Troubled, I stepped over Frank and climbed into bed, where I stared at the ceiling and mulled over my options. Instinct counseled against running to Eleanor and Coileán—surely someone in Virginia would call them directly if there was anything solid to convey. I thought of alerting Bert, but given his apparent distaste for the Minor Arcanum, I doubted he'd be eager to jump into a murder investigation. And so, uneasy but at a loss, I rolled over and tried to sleep.

The Wold house was modest, smaller than my parents' place but plenty big for the elder Wolds and their three cats. The homestead was a detached house with red shutters and a neat front garden not half a mile from the castle, tucked against a field outside of town. Frankly, the place was adorable, a perfect, tidy, quasi-country house, and as Bert escorted me up the front walk, I could smell the unmistakable aroma of roast beef and rosemary.

Bert's father, a wiry, gray-haired man in a white golf shirt, met us at the door before we could even ring the bell. "Bertie!" he exclaimed, and pulled his son close to pound him on the back. "And this must be your friend," he said, turning to me with a wide smile.

I held out a bottle of shiraz, partly in offering and partly to avoid the sort of rib-crushing hug to which Bert had just been subjected. "Ros Bolin. Nice to meet you, Mr. Wold. Thanks for the invitation."

"Oh, of course!" He stepped back and held the door open. "Come in, come in, you two. Maura's just finishing."

From the kitchen, a woman called, "Are they here, Nigel?"

"Yes, love!" Mr. Wold called back. "I'll pour."

I barely had time to shift my purse on my shoulder

before Bert put a glass of wine in my hand. "They're a little excited," he murmured, bending close to my ear. "I've never brought a girl over, and I *told* them you were new to town and that was all, but I think they've got the wrong idea."

"*Ah*," I said, catching Mr. Wold watching us from the dining room. "Are they going to be disappointed?"

"If so, it's their own fault. I tried. But you know how it is, only child, always working, suddenly asks to bring a guest to lunch, and the next thing you know, Mum's going on about a friend of a friend whose son's just got engaged. So if things get, ehm…"

"I'll let them down gently."

"Thank you," he said with a sigh. "Ready to eat?"

As Bert pulled out my chair, his mother emerged from the kitchen with a heaping platter of roast beef, the safety of which I would have strongly questioned if Frank had been anywhere nearby. "Hello, dear," she beamed, clasping my hand once the meat had been delivered to the table. "*So* nice to meet you. Bert's told us all about his friend from the States."

I glanced over my shoulder to where Bert stood, waiting to help my chair to the table. "He…did?"

"Oh, you shouldn't sound so surprised," said Mrs. Wold, heading back to the kitchen for the side dishes. "I'm just glad he's met someone as clever as he is."

"*Mum*," Bert groaned. "Please."

"No need to be modest, Bertie. And go ahead, Ros, have a seat. Be ready in a moment."

I let Bert scoot my chair into position and smirked at him across the table once he was situated. "So," I whispered when Mr. Wold ventured into the kitchen to help his wife schlepp bowls, "dare I ask what you've been telling them?"

"Not what Mum seems to be insinuating," he replied, reddening.

"But you told them I'm clever, huh?"

"That wasn't a lie," he protested. "You'd have to be to make any sense of Marangi without a gloss. Studied Latin long?"

"Not really. My combat coach is Roman, and he gave me what I needed to make sense of it."

Bert's brow knit. "When you say 'Roman'..."

"I mean he predates the Caesars. And if you *really* want to annoy him, get him in the same room with someone using Church pronunciation—drives him up the wall." I grinned. "My dad's old mentor is a priest. Val's confounded that someone as bright as he is can't break himself from the Italian habit."

Before Bert could question me further, his parents carried out the last dishes and sat down to join us. While the platters and bowls began circulating, Mrs. Wold smiled at me and asked, "How long have you been here, Ros? Just come from Arc 1, I assume?"

"About a week," I replied, "and, uh...not directly."

"But you're from Montana originally, yes?"

I cut my eyes across the table, trying to divine what, exactly, Bert had told his parents about me, but from the slightly constipated look on his face, I gathered that it wasn't much. "I was raised in the silo," I told Mrs. Wold, forcing a reciprocal smile. "Lived abroad for a while now."

"That's lovely." She plopped a pair of Yorkshire puddings on my plate and passed me the gravy boat. "I know there's so many who've left Arc 1 in the last years—quite a few came here, in fact. We've got a regular American expat community in the castle," she added, chuckling. "I'm sure they'll have you sorted in no time. Potatoes, dear?"

"Now, you and Bert are of an age, aren't you?" Mr. Wold chimed in as Mrs. Wold heaped food onto my plate.

Bert and I traded glances. "Close," I replied. "I'll be twenty-one in October—"

"I was twenty-two last January," he said, coming in

with the assist. "About two years, then, that's pretty close."

"Ah." Mr. Wold frowned as he mulled that over, then asked, "Were you old enough to have had to sit through the mass trial?"

"What an unpleasant charade," Mrs. Wold muttered at the other end of the table. "First and only time I'd been to Arc 1, and it was *awful.* Such a mess."

"Yeah," I mumbled. Catching Bert's eye, I could see the unease in his face, and I held my tongue.

"So," said Bert, a bit too brightly, "we noticed the roses on the way up. They're lovely this year, Dad, what are you feeding them?"

But his parents didn't take the bait. "I can't believe the Carver girl made all the children sit through that debacle," said Mrs. Wold. Her neat brown coiffure bounced as she shook her head. "It was a kangaroo court of the highest order, and to force children to watch—goodness, what were you, ten?"

"And a half," I said, concentrating on my plate.

She *tsk*ed and stabbed at her potatoes. "I'm surprised more of you didn't have nightmares after that. When they dragged the poor grand magus off to—"

"Maura," cautioned Mr. Wold.

She paused, and though I was doggedly staring at my meat, I felt her eyes on me just before she reached over to pat my hand. "I'm sorry, dear, this isn't fit for the table. Hate to dredge up bad memories."

"Really, Dad, about those roses," Bert tried again.

Fortunately, his second attempt was a success, and the meal turned into a horticultural lecture—it was obvious that Mr. Wold had a massive soft spot for his flower garden. Bert looked my way on occasion, first with relief that the earlier topic had been abandoned, and then with eye rolls as his father droned on about watering schedules and natural pesticides. As for me, I didn't mind the background chatter—Bert hadn't exaggerated about his mother's culinary skill, and I was enjoying the best meal I'd had all week.

By the time Mrs. Wold brought out chocolate cake and tea, I was beginning to loosen up. My hosts were in a good mood, Bert was smiling, and I'd lost the feeling that someone was about to jump me from behind. Congratulating myself on behaving like a mature, responsible adult in polite company, I tried the cake, groaned, and turned to Mrs. Wold. "This is *amazing.*"

She beamed and patted my arm. "Thank you, pet. Bertie, you'll have to bring Ros by more often."

"Seriously, this is great. Am I tasting orange?"

"Cointreau," she stage-whispered. "Got the recipe from my cousin Dora…which reminds me." She turned to Bert. "Dora and Nick are back from London. I saw her in town two days ago—they're in a rental for now, but I said I'd put in a word with you about getting them into the castle."

"I'll see what I can do," said Bert, concentrating on his tea. "What about Nick's, ehm…"

"Sacked. He had too much to drink one night, tried to cure the hangover with a hair of the dog, and wrecked the bus. It's terrible," she said, flipping back to me. "Nick's got loads of talent, but he was in the corps during the Mulligan years, and he got lumped in with the rest, poor boy. It's a travesty how he's been treated. He was only doing his job."

Stunned, I inhaled a bit of cake and broke into a coughing fit, and Mrs. Wold gave me a series of good thumps between the shoulders until I could breathe again. "Sorry," I croaked between sips of water, "the corps?"

"Assassin corps," Bert mumbled.

"That's…what I thought." I drank until my eyes stopped watering, and while I was occupied, Mrs. Wold turned her attention back to her son.

"You know, Bertie, it's been ten years," she began, reaching down the table to clasp his hand. "So many lives have been ruined. Don't you think it's time to consider clemency?"

He averted his gaze from her pointed stare. "Mum, this really isn't the time to talk about that."

"Why not? Nick and Dora are hardly unique— wouldn't it be best for everyone if we could all put that ugly business behind us?"

"Think about Margaret Jenner," Mr. Wold added, pushing his teacup aside. "She was so kind to you, son, and look at her now, out there with nothing."

"She's living with her son in Leeds," he mumbled into his cake. "I wouldn't say she's all alone."

"But to have a career like hers ended that way…"

"Margaret's brilliant," said Mrs. Wold. "You were going to review the instructors for the older children, were you not? She'd make a wonderful teacher if you'd just bring her back and take off the bind."

I sudden, desperately, wished I were anywhere but at that table, and Bert continued his unsuccessful attempt to evade the conversation. "Mum, Dad," he muttered, "there's a *guest*, remember…"

The eyes of the elder Wolds fell upon me. "I'm sure Ros knows someone affected," Mrs. Wold replied. "Surely everyone in Arc 1 had a family member caught up in Carver's purge—isn't that right, dear?" she asked, giving me a sympathetic look and my forearm a light squeeze. "Living through all of that at your age must have been dreadful."

I mumbled something noncommittal and forced another bite of cake down my constricting throat.

"So much talent lost," said Mr. Wold, shaking his head. "Such a shame. I mean, don't get me wrong, I'm grateful that our Bert's had the opportunities he's been given, but what Carver did to the Council was appalling."

"They were just trying to protect us," his wife replied. "And say what you will, but they did keep this realm free of faeries for eleven years, and that's no small feat. Of course," she said with a sigh, "Lowe turned around and invited them right back. But I'm sure, given a few more months, our Bertie will have them on the run again."

Her smile spoke of deep maternal pride, while Bert's expression seemed closer to queasy.

"Vile creatures," Mr. Wold muttered between forkfuls. "If you ask me, we should go back to exterminating them. Maybe that would make them think twice before interfering in this realm."

Bert's head snapped up, and he looked at his father in exasperation. "Could we *please* not discuss this right now? I told Ros we'd have a nice lunch, and—"

"We haven't upset you, have we, dear?" Mrs. Wold interrupted, peering at my carefully blanked face, and her tone softened. "Oh…I didn't think. I bet it's all still rather fresh to you, isn't it? Can't imagine what that must have been like, living there during the purge," she said, reaching over to pat my shoulder. "Were any of your friends magi's children? Or—you didn't have family on the Council, did you?"

"My grandfather," I said, keeping my tone as neutral as possible.

Mrs. Wold's face fell. "Oh, darling, I'm *sorry*. Me and my big mouth—of course you wouldn't want to talk about this. But see, Bertie, isn't it time for a mass pardon?"

"Who's your grandfather?" Mr. Wold asked before Bert could answer her. "Still living?"

I felt discomfort in my left hand and realized that I'd balled it up in my lap, tightening and barely relaxing my fist as I struggled not to explode. But Mr. Wold was watching me, waiting for an answer, and I was too upset to cobble together a convincing lie on the spur of the moment.

"Howard Carver," I replied, looking him in the eye. "And I haven't spoken to him since I was ten, so I really can't say how he's doing these days."

I heard the clatter of metal on china to my right and saw that Mrs. Wold had dropped her fork. Her pretty pink lips had opened into a shocked O, and I suspected I wouldn't like whatever she had to say once she recovered her voice. "Excuse me," I said, rising from the table, and grabbed my purse. "Bert, could you point me to the restroom, please?"

"Down the hall, second door on the right," he mumbled. "Ros, I—"

"Thanks," I said, cutting him off, and made my hasty escape.

Closing the door behind me, I planted my hands on the white porcelain pedestal sink, closed my eyes, and took a few deep breaths. Lunch was almost over. I could politely leave in just a few minutes, no one was going to attack me, there was no need to give rein to the screaming panic in my chest...

From down the hall, the Wolds' rising voices filtered through the thin bathroom door. "How could you?" Mrs. Wold hissed. "Bringing that...that..."

"Mongrel," Mr. Wold supplied.

"Yes. How could you bring that here? To *our* home?"

"And after everything the Carver girl did," his father continued. "Bertie, what the hell has got into you?"

"Oh, God," his mother interrupted, horrified, "are you *seeing* that thing? Tell me you aren't..."

I opened my eyes and stared at the face in the mirror: slightly tanned under my makeup but flushed to my ears, blonde hair falling limp, large brown eyes—my father's eyes, only a shade lighter than Titania's, to hear Coileán tell it—wet with the furious, embarrassed tears I willed away. How, I fumed, could Bert have let that little factoid slip by forgotten before inviting me to meet his parents? Surely he knew their thoughts on the Mulligan fallout—had he been crossing his fingers and hoping everyone would talk football for the afternoon?

"What do you mean, you invited her to the castle?" Mr. Wold cried in the dining room. "Are you *mad?*"

I'd had enough. Faced with two angry wizards and their mumbling son, I took the coward's way out of the house: I opened a gate into my apartment and slipped through before anyone could send a search party.

My bedroom was silent, as was the rest of the flat. On the kitchen table, I found a note in Bee's neat handwriting: *Daisy and I took Frank to a matinee. Hope lunch went well!* She'd signed it with a little pictograph: a cartoon bumblebee flying beside a flower that could only have been a pencil rendition of a daisy. Beneath it, in the unsteady strokes of a kindergartener with a crayon in his fist, Frank had scrawled his name as well, and but for the *N*, all of the letters were facing the correct direction.

I smiled at the note. Bee and Daisy were looking out for Frank, and he'd made so much progress in less than a week. I was grateful for the girls' kindness and so proud of him.

And then I put the paper down, looked around the empty apartment, and had myself an angry cry.

Ten minutes later, drained but still sniffly and with a fresh volley of tears on a hair trigger, I mentally ran through all the things I should have done differently, starting with turning Bert down. I could have told his parents off, right to their smug faces, or I could have shown a spine and returned to the table. Maybe, once the inevitable shouting was over, they'd have listened to me. Probably not. Yelling back at them and summoning forth a few fireballs would have been far more satisfactory in the short term, though something told me my parents wouldn't have approved.

I needed to talk to someone, but my only friends in England were at the movies, and I could imagine what my dad and my uncle would do if I called while a weepy mess. Desperate to talk to someone who wouldn't start a war with the Arcanum, I calculated the time in Texas, hoped Sam was up at seven on a Sunday morning, and dialed.

To my surprise, he picked up on the second ring and actually sounded awake, if quiet. "Hey, Ros. How's it going?"

"Honestly? Awful," I replied, trying not to cry again.

"What's wrong?"

Though I'd meant to keep the conversation light and vague, I broke down twice as I told Sam about my first week in Glastonbury, beginning with Bert and my drafty apartment and ending with the disastrous lunch at the Wolds' house. He listened without interruption, adding monosyllabic responses as needed, and when I came up for air, he said, "I'm really sorry. Sounds shitty. You going to be okay?"

"Yeah." I sniffed, rubbing the back of my hand across one eye and smearing my mascara. "I should have expected it, but…you know…"

"People suck sometimes, and there's not much you can do to change that."

"I know." I filled a glass at the tap and took a long drink. "Sorry, I didn't mean to unload on you, I just—"

"It's okay."

"It's *not*. Way too early for you to be listening to me whine," I said, laughing weakly. "Did I wake you? Please tell me you didn't wake up to that."

"Nah. Never went to bed last night. You're just fine."

I frowned and put my water on the counter. "What's up? Party or something? Cows get loose again?"

Sam was quiet for a long moment, and then, ever so softly, I heard him sniffle. "Mama died yesterday morning," he mumbled. "I'm, uh…I've got to make the arrangements, you know, and…and I don't know what I…what I'm supposed to be doing—"

"*Sam!*" I yelped. "I'm so sorry, why didn't you tell me to shut up?"

"Wouldn't have brought her back, would it?" I heard the sound of glass thumping against wood and wondered what he was drinking at that hour. "Allergies led to bronchitis, she got a summer cold on top of it all, and…" He paused and took a shaky breath. "I've got to get a funeral home lined up, call Mama's friends and some cousins out of state, write an obit, figure out what the hell I'm doing with this ranch, and right now, pretty much the only thing that makes sense is sitting in the kitchen with a six-pack of Bud, so…nice to hear someone else's voice. The house is too damn quiet."

At that moment, my grievances with Bert and the Arcanum seemed rather petty. "Send me a picture of your place."

"Why?"

"Because I'm heading your way. I just need a visual for gate purposes."

"Ros, no," he protested, "you don't—"

"I am *not* taking no for an answer, Rockwell. Photo, stat. Have you eaten?"

After a brief hesitation, he said, "I had a Pop-Tart a little while ago."

"Doesn't count. Hang on," I said as the door unlocked and the moviegoers trooped in. "Bee, is there some place around here that does decent takeout?" I called over their chatter.

Frowning, she nodded. "There's a Chinese place that's not bad, and I know a couple of good Indian restaurants…"

"The chip shop," Daisy added.

"*Ooh*, yes, definitely. Why? Was lunch horrible?"

"Too early for Chinese?" I asked Sam.

"I don't really know what time it is right now," he replied, "but you don't have to do that. I'll be okay."

"Bull. Get the picture, I'll get food."

I hung up before he could try to dissuade me and turned to the curious crowd. "Sam's mom died. I'm on my way to Texas. Could someone point me toward a restaurant?"

"Oh, *God*," Bee murmured, then offered, "Come on, I'll take you there. And how was lunch with…" She leaned closer and squinted at my face. "Have you been crying?

Your eye makeup's all runny."

"Tell you on the way," I muttered, then cast my makeup back into place and headed for the door.

CHAPTER 7

Whatever Sam had been expecting to find when I rang the bell, it certainly wasn't four people loaded down with plastic bags of takeout boxes and booze. He stood on the other side of the front door in navy sweatpants, barefoot and bare-chested, and bemusedly ran his hand through his mussed hair, which was shaggier than I'd seen it in a while. Sam and I had traded hundreds of selfies over the years, but that was the first time I'd seen him in person since I was fifteen, and I couldn't help but notice that his awkward camera angles hadn't done him justice. A touch over six feet tall, broad, well-built, and tanned, Sam was a sight for sore eyes…

…and he was bereaved, newly orphaned, and possibly on his way to drunk, I chided myself, pushing the rest of the previous musing to the dark and slightly embarrassing corners of my mind.

"Hey, you," I said, dropping my bags, and wrapped my arms around his waist. Sam hugged me back, squeezing a little too hard for comfort, and I held on until his grip slackened. "Brought assistance," I told him, turning to the others. "This is my old friend, Bee, that's her girlfriend, Daisy, and *that*, believe it or not, is Frank."

Sam had nodded to Bee and Daisy, but he started and stared up at Frank when the palest member of our party lifted a finger in greeting. "Wait…*the* Frank? How the hell—"

Magic. Aren't you supposed to be fae? he interrupted.

"Yeah, I guess, but last time I saw a picture of you—"

I was much better looking, yes. Hungry? He hoisted his bags and bared his teeth. *You can have anything you want but the spareribs and the Mongolian beef.*

Daisy cut her eyes to him and pursed her lips. "Come on, now, you can't eat all of that."

"Try me," he replied, his basso rumble still jarringly unfamiliar to me but flowing more smoothly.

"And if you're in more of a 'liquid breakfast' sort of mood, we should have that covered as well," said Bee, lifting the bag on her left arm. "I heard you were drinking Budweiser, and that's simply unacceptable."

Sam regarded our knot for a moment, then folded his arms against the warm morning breeze. "Y'all…I don't know what to say, I…"

"We're here to help," said Daisy when his voice faltered. "My gran died two years ago. I know getting everything in order is a monumental pain, and it's the last thing you want to do right now, so congratulations, you have minions to help with the phoning and planning and whatnot," she said, sweeping her unencumbered arm to encompass Bee and me. "Plus Frank, who refused to stay by himself in England."

"I guard Ros," he protested.

"That's only your cover story, and you know it," she retorted. "So," she said, turning back to Sam, "may we come in, then?"

And Sam, whether because he was hungry, outnumbered, or too weary to care, stepped aside.

Within half an hour, Frank had convinced Daisy of his appetite for meat in any form, I'd coaxed soup and eggrolls down Sam, and Bee had introduced him to the wonders of Buckfast. "This stuff is practically medicinal," she said, pouring him a second juice glass full. "Trust me, I'm a med student."

Slowly, we pried a list of tasks from Sam—making

arrangements with the funeral home, getting prices from the florist, writing an obituary for the local paper, and calling his mother's family and friends. "The grave, at least, is taken care of," he mumbled into a plate of sesame chicken that had escaped Frank's notice. "Mama got that arranged years ago. There's a big Rockwell family plot, and…"

He left the thought unfinished, and Daisy, who had been taking notes beside him, patted his arm. "Best eat before it goes cold," she said, looking at his unorthodox breakfast. "Or has it already?"

Frank glanced up from the last of the spareribs. "I could—"

"*No*," Bee and I said in unison.

"I was thinking microwave," Daisy explained. "Let's not burn the place down, all right?"

With food and perhaps a bit too much alcohol in him, Sam grew quiet and lethargic, and I guided him through the house to the bedroom that seemed to be his. "Get some sleep," I said as he landed on the unmade bed. "We'll make progress. Don't worry about it." Exhausted, he closed his eyes, and I drew the shades and slipped out.

Daisy might not have been the world's greatest wizard, but she was an organizational pro and something of a taskmaster. By the time Sam emerged again, blinking in confusion at the late afternoon light, she had set up the funeral—she'd even selected flowers and hired a string quartet, a detail she'd gleaned from a notebook Sam's mother had left behind for that eventuality—and while Bee and I had been given the list of names and Ms. Rockwell's phone, Daisy had gone so far as to draft a rough obituary from Sam's earlier mutterings and what I remembered of our conversations.

"Hey," he said through a yawn, shuffling into our kitchen headquarters. "What time…"

His hair stuck up in odd clumps, and there was a little white crust down one side of his chin, but at least he'd located a T-shirt. "About five," I told him. "Coffee?"

"We're out. I was supposed to get some at the store yesterday, but I never made it." He gazed blearily around the room, then said, "Y'all want some? I could run to town—"

Before he could finish the offer, a steaming mug appeared in my hand. "I'm not great at making food, but I've had some practice with coffee," I told him as he took it from me. "Might need sugar."

He drank, grimaced, then drank again. "It's good."

"You sound surprised," I teased.

"Because coffee usually comes from the Folger's canister, not thin air."

Daisy and Bee looked at each other, and Daisy murmured to me, "Half, you said?"

"Not particularly trained," I replied.

Sam put the mug on the counter and shook his head. "Nope. My teacher moved away, and I didn't want to poke around too much in case of explosions, so..." He shrugged and folded his arms. "Guess all of this is old hat to y'all, huh? You're..."

"Wizards," Bee finished. "Also not great on the food end, but I've learned to produce tea as a survival mechanism, so if that isn't doing the trick—"

"Oh, no, this is great." He lifted the mug again and held it close. "Um...I'm *really* sorry about walking out—"

"Don't apologize," Daisy interrupted. "You're the one who looks like hell right now. Feeling any better?"

"Kind of. But isn't it pretty late for you?"

"Eh, eleven-ish. I'm fine. Could do with dinner, if anyone's in the mood," she added, looking around the table with hopeful eyes. "Is there a takeaway place close?"

"Not unless you're getting pizza delivered," said Sam. "There's a restaurant in town that'll do burgers to go, but the nearest fast food is twenty miles away. We're kind of in the middle of nowhere out here."

Bee nodded and pulled her purse from the floor. "I've

got a driving license. Daisy's still provisional, and Ros…"

"Is useless," I replied.

"Thought so. But if you have an address, Sam, I'll make the run."

He padded to the refrigerator and opened the door. "Mama and I were going to do steaks on Saturday. They're thawed, and they'll just go to waste, so…anyone opposed? Any vegetarians?"

Daisy's eyes went wide. "No, that sounds lovely, but, ehm…" She pointed to the curtained kitchen window, through which we could see part of the Rockwell herd grazing in the distance. "You didn't…*know* those steaks, did you?"

Once Daisy was reassured that the meat was anonymous, Frank, who had been napping out of boredom for most of the day, at last was able to make himself useful. Sam had barely gotten the charcoal arranged in the grill before Frank was flambeeing the briquettes, and while Sam tended the fire, the two stood by the grill and carried on a conversation that was, by and large, monosyllabic and somewhat grunted. Frank remained on hand to char and stoke the fire as needed, and Sam, outfitted with long sleeves and thick oven mitts against the steel, sweated and fussed over the steaks. I could think of a few careers safer for someone with a high concentration of fae blood than grill master, but Sam made it work, and the result was magnificent.

Satiated and finally feeling the hour, Daisy and Bee claimed the guest bedroom, and I stood at the sink to help Sam wash up. I'd offered to do the job with a quick application of spellcraft, but he declined, and so I took up a dishtowel instead. When the plates were dry and the marinade dish was soaking, I said, "Maybe this is premature, but what are your plans? Going to stay here?"

"Don't see how that'd work," he murmured, leaning against the counter, and began to pick at a fresh stain on his grilling shirt. Sam still smelled a little smoky up close, and he'd somehow managed to acquire a black streak down one side of his face, but all things considered, I didn't think the time was right to point that out.

"What about the Browns? Gabriel? Matt Holtz?"

But Sam shook his head. "They all pitched in for Mama, but they can't keep it up for free, and I can't pay them. Not enough in the bank—most everything's tied up in the stock. At least there's no mortgage, but still…you know, a couple of bad years, and we'd be underwater. I can't take on full-time hands."

"So what's going to happen to the ranch?" I asked quietly.

Sam let out a long, slow breath. "Think I'll sell to Les Brown. His place isn't big enough to split between Jobe and Zeke, but with ours added in, they should both have enough to make a living. And they've been really good to Mama and me, so it seems fair to give them the first shot."

"But…Sam, this is your family's land—"

"And I can't work it," he interrupted, turning to me. His hazel eyes looked weary and deeper set than I'd ever seen them. "Not when I can't touch the stock. Don't want to farm, so…you know, this is probably the best plan."

"I've heard there's ways you can work around the scared animal thing, if you can get the enchantment right…"

"Yeah, put that on the list of things I ain't going to trust myself with any time soon," he muttered. "It can be hairy enough going after a bull without having to worry about *magic*."

We stood together in silence for a moment, and then he turned around to begin scrubbing at the soaking dish.

"You sell the ranch, and then what?" I asked, dodging his pistoning elbow. "Travel? Open a barbeque restaurant?"

He snorted and worked at a stubborn patch of grime. "Don't know. Never done much besides this, but…well, you think my aunt would still want to see me?"

"Ellie? Pretty sure she would." I waited until Sam began rinsing the dish, then said, "You know, my parents are empty-nesting right now, and there's a decent guestroom. There's also half a dozen dragons next door, and they're pretty self-sufficient, but I bet Dad would love to have a hand, now that I'm over here. If nothing else, I could put in a good word for you with Georgie."

Sam gave me a fleeting smile. "Yeah?"

"Yeah. And Dad knows horses, anyway, so you two could probably find something to talk about."

"Well, that makes one of us," he replied, handing me the wet dish. "I've been avoiding them to this point—safer than living my own personal rodeo. And believe me, there are few faster ways to be labeled a pansy around here than letting it slip that you can't ride."

"Dragons are different," I assured him. "You just have to put up with the commentary."

He peeked around the wall into the den, where Frank was sprawled across the couch, snoring. "Big guy really loves you, you know."

"Yeah," I said, joining Sam to look in on him. "Feeling's mutual."

"He asked if I wanted to help him fight the, uh...whatchamacallit..."

"Grand magus?"

"*That*. I said I'd need practice first, but I wouldn't mind."

I chuckled. "Well, that's sweet of you both to defend my honor, but maybe you should start by fighting someone a little less adept at magic, eh?"

"Noted." Carrying the dishes to their cabinets, he said, "That asshole really called you a *mongrel*?"

"His dad did. And it's not exactly polite, but it's true. I'm witch-blooded," I said, shrugging.

"Okay, fine, but you don't just call someone a dog," he protested. "They're not all like that, are they? Wizards?"

"Not all." I sat at the kitchen table and conjured up a

fresh cup of coffee—the hour was far past my bedtime. "Bee and Daisy are all right, yeah? And I'm pretty fond of my mom, so that makes three." I paused, running through my mental phonebook. "Badger—she's out with the Fringe. And Bert's predecessor, Arnold, he's decent. I'm sure there are more."

He slid into the chair beside me. "You don't sound all that convinced."

"Been a long day."

"I hear ya."

I made a second coffee for him, and he drank without hesitation.

"It's going to be okay, Sam," I murmured, watching him until he met my eyes. "Not right now, but someday. I'm really sorry."

He nodded and held his mug. "Had the worst of it last night. Just kind of numb right now."

"Well," I said, patting his shoulder, "we'll be here to help. I don't know how long everyone else can stay, but I'm in no particular rush to get back to Glastonbury, so whatever you need, let me know. You can pay me in steak."

Sam grinned briefly. "Thanks for coming, Ros."

"Sure. And let me know if you want to go over when all's said and done—I'll be glad to ask my parents if you can crash with them for a while."

"Will do. And, uh…you can show me how to make those gate thingies, right? Miss Bonnie never got that far with me."

"Cinch." I drained the rest of my cup, weighed the influx of caffeine against my jetlagged exhaustion, and decided sleep was in order. "Going to hit the hay," I told Sam, rising from the table. "How's the recliner?"

"Decent," he replied, following me into the den, "but the couch folds out into a bed…"

We both looked at Frank, who slept on his stomach with one foot over the armrest, the other hanging from the cushion, and his hand dragging on the rug.

"You know what they say about waking a sleeping dragon, right?" I whispered.

"Don't?"

"Yep." Grabbing an afghan, I headed for the chair, ignoring the fading twilight outside the windows.

When I woke Monday morning, it was to the sizzle of frying eggs and bacon, which helped ameliorate the annoyance of the crick in my neck. The couch was empty, but something told me Frank was supervising in the next room. Groggy, I glanced at my phone, only to see a string of unanswered messages from Bert: *I'm so sorry. Where are you? Castle? Did you go home? Can we talk? Are you ignoring me?*

The answer to the last was a resounding yes, and I put my phone away. At least the previous day had settled the question of whether I needed to tell Bert about the murders in the Minor Arcanum—considering what I'd seen of him and his family, I doubted he'd care if every last one of them dropped dead. Hell, I mused, finger-combing my hair, he'd probably call it a win.

The five of us gathered around the table for breakfast, and then, while Bee and Daisy resumed the process of alerting the friends and family to the upcoming funeral, Sam and I climbed into the farm truck and puttered down the road to the Browns' ranch. "This is my friend, Ros," Sam told Les, the sun-weathered patriarch, whose handshake was rough and almost strong enough to hurt. "Brought her along as a witness to show you I'm serious. I'd like to make you a proposition about our property."

Les invited us in from the porch, and when Sam suggested that he take the Rockwell ranch off Sam's hands for a grand, Les blinked hard, then leaned against the kitchen wall and whistled low. "You hit your head or something, boy?" he finally asked. "Land's worth at least a half-mil."

"I figured," said Sam, shoving his hands into the pockets of his homemade jeans—the product of enchantment, perfectly tailored and without any steel bits, one lesson Bonnie had imparted before leaving town. "But I've got to do something with myself, Mr. Brown, and it ain't here. I can't do the place justice, you know that. Mama…"—he paused, collected himself, and swallowed hard—"she'd want it in good hands. Y'all have been like family, and I know you'd take care of the stock—"

Whatever would have followed was cut short when Les wrapped Sam in a quick, back-pounding hug. "You listen to me," he murmured, planting his hands on Sam's shoulders. "Audra was damn proud of you, Sammy. If you're sure about this, I'd be a fool to say no. But if you want to try your hand at it, see if you can make it work—"

"No point in stressing the herd," he replied with a weak smile. "I'm meeting with Mama's lawyer this afternoon. Once everything's square, I'll ask her to draw something up."

He searched Sam's face for another moment, then nodded and released him. "You turned into a good man, I hope you know that. And if you think for one second that I'm going to take your land for a measly thousand bucks, you're out of your damn mind."

Sam smiled in earnest. "Y'all have done so much for us already…"

"Not *that* much. I'm not going to steal your inheritance, boy."

The two dickered for half an hour, and then, with a price agreed upon, Sam and I took our leave. As I climbed back into the truck, Les caught my door and grinned. "Don't think I've seen you around here before. You and Sam—"

"Cousin," Sam interrupted before I could try to stammer out a response that made sense. "Ros came in from Montana to help me settle Mama's affairs."

"Cousin?" he echoed. "Didn't think any of y'all's

people were up that way."

"My dad's people."

The rancher's bushy eyebrows rose. "You found your daddy? *When*?"

"Couple years ago, one of those online genealogy deals," Sam lied. "You know, spit in a cup, they'll tell you if you have cousins in the database? Found a few of mine, we traded notes, and Ros and I have gotten acquainted. My dad still doesn't want anything to do with me, but the rest of the family's been nice about it."

"Well, I'll be," said Les, shaking his head. "Good for you, Sammy. And that's sweet of you to come down, hon," he told me. "Y'all take care, now."

As we drove off, I cut my eyes to Sam and grinned. "Rehearsed that, did we?"

"Les may be the salt of the earth and a little crusty, but he ain't stupid," said Sam, skirting a deep pothole. "The only other option was to tell him I met you on a dating site, and something closer to the truth seemed less awkward."

I bit my tongue before I could blurt out my first thought: *I wouldn't have minded.* The magical community was somewhat limited, after all, and it wasn't as if Sam and I were *close* cousins...but in light of why I'd come to Texas in the first place, I decided it wasn't the time to broach that topic, no matter how nice he looked with his shirt off.

Trying to redirect my rebellious mind to more chaste subjects, I turned up the air conditioning and stared out at the rolling pastures baking in the summer morning. My phone beeped, and I pulled it from my bag to see yet another message from Bert: *Are you alive?*

Yes, I wrote, scowling at the screen. *Out for a few days.*

Seconds later, my phone began to ring, but I silenced it and let it go to voicemail. "Don't feel like talking to Bert right now," I explained when Sam looked my way.

"No judgment here," he replied, and flipped on the radio.

The funeral was scheduled for Wednesday afternoon. Despite the midweek setting and the oppressive heat of early July, seemingly half of Red Plank turned up to see Sam's mother off, and most of the mourners made it to the graveside. We strangers stayed well back, trying not to draw attention—Frank was already uncomfortable enough in a suit without having to field questions—but Sam looked our way for reassurance all the same.

That evening, faced with a freezer full of casseroles from well-meaning church ladies, we heated one that seemed to be heavy on chicken and settled around the table, ties discarded and dress shoes kicked into a pile against the wall. "The worst is over," Daisy told Sam as he picked at his dinner. "I'm not saying it's going to be a picnic from this point, but you've done your duty by her, and the ranch is going to be fine."

"Yeah," he sighed, poking at an egg noodle with his plastic fork. To his surprise, Sam had learned that his mother had been making preparations since his twenty-first birthday, and as he was the sole beneficiary of her will—and her attorney's family had been in Red Plank almost as long as the Rockwells—selling off the ranch had been the work of a painless hour on Tuesday evening. The attorney had raised an eyebrow when she learned the selling price was only ten thousand dollars, but Les brought cash to the closing, Audra had no large debts, and Sam insisted that it was what he wanted. Now a visitor on his neighbor's new land, Sam faced the daunting task of packing up the house, and though the Browns were by no means hurrying him off the property, he was impatient to rip off the band-aid and be done with the business.

As Frank sorted through the remains of the casserole, pushing around the pasta and vegetable detritus in search of chicken chunks, I heard the muffled crack of an opening gate. Frowning at Bee, who was already pulling her wand from beneath her shirt, I slid back from the table, called up a fireball just in case, and headed for the front door to spy on the yard. But before I made it out of the kitchen, the doorbell rang, and she and I shared another look.

"You know," said Bee, rising with Sam to join me, "assassins don't usually buzz."

Still, I kept the fireball behind my back until Sam opened the door, revealing my dad, Toula, and Eleanor on the porch.

"I'm so sorry, dear," the queen began, clasping her hands as he stepped back in surprise. She'd chosen a gray twinset that day, and I suspected she'd be sweating through her cardigan after another minute outside. "Ros told us you were moving, and we thought you might be in need of a crew."

"Oh...uh..." He stuttered for a moment, then managed, "That's really nice of y'all, but I don't even have boxes yet. I was going to the U-Haul place tomorrow for packing supplies, but I think they're already closed tonight."

Eleanor paused, taking that in, then glanced at Dad and Toula and murmured, "We have work to do."

"Val can get him started," Toula replied.

Dad's shoulders sagged. "Come on, he just lost his mom, let's not be *cruel*."

"And for that, I'm telling on you," she teased, poking him in the chest, then brushed past Eleanor and into the foyer. "No need for boxes, bud," she told Sam, running one hand through her dark, purple-tipped bob in thought as she surveyed the scene. "If you want to go out with a bang, we could transport the whole house..."

"I, um...I sold it," he mumbled, watching her poke her head into rooms. "With the land. I mean...uh...that's just the laundry room, nothing exciting..."

My dad sidled up and distracted him from Toula's exploration. "It's Sam, yeah? Joey Bolin," he said, and shook his hand. "Ros said you might be looking for a place to crash for a while. Her mom and I would love to have you."

Relief flickered across Sam's face, followed quickly by confusion. "That'd be great, uh...wait, you're Ros's *dad?*"

He chuckled and absently rubbed his close-trimmed beard, the one obvious clue that Dad, despite the arrangement he'd made with Kura, was a lesser blood. Sam didn't have so much as a trace of five o'clock shadow, and I doubted he'd ever considered putting a razor to his chin, not only because the exercise would have left him with nasty iron burns. "I'm forty-nine," Dad told him, and pointed to Toula, who, given her punkish hairdo, looked barely older than Sam. "She'll be sixty in February."

"And if you idiots put a flock of flamingos in my living room this time around, you're *dead*," she called from the powder room.

"Buzzards," Dad stage-whispered to Sam and me. "Val's idea. And hey, there!" he exclaimed, catching sight of Bee, who'd put her wand away. "Long time, no see. How's Scotland treating you?"

She grinned. "Can't complain, aside from the rain, the wind, my classes...but Daisy here is still putting up with me, so there's that."

Daisy stood slightly behind Bee, suddenly uncertain as she watched the newcomers traipse about the house, and Dad waved from a safe distance. "Nice to finally meet you," he began. "Bee told us, but remind me, you're studying—"

Is anyone going to finish this? Frank thought, broadcasting throughout the building. *Because if not, the chicken is mine.*

Eleanor twitched, then looked up at Sam with sympathy. "You've been hosting everyone?" she asked. He nodded, and she rolled her eyes. "Terrible time for houseguests. If your affairs are straight here, we thought we might store your things with the Bolins until you decide your next step. And Toula's right, you do need instruction...though I don't think I'd turn you over to her brother *quite* yet. Does that work?"

"Sure," he said, still looking somewhat dazed at the influx of people. "But really, I've got a lot of stuff here to pack—"

"Which is why you have us. Bee, dear?" she said, beckoning.

Bee approached, and Daisy, whose wide eyes suggested she'd finally recognized the queen, trailed well behind. "Yes, ma'am?"

"Lovely to see you again, and"—she paused, giving Bee's black dress a closer look—"ooh, that *suits* you. Well done. We have it in hand from here, so if you and your...ehm..."

"Partner," she supplied.

"Wasn't certain, thank you. If you two want to go on your way, we'll manage. Ros—"

"I thought I'd go back long enough to make the introductions," I interrupted. "If that's okay—"

"Of course. And him?" she asked, nodding toward the kitchen.

"We'll take Frank back to Glastonbury," Bee offered.

"Wonderful," said Eleanor. "Come on, Sam," she said, taking his hand, "show us what we're up against, hmm?"

As she led him off, I looked at Daisy, whose jaw had begun to sag. "That would be Sam's aunt," I murmured. "And exactly who you think she is."

"His *aunt?*" she whispered. "You didn't say anything about—"

"There was nothing to say. Sam is...well..." I swept my arm toward the decorative antelope skull on the dining room wall. "Sam."

"And she's always treated me well, so there's no need to wet yourself," Bee added, steering Daisy toward the kitchen. "Frank!" she called. "We're leaving!"

He looked up from the picked-over remnants of the casserole. "Now?"

Seeing that we were alone, Bee hurried to the freezer and extracted a foil-wrapped pack of steaks. "Now. Come along, I'll make you another course."

With a bit of coaxing, Frank agreed to be separated from me for a few hours, and I stood back and watched as the impromptu movers did the heavy lifting. Once they had a gate stabilized, Dad and Toula floated items through, room by room, and Eleanor shrank everything to the size of dollhouse furniture before packing it into a plastic tub. When an item was too iron-based to enchant easily, Toula offered a casting assist. They'd cleared the house and packed the tub within an hour, and Eleanor had built in little dividers to keep the contents of the rooms from getting mixed up in storage. Sam took one last walk around his emptied childhood home, running his fingertips over the wallpaper and the old paneling, and finally stood in front of the window overlooking the back pasture, watching the cattle graze in the fading light. The first stars had come out, and the herd was no more than silhouettes against the sky.

"It's never easy," Eleanor murmured, coming up behind him. "Believe me, I've done it enough times. Take as long as you need."

"Mama loved this place," he mumbled, resting his hand on the painted sash.

"And it will be here," she said, standing beside him. "Not always as it is now, but in some way, home endures. In *here*," she added, patting her chest. "You know, last year, I went to see my parents' home for the first time in ages. There's only part of one of the towers left—it's a scheduled monument these days. But I remember it as it was…the castle at its prime, the people, my brothers and their horses, the *stench*…" She mock-shuddered. "At least something's improved. But we do what we must, dear, and you're not a bad son for leaving."

Sam stood beside her for a moment longer, then sighed and turned to go. Before he stepped through the gate, however, he paused and peered down at Eleanor. "You really grew up in a castle?"

"Not a huge one," she replied, "but yes, towers and walls and such."

"How old *are*—"

"Old enough. This way, now," she said, stepping between realms. "I smell dinner."

The fact that Sam had already eaten that night made no difference to Gran, who had commandeered my parents' kitchen that afternoon when she learned of Sam's imminent arrival. "Here," she said, plopping a plate of chicken and dumplings in front of him, "you eat up, sweetie. There's plenty more, so don't be shy."

As a native Virginian and the daughter of another southerner, Gran's first impetus when confronted with a person in crisis was to feed him, and since she was a whiz in the kitchen, no one complained. By the time I'd finished my second dinner—Gran had insisted, and I wasn't about to argue with her—Sam had begun to relax through a combination of home cooking, wine, and Pop's litany of bad jokes. He almost jumped out of his seat when Georgie's nose appeared at the open wall, but soon enough, Dad had him and Pop out in the barn, and Mom and Liza shook their heads as the men's excited voices filtered back into the house. "Boys," Liza said with a sigh, and looked at Gran, who was plating dessert. "Rebecca, honey, want a hand with that?"

She held up a bowl of whipped cream in invitation. "It's your recipe, Grandma."

"And you're doing a fine job, but you've been working for hours," she replied. With a snap, the dessert arranged itself, and she grinned. "Wish I'd known how to do that fifty years ago. It'd have made running a bakery so much simpler." She helped herself to a finger of whipped cream, then leaned toward me and murmured, "He's cute, you know."

"He's your *cousin*," I mumbled, reddening.

"Half. And since there's, oh, four generations between you…"

"*Liza!*"

She raised her hands in surrender. "I'm just saying…"

My mother's and grandmother's expressions gave me no hope of assistance, and so, blushing furiously, I hurried out into the yard to cool down.

Alone, I took in the lovely night from the porch, realizing I'd missed this in Glastonbury. Though unpredictable in their movement, the stars were bright and abundant in Faerie, and the usual chorus of frogs had started up from the sheep pond. As my reddened face resumed its usual color, I checked my phone for word from Amy, but there was no news. That wasn't a bad thing—no message presumably meant no new bodies—but I also had no idea if the Fringe was any closer to finding the culprit.

"Hey, Kura?" I asked the night. "Can we chat? There's something you might want to know from the Virginia folks."

But although I stood on the porch for ten minutes, hoping for the flash of her appearance, the realm declined to show herself. She didn't need to—Kura could pull the information from my thoughts more quickly than I could tell her—but still, I was disappointed. After the last week and a half, I'd hoped for a word of reassurance.

My phone beeped, and I found a new message from Bee: *Sleepover at your place. Frank's on the floor, Daisy fell asleep on the couch. Mind if I take your bed?*

Be my guest, I wrote back. *Or use Frank's—he never has.*

Got it, she replied. *And Bert left a note for you under the door.*

"Hey, Ros!" Dad called from the barn door. "Come here a second! Georgie's going to take Sam and me up. Pop's shooting from the ground, but Horus says he's willing to give you a lift if you'll do the aerial photography."

Back soon, I told Bee, then hurried off to find a flash. Sam would be mourning his mother for a long time to come, but at least I knew I was leaving him in good hands.

CHAPTER 8

"I was worried about you."

Bert stood in my entryway, arms folded across his thin chest. His robe, a muted scarlet, swished as he shifted from foot to foot. "I didn't know if something had happened, and you wouldn't take my calls."

I cut my eyes to the quiet kitchen. Bee and Daisy had hidden themselves in Frank's room when Bert showed up unannounced on my doorstep, but Frank, unperturbed, sat at the table with their abandoned cereal bowls and continued to eat his platter of bacon, methodically breaking each slice in half and dipping it in ketchup.

"Would you have taken my calls if you were in my place?" I retorted, glaring back at him. "After those *lovely* words from your parents—"

"They were surprised," he protested.

"And whose fault is that? Moon and stars, you didn't think to warn them before dropping me at the table? Really, given their feelings about my family and me, what the hell made you think that was a good idea?"

"It was a mistake," he admitted, "but honestly, Ros, I didn't know the extent of their sympathy toward the probationers."

I crossed my arms and cocked an eyebrow. "Come on. What about good old cousin Nick, too sloshed to drive a bus? You expect me to believe you didn't know?"

He shrugged. "I studied a lot. We didn't talk politics much, especially since the grand magus was being so kind to me, and I suppose I didn't pay attention, and…and

Dora and Nick were down in London, and it's only lately that Mum and Dad have brought up the issue of pardons—"

"It is your *job* to pay attention," I snapped, cutting off his rambling explanation. "You want to end up like my mom? She took the Council for granted, and we both know what happened next."

"I am *nothing* like your mum," he replied, taken aback.

"Obviously. Not if you're considering pardons."

Bert stopped, took a step away from me, and closed his eyes. "That came out poorly. Grand Magus Carver is an exceptional talent, and I respect her. But I don't have nearly the sort of friction with the Council that she did. We're apples and oranges."

I leaned against the door frame and continued to stare at him. "So you think. How many Mulligan sympathizers are on the Council, Bertie? What if they decide they don't like you? What if—and here's a thought—what if you don't pardon your *murderous* cousin Nick?"

"Ros—"

"What's his body count, anyway?"

"He was following orders!"

"How many bodies, Bert?"

"I don't know," he finally muttered, reddening as his temper grew short. "And while we're on the subject of my family, would it have killed you to not make a scene?"

I straightened, momentarily speechless, then spat, "*Excuse* me?"

"You heard me. You could have let it go, you know."

"You dad asked me who my grandfather is. What did you want me to do, lie?"

"Maybe! I don't know, anything but drop the Carver bomb. I mean, if you were going to do that, why not just go ahead and spit in their faces? And then locking yourself in the toilet and running away—really helpful of you, thanks. I got an earful, I'll have you know, and—"

"Leave," rumbled Frank.

I stepped back into the apartment and looked to the kitchen, and Bert followed me over the threshold. "Who the hell is…"

The grand magus fell silent as Frank unfolded himself—all six and a half muscle-bound feet of himself—from his seat, wiped his hands on his napkin, and calmly marched to the door. "Leave," he repeated.

Bert looked up at him, suddenly far less confident than he'd been. "I…ehm…I thought you were a mute."

"Selective," I replied.

"You insult her," Frank continued, never raising his voice. Then again, if he'd shouted, he'd have rattled the windows. "Get out."

Grand magus or not, Bert did as he was told, and Frank firmly closed the door behind him. "Thank you," I murmured, shuffling to the kitchen table. "I had it under control, you know. You didn't have to jump in."

Well aware, he replied, resuming his breakfast. *I was attempting to prevent you from showing Bert just how under control you had the situation. Probably best if you didn't beat him senseless, right?*

I laughed weakly and took up my spoon. "Probably."

But if you change your mind and want him crisped, he added, snapping a piece of bacon in half, *just say the word*.

Jetlagged from our days in Texas, I abandoned my attempt to quickly reacclimate to Glastonbury time and crawled back into bed after Daisy and Bee took their leave. Ever the champion napper, Frank raised the shade just enough to let in sunlight on the far third of my bed, then flopped into the bright spot and sighed contentedly. I slid close to him, letting him warm my back, and slept deeply until noon.

Trying to avoid Bert, I took Bee's recommendation and walked to a hamburger place in town, across the street from a New Age shop doing a modest trade in crystals and faux Arthuriana. With a cheeseburger for myself and a bunless triple for Frank, we settled in at a quiet corner table to watch the tourists stroll by and not talk about the lousy job I was doing as Faerie's ambassador. Our waitress was only too happy to bring a second pop for me and refill Frank's water glass, and I snickered as she kept sneaking looks at him as she made her rounds.

"What is it?" he mumbled through a mouthful of meat.

"You've got an admirer," I whispered, glancing across the restaurant.

He followed the direction of my stare, noticed the bubbly waitress, then groaned and slouched lower in his chair. "Why me?" he muttered, squirting a fresh glop of ketchup onto his lunch.

"Take it as a compliment."

Would you consider it a compliment if my brothers wanted to mate with you?

I snorted. "Drama queen. She just thinks you're cute."

No, that is definitely not all she thinks, he replied, glowering at his plate. *Trust me, I checked.*

Before I could comfort him, an older man paused beside our table and smiled. "Looks good. May I?" he said, taking one of my fries, and slid into an empty chair.

Thinking quickly while he ate, I tried unsuccessfully to place him. He wasn't someone I knew from Faerie—he looked to be in his mid-sixties, judging by his modest wrinkles and the gray scattered throughout his neat blond curls. His accent pegged him as American, maybe Midwestern, and his pressed khakis, black polo, and sunglasses hanging from a sport strap suggested he was one of the horde of tourists. After he helped himself to another fry—and since they were done with parmesan and sea salt, I couldn't really blame him—he pulled out his wallet, then passed me a black card without a word.

The card appeared to be nothing more than a piece of black cardstock, but my fingertips detected the embossing, and I fought the urge to drop it on the table. I could think of only one organization that used black-on-black business cards—well, only one whose representative would help himself to a stranger's lunch.

"Mr. Adler, I presume?" I murmured, returning his card.

Our new companion smiled. "I see my reputation precedes me. And it's Tanner, please, Ms. Bolin." He paused, considering Frank, who had wrapped one arm protectively around the remains of his burgers. "I'm not here to hurt either of you," he told Frank. "And it would be a poor idea to incinerate me in public, don't you think?"

Frank stiffened, and Tanner bit into another fry. "Oh, yes, Mr. White, you're on our radar. But go ahead, finish your lunch. I'm not going to steal from you—I prefer my fingers in their current configuration."

"Tanner Adler is the head of the Dark Company," I quietly told Frank. "Shapeshifting spies."

"Exactly, but I prefer the term 'information brokers,'" said Tanner, sounding far cheerier than I felt. "And take it from a shifter that you're doing well at acclimating to that form," he said as Frank's eyes narrowed. "I realize you have the balance issue to negotiate, but it's tricky shifting the other way, too. Way too many feet to worry about."

"I assure you, Frank isn't going to go on a rampage," I said quickly. "There's no need for the Company to worry about—"

"We're not. This meeting has nothing to do with your draconic associate." He reached for my fries again, then hesitated. "May I? These aren't half bad."

I passed him the bowl. "So why are you stalking me?"

Tanner grinned. "*Stalk* is such a strong word. You're easy to follow, kid—I mean, it took us a day to find you when you dashed off to Texas, but other than that, you don't exactly disguise your movements. But that's neither here nor there right now." He borrowed my unused bread plate and Frank's bottle of ketchup, then tucked into the remains of my lunch. "I want to know what you know about the recent spate of deaths in the Minor Arcanum."

That gave me pause. The idea of supplying the Company with information sat uneasily with me, and so I hemmed and hawed for a moment, grateful that shifters couldn't read minds. "I, um…I don't really keep tabs on them, so you'll have to be more specific…"

"We know about the murders," he murmured, leaning closer to me. "Quite a bit about them, actually, and quite probably more than you do. I just didn't want to waste your time by repeating information you already had."

"Then yes," I said, meeting his dark eyes, "I know of three recent deaths. Badger and Seamus are on it. That's about the extent of what I've been told."

"All right, then let me flesh it out for you." Tanner didn't bother to so much as pull out a notepad. "Helmut Moser, fifty-seven, found dead on June 1 in his home in Westendorf, Austria, with a dime-sized hole through his head. Michelle Parkinson, twenty-three, found dead on June 13 at her boyfriend's apartment in Queens with a similar injury. The boyfriend, who's mundane, is a pizza delivery driver, and he has an ironclad alibi. And then there's Muhammad Faris Ismail, seventy-two, found in an alley behind a mosque in Giza after Friday afternoon prayers."

"Headshot?"

"Bingo. No one had any known enemies—a florist, a preschool teacher, and a convenience store clerk, pretty low on the usual hitlists. Ismail was twice married with a pack of kids and grandkids, Parkinson was in a long-term relationship, and Moser never married. No similarities at all beyond affiliation with the Minor Arcanum and method of death."

"And missing wand," I muttered.

"Heard that too, hmm? What do you know about the wands?"

"Nothing," I admitted. "Amy said they were missing from the victims' bodies, but that's all I've been told."

Tanner planted his elbows on the table and continued to pick over my fries. "If my intel is good—and I have no reason to doubt it—all of the wands were Levey specials."

I frowned. "As in Amy Levey?"

"The same. I mean, I'm no expert, but it's common knowledge that Ms. Levey's one of the Fringe's greatest assets. The woman's got an exceptional gift for wandcraft. And since the Fringe here and the Minors have been cooperating for the last twenty years—"

"She's been crafting for them, too," I finished.

"Mm-hmm." He signaled to the waitress, then ordered a Coke and another basket of fries. "I have a weakness for a good potato," he confessed as she headed for the fountain behind the bar. "Now, here's the thing with the Levey wands. When she crafts for the Fringe, she uses stronger materials, yeah? What's the wood…"

"Rowan," I said. "Or oak. Witch wands."

"Okay. But the Minors aren't witches, by and large, so when she crafts for them…"

"It's something a wizard could use." Though the fries *were* good, my appetite was quickly fizzling. "Someone's killing them for their wands. Another wizard."

"That's where my money would be." He paused and smiled as the waitress deposited his drink, but when he turned back to me, his expression was serious. "You've got a problem on your hands."

"Not to be rude," I replied, leaning closer to him, "but why is the Company concerned here? What's your angle?"

Tanner's smile flickered across his face and faded. "Some years ago, Badger Parsons did this realm a massive favor. She's been holding the line against the Gray Lands all this time, and some of my people and I believe we're in her debt. None of this is on the books, of course, but considering what may be at stake, we've reached the conclusion that the time's come for repayment." He spread his empty hands. "At the very least, her interests are threatened if her known associates are turning up dead. In order to start balancing the ledger, so to speak, I've come to you with information for your bosses. Gratis."

"Why—"

"Because despite what Arnold Lowe's done, large chunks of the Arcanum are still apathetic, if not hostile, to the other non-mundane organizations in this realm," he murmured. "And even if the Arcanum has its head up its ass, the courts would have the firepower to step in if things go the way the tea leaves are suggesting." He sat back and sipped his pop. "You're the envoy, are you not?"

"Well, yeah, but if you think it's that important, you could go straight to—"

"Nope. Oddly enough, the courts don't take kindly to uninvited visits from my people. And I...*may* have stepped on some toes a few years back, so rather than risk it, I thought you could carry the message. Agreed?"

I waited while the waitress put the fresh fries in front of Tanner, then nodded and pulled a notebook and pen from my purse. "What do they need to know?"

"Plenty. Put that aside for now," he said, tapping the blank page. "Let's bring you up to speed." He drizzled ketchup all over the basket and dug in, and Frank, to whom almost everything was a new food, began to experimentally pick at the leavings of my lunch. "First things first," said Tanner once his fries were sufficiently covered. "What do you know about the probationers?"

"What probationers?"

"The ones your mother and the tribunal decided not to execute."

"Well," I said, swirling the melting ice around my glass, "I know at least one of them was driving a bus until recently..."

"Nicholas Briarfield, yes," he said, nodding. "What about the others?"

"Don't know. I guess I'd assumed they were living in Montana."

"Some, but not nearly all. Most have actually moved

away from the installations."

"Arnold *let* them?"

"Arnold is, at heart, a kind soul who doesn't believe that probation should be tantamount to incarceration. I tend to disagree in this case, but it's not my arcanum, is it?" Tanner popped a pair of fries in his mouth and chewed thoughtfully. "If you think about it, there isn't much for the probationers in the installations. They're bound and wandless, and that's quite a stigma, especially for the former magi. So yes, they were allowed to move away, but they're supposed to make quarterly reports to their parole officers...the Arcanum calls them 'welfare coordinators,' but it's the same difference, practically speaking," he explained. "Trouble is, they've all grown somewhat lax about getting those reports in on time."

"Sounds like a bad idea," I muttered.

"Maybe, maybe not. The probationers have kept their noses clean, by and large, so I suppose those responsible for maintaining vigilance have...slacked off, shall we say?"

Frank grunted as he covered my leftover fries in a mixture of ketchup and brown sauce. "How bad?"

"Could be better," said Tanner. "The last reports we've seen on some of them are six months old. That might not be a problem, in and of itself, but for the fact that a certain subset of them seem to have skipped town. We've been watching, too," he said, leaning toward us as if sharing a great secret. "Not as carefully as we could have, though. Some of our targets appear to have run off in the middle of the night."

My stomach knotted at the thought. "Who's missing?"

He began counting off on his greasy fingers. "Russell Mulligan, Allen and Stacy Morse, Brandon and Marcie Conrad...your grandparents..."

"*Shit*," I hissed into my drink.

"The Morse and Conrad boys are still in Florida, if you were wondering. We're keeping tabs on their calls and correspondence for now, hoping to find their parents, but no dice so far. These are magi we're dealing with, and you people do have your methods," he said with a sigh. "But here's another consideration for you: who crafts for the Arcanum?"

I snorted. "Not Amy."

"No, I wouldn't think so. From what we've seen, there are only two crafters who are willing to do Arcanum work these days, Anvi Singh and Oluwa Iwe. Both live in Faerie, and their output is *highly* monitored—there isn't much of a wand surplus these days."

"And for good reason."

"Granted. Singh and Iwe products seem to be well-received—and with the price tags we've seen on them, they'd better be—"

"How much?"

"About twice what the average crafter would have charged before the Mulligan years. Proceeds have been going to support the Fringe in this realm, I believe, but don't hold me to that. Anyway, you've got bound wizards without wands, no legitimate source for wands, and suddenly, the wizards start going off the grid—"

"Oh, my God," I whispered, seeing the puzzle come together. "They're killing off Minor Arcanum wizards just for the wands."

"We're not completely certain, but signs point to yes," said Tanner.

"But who would have unbound them to begin with?" I pressed. "A wand wouldn't do them any good if they couldn't use magic at all."

"Not all of the probationers were bound, were they? I thought that was just the magi."

"No, the assassins were bound, too...but the killings look like wandwork, don't they? Clean shot, not a gun—that's a wand blast. And the unbound probationers or their spouses wouldn't be strong enough to break those binds—Mom and Arnold made sure of it." I gnawed my lip in thought, then said, "If they'd crossed into Faerie, that would break their binds, but I'm sure Kura would have reported it if they'd come over. So...someone else might have helped them. Someone *strong*."

"That's our deduction, too."

My mind flashed to Bert's parents, and I wondered just how talented the Wolds might be. "Any idea who might be involved?"

Tanner paused to eat a few fries, then caught Frank's hungry look and slid his basket into sharing range. "Like these, huh?" he asked.

"Crunchy," said Frank. "With...uh..."

"Sauce?"

"Sauce, yes. Not bad."

"Go ahead, knock yourself out," he said, then turned back to me. "What do you know about Moyna?"

I knew plenty. My parents had mentioned Coileán's missing daughter many times before, and I'd been told that she'd disappeared with a good portion of Mab's former court—the so-called shadow court—after making a disastrous attempt to invade Faerie, but I'd never met her. She'd been missing longer than I'd been alive.

And though I knew *damn* well not to raise the issue around Val, it was no real secret that he was Mab's heir—her eldest living child, though she'd never claimed him. If anyone had a right to the shadow court, he did, but I'd never heard so much as a whisper suggesting that he wanted to convince them to follow him. Ignorant of his parentage, Val had sworn himself to Titania long ago, and then to Coileán. He'd fought his half brother's forces in the Gray Lands, and he'd helped hold them off when Moyna tried to invade. Rather than attempt to rule a people who had, at best, mixed feelings about him, he seemed content as the captain of Coileán's guard.

But I wasn't about to spill everything I knew in front of a spymaster. "Just the name," I fibbed. "Moyna partnered with Oberon to kill Coileán and attack the Arcanum, and then she tried to take on Coileán and Eleanor, but no one's seen her since."

His little smile spoke volumes, and I gaped at him. "You *found* her?"

"No. We continue to find her, every so often, but she's a regular pain to track." He leaned toward me and murmured, "Moyna's young, as faeries go—maybe forty, I guess—but she's surrounded herself with much older advisors. Faeries who know how to keep her safe...and an ally with a wand."

"*Who?*"

"Grace Mulligan. Not a magus, not on probation, and she has scores to settle. Can't imagine why. We think she sought them out shortly after her husband's execution," he explained as my face worked. "She's been helping them for the last ten years, but whatever spellwork she's been doing to hide them hasn't been perfect. Oh, I imagine it blocks blood traces," he added, "but she hasn't considered every contingency." He tapped the tip of his nose and smiled again. "The human sense of smell is barely a sense at all. But when there are shifters involved, especially once a few old lupines can be reactivated from retirement...see where I'm going?"

"But why would she help them? And more importantly, how could Moyna keep the support of a court? She lost."

"That was twenty years ago. Besides, if something happens to Coileán, his court's hers by right. Once she's in power, she can bring the shadow court back into Faerie and do whatever she likes with the rest."

"And you actually found her," I said, still not quite believing it.

Tanner nodded. "They've been licking their wounds for a while. Their camp's always well protected, and they move every few weeks, but we do our best to keep an eye on them."

"So why haven't you mentioned this to Coileán?" I demanded, flabbergasted. "Didn't think that would be important?"

But Tanner just shrugged. "No one's ever retained us for that purpose, have they? Besides, I'd have said something before now if I thought they were planning to make a major move. They haven't been hurting anyone...to speak of," he muttered. "And in all honesty, if there's going to be a civil war with the courts, I'd much prefer that it take place somewhere other than this realm."

"Unbelievable," I groaned.

While my attention was distracted, Frank had summoned our waitress again. "Yes...more of this," he said, pointing to my empty fry bowl. "Please."

She dimpled as she wrote down his order. "Anything else, love?"

His brow furrowed in thought. "Meat?"

"Sure. What kind?"

"Surprise."

The waitress smiled again—a little too widely—and sashayed off to the kitchen. *What?* Frank asked, seeing my expression. *I'm still hungry.*

"We'll talk later," I told him, and turned back to Tanner, who was cleaning up the few fries from his order that Frank had left untouched. "All right, so Moyna's still around. Are you going to tell me where to find her, or does Coileán need to pay in advance?"

"Can't tell you, unfortunately," he replied.

"What, it's a Company secret or something?"

"No." Tanner licked a glob of ketchup off his finger and wiped it on a spare napkin. "I have no idea where she is now. Camp vanished again about three days ago."

"But you'll find it soon."

"I don't know. We've been on it, but we're having a hell of a time finding their tracks this go-around." He met my stare and held it. "The last time Moyna went completely off the map, she did so only with the help of your grandfather. I mean, we aren't one hundred percent certain, but it looks like Grace is finally getting some assistance. Do you see what I'm getting at?"

I did, and the realization made me queasy. "Oh, *shit*."

"What?" Frank asked.

At a loss for words, I tapped my forehead and felt his delicate touch as he entered my thoughts. And there, I assembled the picture for him: Moyna and her shadow court living in uncomfortable exile in the mortal realm for two decades, biding their time. Their old allies, my grandfather and his ilk, bound and rendered magically inept, forced to report to the Arcanum for years...until the reporters grew lazy, their guard dropped, and the former magi went on the lam. The old, uneasy allies had come together once again. I doubted that Moyna was strong enough to break the magi's binds, but surely someone in her party could do the job. And then, once again back at their full strength after a decade in purgatory, they'd struck out to find suitable wands—and in return, they'd fully hidden Moyna from prying eyes.

"The writing's on the wall, I think," said Tanner as Frank withdrew from my troubled mind. "They've all got scores to settle. And since the last successful faerie–wizard team-up temporarily sealed Faerie off, I think this is information that needs to be shared."

"I've got to tell Bert," I said, staring dazedly at the tablecloth.

"*Bert?* Heavens, no," he replied in the same tone he'd have used if I'd suggested ritualistically slaughtering kittens. "Not directly, at least. He's still too much of a cipher to be trusted."

"But he could get the security team after them—"

"Unless someone gets to him first." Tanner leaned close to my face and murmured, "Bert's predecessors were savvy enough to recognize that their offices were almost always bugged, and not just by the Company. You can't discuss this anywhere within the castle. I wouldn't be surprised if there are microphones in your quarters as well. And think about it—no one has reported the probationers missing yet, right? How many people know? Who else in that organization is compromised?"

"So what do I do?" I asked him. "Bert needs to know—"

"Not just yet. Tell the king and queen—and be careful, girl," he added, gripping my wrist. With a final squeeze, he rose from the table, then pulled a couple of bills from his pocket and laid them by his empty basket. "That should cover your lunch. Might want to ask your new friend to put the rest of it in a takeaway box," he told Frank.

"I'll talk to them as soon as I can," I said. "Today, if they'll see me."

Tanner nodded and turned to go, but paused and stepped back to the table. "By the way, do you know Poppy Kane? She might go by Stowe these days."

His practiced ease told me the question was rhetorical. "Sure."

"You know, it's a real shame that her parents have yet to meet their grandson. How old is the boy now, eleven?"

"Twelve."

"Mm. That's a long time with no word."

I hesitated, trying not to make promises I couldn't keep. "If Poppy asked permission, then the powers that be might let her family visit. Assuming they meant no harm."

"Of course. Tell me, how *do* the powers that be plan to handle Malcolm? Fae blood, shifter blood, a quarter mundane—that's quite a combination."

"Not much to handle. He enchants about as well as any other lesser blood—he can do a bit, but nothing spectacular."

"Is that so?" Tanner smiled and leaned over the table. "Boy's going to hit puberty before long, don't you think?"

"So?"

"So that's when we tend to first learn to use our gifts," he replied. "And Poppy has lupine shifters on both sides. Might be interesting." He straightened and nodded to the waitress, who was bringing Frank's second course. "Take care, my lady. And do give your aunt and uncle my regards."

As he slipped out of the restaurant, I handed the money to our waitress. "Box, please," I said. "Keep the change. And he's taken," I added, glancing at Frank. "*Very* taken."

Thank you, he thought as she hurried off to find a container.

"Sure, bud," I said, grabbing a last sip of my pop. "What are platonic life partners for?"

That afternoon, after debating the best way to contact my bosses without being presumptuous or causing offense, I settled for a group text: *Had unplanned lunch with Tanner A today. Need to speak with you ASAP.*

Not two minutes later, I had a response from Coileán: *My office, half an hour.*

I freshened up, left Frank with a marathon of an old murder mystery show, and headed back a few minutes before the appointed hour in order to clear security, having decided that Coileán's guards would like me a whole lot less if I popped through unexpectedly in his inner sanctum.

Val was waiting for me at the palace's main door and quickly escorted me through the hallways and upstairs. Before we reached Coileán's office, he murmured, "Did the Company threaten you?"

"No. Worse than that, I think."

He grunted and rapped on the door, then opened it to reveal the king and queen, already sitting across from each other on Coileán's pair of leather couches. Eleanor's captain, Nico, stood against the wall behind her and nodded to Val, who locked the door and nudged me into the room.

"So," said Coileán, raising a half-full tumbler of bourbon, "what's up, Ros?"

"Long story short," I replied, approaching the couches,

"Grandpa and a bunch of the old magi have gone missing, they're probably the ones killing Minor Arcanum wizards for their wands, and the Company, which has been keeping an eye on Moyna until now, can't find her anymore."

I jumped aside barely in time to avoid the spray as Coileán choked and spat out his drink. "*What?*" he managed through a coughing fit.

As he caught his breath, Eleanor slid down her couch and patted the cushion beside her. "Have a seat. I think we're going to need more than the short version."

They listened, growing agitated as I recounted my conversations with Tanner and Amy, and then Coileán rose and headed across the room to his bookshelf. "What on earth are you looking for?" Eleanor asked, watching him toss items onto the floor.

"Answers," he muttered.

By then, he'd cleared a couple of shelves, revealing the small hole hiding in the back of the bookcase. With an impatient gesture, the shelves moved aside, and the hole widened into a proper gate, which led straight into a modest den, judging by the plush sofa and recliner. As soon as the gate was big enough, Coileán stepped through and called, "Badger! Seamus! Are you here?"

A door down the hallway creaked open, and a gray-haired man in a wrinkled T-shirt and sweatpants padded toward us, squinting blearily. "Something wrong?" he asked.

I recognized Seamus's voice, even if the face didn't match the one I knew. Past about thirty, the only way a faerie looked his age was with glamour, and Seamus had done heavy work. Though close in age to my dad's parents, who had been evacuated to Faerie in their early fifties and hadn't aged a day since, he appeared to be considerably older. Then again, his partner was mortal, and so he glamoured up to prevent questions. Seamus and Badger, childhood sweethearts who'd finally married when

I was a kid—once they were confident enough in their skill at magical forgery to produce the necessary documentation for a civil service, that is—were on the downward slope to seventy. Badger had an open invitation to Faerie, but since her presence in the mortal realm was the one thing keeping Nath out, she refused to give up her watch—and so Seamus changed his hair color and added lines as necessary to keep up appearances.

Coileán gave his attire a cursory once-over. "Did I wake you?"

He yawned. "No worries, late night. Badge's still sleeping—what's going on?" he asked, catching sight of Eleanor and me on the far side of the gate.

"It's to do with—" Coileán began, then stopped, glared at the corners of the room, and beckoned Seamus closer. "Join us, please," he muttered, and stepped back through the gate with Seamus close behind.

By the time Coileán had shrunk the gate, Seamus had greeted his watchful uncle and was sitting on Coileán's vacated couch, once again black-haired and youthful, if still sporting old pajamas. "All right, want to tell me what's so important?" he asked as Coileán resumed his seat.

"Ros had a sit-down with Tanner Adler," he replied as his tumbler refilled itself.

Seamus's eyes, dark blue like Toula's—and, I'd been told, Mab's—widened briefly before narrowing as he scowled. "If those sneaky bastards are bugging our building again, so help me—"

"I don't think you're the target this time, but can't be too careful, right?" He slugged back at least a finger of bourbon and screwed his eyes closed with the burn. "Bring him up to speed, Ros."

I did as instructed, minimizing my conversations with Amy, though Seamus still looked peeved when he realized she'd alerted me. "Badge and I have been on it," he told us. "We've set up traces as well as we can—"

"Which are useless if Mulligan's people are hiding their

tracks," Eleanor interrupted.

"You know, boy," Val quietly added from the wall, "you might have mentioned this before now."

The king and queen nodded, and Seamus looked at the three of them in exasperation. "We thought we had it in hand. Homicide's in our wheelhouse, yeah? But if Adler's being straight with us…" He propped his chin in his hands and sighed. "Well, that would explain why the traces have gone nowhere."

"There's probably no point in setting up a blood trace," said Coileán, "but I'll ask Toula to try anyway."

"In the meanwhile, you need to share this with the Minor Arcanum," Eleanor told him. "As much as you think wise, but make it plain that anyone with known talent is in danger. Particularly if Moyna's people are involved," she muttered. "If they need to run, they can shelter in the settlement for now. And I don't expect to hear anything about it," she added, raising her voice and looking at the ceiling. "*Understood?*"

If Kura had an opinion about opening the doors to refugee wizards, she kept it to herself.

While Seamus talked logistics with the king and queen, I stepped into the hall, then wound up across the way on one of the palace's many balconies. Leaning against the railing, I tried to relax in the breeze, but I felt like the world had come crashing down upon me.

Bert needed to know, period. As frustrating, condescending, and unintentionally insulting as he'd been in our brief acquaintance, he still needed to know that there were rats in his cellar. But how was I supposed to tell him? If I dropped the bomb on him, would he even believe me? And say he pressed me to name my source—I didn't want to antagonize the Dark Company, not if they were trying to be helpful.

Or suppose I told him the news and he leapt into

action—unlikely, given what I'd seen thus far, but possible. Surely the missing probationers would get wind of it if the Arcanum sent security or assassins after them. They had to have sympathizers within the organization who would send word before they could get caught.

Frustrated by my lack of options, I paid no attention when the door opened and yelped when Coileán's hand landed on my shoulder. "Sorry, Ros," he said, stepping back a pace while I clutched my chest. "Lost in thought?"

"Lost, at least," I mumbled, feeling my heartbeat slow. "Did Seamus—"

"He went home. So did Ellie." He rested his back against the railing and looked up at the cloudless blue. "I know this is hard to believe, kid, but you don't actually have to solve the universe's problems by yourself."

I weighed the risks of coming clean, then decided to be honest—it wasn't as if Coileán couldn't poke around in my thoughts, anyway. "I don't think this envoy gig has been working out."

"No?"

"No. Bert and I haven't exactly hit it off, and…and then I skipped town for a few days to help Sam, and—"

"Hear me," he interrupted, sidling closer. "You're doing exactly what we need you to do. I don't care if you're living sandpaper to this Bert cretin—oh, don't look surprised, Sam told your parents what happened with Mummy and Daddy Wold."

"I'm sorry…"

"Don't be. I told Joey he could go pound the little weasel with my blessing, but Helen talked him down. Aiden took some convincing, now, but you know your uncle," he said with a shrug. "If you're miserable, you don't have to go back. Honestly, if this thing comes to a head, you shouldn't be in the middle of the fray. Not this time, at least," he added, smirking. "But if you're willing to stick around in the belly of the beast for the time being…"

Coileán left the thought unfinished, and I nodded.

"Someone needs to be there. Bert needs to know what's happening, and..." I paused as inspiration, which had been stubborn to that point, finally graced me with its presence. "I *might* just have a way of getting through to him. No promises," I insisted, "but give me a few days, and we'll see."

"Mm. And when your parents get wind of these developments and demand that I drag you home, any idea of what I'm supposed to tell them?"

I forced myself to smile, even though my guts felt like lead. "Tell them this isn't my first rodeo. And I've got Frank, Bee, and Daisy this time around, so I'll be all right."

"And maybe more than that in the near future," he replied, turning his gaze toward the distant sea. "Ellie's contemplating sending her own envoy. You haven't done anything wrong," he rushed before I could apologize again. "It's just the proper thing to do, and she has a candidate in mind. So when next you see the myopic asshole-in-chief, tell him to get another apartment ready, why don't you?"

I grinned in spite of my unease. "Thanks, Coileán."

He ruffled my hair, then left me to my contemplation.

CHAPTER 9

Three minutes into my audience the next morning, Bert regarded me over his laptop, the one item on his cluttered desk that detracted from his careful air of the traditionalist wizard at work, and finally stopped typing. "A second envoy?"

I didn't think I was imagining the note of suspicion in his voice, but I played it cool. "It's proper. You wouldn't ask England and France to share an ambassador, would you?"

"I thought there was cooperation between the courts."

"There is—for now. The queen would prefer to have her own liaison on the ground here, as long as we're doing this." I paused as he yanked off his glasses to clean them. "Maybe she'll send someone more to your liking."

He shoved them back onto his nose with a flash of annoyance. "I don't *dislike* you, Ros. You're...well... ehm..." he struggled.

"Prickly?"

"Challenging. But perhaps we could see our way to a better working relationship, hmm?" He closed his computer, the better to stare at me. "Let me take you out. No parents, no ambushes, just good, old-fashioned alcohol, and maybe crisps, if we're feeling daring. There's a hole-in-the-wall pub on the far side of town, and I...*might* have sneaked off every so often when my tutors were distracted."

I considered the gesture in light of my growing aversion to spending time alone with Bert—so far, that had never gone well—then chose diplomacy. "Sure. Saturday night at the pub—no harm in that, right?"

Bert's brows knit. "Oh, you were thinking *tonight?* I've got a Council thing, and tomorrow's booked. Monday?"

"Uh...sure. I'll pencil it in," I replied, and left him to his working weekend.

Though I'd have preferred to get my pub meeting with Bert out of the way and be done with it, at least my schedule was clear through the weekend—a fact I intended to rectify posthaste.

Half an hour after leaving the grand magus's end of the magi office suite, I pulled Frank away from our television and rapped on Arnold's door. Fortunately, he, too, was putting in a few hours of work that Saturday morning, but he seemed far less irked than Bert had been to be interrupted. "Morning, Ros," he said with a smile, bookmarking the leather-bound tome on his desk. "Come in. Frank, good to see you," he added, noting my quiet companion. "Have a seat. Tea?"

"Don't go to any trouble," I told him.

"Oh, none at all. Water's already warm." As he prepared cups, he casually said, "I'm going to assume this visit has something to do with last weekend's lunch with the Wolds. Yes?"

"No, we've put that behind us," I lied, earning a surprised glance from the magus. "Actually, I was hoping for a tour."

"Of what? And here you are...sugar?"

I helped myself to the bowl, though Frank left his tea untouched. "Glastonbury. I've been out a little with Bee, but I don't want to monopolize her summer break or her time with Daisy. You know, my parents speak so highly of you, and I'd like to get to know you better. Do you think you'd have time to show us the highlights?"

Arnold looked quizzical, torn between confusion and

the dictates of manners, until Frank stepped in. *There's a problem with the Arcanum, and the Minor Arcanum and Fringe are in trouble. Maybe the Arcanum, too. But Ros thinks someone may be listening to your office, so she can't tell you about it here.*

His eyes widened as he received the thought, and then he nodded and sipped his tea, giving himself time to recover. "Of course, dear, I'd be happy to. I'm a bit snowed-under today, but what would you say to dinner tonight? I know a great little place. And then I'll give you the walking tour—how does that sound?"

"Perfect," I replied.

"Seven?" Arnold asked, then looked at Frank and, with practiced casualness, tapped his temple.

Frank's head cocked ever so slightly as he looked at the message Arnold was trying to convey. *No hard proof of a bug,* Frank thought, *but since a lot of what you need to know came from Tanner Adler...*

Arnold drank again, deeply.

Dinner out on the town was pleasant, a quick bite at a casual Italian restaurant. As Frank plowed through a plate of meatballs and sausage links, Arnold told us about the mundane side of Glastonbury, keeping the conversation light, a mixture of historical anecdotes and recommendations for local beer. He laughed easily for a man with a weight on his mind, but then again, Arnold had been a member of the Fringe resistance team during the Mulligan years—he would have had to learn to cope along the way.

After tiramisu—Arnold insisted, though Frank pushed his away with a wrinkled nose after a single bite—our host paid, then led us out into the warm summer night. "Hen do," he muttered, steering us past a cheerfully yelling group of young women in stilettoes and pink sashes. "Come on, I'll show you the view from the top."

Technically, he told us, the Tor was closed at dusk, but

such trivialities as opening hours meant little to a wizard on a mission. He directed us toward the tower on the hill, prepared to create a distraction in case of police interference, but the only surprise came when we accidentally flushed a pair of teenagers out of the bushes, who scampered off in their underwear. "Ah, memories," he muttered, watching them run, and pressed on for the summit.

A short walk later, the three of us stood together at the base of the ruined tower, taking shelter from the night wind. I leaned close to Frank, trying to surreptitiously use him as a space heater, while Arnold turned his back to the town and closed our triangle. "No Arcanum or Company surveillance here, I bet," he said, keeping his voice low. "What's going on?"

He said nothing for five minutes while I filled him in, then sighed, muttered, "*Christ*, not again," and turned and walked off.

I traded uncertain looks with Frank while Arnold, arms folded, glared out at the stars and the patchy clouds flying over the peaceful night. After a moment, I joined him and cleared my throat. "You okay?"

"No."

"Want us to go—"

He gave his head a curt shake. "Just trying to sort out how I messed up this badly."

"This…isn't your fault," I tried lamely.

"Bollocks." His jaw clenched as he stared into space, and he finally said, "I was a rubbish grand magus. Tried to tread water for ten years, but that's all. And seeing as I overlooked a bloody *jailbreak*…"

I let him stew in silent self-castigation for a time, then murmured, "I need your help, Arnold. I've got a plan, maybe, but I can't do it alone."

"I'm listening."

"We can't go straight to Bert with this, right?"

He turned to me with a look of horror. "Absolutely

not. Never mind the fact that we're missing probationers—if Bert had any inkling of how compromised our security situation is when it comes to the Company, he'd flip out. He's already wary of them."

"Better not give him any more ammo, then. Listen," I said, sliding closer to him, "I need someone who knows the Arcanum's IT system and can access the Archives, preferably without using the old loophole credentials Aiden gave me. Someone who wouldn't attract any notice if he or she started poking around."

Arnold mulled that over, then dipped his head in a slow nod. "I might know just the person. We can't discuss this in the castle, naturally...have you got lunch plans tomorrow?"

Not yet, thought Frank, who'd been following along by peeking through my thoughts.

The magus turned and smirked at him. "Tricky, aren't you? And what are your opinions as to curry?"

As it so happened, Frank adored curry—the hotter, the better. Having arrived at the restaurant Arnold suggested an hour ahead of him and his IT connection so as not to give the impression that the four of us were meeting, we had plenty of time to sample the menu. When our waiter realized we were virtual novices, he brought us a sampler platter of appetizer-sized portions, a variety of meats and spice levels with heaping sides of rice and naan. I didn't venture above medium heat, but Frank—who, granted, could shoot fire from his throat without incinerating himself—fell in love with the triple-pepper offerings. By the end of the hour, he was adding hot sauce to extra-spicy curried goat, to our waiter's horrified amazement, and cleaning the caustic leavings with any convenient starch.

While Frank leaned back in his chair and patted his stomach in anticipation of the next course, the front bell jingled, and I saw Arnold walk in beside a thin figure in a navy hoodie. By the time Arnold had spotted us, I'd recognized his companion, and he soon recognized me.

"Ros?" Antony asked in bewilderment as Arnold pulled out a chair. "Uh…hi. Grand Magus Lowe said he had someone in need of technical help…"

He let the thought dangle, and I quietly asked Arnold, "You're sure about this?"

"Positive," he replied, unfolding his napkin. "Antony is trustworthy."

"Clean," Frank rumbled, staring up as Antony shifted from foot to foot. "I see no deception."

"Deception?" Antony echoed, looking around the table for a clue.

"Have a seat," I told him, and nodded to my companion. "This is Frank. Frank, Antony. He's a librarian."

Antony stuck out his hand, and after a brief hesitation, Frank clasped it. "Are you, um, Fringe?" Antony began. "Or—"

"What *is* that?" Arnold interrupted as our waiter, wearing protective gloves, plopped a plate of rice and a metal bowl that was more brown sauce than meat in front of Frank. The smell coming off the dish was enough to make my eyes water, but Frank pulled his chair closer and took up his spoon in his fist.

"Phaal," the waiter said, depositing a small dish of raita within Frank's reach. "And you will need this."

Frank took a test bite, chewed slowly, then licked his lips and smiled. "Unlikely."

"Chicken tikka," Arnold mumbled, keeping a safe distance from the noxious curry. "Mild, if you please."

Once the waiter departed with the new orders, though not without casting a last worried look at Frank as he continued to devour his phaal, Arnold murmured to Antony, "I asked you to join us because we have good reason to believe there's a problem with several of the Montana crowd."

"What sort of problem?" he replied.

"The kind that's discussed on a need-to-know basis. And since I think you'd prefer to have plausible deniability, that's as much as you need to know. All right?"

He thought it over for a moment, then nodded. "Okay. What do you need from me?"

"We need to do a deep delve in the Archives," I explained. "One that wouldn't set off any alarms."

"Well, I certainly have credentials for that," said Antony, "but if you're looking for access to, say, personal files, I can't help you. I can set you up with Arcview and make your computer look like mine, but as far as getting into the encrypted docs..." He shrugged. "I'm just a librarian, you know?"

"That'll do," I replied, "assuming you wouldn't mind patching some remote users into the network."

Antony's eyes narrowed as he asked, "How remote?" When I said nothing, he huffed a frustrated sigh. "I don't need names right now, but I'm going to need to know what sort of systems I'm trying to connect."

I leaned toward him and lowered my voice. "My uncle will help you."

Antony sat back, surprised, then ran a hand over his face and turned to Arnold. "You really want me to open up the Archives to *Faerie*?"

"Temporarily," said Arnold.

"Aiden and some Fringers have solid password-cracking tools," I explained. "We need to get into a few people's personal files, see what's in there, then plant whatever we find somewhere that Bert can stumble across it and think himself clever."

"And hopefully act," Arnold muttered.

Frank, who had been listening while he inhaled his lunch, finally wiped his mouth and pushed his dish aside. "You are scared," he told Antony.

"I'm not thrilled, no," Antony retorted. "This is getting dangerously close to treason."

"Mm. What 'plausible deniability' mean?" he asked me.

"It means that if anyone finds out about this and asks him what he knows, he can honestly say he had no idea," I replied.

Frank considered that, then said, "He is uncertain. That not work. I show him."

Suddenly, Antony gasped and gripped the edge of the table, hyperventilating for a few seconds until Frank blinked and picked up a piece of naan. "Better?" he asked as Antony clutched his head and gawked at him.

"What…how…what the hell was—"

"He got in your head, didn't he?" I said, giving Frank a long look. "How much did he show you?"

Antony took a deep breath, then squeezed his eyes closed and steadied himself. "Enough. Just tell me what you need from me."

I gave Antony my specs, my uncle's phone number, and a warning to do *nothing* within the confines of the castle. He told me that it would take him at least a few days to work out the setup and make it secure, but he promised to deliver a solution as quickly as he could. That was good enough for me—whatever Frank had shared with him unsettled him enough to take a few pieces of naan and run.

Leaving Antony to his own devices, I passed a quiet Sunday evening with Frank, then spent most of Monday in the library, keeping up with my reading, while my roommate binged on his new favorite shows. But as comfortable as the library was, I couldn't avoid the inevitable, and so, after dinner, I made myself presentable and met Bert in the entrance hall for our night out.

At least he'd left the robe off, but his ensemble had little else to commend it. Bert sported a dress shirt and green knit vest over pleated khakis and loafers, the sort of sensibly drab garb of an accountant on casual Friday, and he seemed flustered to find me in a sleeveless red summer dress. Still, he pressed gamely on, and we soon found ourselves at his dingy favorite pub with a pint and a pack of vinegar-flavored chips each.

For once, after two weeks of acquaintance, he and I were able to make it through an entire social outing without disaster, albeit by limiting our conversation to safe, mundane topics like the summer weather, the tourists, and football. Bert stumbled as he tried to bluff his way through the unfamiliar terrain of movies and music—sadly, it seemed that I had a better handle on pop culture than he did, despite having learned what I knew by streaming it into Faerie. At first, I wondered how many weekends little Bertie had spent hiding in the library instead of goofing off with his friends, but that led me to the root enquiry of whether little Bertie ever *had* any friends, and if not, whether he had attempted to rectify the situation. Oh, he seemed pleased enough to be drinking out in public, and he wasn't exactly gibbering to himself, but his demeanor revealed a sort of awkward anxiety that suggested he had no clue what he was doing in the company of another person when there were no clear guidelines as to the purpose of the interaction.

But at least he was polite. He insisted on paying for our drinks—"The Arcanum isn't hurting," he joked—and he listened with an almost uncomfortable intensity when I spoke. I got the feeling he was studying me, but I let it go. One vodka tonic later, I told him I had to write a progress report for Coileán before morning, and he took the hint and called it a night.

Bert saw me to my door and waited while I fumbled with the key. "Thank you for the evening, Ros. I had a nice time. Hope you did as well."

"Oh, sure," I said, showing him a brief smile, and finally turned the lock.

"I, ehm…I hope you don't still think I'm awful."

In that moment, he seemed almost pathetic, an inexperienced boy parroting his father's wardrobe, proud of a successful outing and searching for a pat on the head.

"I don't think you're awful," I replied, which was close enough to the truth. "Goodnight, Bert."

When his footsteps receded, I flipped the bolt, leaned against the door, and let out the long breath I hadn't known I'd been holding. Frank, still lounging on the couch where I'd left him, paused the show and pulled himself just upright enough to see me over the back. "And?"

"He's not dead, is he?"

"You want me fix that?"

"Do I want you *to* fix that? No," I replied, heading for the kitchen, only to get a decorative pillow upside the head. Frank might not have had the nuances of spoken English down pat, and he still had a tendency to hold utensils like a toddler, but his aim was *superb*.

It took Antony the better part of two days to work out the kinks on his end, then another two to work up the nerve to call my uncle. "He was really nice about everything," Antony told me on Friday, sounding surprised, as he debriefed me in a café on the other side of town. "Actually showed me a few shortcuts, which isn't worrying at all."

I grinned. "Aiden knows his stuff. He got into the restricted bits of the Archives before he ever left the silo."

"And the fact that he still knows workable loopholes tells me everything I need about the state of our network security," he muttered. "Anyway, he got your people in Virginia patched in, so that's two servers more or less dedicated to trawling Arcview. Let's just hope they finish before anyone figures out there's been a breach." He sipped his coffee, his face betraying his tension. "They're just looking at records for the probationers, their families, and the people who're supposed to be monitoring them, right? Nothing else?"

"That's it. No one's trying to bring down the Arcanum," I replied.

I decided not to mention the request I'd made for the computer team to add the Wolds to their research list. Antony was no great fan of the grand magus, but he was conflicted enough about serving as our connection without knowing we were investigating Bert's family.

"Password cracking will take longer than anything," I added. "They'll copy the files they need and log out before anyone suspects there's a problem." I reached across the table and gripped his hand. "Thank you, Antony. I mean it."

He nodded. "If half of what your friend told me is accurate…"

"What *did* he tell you?" I asked, releasing him.

Antony took a moment to drink deeply. "Stuff about the Company and the folks who've turned up dead of late. And, uh…other things."

"Oh?"

"Your friend's a mind reader, yeah? He's picked up on some of your memories, I think."

"Frank's never been shy about that," I said, and swirled my tea. "What did—"

"I never knew how rough you had it back then," he mumbled in a rush. "Not just from me and the guys, but…we didn't exactly help. He reminded me that I owe you."

I lifted my teacup and smiled over the rim. "You're all right, Copeland."

He shrugged. "Frank also told me that if I didn't help out, I'd regret it, and since he's, like, ogre-sized and has the scary eyes down pat—"

"Oh, you have *no* idea," I replied, laughing to myself as Antony squirmed.

I was enjoying a nice, long Saturday lie-in the next morning when my phone rang.

Grunting, I rolled over and pawed at the nightstand

until I located the culprit, and I mentally cursed the person on the other end. I'd been good, hadn't I? I'd made it a week without blowing up at anyone important and coordinated the latest round of computerized espionage—surely, I reasoned, that entitled me to a few extra hours of sleep. But no, the phone wouldn't shut up, and I blindly hit the button and held it to my ear. "Hello?"

"Ros? Sorry," said Sam, surprised, "did I wake you? You're more than halfway to lunch."

I peered at the clock—twenty of ten—and flopped back onto my pillow. "We're not all up with the chickens, man," I said, yawning. "And what are you doing up already? How far behind is Faerie right now, five hours?"

"Closer to six, I think, but you know what a pain that is to nail down," he replied, sounding far too pleased to be awake. "How's it going?"

"Okay. Bed's comfy," I mumbled, pulling the covers to my chin. "Mom and Dad treating you all right?"

"No complaints here, except I think I've gained five pounds since your grandma started feeding me. By the way, I got a job offer."

"Really? Trainee dragon wrangler?"

Sam chuckled softly on the other end. "Nah. You were right, they mostly look after themselves. Actually, Aunt Ellie asked if I'd be interested in this envoy gig."

That pulled me closer to properly awake. "Yeah? Considering it?"

"Well, I'm standing outside the castle right now, so take that for what it's worth. Uh...is there a front door to this place, or what?"

I bolted upright, clutching the phone so hard my fingers ached. "Wait, you're *here*? Now? Glastonbury?"

He laughed again at my excitement. "I got dropped just inside this bubble thingy, know what I'm talking about?"

"That's the illusion spell."

"If you say so, it's all just pretty lights to me right now. Anyway, Aunt Ellie said it'd be safer to not actually walk straight into the castle from Faerie…might give the wrong impression or something. So I'm trying to figure out exactly how to get into this place, and if you've got any tips—"

"Don't move," I interrupted, pinning the phone to my ear with my shoulder as I grabbed a pair of pajama pants. "I'm on my way down."

He sighed with relief. "Thanks. Be a pretty crappy first day at work if I couldn't even get into the building, huh?"

"Down in five," I said, and ended the call. Pulling a light sweatshirt on over my tank top, I yelled, "Frank! Sam's here! You coming?"

Sam? he replied, the thought tinged with curiosity. *Where?*

"Outside." I hurried to the door, and Frank jumped off the couch to join my mad dash through the towers.

One long sprint and several flustered wizards later, I ran through the courtyard and into the entry tower. Ignoring the ten-foot ceremonial doors, I smashed open the more reasonably sized modern door beside them and looked around wildly—and there he was, standing just inside the protective spell, looking like he'd strolled off a ranch: black T-shirt, crisp jeans, well-worn brown boots, and a matching cowboy hat tipped low over his eyes. A duffel bag and a computer case were slung over his shoulder. Startled by the commotion of the slamming door, he spotted me, waved, and started up the rolling green lawn.

Strange hat, Frank thought.

"Completely wrong for here," I agreed.

But you're pleased.

"It suits him."

Frank snorted, and when I glanced his way, there was an odd, sly look on his face. "What?" I asked.

You know.

"Know what?"

He rolled his eyes and said no more, but before I could

press him, Sam had almost reached us, and I hurried through the grass to hug him. "Good to see you again," I said. "I'm a mess..."

He grinned and clumsily patted a clump of my sleep-snarled hair flat. "There, all better. Sorry to drag you out of bed, but thanks for coming down to rescue me."

I noticed a few curious passersby staring our way, realized that I was barefoot and wearing mismatched clothes, and tugged at Sam's arm. "Come on, let's get you inside. Bert's probably working by now, so I'll take you up and make the introductions. And would it have killed someone to let me know you were coming?"

"Thought it'd be more fun to surprise you. Morning, Frank."

The two shook hands, and though Frank's unusual expression never changed, Sam seemed unaware that the dragon was quietly amused for reasons he refused to divulge.

Before I took Sam around, we stopped by my apartment so that I could make myself presentable, or at least acquire shoes. Sam left his bags and hat by the couch at my suggestion, and when I emerged with tamer hair and real pants, I found him at the window, taking in the view of the town beyond the dome. "Bit of a change, huh?"

"I mean, it's the second place I've moved in just over a week, so everything's a change right now. But it seems nice enough."

"I'll get Bee to show you around later—she's native. But let's go tell Bert you've arrived."

Sam and Frank followed me as I made my winding way toward the grand magus's office. Once we'd entered the next tower, Sam asked, "This would be the Bert who was giving you fits?"

"The same, but it's getting better."

He grunted noncommittally.

I've made offers, Frank added.

"You're a dear," I replied, glancing back at him, "but

the official point of our presence here is for us all to be civil to each other."

Sure. The offers stand.

I shook my head and pressed on.

Soon enough, I led our little party up the last staircase and rapped on Bert's door. As I'd predicted, he was hunched over his laptop, sporting a basic black robe over his weekend polo—in all honesty, I doubted he had anything more relaxed in his wardrobe. "This is Eleanor's envoy," I explained as he came around the desk. "Bert Wold, Sam Rockwell."

Bert didn't look nearly as small beside Sam as he did next to Frank—well, to be fair, almost anyone looked small beside Frank—but Sam still had about four inches and at least fifty pounds on Bert, much of which was muscle. The grand magus was relatively slim and pasty, and with his thick glasses factored in, his overall appearance suggested he'd grown up in a library carrel and wore his older relatives' hand-me-downs. Sam, by contrast, came with a modest tan and the cowboy version of business casual, giving him the look, at least, of a man who knew which end of a horse to avoid.

"Howdy," said Sam, extending his hand.

Bert winced at the strength of Sam's grip, but he forced a polite smile. "Good morning. You've, ehm…just come?"

"Left my things in Ros and Frank's apartment. Hope that's okay."

"Certainly." His eyes darted toward me, then turned upward again to meet Sam's. "I'll have a flat readied for you. A little forewarning would have been appreciated."

"He can crash with us for now," I interjected. "Don't put anyone to trouble on our account."

"No, no, quite unnecessary," Bert replied brusquely, returning to his desk. "I'll see what's available."

I told him we would be in my rooms whenever Sam's accommodations were ready, and the three of us headed back for breakfast. Sam offered to cook, but I sat him down at the table with an oversized cup of coffee and chatted while I pulled together eggs, bacon, and toast. "Nothing fancy," I said as I brought the finished platter forth, "but we're pretty big on protein around here."

"Don't blame me," said Frank, grabbing a plate. "You like bacon."

"Beats the heck out of the traditional bowl of Rice Krispies," Sam added, and grinned. "Your dad tried to teach me to cook via enchantment, but I haven't gotten the hang of it yet." He paused suddenly as a thought occurred to him. "They *do* sell Rice Krispies in this country, right?"

By the time Frank was mopping up the last of the bacon grease, one of Bert's assistants showed up to escort Sam to his apartment—which, conveniently enough, was 2031, down a floor and across the hall from me. Promising to join him shortly and help with furniture and paint colors, I started cleaning up the kitchen while he headed down to inspect his new place.

Frank laughed softly as he brought the dishes to the sink, and I looked up from the soapy basin with mild annoyance. "Okay, *what* is so funny?"

"Bert will not like Sam's room."

"Why not?"

"Too close."

I cocked my head, baffled, and he smirked at me. *You didn't notice the look on his face when Sam shook his hand?*

"Maybe a little pained, but what does that have to do with anything?"

Frank chuckled again. *Maybe it wasn't evident to you because you're not hearing the subtext.*

I dumped the dishes into the sink, then turned back to him and planted my hand on my hip. "*Oh*? And what would that be?"

When Bert saw us, thought Frank, hoisting himself onto the counter, *he was immediately intimidated. Confronted with two larger males—that's reasonable, and he moved past it in seconds. But he kept watching you and Sam, gauging distance, familiarity…* He screwed up his face as he sought the right phrasing. *No matter how much noise you people make, much of your communication is physical—how you stand, how you gesture, your expressions. It's why Daisy's tried to teach me to smile in a way that isn't so off-putting.*

"It's not *that* bad…"

Neither is it good, apparently, but I digress. Bert was paying attention to what you and Sam weren't verbally saying, and it flustered him.

"And what, pray tell, were we saying?" I replied. "I thought it was all pretty professional."

You were excited. You conveyed a familiarity with Sam, but more than that, your demeanor showed a fondness for him. Bert was threatened.

"Threatened?" I echoed, raising an eyebrow. "By what?"

You really don't get it, he thought, and shook his head. *Bert's interested in you as a mate.*

I threw back my head and laughed at the absurdity. "What would give you that idea?" I finally asked, wiping a tear away. "Bert's not into me."

He is, Frank insisted. *Communicating it poorly, but I guess he doesn't know better. He's of two minds about it, now,* he clarified. *Part of him is intrigued, and part is upset that he feels that way. Conflicted, definitely, but there's an interest there, whether he likes it or not.*

My thoughts ran back to our brief pub night on Monday, the awkward small talk and scruffy ambiance of Bert's favorite watering hole, and I looked up in time to see Frank nodding. "Damn it," I muttered, rubbing my forehead, "I don't need this."

I'm not telling you to upset you, only to make you aware. Watch for dominance posturing.

"If I just play it cool and don't give him any indication that I'm interested—"

Ros, he's more clueless about the nuances of your communication than I am. He's not going to give up unless it's clear to him that he doesn't stand a chance. Think about Horus and Rego. Remember that day last summer when they came home bloodied and slept on opposite ends of the barn?

"Yeah, but no one would ever tell me what happened."

Frank smiled—and yes, it *was* looking closer to acceptable. *They found a female ready to mate while they were out together, and they turned on each other. Horus is bigger, so immediate points there, but Rego challenged him to impress her, and he's the quicker fighter. She might have chosen him if an older male hadn't come along and chased them both off,* he added with a flash of amusement. *Now, translate that to your males. Sam's the larger of the two, but Bert might challenge him to prove himself the better mate material.*

"Except Sam's just my friend," I pointed out.

You think so?

Before I could come back at that, someone knocked at our door, and, assuming it was Sam, I yelled, "It's unlocked!"

When the door opened, however, it was Bert on the threshold, peering through the opening as if there might be something untoward going on in the foyer. "Ros? Hello?"

"Oh—hey, come in," I said, throwing a damp dishtowel over my shoulder to suggest I'd been doing more in the kitchen than gossiping with Frank. "Sam's gone to get moved in, if you're looking for him."

"I was looking for you, actually," he replied, and gingerly stepped into the apartment. "Work's not bad this weekend, and I was, ehm…well, Grand Magus Lowe said he took you around, but I'm positive he didn't hit all the good places, and I know of this pub near the Tor, great view, beer garden, so…dinner?"

I could practically feel Frank smirking behind me, and I thought fast. "Sounds nice," I told Bert, aiming for enthusiastic. "Is this an official thing, or can the guys join us?"

"The guys?" he asked, momentarily thrown.

"Well, Frank's a menace with a good burger and a bottle of hot sauce, and Sam doesn't know jack about Glastonbury, so why don't we make this a foursome?" I asked.

Bert's mouth hung open for a few seconds, and then he snapped it closed and gave me a weak smile. "Good idea. Six?"

"Perfect," I replied, and looked at Frank in triumph as Bert made his hasty exodus.

Whatever Bert had in mind when he issued the invitation, all he got out of the original plan was the menu and the view. While I'd assisted Sam with decoration that afternoon—his beginner's enchantment couldn't hold a candle to my spellcraft when it came to bathroom remodels—Frank had texted Bee and Daisy to try to make our group a sextet. Once he'd explained the situation, they proved more than willing to help a sister out.

The six of us crowded around a wooden picnic table built for four that evening, eating burgers and fries and drinking draft pints (and one bottomless Bloody Mary) as the sun went down. The proprietor had hung dozens of strings of white Christmas lights across the back garden, and as soon as dusk was dark enough, we found ourselves beneath a glowing canopy. We took turns putting in orders at the bar, and as the night wore on, our voices rose and crashed into laughter with surprising ease. The girls did their best impressions of their stranger neighbors, sometimes from atop the empty table beside us, and by the time Sam finished recounting his one and only disastrous attempt to tag a cow, I was almost in tears. The only member of our party who seemed less than enthusiastic about the evening's entertainment was Bert, who nursed a single pint for the duration, said little, and generally frowned at the beer-fueled antics, especially once Daisy made a game of trying to steal Frank's fries.

I thought having a couple of additional females at the table might help, Frank told me as I brushed my teeth that night. *A distraction, as it were. I mean, I'm no judge, but I don't think Daisy and Bee are hideous, are they?*

I spat and wiped my mouth. "Not by a long shot. But they're also pretty obviously a couple, so in terms of giving Bert other women to hit on, that might not have been the most effective tactic."

Do you really think he's savvy enough to have caught on to that? he retorted, leaning against the doorframe with his arms folded. *This is the same guy who thought taking you to meet his parents was a wise idea.*

"True." I turned and hugged Frank, and he awkwardly patted my back. "Thanks, bud."

Of course. He rested his chin on top of my head and let out a little sigh. *If you'd prefer him crispier—*

"Frank."

Just offering.

CHAPTER 10

Despite my apprehension over the missing probationers—I kept my phone close in case of an update from Aiden or the Virginia Fringe—alcohol al fresco proved to be an effective sleep aid, and I barely moved once I hit the sheets…

…until, that is, someone grabbed my shoulder, rolled me onto my back, and pinned me to the mattress.

I shrieked as my eyes flew open, trying to focus on my assailant in the blue predawn light, and finally picked Val's face out of the confusion of shadows around me. "What the *hell?*" I yelped, ceasing to thrash under his arm. "How did you get in here?"

"You sent your parents pictures. I appropriated one," he replied, and lessened the pressure against my chest. "Where's your practice room?"

I pushed him the rest of the way off of me and sat up, grateful I'd slept in decent pajamas. "There's a climate-controlled suite in the old dungeons, and Arnold said I could use that if I needed—"

"Anything more private?"

Visualizing what I remembered of the castle tour, I told him, "Yeah, but it's less pleasant. There's an old one at the base of tower ten, but it's mostly used for gardening tools, I think. Why?"

I felt the quick intrusion as Val pulled the directions from my mental map, and then he nodded and headed for the door. "Meet me there as soon as you're dressed. Bring Sam," he added, and let himself out.

A few minutes later, I'd pulled on sweats and woken Sam, and Frank accompanied the two of us out into the chill of the morning. The courtyard was empty—five a.m. on Sunday was a quiet time around Arc 2—and when we let ourselves into the old practice building, Val was sitting atop a pile of musty, folded mats, well away from the gardeners' rakes and shovels. He had always taken my training seriously, but that morning, there was an unusual tension in his face and arms, and he didn't smile.

"What's the big idea?" I demanded as Frank latched the door. "What couldn't wait until breakfast?"

The look in his eyes deflated much of my bravado. "Tell me about the security on this place," he said, tapping one foot against the cement floor.

Sam could only shrug, and I took the lead. "There's the illusion spell, and the one that warns strangers away—"

"Not defensive."

"—and if you'll let me *finish*, there's a ward system that can be engaged as needed. Or so said Arnold. They keep it down so people can come and go without having to walk outside the castle."

"Anything else?"

I shook my head. "Why?"

"Because," said Val as his foot picked up its tempo, "at the moment, anyone—and I do mean *anyone*—could stroll into your room and strike you dead." He stared at Sam and me in turn, letting that sink in. "There was nothing keeping me out of your quarters, Ros," he continued, sounding disappointed. "What if I'd wanted to kill you instead of wake you?"

"I'm a decent fighter," I started to protest, but Val was having none of it.

"Against what? A wizard your age? *Him?*" he asked, pointing to Frank. "Need I remind you that Moyna and her camp may be with the missing wizards, and not even the damn Company can locate them?" He pushed himself off the mats and marched toward us, and though we were almost of a height, I suddenly felt quite a bit smaller than usual. "I know some of Moyna's followers," he murmured when we were nearly nose to nose. "I have *peers* among them. Do you understand how serious this is, Roslyn?"

"Sorry," Sam interrupted, "but I don't see what the problem—"

Without so much as glancing his way, Val flung Sam against the far wall and pinned him six feet above the ground. "*That* is the problem, boy," he replied, finally deigning to glance at the result as Sam kicked at his unseen bonds. "Neither of you has the skill or the power to defend yourselves. You need to return to Faerie."

"That's not an option right now," I said as Sam fell to the floor. "Not for me. I've got a project—"

"Aiden and the Fringe are more than capable of searching the Archives without your continued assistance."

"They don't know Bert. If they find something, if I can get it to him in a way that he'll accept—"

"Arnold can do that at least as well as you can."

"But it's not *his* grandparents killing people, is it?" I blurted, flushing with sudden anger.

Val paused and considered me—reddening, tense, my hands clenched into fists—then shook his head. "This is not your responsibility, child."

"I'm making it mine. Take him back with you if he wants to go," I told Val as Sam, wincing from his fall, shuffled toward us, "but I'm staying here."

My coach sighed and rubbed his face. "Foolish. But if you won't be swayed by reason, then I insist that you improve your defensive skills. Your training begins today, and it will continue at the same hour until I'm satisfied. Agreed?"

"Dawn?" I snapped. "*Really*?"

"Those are my terms."

I turned to Sam, who was rubbing his bruising shoulder, then nodded at Val. "Agreed. Can we at least put the mats down first?"

He responded with a blast of force that, even with my shield in place, sent me halfway down the room and onto my back. "Mats make you complacent," he replied. "On your feet."

As I pushed myself off the unforgiving floor, Frank snorted and started for the exit. *If you're not going to let me help you, Ros, then I'm going back to bed,* he thought.

"*I* am helping them," Val replied.

Frank turned, looked pointedly at me, then locked eyes with Val and snorted thin curls of smoke.

At last, Val cracked a smile, though there was no warmth to it. "You think I'm afraid of you?"

I don't care if you fear me. But if she comes back in pieces…

He left the end of that thought unformed and took his leave. Val waited until the door slammed behind him, then turned to me and shook his head. "Children," he muttered, and sighed. "Now, that last shield was sloppy—do it again."

Not until the castle clock chimed seven did Val let us crawl away to lick our wounds. "Tomorrow," he reminded us, opening a gate. "Should you forget, I'll find you."

Sam and I were quiet until we got back to my apartment—I ached too much to do more than concentrate on walking—and when I unlocked the door, I collapsed onto the couch without a word. Sam draped himself over a chair, similarly exhausted, and at the sound of our groaning, Frank emerged from his room. "Finished?" he asked.

"Dead," I moaned.

His eyes narrowed. "Val did not fix you?"

"Guess he had somewhere to be. *Ouch.*" I hissed as I shifted against the cushions. "Sam, are you any good at healing?"

"Never tried," he mumbled.

We lay still for a moment, and Frank, considering the

sorry sight, shrugged and headed for the kitchen. "I make breakfast. You do magic."

Fearing a stovetop inferno, I struggled to rise and called after him, "It's okay, bud, I'll get it—"

"Bacon is not difficult." He poked his head back around the wall and grinned. "And eggshell not edible. Got it."

I couldn't stay horizontal all day, especially not if Frank was going to try his hand with a skillet, and so, moving slowly, I cast a healing spell around myself, then added a generous layer of numbing magic. When I could move without wanting to cry out, I hobbled to Sam and did the same for him, and he sighed in relief. "You've got to teach me how to do that," he said as the spell took full effect.

"It's casting, you can't do it. Val can whip up an enchantment that works even better, but he was in a weird mood today." I offered Sam a hand and pulled him from his chair, and then we shuffled to the kitchen to supervise Frank and make coffee. "Don't know what set him off," I said, measuring out grounds. "He's never been that rough before."

"He beats you on the reg, does he?" Sam asked.

"He's been teaching me for years. But he's always kept things fair before now—I mean, did he even break a sweat this morning?"

"Couldn't have proved it by me." Sam filled the carafe, using a potholder to turn the steel spigot. "That guy's a *beast*."

Frank looked up from the sizzling bacon and grunted. "Scared?"

"Of course I'm scared of him! He wiped the floor with me!"

"Nothing new from Val." He considered the bacon, blew a short blast of flame over the top to speed along the cooking, and nodded in satisfaction. "Plate."

Sam passed him one, and as I pulled the eggs from their carton, my phone trilled. Moving as quickly as I could with my injuries, I returned to my room, hoping for a word from the password crackers.

It was from Amy, all right, but it was terse: *MA won't evacuate. Two dead overnight in Japan.*

The next two days showed me, in exquisitely painful detail, just how much Val had been holding back all along. In the past, he'd been tough but encouraging, putting me in scenarios in which I had a chance of winning if I kept my wits about me and cast as I'd been taught. But now, there was no more handicapping, no more training wheels. Val was a master with two millennia's experience, and in his shadow, even with ten years of top-notch tutelage, I was nothing more than a novice.

But if I had it bad, Sam had it abysmally worse. I knew the basics of combat—if not all of the techniques, at least the likely attacks. Sam's mentor had taught him just enough about his talent to prevent him from burning the house down, however, and I doubted she'd anticipated him getting into a fight with a faerie a hundred times his age, much less one who'd spent most of his life as a guard. I couldn't tell if Val was actually bored as he continued to shatter our shields and swat us into every hard surface in the practice room or if he was trying to provoke me with nonchalance, but the effect was, at best, disheartening.

Twice more, he beat us into paste and took his leave with a warning to be ready in the morning, and Sam and I spent as much of the next precious hours horizontal as we could, letting my spells work. I crawled off to my room with a stack of books Arnold had checked out of the library for me—at least I could make *one* of my tutors happy, I decided—while Sam, who had no such reading list, flopped on the couch beside Frank, who brought him up to speed on his new favorite police shows. There was no question as to which of them had laid claim to the remote, and Sam was wise enough not to fight Frank for it.

We were both feeling glum as we trooped downstairs Wednesday for a fresh administration of bruises, and Val didn't disappoint. Sitting atop the practice mats, sipping a cup of espresso, he deflected every shot, ripped every shield apart, and finally threw Sam hard enough to break his leg. I ran to Sam's side, yelling for a timeout, and started cobbling together a healing spell, but in the next instant, the wind was knocked out of me as I once again met the unforgiving wall. "There is no timeout in battle," Val called from the other side of the room. "You fight injured or you die. Get up."

Battered, bleeding, and seeing red, I scrambled to my feet while Sam did his best to stand. "Come on, then," Val goaded from his perch, "take your shot. What are you waiting for, permission?"

In my frustration, my eyes landed on the stack of gardening tools, and I darted to the pile for a weapon. The nearest to hand was a rust-flecked shovel, and with a yell of rage, I yanked it off the floor and ran at Val, wielding it like a blunted pike. Without batting an eye, he shielded, but before he could toss me again, I threw the shovel as hard as I could, straight toward him. It barely pierced his shield before he managed to deflect it—but then, I realized with a tinge of satisfaction as I flew backward, that was the closest I'd come to touching him in days.

My skull bounced off the concrete, and I moaned, dazed with the impact, until my eyes focused enough to see Val standing over me, holding the shovel. "Finally," he said, knocking the blade against my leg, "she uses her head as more than a target. I was beginning to wonder."

"Wha…"

"You have access to any number of iron implements in here," he continued, pointing the shovel toward the gardeners' stash, "and it takes you four days to consider *employing* them? I thought I taught you better than that."

I groaned and sat up, closing my eyes against the wave of dizziness. "You *want* me to come at you with iron? Since when?"

He said nothing for a moment, and when I was able to see straight again, I found him crouching beside me. "I've taught you technique," he said quietly. "Defenses for different styles of attacks. But I cannot teach you to defeat me in a fair fight. I can't. There's nothing I can show you that will give you any chance. And I am *still* holding back," he pressed. "In a real fight, I'd have killed you in the first minute. That's not an empty boast, child. So what I am trying to impress upon you is that if you're going to be stupid and stubborn enough to remain here, knowing what could come for you, then you absolutely cannot fight fairly." He stood and watched as I found my feet again. "Incidentally, if someone is doing his best to introduce your head to unpadded surfaces at high speed, you're allowed to counter with appropriate measures."

I swayed as the world spun, and Val grabbed my shoulder before I could list too far. "This isn't about technique any longer," he continued. "It's not about style or points or prizes. It's your life or your opponent's, and I need to know that you can be ruthless in that moment, because I don't want you falling due to of a sudden attack of conscience." He held me at arm's length, letting me test my balance, then released me and watched for signs of imminent collapse. "There's no rule against reaching for iron in time of need. Your father and Aiden have done it to great effect, and the gods only know how many times Coileán has used it."

"I didn't want to hurt you," I protested.

"I won't allow you to hurt me," he countered. "But I had to provoke you to that point." Val frowned, studying my unsteady stance, then waved a pair of cots into existence. "Lie down, both of you. I'll put you back together."

We gratefully stretched out as Val crafted the necessary enchantment, which worked far more effectively than my healing spell. Then again, he'd had ample opportunity to refine it. "Clean break," he said as he straightened Sam's numbed leg. "You'll be walking by nightfall. Be careful until the bones solidify."

Sam—bloodied, sweating, and streaked with the practice room's dirt—rolled his head to look at me and mumbled, "I'm beginning to think your teachers were a little tougher than mine."

"But effective," Val said cheerily, stepping back to consider his handiwork. "So, on to diagnostics. Ros, remember that you're working in a lower-magic environment. Toula has taught you amplifying techniques, has she not?"

"Yeah, but in the heat of the moment—"

"No excuse. Drill until it's instinct. And Sam…" He folded his arms and frowned. "You're not the worst I've trained," he said after a moment's contemplation, "but I wouldn't pit you against a well-armed witch. You need to work on basics. That, at least, I can show you. Now, in light of the situation here," he continued, addressing us both, "you need to be armed with iron at all times. That includes having a weapon close at hand when you sleep."

Sam lifted a finger. "Will a boxcutter do?"

Val glanced at me, and I felt him pluck the answer to his question from my thoughts. "Yes, at long as you trust the blade not to fall out. Ros—"

"I'll buy a decent knife."

"Good. Keep them close—a surprise attack can save your life. We'll resume tomorrow," he added, stepping away from our cots. "Rest, mend, arm yourselves."

Thursday morning, Sam's leg was almost as good as new, my bruises were fading to green, and Val was back to his old self—demanding and perfectionistic, but disinclined to see how many of our bones he could break for fun. Triaging, he focused on Sam, showing him the fundamentals of magical combat by using me as his guinea pig. To keep me from slacking off, Val occasionally shot a blast of force or fire my way without warning, forcing me to pay attention and keep a shield at my fingertips. We ended the session tired but otherwise whole and hale, and once Val was satisfied that we were carrying our weapons as instructed, he let us take our leave.

Friday began with more of the same, but once Val had set Sam up in a beginner's shielding exercise, he told me to draw my knife. "This is for demonstrative purposes," he explained, standing about ten feet from me, and put up a thick shield. "Throw it."

I hurled the knife his way, speeding it along with a blast of spellcraft. Though the blade penetrated the shield, it did so only by an inch, then clattered harmlessly to the floor.

"I was prepared," he said, dropping the barrier between us. "My shield was solid and far enough from me that the knife was never going to be a problem. You don't have the strength to *make* it a problem under these conditions," he added with a slight smirk. "So with that in mind, your only chance to win with iron will be if you can use it in a surprise attack." He nudged the knife toward me with his boot and watched as I folded it back into my pocket. "You wouldn't have a nail gun, by chance?"

"Like Dad's?" I laughed. "That old piece of junk—"

"Helped kill Titania," he murmured. "If my reconstruction is accurate, he shot her before she expected it, and once a few nails were stuck in her and burning, she was in too much pain to retaliate. You might consider acquiring something along those lines."

"Ninja throwing stars," I replied with mock solemnity.

Val grunted and shoved me off my feet. "Has anyone ever told you you're impertinent?" he asked, hiding a smile, as I picked myself up.

"Once or twice. Mostly you."

He came closer while I dusted myself off and lowered his voice. "I know why you want to be here," he said, gripping my shoulder. "If nothing else, you are your parents' child. But I would be lying if I said I haven't been pressing Coileán for the last ten days to recall you."

"You think I can't handle myself?"

Val hesitated. "I have every confidence in your skills, but I doubt they would be sufficient unless you were to be very, *very* lucky, and luck is a terrible variable. If I were Coileán, I'd have ordered you home by now."

"So why hasn't he?" I asked, meeting his stare.

"I think you know. A certain someone is rather anxious, and she protests whenever I broach the subject with him."

"Kura?"

He nodded. "For reasons she declines to share with me, she wants you to remain here. And since that's the case…" He turned to watch as Sam shielded, charged at the wall, then rebounded and stumbled. "I'll do what I can to prepare you, but I promise no miracles."

"You know," I said as Val walked off, "I'm better with magic than Dad was at my age, and look what he was able to do."

He glanced back at me with disapproval. "*Luck*, Ros. Never count on it."

Even with Val's pessimism and Sam's inability to throw a fireball more than a few yards without it sputtering out, I counted the morning session a success. The sun was well up by the time Sam and I headed inside, and my thoughts drifted toward breakfast like a compass needle to a magnet. Bacon. Pancakes. Maybe bacon *in* pancakes. It was amazing what sort of appetite I could cultivate when I wasn't ready to pass out with pain. As had become our tradition that week, I invited Sam to join Frank and me, and we parted ways at his landing so that he could clean up before eating. Sam had come a long way in only two sessions, but he still didn't feel comfortable using enchantment in lieu of a shower.

Frank was already in the kitchen when I returned, doctoring a cup of coffee with hot sauce, the only condiment he loved as much as ketchup. I changed out of my sweats, pulled my damp hair back in a neater ponytail, and joined him at the stove. "Okay," I began, turning on the burner, "you don't have to eat it, but if I make French toast, will you at least try it?"

Before Frank could ask for details, someone pounded on our door—an agitated knock, not Sam's usual quick knuckle rap—and we eyed each other in surprise. "Bert," Frank muttered. "Angry."

"Shit," I sighed, and, putting on the most innocent face I could summon, I opened the door and pretended to be surprised to find the red-cheeked grand magus standing there. "Morning," I told him, and stepped aside. "Come in. You okay?"

Bert waited until I closed the door behind him, then wheeled on me. "No, I most certainly am *not* okay," he snapped. "I demand to know what the hell is going on."

"You're going to have to be more specific—"

"I've seen the footage! You, your associate, and an unknown male, meeting in the shed every morning this week. Security reports massive surges in active magic during those periods, and two-thirds of the bloody installation is still asleep. So who the devil is that, and what are you doing?"

With his old-person's glasses, gray sweater vest, and bowtie, it was difficult to take Bert's anger seriously, but I tried to be pacifying. "That's my coach. He thought I was slacking off and put me through my paces," I replied, bending the truth. "Sam got sucked in, so he might be reconsidering our friendship right now."

Bert was neither mollified nor amused. "You invited a faerie into this installation without my approval?"

"I didn't *invite* him. He just showed up. Seriously, this isn't nefarious—he's been dropping by to make me sweat, that's all."

Bert jutted his finger toward me, and I took a step back in surprise. "This is *my* installation. It's a secure facility. I have a right to know who's coming and going, *especially* where faeries are concerned, is that understood?"

"I'm sorry, I didn't—"

"Are you trying to make me look weak?" he continued over my attempted apology. "Undermine me in front of the Council? Is that your game?"

"There's no *game*, I just—"

His finger pressed against my sternum. "You are not to have any visitors without my explicit permission, in writing, signed. And you are not to leave the castle until further notice."

At that, I laughed incredulously. "You can't *ground* me."

"I most certainly can. *I'm* the grand magus here," he yelled, shoving me backward, "not you, and you *will* respect my authority!"

I took another step away from him, putting a little distance between us. "Okay, look, you need to cool it," I said, raising my palms in surrender. "I'm sorry about Val, I'll let him know, but back off and stop shouting at me."

But that only incensed him further. Before I could put up a shield, he closed the gap I'd made, grabbed the front of my T-shirt in his fist, and snarled, "I don't take orders from a damn mongrel—"

Suddenly, the door slammed open, and a pair of bare arms snaked around Bert and yanked him off of me. In a matter of seconds, he was pinned on his belly beneath Sam, who had put on jeans but was still shower-damp and barefoot. Sam pulled Bert's bent right arm back and sharply upward in a painful lock, and his knee kept Bert's left hand on the ground. "What did you say?" he growled, pressing Bert's face into the rug.

Bert yelped with the pressure on his shoulder. "I—"

"What the *fuck* did you call her?"

"I'm sorry, I'm sorry," he squealed, wriggling in pain. "Don't break it, please, I'm sorry…"

"Let him up," I muttered, and watched with folded arms as Sam crawled off of Bert and the disheveled grand magus climbed to his feet.

Straightening his robe, Bert turned to me again, but all the fire had gone out of his eyes. "I apologize, Ros, it slipped out," he said, and began to move toward me. "I didn't mean—" A very low, very *inhuman* growl stopped him in his tracks, and he cast a quick glance at Frank, who watched from the kitchen with his teeth bared. "Really, I didn't mean that, it was uncalled for, but you—"

"I was actually starting to think you were better than that," I murmured, cutting him short. "Guess I was wrong."

"Ros—"

"I'll tell my coach to stay away. Now *get out.*"

Bert gave me no quarrel, but I was shaking by the time he slunk into the hall, far more stung by the slur than I'd expected. Of course I was witch-blooded—I'd made no secret of that fact—but to have it thrown in my face like I was somehow lower than human because of it...

"Hey," said Sam, wrapping his arms around me, "you all right? Did he hurt you?"

"Fine," I lied, shaking in his embrace. "I'm okay."

"Sorry about making a scene, but I didn't know—"

"No, I appreciate it. Thanks for caring."

Sam grinned and nodded to Frank. "He's the one who told me to get my ass up here. I was getting the conversation broadcast."

Frank shrugged it off. *Since my opening gambit would have been to set that stupid robe on fire and toss him from the window, I thought it best to let Sam wrangle him first.*

"That's sweet of you," I told him. "We should probably keep the murder to a minimum."

Provocation manslaughter, he replied, and plucked his key from the counter. *Partners take care of each other. I'm going to the canteen to pick up food*, he added, heading out. *Back in a few minutes. Incidentally, Sam*, he thought before closing the door behind him, *if you and Ros want to mate, that's fine with me.*

"Sorry—*what?*" Sam asked, but Frank was already gone,

leaving us too flabbergasted to do more than awkwardly laugh, separate, and make small talk about the quality of the coffee and the chances of rain.

I was hurt by Bert's temper tantrum and his choice of words, but more than that, I was disappointed. Sure, we'd gotten off to a rocky start, and in no way, shape, or form did I want to date the man, but I'd thought we were on the road to forging at least a cordial relationship. But if that was truly all that Bert thought of me…well, I told myself, I couldn't win them all, but it still smarted.

I'd planned to keep the morning's events to myself, but Frank sent Daisy a message while the dining hall cooks packed up several takeout clamshells of sausages for him, and by the time we'd finished breakfast, Bee was beating down my door. "Little wanker," she said in greeting, and hugged me. "Frank spilled everything. You're all going to Edinburgh with Daisy and me for the weekend, and I don't want to hear any complaints, got it?"

Her tight mouth and narrowed eyes warned me to go along with the program, but I couldn't help questioning her logistics. "Do you have *room* for us?"

"Barely. Daisy and I will take our bed, and you three can either fight over the futon or make your own furniture. Agreed?"

Sam waved from the kitchen table to draw her attention. "That's really nice of y'all to invite us, but I think we're supposed to stay here—"

"Beat you to it," she interrupted, holding up her phone. "Behold, permission texts from your bosses. Your aunt wants photo documentation of you trying haggis," she added with a wicked grin, "but I think that's doable, don't you?"

Within half an hour, thanks to Bee's facility with gates, the five of us were dropping overnight bags in the middle of Bee and Daisy's modest flat, and then the girls dragged us out to play tourist on the town. By late afternoon, we'd been up and down the Royal Mile twice—Sam had a thing for castles—bought far too many souvenirs with tartan wrapping, and had plans to see some of the buried bits of the city that evening. While we settled in at a little restaurant with traditional dishes on the menu, Daisy scrolled through her phone looking for cemetery tours, Sam proudly showed off the wool scarf he'd purchased at a discount before Bee broke it to him that the sale sign in front of the store was a permanent fixture used to lure gullible visitors, and Frank sighed and nursed a glass of water, happy to be off his feet. We ordered too much food, laughed as Sam grimaced for the camera in front of a plate of minced offal, and swapped stories about Bert's failings, real and imagined. After another couple of evening tours, we caught a bus back to the flat, and as Daisy attempted to sell us on the notion of taking a dawn hike up Arthur's Seat, Sam pulled a paper sack out of one of his shopping bags and said, "Not so fast. I've got twenty-five-year-old scotch here that doesn't need to go back to Glastonbury."

That wasn't all he had—Sam's surprise purchase turned out to be a dozen miniatures of varying ages and descriptions, most of them single-malt—and the five of us passed a pleasant evening together, even Frank with a pitcher of Bloody Marys, until crashing in the wee hours to sleep it off.

I hadn't planned to see sunrise—Scottish summer mornings came quite early, after all, and I'd had more than enough to drink—but my phone trilled just after five, and I made myself answer it before Sam, who was snoring beside me on the folded-out futon, could wake. "Hang on," I muttered without looking at the ID, and grumped my way out the kitchen window and onto the quiet fire escape. The light hurt my head, and my mouth tasted like something had been fermenting between my molars all night, but I had to admit that Daisy was right—the hill in the distance did seem pretty by dawn's light, though I had no desire to scale it in my condition. Finally looking at the screen as I settled onto a stair, I saw that the caller wasn't Val, as I'd feared, wondering why we'd boycotted our workout, but rather Aiden.

"Sorry about that," I said, squinting at the morning. "Hey, have you seen Val today? I need to tell him—"

"Frank sent him a message about Bert's blow-up yesterday," my uncle interrupted. "He's not happy, but he understands."

I let out a sigh of relief and rubbed my stiff shoulder. "Did he mention we're up in Scotland? It's nice."

"Well, glad to hear at least one of us has been having a good weekend."

I did the mental calculation and realized it was late in Faerie. "Sorry," I mumbled. "So, uh…how's the Archives situation?"

"That's why I called." Aiden's chair creaked, and I could imagine him sitting in the dark in front of his bank of monitors, his face pale in the artificial light of the screens. "The crackers have been busy."

"Anything useful?"

"Not directly, but there's enough to be concerning. I started with Dad's files," he explained. "Figured Russell would be too stupid to have much of use in his folders—and I was right, as it turns out, though he does have a magnificent stash of German porn. Maybe a hundred gigs of the stuff. At least we know how he's been keeping busy…but I digress," he said, and cleared his throat. "Anyway, Dad had a lot of junk, too, most of it in document files, but several of those files were huge—way too big for a report or whatever. Turns out most of them are the result of consolidation, you know, putting all his paperwork into one file."

"But…"

"But there's an exception. He named this one file just like the others, and for the first hundred pages, it was more of the same—he may well have cut and pasted to make the buffer. The real meat of the file was hidden in the middle, almost two hundred scanned pages from a handwritten book. I couldn't figure out what it was, but Toula knew right away. Turns out someone digitized Simon Magus's diary."

I'd heard of the diary—the musings of the first grand magus, but more importantly, his theoretical jottings, a book so dangerous in the wrong hands that he'd bound it with spells so that no one who wanted to use it could even read it. "Why on earth was it *scanned*?"

"Shouldn't have been," said Aiden. "Toula said that one is highly restricted—we're talking accessible to the grand magus, the head archivist, and no one else without special permission. I have no idea how or when Dad got a copy, but considering how long he worked in the Archives…"

Aiden didn't have to finish that though. Grandpa had been an archivist before he conspired with Mulligan and was elevated to magus, and with those credentials, surely he would have had an opportunity to get close to that book during Mulligan's eleven-year tenure. Or maybe Grandpa still had a friend in the Archives, someone who wouldn't mind satisfying an old man's curiosity.

"What I'm afraid of is that he took a copy of this file with him," Aiden continued. "Toula says that Simon's more impressive procedures are way too complex for Dad to pull off alone, but she and your mom are reading the scan right now, looking for clues as to what the probationers are up to."

My phone began to beep with an incoming call, but I ignored it. "Do Coileán and Eleanor know?"

"I'm keeping them apprised. Needless to say, they aren't happy. I'll call back once we have something more concrete. Have fun in Scotland, okay? Tell Bee and Frank hi for me."

I'd barely hung up before Bee, a wide-eyed spectacle of

rumpled nightclothes and wild red curls, threw open the window and jutted her phone toward my face. "Hello?" I asked, holding it to my ear.

"Where are you?"

I recognized Badger's clipped tones, though uncharacteristically for her, she sounded like she was on the verge of panic. "Edinburgh, we're weekending up north. What's wrong?"

"Another dead wizard," she replied. "Just outside of Glastonbury. Give me your address and stay where you are, we're coming."

CHAPTER 11

Badger knew Edinburgh intimately enough to open a gate near Bee and Daisy's building, and within ten minutes of hanging up, she and Seamus were standing by the futon, chastising Bee for not properly warding her home. "Anyone could waltz in!" Badger exclaimed, thrusting her hand toward the open door. "What were you *thinking*, kid? You're meant to be clever!"

While Badger set to work rectifying the defensive oversight, Seamus checked the block for signs of disturbance, and the five of us congregated in the bedroom to stay out of the way. "Well, that's one way to start the morning," Sam muttered, rubbing the sleep from his eyes. "Y'all got aspirin?"

Bee handed him a box from the nightstand. "I know there's a way to cure a hangover with enchantment, but something tells me Seamus isn't in the mood to play medic."

"If there is, it's news to me," he replied, then dry-swallowed a pair of capsules and grunted. "Badger's got a short fuse, huh?"

"Badger's my cousin," Bee explained, flopping back onto her pillow. "Once removed, I mean, she's cousin to my mum. I think she was just worried."

You're right.

We turned as one to Frank, who, having been forced to vacate his patch of rug, had sprawled facedown across the foot of the bed. "Listening in again?" Sam asked.

It's not difficult when they're practically shouting. They're thinking of another time and place, particularly Badger. Something to do with her parents, but… He limply raised one hand, slapped it against his face, and let it fall. *Honestly, it hurts too much right now to work through it.*

Bee frowned at me. "Can he handle aspirin?"

Let's not experiment.

I stood over Frank and began rubbing his head, and he responded with a wordless flash of gratitude.

It didn't take much hypothesizing to figure out why Badger and Seamus were on edge. They'd spent the Mulligan era trying to find and evacuate Fringers before the assassin corps could locate them, and now, ten years later, people they cared about were winding up dead yet again. No wonder Arnold had been so willing to help me break into the Archives, I mused—he'd been on the extraction team, too.

Nearly an hour later, Badger was finally satisfied with her handiwork, and Seamus hadn't seen any sign of wizard activity for blocks. "Be *careful,*" Badger stressed as she showed off the lattice of the new ward system, which glowed in a spectrum invisible to mundane eyes. "This is good, but it's not unbreakable."

Bee nodded in appraisal at the fine spellcraft. "Don't worry about us, guys, we'll be safe."

"Too late for that," Badger muttered, giving her a one-armed hug. "And I'd feel loads better if you lot went back to Glastonbury."

Daisy cocked her head in confusion. "But didn't you say there was another murder—"

"Outside the castle, yes. Inside…well, safety in numbers, yes?" Her gaze traveled around the room, looking for signs of imminent compliance. "Seriously, make me feel better and head south. And ward your flats," she ordered as Bee headed toward her room to pack.

We knew better than to argue. Shortly thereafter, I made a gate back to my apartment, and as Bee and Daisy headed to Bee's family's place, I got to work constructing my own wards while Frank settled in with the television. Ten minutes into the job, I was so fixated on casting and connecting channels that I screamed and jumped when Sam tapped my shoulder.

"Sorry, sorry," he said, backing off as I clutched my chest. "You didn't hear me, did you?"

"No," I panted. "What's up?"

"Well, uh…" He considered what I had done already, which looked rather like a dark blue chain-link fence across my door. "Could you teach me? I have no idea how to build one of those, and Badger seemed pretty adamant that we put them up…"

His expression was an even mixture of confusion and hopefulness, but I had no choice but to disappoint him. "This is pure spellcraft," I explained, calling into creation a new channel to lengthen the ward in progress. "You can build wards with enchantment, but they're a lot messier, and I can't show you how to do it. But I'll put one together for you," I assured him. "Just give me an hour or two to tweak this bad boy."

Sam sat on the back of the couch and watched as I pulled another channel from the ether like molten glass and bound it to its new neighbors. "How does it work, anyway?"

"What, wards?" I asked, continuing to weave. "You want the theoretical thaumaturgical explanation or something in layman's terms?"

"Let's just pretend I'm an idiot and start there. And shut up, Frank."

I glanced back in time to catch Frank smirking at him from the other side of the couch. "*Boys.* To answer your question, Sam, think of this as a fence, only instead of just going around the circumference of a space, it surrounds it on all sides—a sphere, a cube, a dome, whatever. That big construction around the castle is a partially active ward system."

"Okay…"

"So, when most people think of wards, they think of defense. When this thing is active, it forms a solid barrier of magic—a shield. I mean, it's certainly possible to breach a ward, but it takes extra work, particularly if the ward has some elasticity built in. Rigid ones are easier to shatter."

He came up beside me and studied my work. "If I were to shoot at this right now—"

"It would go through. Ward's not active. But if I turn it on…" I passed my hand over the door, and the lattice glowed like a neon sign. "Watch," I said, and lobbed a small bolt at the ward. The bit of active magic that had flown from my hand smashed into the ward, which flared and ballooned outward ever so slightly before the bolt fizzled out. "Good wards block magic, but great wards absorb it. Now, they don't just stop magic—a ward is useless if it can't block the movement of matter as well," I continued. "So you have to cast exceptions into it. I'm designing this one to allow Frank and me, Bee and Daisy, and you access when it's active, but for everyone else, it'll be like running into an electrified wall. *If* I do it properly," I muttered. "This takes practice."

"Wonder why Miss Bonnie never taught me anything about them," he replied, holding his palm as close to the active ward as he dared.

I turned it off and resumed construction. "She may not be any good at them. A lot of faeries aren't."

"Huh?"

I created a pair of channels, wrapped them around each other for reinforcement, and wove them through the fence. "Wardwork is technical stuff. Spellcraft and enchantment can accomplish most of the same things, but they go about it differently. Enchantment's great if you want to mess with someone's head—you know, glamour, stuff like that—and if you want to do something quick and massive like throw lightning. You put an equally matched faerie and wizard in a dark alley and tell them to rumble, and the faerie's going to have the early advantage because he's packing a bigger gun that's preloaded with ammo, see?"

Sam rubbed the back of his neck. "I...guess?"

"You can throw lightning by casting, too," I continued, "but it's usually smaller unless you've had time to prepare. But if you give a wizard sufficient time to get her wards and such in order, she can hold her own." I paused to tweak a channel until it ran parallel to its fellows. "That's not to say you can't work on your weak spots. My mom can make explosions in short order, and I've seen the kind of wardwork Coileán can do—it's nearly on par with a quality wizard-made ward in terms of technicality. Anyway, that's all for another day," I said, and patted his arm. "I'll get you covered."

"Sorry to put you to the extra trouble," he began, but I cut his apology short.

"Don't worry about it. Look, I've been training to do this since I was ten," I told him. "And if you think Val's tough as a combat coach, you should see how rough his sister can be on the spellcraft side. Toula's fantastic, but she is *merciless* when you slack off." I mock-shuddered and began braiding the next set of channels. "You can pay me back someday. It's not like you're crunched for time. I'll call in a favor when you're, like, a hundred and useful," I joked.

"Deal," he replied, and moved closer to me—so close that I could feel the warmth from his skin. "But since Frank's hogging the TV, why don't you show me how you're doing what you're doing?"

"That's as exciting as watching paint dry," I said, but when I glanced up at him, his hazel eyes were studying me with an unfamiliar intensity, and I raked my teeth over my bottom lip as I looked away. "Hey, it's your Saturday down the drain. Welcome to Spellcraft 101."

Maybe he was just looking for an anchor, I told myself as I worked. He'd lost his only family three weeks before, he was alone in an unfamiliar country, and I was the most familiar person for thousands of miles. But all the same, I couldn't shake the feeling that there was more than a spark between us, and...well...I liked it. I liked seeing Sam in person, I loved it when he threw back his head and laughed so hard that he cried, and even with that morning's rough wakeup call, I had enjoyed the ease with which we'd fallen asleep beside each other on that awful futon, especially when his arm, ever so tentatively, had snaked over my side.

It didn't help my concentration when Frank, who'd obviously been listening in on my mental clutter, interjected, *You're overthinking this. Really, I won't put up a fuss if you want to mate.*

I focused on the words *Butt out*, picturing them in flashing red letters and hoping he'd get the message, and a quiet chuckling from the couch told me all I needed to know.

Hours spent at the mind-numbing task of warding, especially after the festivities and poor sleep of Friday night, should have put me straight to bed. Instead, I lay awake long after Frank had dozed off, staring at the black ceiling and trying to make my mind go quiet. But like a dog with a favorite bone, it refused to put aside the Minor Arcanum deaths. They nagged at me, and I couldn't shake the feeling that I was overlooking something.

Six dead wizards in six weeks. I knew almost nothing about the victims beyond their manner of death, but I assumed that Amy, at least, would know what sort of wands they had been carrying. Russell would need something stronger than pine, and so would both of my grandparents...but what about the other magi? Were any of them able to cast reliably without help, or were they wand-dependent, too? How many had gone on the run already? How many more were thinking of joining them?

And why would Moyna, of all people, help them?

Grace had been camouflaging her for a decade, but how had they struck that bargain to begin with? Surely Moyna didn't care who ran the Arcanum, so what did the probationers have to bargain with?

Unless camouflage was enough. Coileán and Eleanor hadn't pursued her after her failed assault on Faerie because doing so would have required a trip into the mortal realm, and Mulligan held his hostages to prevent any such incursions. But after the regime change, what would have stopped them from hunting her down? She'd have needed help then, and maybe Grace had come to her with a back-scratching proposal. Maybe the probationers were finally cashing in their chips.

To what end, though? If the probationers thought they could take on the Arcanum from the outside, especially with Faerie ready to jump in, they were insane. Even if they were backed by Moyna's forces, they had no real hope of success. And a handful of wizards wouldn't be enough to help Moyna overthrow her father...so what did they hope to accomplish?

Though my troubled mind continued to circle the drain, I finally fell asleep.

It's nearly impossible to keep track of time when dreaming, but I didn't think I'd been out long when I became aware of myself once again...only that time, I seemed to be standing on nothing in the middle of a void. Before I could grow too concerned, a familiar voice called my name, and I spun around to find Kura behind me, luminous in the darkness but looking drawn. Her long blonde tresses seemed almost flat, her eyes were sunken in her delicate face, and strangest of all, in lieu of her usual wardrobe of diaphanous shifts, she appeared to be wearing leggings and an oversized gray hoodie.

"Are you...*sick*?" I ventured, though the question sounded ludicrous to me. Kura was ancient and generally incorporeal, and the idea that she could be under the weather was laughable.

To my surprise, though, she only hugged herself instead of denying it. "I'm being attacked," she said, her voice low with exhaustion. "I don't know exactly how or by whom, but something is sapping my strength. What have you found?"

"Nothing new since my last trip over, except there's been another death in the Minor Arcanum. Is there anything I can do—"

"Find the source." She stiffened suddenly and grimaced in pain, and she almost faded away before she recovered sufficiently to focus herself in my dream once again. "Find it *now*, Ros. The attacks are getting stronger." A note of pleading crept into her voice. "Has there been any sign of Moyna? Anything?"

I shook my head. "No word from the Company, and if Toula had been able to work a blood trace, I'm sure you'd know. I wish I had a faster plan," I said apologetically. "Once the Archives delvers go through their findings and get concrete evidence of a conspiracy, I'll figure out how best to present it to Bert, and then he'll have no choice but to raise the troops against the probationers. If he thinks I'm trying to undermine him now, I'm sure he'll be thrilled once he sees what we've found," I muttered, "but if I go to him with only a suggestion of a problem, it might not be enough to sway him. I mean, I *am* just a mongrel—"

"Forget him," she interrupted before I could properly vent. "Unless you believe he knows who is behind this and how to stop him, he is a waste of time. Find the source," she repeated, reaching out to grip my hands. "*Someone* inside the Arcanum must know what's happening to me. Force him to tell you, if you must."

The strength of her grip and the intensity of her gaze scared me. "I'm sure there's a diplomatic way to find out—"

"There is no time for diplomacy, child. Help m—"

Kura cried out in pain once more and vanished, and I woke in a cold sweat, grateful to feel the mattress beneath me and hear Frank growling in his sleep on the floor. Shaken, I pushed back the blankets, dug my old laptop from its bag in the wardrobe, and padded carefully past the sleeping dragon into the main room. I feared that I would be seeing dawn from the wrong side, but as long as I couldn't sleep, I might as well work. I cast myself a cup of tea, one of the few food items I could reliably produce on the fly, then plugged in my computer to power its weak battery and waited for it to boot.

Aiden had custom-built three laptops for me over the years, each with top-of-the-line components and all the useful software I could need, but still, I kept the computer my grandparents had given me for Christmas when I was ten—my last gift from them, though I couldn't have cared less about whatever slight sentiment might have been behind it. The thing was a clunker, old when I'd inherited it, a piece of Council surplus incompletely wiped for reuse. Aiden had discovered a hidden copy of Arcview on the hard drive, and I'd made a copy of all the backdoor login credentials he could remember. Some of them had been blocked over time, but not all. Regardless, my uncle had cautioned me against using them. "Arnold knows how I got in here before," he'd explained, "and I wouldn't be shocked if he's had an alert built in case anyone logs on with the old credentials."

"Why not just delete them?" I'd asked.

Aiden had waggled his eyebrows in response. "Honeypot. The ones that still work might have limited access, so if someone unauthorized uses them, he won't find anything important, and Arnold will know someone's snooping. See?"

I did, and it was why I'd relied on Antony's help instead of giving Aiden my old laptop. But Kura was being attacked, and I didn't have time to worry about covering my tracks. Working quickly, I logged into Arcview and began my hunt through the more public side of the Archives.

It didn't take much digging to uncover what I was after: the Arcanum's address database. I scrolled through the listings until I found the H section, then wrote down my target's address and pulled up a map.

Toula had surrendered Simon Magus's diary to the Arcanum, where, except for one teensy, insignificant trip to the scanner, it had been kept out of the hands of almost the entire organization. But if anyone had studied it, I reasoned, it had to be Greg Harrison—and unless he, too, had gone on the run, he was living on probation in Louisiana.

Hoping Sam would forgive me for the predawn wakeup, I called downstairs and waited only two rings before he mumbled a greeting. "Sorry to bother you," I said, "but have you ever been to NOLA?"

"Once," he grunted. "Senior class trip. Why?"

"Do you know it well enough to point a gate into the city?"

I could hear his mattress creak as he sighed and rolled over. "I remember it, but I don't do gates. No one's taught me how."

"Good enough. See you in a few hours, okay?"

"Wait, wait," he said before I could hang up, "*why* do you want to go to New Orleans at two in the damn morning?"

"Research. Go back to sleep," I told him, and cut the connection before he could press for details.

Before any excursion could be mounted, there was the slight matter of the time difference to consider. Louisiana was six hours behind us, and so I forced myself to go back to bed and at least doze until it was decently morning. Around nine, I shook off the worst of my grogginess and messaged Sam, Daisy, and Bee to come over, promising Sam breakfast to make up for the night before.

Pancakes seemed to smooth over my transgressions,

and while everyone ate, I recounted my conversation with Kura and my trip through the Archives. "Was that wise?" Bee asked, peering at me over her second cup of tea. "I'm sure Antony could have found that for you."

I shrugged. "Got what I needed, and no alarms went off."

"That you know of."

She had a point, but I couldn't dwell on it. "Anyway, I need to get to New Orleans. Anyone else want to go?"

"Sure," said Sam, "but as I think I told you last night, I can't make gates."

"No problem," Frank cut in from the kitchen, where he was microwaving another plate of sausages. "You think of place, I show it to Ros. It can work."

"If you say so." He popped a bite of pancake into his mouth and chewed thoughtfully. "This guy you want to see, now…"

"Former grand magus," Bee explained. "He *claimed* he only went along with Mulligan because Mulligan threatened his family—"

"Mundanes and duds," I added. "Or so said Mom."

Bee nodded. "Yeah. So maybe he'll be willing to talk, but that's assuming we can get to him. I bet his home wards are watertight."

"*What* home wards?" said Daisy. "He's still on probation, isn't he? Weren't they all bound?"

"The magi certainly were," I replied as my guts began to clench. "Guess we'll find out if it held, won't we?"

After some quick calculation and a discussion of exactly how early was unforgivably rude to make a Sunday-morning house call, we parted until one that afternoon, then reconvened in my apartment. "I did some research after breakfast," said Daisy as I turned on my wards, "and assuming all goes well, there's a place that sells nothing but coffee and beignets, and it's open twenty-four hours, and I'm thinking out loud, here…"

"Noted," I replied, smiling to hide my nerves, and

turned to Sam. "How close to the target can you get us?"

"Actually," he said, sounding embarrassed, "I was going to shoot for the beignet place. We all kind of got wasted one night, and we sobered up there, and I remember it pretty well."

"Oh, you and I are going to get on *smashingly*," said Daisy.

Before I could remind them that pastries had to come later, an image blossomed in my mind's eye—a short, columned building decked with green and white striped awnings, tucked beside a park on a crowded street. Aiming for the relative cover of the trees, I opened a pinhole gate, then began scanning my surroundings for surprised mundanes. The city seemed quiet, however—relatively speaking—and I was about to widen the gate when someone knocked on the apartment door.

"Ros?" came Bert's voice, muffled through the wood. "Are you in? I need a word with you."

Too late, I remembered that although I'd engaged the wards, I hadn't locked up. The door opened, and Bert scowled in confusion to find himself on the wrong side of a magical fence. "What's this?" he asked, scanning our faces for a clue. "And what are you lot doing? Where were you Friday night? We need to talk, Ros, *now*."

Seeing the grand magus stymied on the threshold gave me enormous satisfaction. "It'll have to wait," I told him. "And since this installation has almost no security, I took my safety into my own hands. Can't blame a girl, can you?"

"There's no need for this," he protested, holding his palm close to the glowing wards. "And it's unauthorized. I'm afraid I must ask you to take them down."

"Ask all you like," I retorted, "but since it's obvious that I'm not among friends here, I have to watch my back. See you later, Bertie," I said, then widened the gate, slipped through with the others, and closed it on his exhortations to be reasonable, damn it, and let him in.

There are far more pleasant places to visit than New Orleans in mid-July. Certain circles of hell come to mind as alternatives.

Faerie's mild climate had spoiled me, and I had no quarrel with Glastonbury's idea of summer, aside from the regular rain. But even at seven in the morning, the mercury hovered north of eighty in the French Quarter, and the sodden air pressed in on us like a warm, wet blanket that smelled slightly of stale beer. The sky was nearly a perfect blue dome, marred only by the faintest of wispy clouds, and the rising sun warned of the broiling to come.

At least the overnight crowds had dispersed. But for a few insane joggers and a couple of drunks passed out on the park bench beside our gate, there was no one to witness our arrival—anyone with sense was sleeping off the night's revels, and those who were still around were mopping up the alcohol with a healthy dose of beignets, the odor of which was enough to make me salivate. Still, I ignored Daisy's longing looks toward the awnings, pulled up my map, and led the pack on a mile-long march into the colorful cottages of the Faubourg Marigny neighborhood.

The Harrison house was hardly a showstopper. Dark green and smaller than its neighbors, it was almost invisible behind the overgrown foliage of the small front yard, and the only indication that it wasn't abandoned was the swept concrete walkway to the door. A wooden ramp covered the front steps—unsurprising, as the former grand magus was just over a hundred years old. Wizards generally ignored mundane mortality tables—magic wasn't a cure-all, but it helped—but even so, a wizard past his centennial would hardly be considered spry.

We stood together in front of the silent cottage, watching and listening for signs of life, but aside from a few cars heading toward Mass, the neighbors appeared to be asleep. After a moment of observation, Bee muttered, "Think we should come back later? Maybe he isn't awake."

The threat of another long march through the increasingly uncomfortable morning spurred me to action. Pushing caution aside, I headed up the walkway, dodging the wide, overhanging leaves of the tiny jungle, then climbed the ramp and hesitated only a second before I rang the doorbell.

To my surprise, the door unlatched and creaked open with a blast of blessedly chilled air. Curious, I poked my head through the crack and looked around, but the foyer was shadowed and silent, bare but for a decorative side table and a trio of what appeared to be suspiciously like fertility figurines. "Hello?" I called. "Is anyone here?"

"Come in if you're coming in," rasped a voice from down the hall. "You're letting all the air conditioning out."

By then, the rest of the group had joined me at the door, and we hastily made our way into the house. As the others looked to me to take the lead, I said, "Uh...Grand Magus? It's Roslyn Bolin. Could we talk, please?"

"In here," was the curt response, and with a last glance at the rest of my party, I followed the oriental runner toward our host.

The cottage's dining room was proportionally small, and much of its space was filled by a mahogany pedestal table beneath a brass chandelier topped with faux candles. Greg Harrison sat in a motorized wheelchair at the head of the table, a dark-skinned man with a horseshoe of white hair left to him, swaddled in an oversized navy bathrobe and dealing out a hand of solitaire with a well-thumbed deck of cards. He watched us enter and take spots along the wall, but he didn't say another word until his setup was complete across the red placemat.

"Whatever you're here for, keep the magic to a minimum," he began, putting the rest of the cards aside. "Does a number on my chair."

"How'd you open the front door, then?" I asked.

His bony shoulders rose and fell. "A little twitch every now and then seems to be all right. And that's the extent of what your mother left me," he added, staring at me over his thick glasses. "Just a little twitch. I haven't broken my bind." He held my gaze as if daring me to argue, then turned back to his cards and began play. "There's a lot of Helen in you, as I predicted. And Ms. Powell, I see you're doing well."

"Grand Magus," she mumbled.

I took the unspoken hint and made the rest of the introductions. "This is Daisy Hornby," I told him, "a late discovery from London, and those two are Frank and Sam."

To my relief, he didn't press for more specifics. "May I ask why you're here?" he said, moving an ace to the top of the placemat. "I checked in with my welfare coordinator three weeks ago, and she told me everything was in order."

"Maybe it is with you, but the Arcanum's in trouble. We need information."

He paused, sighed, then swept one long-fingered hand toward the empty chairs around the table and continued playing cards.

As I took the chair on his right, I noticed the half-empty jelly jar of golden liquid sitting on a coaster beside the placemat. Even from a distance, my nose told me it wasn't apple juice.

"So, ehm," Daisy began, smiling politely as she settled into the chair to his left, "you're from Montana, yes? What brought you down here? Never wanted to see snow again, eh? Or did you move closer to family?"

Harrison didn't look up from his cards. "I have no family."

"Oh," she replied, momentarily thrown, then tried to recover. "Well, in any case, I suppose the humidity is better than blizzards, isn't it?"

"What do you mean?" I interrupted, ignoring her attempt at changing the subject. "I thought you had kids."

"Cindy and Abby," he said, and took a long swig of what I strongly suspected was whisky.

"Did something happen to them?"

"Don't know. Haven't spoken to them in ten years."

"I'm sorry."

That, at least, made him put his cards down and look at me. "*You're* sorry? I figured this would be right in line with Helen's idea of justice," he snapped. "It's her damn fault."

"What, for kicking you out of office?" I replied, momentarily letting my anger override my need for civility.

"For calling them in. Making them sit through that goddamn trial. They didn't have to know," he said, glaring at me with dark, bloodshot eyes. "She didn't have to do that."

"Sorry to interrupt," said Daisy, lifting a finger, "but I missed the whole trial, so *what* happened?"

He turned to her and knocked back another gulp. "My wife and I had two daughters," he mumbled. "Five grandbabies. Four great-grandbabies. And except for the girls, none of them were stronger than witches. Most of them were duds. The girls married mundanes and moved away years ago." His hand clenched around the jelly jar. "So when James Mulligan got the bright idea to seize power, he and his goon squad came to Missy and me and said they'd let the girls and their families go on with their lives if we played ball with the new regime. And we did."

Daisy's expression struggled to stay neutral, but beside her, Bee watched the former grand magus with unhidden scorn.

"Tell me what you would have done differently," he said to Daisy. "Someone's going to die, either your kids or someone else's kids. What choice do you have when there's a gun pointed at the people you love the most?"

"Not a good one," she murmured.

"There isn't one. Because let me tell you, girls and boys," he continued, glancing around the table, "when the bomb's ticking, you'll do *anything* to keep it away from the people who matter the most to you. I'm damn sorry that he did what he did to the Fringe. I surely am. But the kids in the framed pictures on your desk—those are the ones who count when you get right down to it."

No one said anything as he drank his whisky.

"We kept them safe," he resumed, looking back to Daisy. "They never asked much about the Arcanum. Got miffed back in the day when their mom and I weren't jumping for joy over the mundanes they brought home, and they didn't have anything to do with the silo after that. They got to live their lives in peace, just like they wanted, and then Helen waltzed in and made the girls come home to see their parents tried for treason."

"Mom recalled everyone, not just your daughters," I pointed out.

But he ignored me. "Our girls sat there through all that testimony. All those stories, and then the glass statues…" He shook his head, almost as if shuddering. "It was horrible. They saw us convicted. And once the binds were in place, they called us monsters and said they'd never speak to us again."

While Daisy struggled to find a polite response, Harrison picked up his cards and continued his game. "If they'd ever get off their damn high horses, they'd understand why we went along with James, but they won't give an inch. Too much like their mother." He put a two on top of the ace, a three, another ace beside the first stack. "So, to answer your question, we didn't give two shits about the weather in Montana. Cindy lives in town, and since she's always been more of a peacemaker than her sister, we relocated and tried to reach out to her. Nothing. Letters come back unopened. Knocked on her door once, and her husband threatened to call the cops. The *cops*. On her parents." He drank with barely a pause in his play. "I see how it looks bad. Two of her kids and all her grandkids are duds, so I know why she's sensitive about the way the Fringe was treated. But she blamed us for everything, and it wasn't our fault. We couldn't have stopped James and the entire Council by ourselves."

Daisy cleared her throat, then offered, "Maybe it's all a matter of time. If you keep trying—"

His harsh, barking laughter cut her suggestion short. "Time? It's already too late. Missy could only take five years of being shunned by her own babies before she overdosed on sleeping pills. They didn't even send flowers to her funeral, can you believe that? Their own *mother*. Everything we did was for them." He drained his glass, then slammed it back onto its coaster and moved the next ace. "But you didn't come here for family therapy. What do you want from me?"

"Like I said," I began as he cut his eyes toward me, "information."

"And why should I tell you a damn thing?"

"Because some of the other probationers have disappeared, the Company can't find Moyna anymore, and Minor Arcanum wizards are being killed for their wands. Oh, and Faerie's being attacked as we speak."

He softly snorted his contempt. "If those idiots think they have a snowball's chance of taking Faerie by force—"

"Not that kind of attack. They're hurting the soul of the realm. I've seen her, she's…bad."

Harrison kept playing.

"And I think my grandfather has a copy of Simon Magus's diary," I continued, staring at him while he focused on his cards. "So if there's something in there we should know about…"

For a long moment, there was no sound but the ticking of the grandmother clock down the hall and the slap of the plastic-backed playing cards. As I tried to think of anything else that might pique his interest, Harrison finally paused his game again and looked up at me. "What do you mean, he has a copy? There's never been a copy made."

"Digital. It's in his personal files in the Archives."

I couldn't quite make out Harrison's mumbling, but it sounded decidedly profane. "Howard *knew* how I felt about the diary. It's far too dangerous to be in just anyone's hands." Agitated, he flipped on his chair and backed away from the table toward the sidebar, where a crystal decanter of his morning beverage waited to refill his glass. "You're sure it's the Magus's diary?"

"Toula verified it."

"She would know. Can't say if she's read it cover to cover, but she would recognize it." He drove the whisky back to the table and poured a healthy triple. "And you say Faerie's being affected? How?"

"She doesn't know," I told him as he drank, "but I've seen her, and she's a wreck. Is there something in the diary that could hurt her?"

He pushed the glass aside, folded his arms on the tabletop, and looked me in the eye. "Yes. It's theoretical, but the underpinnings are solid."

"I'm sorry," Sam interrupted, "but what's this diary y'all keep going on about? Who is—"

"Simon Magus?" Harrison finished, cocking an eyebrow. "Not Arcanum-trained, I see."

"Not exactly."

"Mm. In furtherance of your education, then, Simon Magus was probably the greatest wizard who's ever lived. Founder of the Arcanum. Managed to unite the magically gifted of this realm under his rule."

"Most of them," I muttered.

"He left behind his diary," said Harrison, ignoring me, "which, aside from its historical importance, contains some incredibly high-level theoretical magic. He had a change of heart before his death, put spells on the book to keep anyone who would want to learn from it from reading it, and hid it away, and so some of his musings weren't rediscovered until centuries after his death."

"So how'd you read it?" Sam asked.

Harrison smirked down the table at him. "Guess you weren't around when Faerie was sealed off, were you?" Sam shook his head, bemused, and Harrison sipped his breakfast. "Long story short, this realm was cut off from its supply of magic for about a week. When that happened, spells failed worldwide, including the ones protecting the diary. It was left in my keeping, and I studied it for *months*. Whatever else can be said about the Magus, the man was a genius in his field."

"He figured out how to hurt Faerie?" I pressed.

"Untested, but he had a strong theory," said Harrison, pivoting back to me. "Near the end of his life, he got a little...*paranoid*, shall we say, about protecting the Arcanum from the courts. I think it was the merrow who told him that Faerie has a consciousness running the show, empowering the Three beyond their normal limits. He theorized that if that consciousness could be contained, the wizard on the other end of that spell could hold it for ransom...or he could depower the Three long enough to make an assault on Faerie possible."

"But that's just theory, yes?" Bee interjected.

"Yeah. He worked out in detail what sort of construction could accomplish that, and then he spent two pages talking about all the reasons why that should only be a last resort. Far too risky to test."

"How so?" she asked.

Harrison cocked his head and faintly smiled. "Thought you were a smart girl, Ms. Powell. Did something happen?"

"Elucidate it for me, then," she muttered, staring daggers at him.

"Think of it like this: what's a body without a soul?"

"A corpse."

"Mm-hmm. So if Faerie's consciousness is trapped outside the realm for too long, or if something happens to it..."

"Faerie dies," she finished, eyes widening.

"He didn't test it because if something went wrong, he thought there was a possibility that we could lose magic forever—not to mention what might come spilling out of the Gray Lands if the balance tipped," Harrison explained.

"And he also realized that he couldn't channel the power needed to run such a spell. I mean, the amount of magic needed to extract Faerie's consciousness and pull it across the border would be astronomical. Even so, I decided that there was no need for idiots to get access to his work, so just in case, I extracted one of the pages from the diary," he said with a smug smile.

"Maybe you should have pulled more," I countered, drawing his attention back to me, "since *something* is attacking her."

Harrison shrugged. "If Howard and his friends are trying to use that spell, one, they aren't strong enough to see it through, and two, they're missing the Magus's discussion of boosting through complex power channeling. Faerie will be fine."

"Where's the missing page, then?"

Lesson delivered, he returned to his cards. "It's safe."

I squeezed my fist under the table, trying not to lose my temper with him. "You may *think* so, but in light of what's happening, wouldn't it be a better idea to put that page where the probationers can't possibly get to it? Like, you know, *Faerie?*"

He found the fourth ace and added a short sequence of cards, considered the spread, then deigned to face me again. "You have nothing to worry about. It's very safe, and…" He jerked, then glared down the table at Frank, who had watched our interrogation in silence. "*You.* Sneaky little bastard, aren't you?"

Frank dipped his head in faint acknowledgement. "You are sensitive."

"I'm experienced. You don't just get past my blocks," he snapped, tapping his temple. "So whatever the hell you think you saw, that's all you're getting."

"It is enough," he replied, and showed his teeth. "The woman in the painting is your mate, yes?"

I gasped as the answer hit me. "The magus portraits," I said, going to my feet. "The official ones in the Council wing. It's in her portrait, isn't it? You hid it with Magus Harrison?"

He considered the cards, then shuffled them back together and began dealing a new game. "You have what you came for. See yourselves out."

There was nothing more to be gained from antagonizing the old man, and so Bee opened a gate back into her family's apartment and led the way over. Before I could cross, however, Harrison murmured, "Missy asked Helen what she should have done, and she never got an answer. Tell your mother I'm still waiting."

CHAPTER 12

Unsurprisingly, Antony was less than enthusiastic to see the five of us in front of the circulation desk that afternoon. "Can I help you?" he asked in a carefully blasé voice, and I smiled to myself—Antony was trying so hard to be sneaky, but his shifting eyes betrayed his unease.

"Looking for a book," said Bee. "I've got a bet going with these illiterates about a diagram, and I've misplaced my copy of *Humanum Transformatio*."

Antony blinked once, twice. "A diagram?"

"*The* diagram. You know the one."

He sighed and beckoned us toward the back. "Yes, the udder popped out first, and yes, it's as weird as you think. We scanned that book years ago—I'll pull it up for you."

When we'd crowded into his office and Antony had locked the door, Sam sheepishly asked, "So…what diagram would this be, again?"

"Series of woodcuts," said Antony, plopping into his swivel chair, "made circa 1580, chronicling the misadventures of this crazy wizard's assistant. He turned the poor bastard into a cow, and he did it over the course of an afternoon—thought it would be easier on his mind to do the transformation piecemeal rather than take the usual rip-the-bandage-off approach."

"It *is* a shock," Frank muttered, leaning against a cluttered bookcase with his arms folded.

Antony glanced up from his computer. "You've done transformation before?"

"You have no idea."

"Noted. And…here," he said, spinning his monitor around to show us the open pages of the notorious book. "Ride 'em, cowboy. Last April, we made this the head librarian's lock screen and changed her password, so I've still got it bookmarked."

Sam studied it over my shoulder, then muttered, "This is what y'all study, huh?"

"That's not the half of it, I'm afraid," Antony replied, closing the viewer. "And who're you, again?"

"Sam's my counterpart from Eleanor's court," I explained. "And Sam, this is our unofficial connection to the Archives."

"Antony," he said, shaking Sam's hand across the desk. "Well, now that we're all thoroughly scarred by the worst woodcuts in the library, what's up?"

Quickly, keeping our voices low, Bee and I filled him in on recent developments and our fears concerning Simon Magus's digitized diary. "We need to find Missy Harrison's magus portrait," I concluded. "I know it's not on the hall with the others. Arnold said he put all of the Mulligan magi's portraits in storage…"

By then, Antony had begun to look queasy with the tidings. "Archives," he murmured. "I've seen them. They're in a climate-controlled room with the older portraits."

"Can you get us in there?"

He hesitated, then nodded. "But not until tonight. It's restricted, and if I tried to walk all of you in there right now, I wouldn't get far. Wait until the archivists knock off for the day, and then we can try to sneak in."

I'd expected that gaining access to the most well-guarded collection of magical books and artifacts in the mundane realm would take at least a bit of spellcraft, but as it turned out, all we needed was Antony's fingerprint on the scanner and a magnetic card. I could see the thick layer of spells coating the electronics at the door, protecting them from the surges of magic that could easily fry them, but they let us through without complaint or alarm.

The lobby of the Archives was empty—even the most diehard archivist was home by eleven on a Sunday night—and the few lights left on had been dimmed. Antony led us past the abandoned security desk and cloakroom, down three flights of stairs, and into the former dungeon of one of the original towers, now expanded and retrofitted to serve as protected storage. We traveled deep into the heart of the storage area, and Antony used his phone to read the brass plaques on two dozen doors before he smiled and opened one. "All right, folks, time for art appreciation," he said, and stepped aside.

The room was nothing short of an art gallery, a long, white-walled chamber full of thin quarter-walls marching in parallel lines from one end to the other. Almost every vertical surface was covered with a painting, some modest, some life-sized or larger, some in heavy golden frames worth a small fortune. The artwork covered a thousand years of Arcanum history, though jarringly, most of the paintings of the first magi had been done in the eighteenth century, making the transition to the rows of authentic medieval portraits awkward. Still, the gallery was staggering in its scope, and I paused just inside the door to try to take it all in.

"This way," said Antony, heading toward the far end of the room as we dawdled behind him. "There's a separate chamber for the black sheep, so to speak—pretty much anyone who left office under unsavory circumstances winds up in here." He opened another door, revealing a much smaller but just as packed room…and there, hanging in a corner beside her husband's official grand magus portrait, was Magus Harrison.

She had been a handsome woman when she sat for it, I thought as I approached, maybe forty-five, her night-black hair straightened, perfectly flipped, and hanging just below her shoulders. Her eyes were her best feature, round and golden-brown, and they seemed to track me as I neared. She wore a deep violet robe with a silver Celtic knot clasp at the neck, and it hung open for most of its length, revealing the matching pantsuit beneath. The cut and style of her clothing dated the painting to the eighties, but that did nothing to detract from her look of serene determination.

I paused in front of the painting as the others crowded around, not quite daring to touch it. "Where do you think he hid the page?" Sam asked, rubbing his chin. "Like…is there a spell or something binding it to the canvas, or is it hidden in the background?"

Antony looked at him like he was crazy. "It's probably somewhere inside the frame," he replied, and carefully flipped the painting over to show the brown paper backing. "Easy enough to replace. I bet it's sitting between that and the canvas."

"One way to find out," I said, pulling my new knife from my pocket. "Let's see what we have—"

"Wait."

As one, we turned to Frank, who was scowling at the flipped painting. "Wait for what?" I asked.

"The face…it was different in Harrison's mind."

"How so?" Bee asked.

He struggled for a moment, then said, "I could be wrong. You blend together."

"Oh, *thanks*," Daisy muttered.

"Nothing personal. But I think the face he remembered was different."

"Could it just be a function of memory?" Sam ventured. "Guessing it's been a while since he's seen this painting, so maybe the details have gotten fuzzy."

"Possibly," said Frank, then shrugged and shook it off. "Never mind. Stab it."

"We're not *stabbing* it, we're making a careful incision," I protested, and pressed the tip of my knife close to the bottom of the frame, intending to cut a small flap and see what shook out. But before I could even dent the paper, all of the lights flared to full brightness around us, and the door into the main gallery slammed open. We barely had time to look at each other in alarm before our door flew open as well, and then Bert, black-robed and fuming, was upon us.

"What the *hell* do you think you're doing?" he shouted as he ran into the room. "Get away from that!"

"Whatever you think we're up to, you're wrong," I tried, but Bert wasn't in the mood for placation.

"Really? I see you defacing a dead magus's portrait. Have you no shame at all? The poor woman was punished enough without you coming along to destroy what's left of her legacy!"

Before I could counter that, Antony stepped into the fray. "Grand Magus, please," he began, showing his empty palms, "no one's hurting the painting. We just need to have a look inside the—"

"*We?*" he snapped, rounding on Antony. "Oh yes, it *is* 'we,' isn't it? You'll never guess what IT told me just this evening," he said, his voice thick with sarcasm. "Seems there's been loads of activity in Arcview on your credentials—thousands of files accessed and downloaded at all hours of the day and night. They saw past your tricks, and they traced the pipeline you tried to hide. Straight to Virginia, as it happens. Somewhere on the coast—which, if memory serves, is a nerve center for the Fringe. What do you have to say for yourself?"

Antony remained unruffled as Bert's color rose. "I'm trying to save the Arcanum," he said calmly. "And if you'll shut up for two seconds and let us explain what we're doing down here, you'll understand."

In reply, Bert muttered a word and flung Antony against the far wall. He bounced and collapsed, a moaning ragdoll, and Daisy and Sam ran to help him as the rest of us moved between them and Bert. "The fuck is wrong with you?" I yelled. "The walls are stone, you could have killed him!"

"Last time I checked," said Bert, "death was an appropriate punishment for treason."

"*Treason?*"

"Opening the Archives to outsiders? Not to mention bringing the lot of you in here—IT rang me as soon as he used his credentials tonight. It seems someone hacked into Arcview today with old credentials, and they've been on alert ever since. I never expected much from the witch, but this is unforgiveable." His voice began to rise as he worked himself up. "Here I am, trying to forge a diplomatic channel with the courts, allowing their representatives to live on Arcanum property, and what do I get for my trouble? Espionage and desecration." He pointed to the wall of paintings and snapped, "How many would you have ruined had I not caught you? What is this, part of your little vendetta against *Grand Magus* Mulligan? It's petty and childish! Your mother won, their lives were ruined, so what else do you want?"

I knew he was trying to get a rise out of me, and I could feel the fireball itching to spring to life in my hand, but something told me that starting a conflagration in a room full of artwork would send the wrong message. "We're in danger," I told him. "You, me, the Arcanum, the courts, the Fringe—all of us. And *we* are trying to stop the problem before it becomes worse. So *back off* and let me work," I said, holding up my knife.

"Is that the best you've got?" Bert taunted. "Can't outcast me, so you reach for a pocketknife?"

"Keep that up," I replied, "and you're going to learn what it's like to get your butt kicked by a mongrel. Now excuse me, I have work to do…"

I felt the bolt coming an instant before impact, and instinct created a shield in the nick of time. "Really?" I said in frustrated disbelief. "You want to rumble in the *Archives*? I thought you were trying to keep your paintings intact."

"Get out," he growled, moving into a defensive stance. "All of you. The three of you are expelled as of now," he said, pointing to Sam, Frank, and me, "and as for the traitors, you will accompany me back to my office, you will be held until morning, and then formal banishment proceedings will commence. I'll be merciful."

Frank sighed and looked down at me. "Can I do it now?"

"Not yet," I muttered, then put the knife away and marched toward Bert. Unprepared, he tried to put up a shield, but he hadn't had the benefit of a decade of pummeling from Val to make his shields strong. I reached through the shield before it could crystalize, grabbed Bert by the collar, and yanked him close to my face, knocking his glasses askew. "Listen closely, you little shit," I said, fighting the urge to throttle him. "We are all in *deep* trouble because you haven't done your job."

"What are you talking—"

"When was the last time you checked on my grandparents? Or the Mulligans? Or any of the other probationers?"

"Their welfare coordinators—"

"Are lazy, incompetent, or swayable," I interrupted. "But the Company's been watching, and they say a chunk of the probationers have vanished."

Bert's mouth opened, but for once, he could do nothing but gape at me, and I pressed my advantage. "Know who else has gone missing? Moyna and her friends. Company keeps an eye on them, too. So yeah, I asked Arnold for a secure line into the Archives so that we could look for clues to the probationers' whereabouts, since *you're* obviously useless. I mean, heavens, Bertie," I said, dropping into a bad impression of his mother, "isn't it time you pardoned them all, anyway?"

His face, already a splotchy red with his anger, darkened. "You had no right—"

"What, to do your homework for you? Want to guess what we found? My dear old grandpa had a copy of Simon Magus's diary in his files."

That finally took the wind from his sails. "Impossible," he said, though he sounded uncertain. "The Magus's diary was never digitized. It's too dangerous—"

"And yet, somehow, someone with Archives credentials—oh, I don't know, like *Grandpa*—managed to get it close enough to a scanner," I retorted. "Greg Harrison says there's a theoretical section in there about extracting Faerie's consciousness from the realm. We don't know if they're trying to use it, but the realm is *hurting*, and if something happens to her…"

I let the thought hang, and Bert's eyes widened. "You're joking."

"I wish." Giving him a last shake for good measure, I released his shirt and stepped back. "But Harrison pulled a page in that section out of the diary, just in case it fell into the wrong hands. He's hidden it in his wife's painting, which is why we're down here. Once I get it, I'm going to take it back to Faerie and let Mom and Toula work on it. So why don't you get out of my way?"

He mulled it over for a long moment as Antony, leaning on Daisy and Sam, shuffled back toward us, then nodded curtly. "Don't hurt the painting."

"Wasn't planning on it," I muttered, pulling out my knife. I made a quick incision in the paper, then lifted the flap and reached inside, feeling for the missing vellum.

My fingers brushed only the back of the canvas.

"I don't…*shit*," I muttered, withdrawing my hand, "Frank, I think he played you. It's empty."

Bee swore, but before she could do more, Bert's phone began to trill. "Yes?" he said impatiently. As he listened, his expression softened toward disbelief, and by the time he put his phone back in his pocket, the color had drained from his cheeks. "Grand Magus Harrison is dead," he murmured.

"*Dead?*" I echoed. "He was fine when we left him, just buzzed—"

"The blood's still warm. He called for help ten minutes ago, but he was dead before the medics arrived." He shook his head, stunned, then recovered enough to stand up straight and adjust his glasses. "You know the way?"

I opened a gate into his foyer with barely a second's thought. "After you."

The air conditioning was still running in the Harrison house, which was a small comfort. I couldn't imagine how quickly the situation would have gone south had the body been lying there in the hundred-degree heat.

Someone had pulled a sheet from the closet, but all it was doing was soaking up the blood on the kitchen linoleum. Even with the dark dining room rug hiding some of the stains, I could piece together Harrison's last moments: he'd been shot in his wheelchair, judging by the blast marks and bloodstain on the gray seat cushion, and then he'd been removed from the chair, either by force or by his body collapsing. The tracks on the rug showed how he'd crawled to the kitchen, and he'd died on the floor with his phone in his hand, which peeked from beneath the sheet.

"Jesus," Sam whispered, standing over the body. "He bled out, didn't he?"

"A bolt shouldn't have done that," said Bee. "They tend to cauterize…" With clinical detachment, she lifted the sheet sufficiently to give her a private view of the corpse, then lowered it with a grimace. "The bolt may have been the primary cause of death, but there are stab wounds, too, at least half a dozen. Difficult to tell with his clothing on, but that's where the blood's coming from."

I wanted to be sick—my eyes kept drifting to the bloody shoeprints of the medics who had tried to save him—but I knew that vomit was the last thing needed in that house. "Can't believe he's dead," I muttered.

Bert walked in from the dining room, but he and his loafers stayed well clear of Harrison. "Blast marks on the walls and carpet. Maybe they fired warning shots."

"Did he say who came after him?" I asked.

"No. He just called for a medic…damn it." He sighed, rubbing his face. "Who would have killed him? He was an old man, bound, harmless…"

Before any of us could advance a theory, Frank yelled my name from down the hall. The others trooped after me into the master bedroom—pale green walls, messy cream-colored linens, a fake banana plant in a black pot beside the window, and Frank, who was staring at something on the wall. "*This* is what I saw," he said, and stepped aside.

Facing the bed, directly in the line of sight of its occupant, was Missy Harrison's bridal portrait.

The slash across the middle of the canvas was, I assumed, a recent addition.

"Too late," I murmured, and pulled out my phone. "Bert, is there a cleanup team on the way?"

"They've been notified," he mumbled, examining the damaged painting. "I need to call his family—"

"Let Arnold handle that." Stepping aside, I dialed and waited through two rings until the line opened.

"Everything okay?" Coileán asked without preamble.

"No. Greg Harrison's been murdered, and we're in trouble."

I heard footsteps on stone—his office, presumably. "Moon and stars," he muttered. "Where are you?"

"New Orleans. I've got company, and we need to evacuate."

"Mm. Anyone who's going to give the realm fits?"

"Maybe, but she's got bigger things to worry about," I replied. "I need to talk to the two of you, pronto."

"Not a problem. I'll call Ellie." He paused briefly, then said, "How did he die?"

"Looks like a wand blast and several stabs."

"Quick, I hope."

I decided it wasn't the time to tell Coileán about the rest of the scene. "Probably. We'll be there in a minute," I said, and hung up.

A few seconds' concentration was all it took to rip open a gate onto the immaculate lawn of Coileán's palace, a sprawling green carpet warmed by the afternoon light. "We've got clearance," I told the others. "That means everyone."

Bert's eyebrow rose. "Is that...*Faerie*? I can't—"

"You're an asshole, but I'm not leaving you here to let you wind up like Harrison," I said, cutting him off, and thrust my finger toward the gate. "Move it, Bertie."

"But—"

"But nothing. If we're right, the exact wrong people have everything they need to do something incredibly stupid, and if you go back to Glastonbury right now, you'll be a sitting duck. Go on," I said as the others hurried across.

Though he looked like he'd rather hug a wasp nest, Bert reluctantly did as I told him, even if I had to give him a little shove between the shoulder blades when he hesitated on the edge of the gate. Carried by momentum, I followed him over and looked back to find Frank still in New Orleans, watching us with his arms crossed. "You, too," I said, reaching for him between the realms. "Come on, let's go home."

"Toula might not be pleased if I ruin her work," he replied.

"She'll understand."

He weighed his options, then nodded and waved me aside. "This breaks when I cross, yes? Make room."

I didn't have to be told twice, and I shooed Bee and Daisy away in the other direction. Frank let out a long breath, then took two steps back and ran at the gate, leaping the last few feet like he was trying to steal a base. The spell crumbled the instant he came through, and suddenly, with a flash of magic and a puff of shredded clothing falling like confetti, he was back to his old self. As he rumbled and stretched his wings with a look of reptilian bliss, Bert turned around, noticed what had materialized in our midst, and shrieked like a little girl.

"*Whoa,*" Antony muttered, taken aback, but he proved to be quicker on the uptake than the spooked grand magus. "Uh...Frank?"

The dragon nodded and flopped onto the grass. *I can't tell you how good this feels. Stuck like that for a month...ahhh.* He broadcast pure pleasure as he rolled onto his back and rubbed his scales against the lawn. *Oh, that's better. And I'm starving, Ros, so unless you desperately need me, I'm off to the sheep.*

"Enjoy, bud," I told him, stepping clear of his wriggling radius. "And thanks again."

Wouldn't have missed it. He rolled upright and stood, gave Bert his version of a smirk, then looked the other way and found Daisy staring up at him, mouth agape. *What?* he asked her. *This shouldn't be a surprise.*

She clasped her hands beneath her chin, blinked a few times, then finally broke out in a squeal. "Oh, my gosh!" she cried, jumping in her excitement. "You're so *pretty*!"

The cast of discomfort in his thoughts made a perfect counterpoint to Daisy's exuberance. *Keep that up, and I will eat you,* he replied, taking a precautionary step away from the overjoyed wizard.

"Liar."

With hot sauce. Try me.

He stretched his wings again, casting all of us into sudden shadow, then broke into a short gallop and was airborne. Only once he had vanished over the trees did Bert recover his voice and his nerve. "That...ehm... that—"

"That's Frank," I said. "Minus the transformation spell."

"And that explains a lot," Antony mumbled, then pointed to the palace. "So, uh...what's the plan?"

I looked at Sam, who, like Bee, had been nearly unfazed by Frank's new appearance. "We go have a chat with the bosses. Come with me," I said, linking my arm around Sam's. "I don't want to deliver this news on my own."

As before, Val was waiting at the front door, and he gave our group a careful once-over as we slipped past him. "You've made friends, I see," he said in quiet Fae, and noticed the mound of curls behind me. "Ah, Bee. You're unharmed?"

"Hi, Val. Still intact," she replied in kind. Daisy looked at her questioningly, and Bee shrugged. "The king taught me the language when I was ten," she explained to her girlfriend. "Instant transfer, more like. Comes in handy every now and again."

Val smiled faintly, then took a closer look at the back of the line and blocked their entry. "Ros?"

"The blond is Antony, who's been working with Aiden and the Virginians," I told him, and Val let him pass with a nod. "And that's, uh...Bert."

"Bert?" he repeated, arching an eyebrow. "As in—"

"Yeah. *That* Bert."

The subject of his inspection stood stiffly on the wide staircase, curls mussed, glasses smudged with fingerprints, black robe slightly stained with blood on the hem. Even with the hour in Glastonbury, he still wore pressed chinos and a blue polo, but overall, he looked like he'd just witnessed a flaming car wreck—and in light of the last half hour, I couldn't entirely blame him.

"*That* is Arnold's replacement?" Val muttered.

"He's had a bad night."

Bert cleared his throat. "If someone would be so kind as to translate and tell me what the problem is, I'd appreciate it."

"The problem," said Val, switching tongues, "is that I neither like you nor trust you, but if the lady insists..."

"I can handle him," I said, following the captain's

linguistic lead, and Val let him pass. "And I can assure you that he wouldn't be stupid enough to try anything here."

"Oh, I wouldn't be so sure about that," said a familiar voice across the cavernous entryway, and I turned to find Mom hurrying toward us with Toula on her heels.

I met her in the middle of the room and hugged her tightly. "Coileán called you, too?"

"Diary review team," Toula explained. "Do you know who got to Greg?"

"I've got a decent guess," I replied, and followed Val upstairs.

When he ushered us into the office, I found the king and queen waiting—sitting on the same couch, for once—and Nico standing guard by the door. They watched silently as our crowd filed in, and then Coileán beckoned to Sam and me with a crooked finger and pointed to the facing couch. "What don't we yet know?" he asked as I slid onto the leather seat across from him. "Don't leave anything out."

As succinctly as I could, I told them about the discovery of the diary in Grandpa's files—"Aiden's kept us apprised," said Eleanor, motioning me along—then of the latest Minor Arcanum casualties, my conversation with Kura, our trip to New Orleans, and the disaster with the paintings. "I didn't know he had another one," I said, trying to apologize. "Frank saw Magus Harrison in a painting, and—"

"You assumed it was the official portrait," Coileán finished. "Greg always loved that picture of her in her wedding gown, but there's no way you would have known about that." He paused, then looked toward the bookshelves, where Bee was muttering a translation to the others. "Ms. Powell, are we making your life difficult?"

She looked up and smiled wearily. "No more than usual, sir."

Val snorted, and Coileán smirked in acknowledgement. "Touché. Tell the two of them who aren't Bert that no one's going to bite them."

Eleanor cut her eyes to Toula and Mom, who stood together near the captains. "Well? You know the diary better than we do—any thoughts?"

"We did notice the missing page," Mom began, "but considering the rest of that section and the physical limits of spellcraft...I mean, the power it would take to bind the *realm* would be unheard of. I know I couldn't do it."

"Neither could I," said Toula.

"But something is attacking the realm, all the same," Eleanor pointed out. "If you worked in tandem—"

"Still insufficient," Toula interrupted. "I could make stacks for the next decade and not have the oomph to do more than punch at the realm. *But.*"

"But?" Coileán asked.

She crossed her arms and looked him in the eye. "Remember that one time my parents teamed up?"

"You think they're—"

"I think Moyna's got a cadre of senior faeries at her back and a band of pissed-off wizards holding an instruction manual to magical doomsday, yeah. If Greg was right and the missing page was a list of Simon's bright ideas to channel power more effectively, then we're in deep trouble."

As soon as Bee finished her translation, Bert stepped forward and waved for attention. "Did *no one* think it might be a good idea to tell me about this before now?" he said, glaring at Sam and me. "If I'd known the probationers had fled, I might have been able to—"

"Warn them?" Coileán interrupted in English, then shrugged. "Too risky. Arnold wasn't convinced of your loyalties."

Bert stared at him, momentarily dumbstruck, then snapped, "You speak—"

"Of course," he replied, rolling his eyes. "But Bee was doing such a nice job, and I didn't want to be rude to Nico," he added, gesturing toward the pair of guards at the door.

The grand magus caught himself, took a deep breath, then closed his eyes and pinched the bridge of his nose. "Why would Grand Magus Lowe doubt me? Everything I do is for the Arcanum, everything I have ever done is for the Arcanum, my *life* is the bloody Arcanum—"

"Yes," said Eleanor, "and we've heard all about your wonderful plans to better the Arcanum. Let's see, what was it...*right*," she said with a snap, "you're going to send all the Fringers over here and bind your witches if they won't go, and then you're going to take the Minor Arcanum under your wing—this is all by force, I assume, since they don't trust you, either—and what was that about pardons?"

"Yeah," Mom cut in, cracking her knuckles, "about that. I'm going to go out on a limb and guess you didn't lose anyone during the Mulligan years, did you?"

Bert looked at the three of them, and his eyes finally settled on the least threatening. "Grand Magus Carver," he began in a rush, "you must understand—"

"No, sweetheart, *you* have to understand," she interrupted, marching toward him as he backed away. "That's not the Arcanum's realm. It never was! It's the great mixing ground, and like it or not, you can't set yourself up as a dictator for every other organization in the realm and claim it's your right."

My mother wasn't a large woman, but she carried herself with all of the confidence befitting a magus at the top of her game, and Bert seemed to shrink before her. "You know who taught me that?" she asked, bearing down on him. "Greg. Before you were so much as the proverbial twinkle in your father's eye. So don't come in here and try to tell me what I *must understand* about the Arcanum and your grand plans for it, little boy."

He took a moment to choose his words. "I, ehm...I apologize if I misspoke, but as Grand Magus Lowe taught *me*, your great failing was that you never fully understood the Arcanum."

"Never said I was perfect," Mom murmured, "and there's a hell of a lot I've learned from my mistakes—such as what a terrible idea it is to set up a twenty-something as grand magus. You may be the finest caster in a hundred years, but you still don't know shit. I certainly didn't, and people died because of it. I think Arnold was a fool to let the probationers live outside the installations, but that was his call. The least the two of you should have done was keep tabs on them."

Bert tried to defend himself. "The welfare coordinators said—"

"*When*? When was the last time you reviewed their records? Talked to them in person?"

"I've had a lot on my plate!" he protested. "I've only had the job a month and a half!"

"And I only had a month longer than that. If the Council could turn on me, then they sure as hell could turn on you. Or forget the Council—there's already a group of wizards with a grudge and a taste for blood, and if you don't sympathize with them, then I wouldn't be surprised if you're in their sights."

"I think it might be time to reconsider their probation," he replied, "but in the proper course, not by…whatever it is you think they're doing."

"Your probationers got their hands slapped," Coileán interjected from the couch. "If the decision had been ours, they'd all have been executed."

"Right," Bert retorted, glaring down at him, "and you wonder why we don't deal with your kind."

The king just smiled at his petulance, and Mom sighed. "I'm not saying this is all your fault, Bert," she resumed. "Arnold trusted his welfare coordinators way too much. But knowing what we do, it's imperative that the Arcanum work with the courts on this one."

"And what *do* we know?" he countered. "Fine, your father had a copy of the Magus's diary, and someone armed with a wand took the missing page from Grand Magus Harrison. And yes, I suppose some of the probationers are unaccounted for. That doesn't mean—"

"Faerie's being attacked," Toula interrupted. "The diary could at least point someone in the right direction for accomplishing that. More importantly, if we assume that a known holder of said diary is able to do anything with it, he's unbound. How many dead, wandless wizards is it going to take before you consider it a pattern?"

"The Minor Arcanum is not my concern—"

"It is now!" she shouted. "Let's assume the worst, shall we? Moyna and her merry band break the binds on Mulligan's buddies, they go after Minor Arcanum wizards to steal wands—I mean, why would *you* care if they wind up dead, right?—and then they scratch Moyna's back by sharing the diary."

"But why would a *faerie* want to hurt this realm?" he said, spreading his arms. "Counterintuitive, don't you think?"

"You know, dear," said Eleanor, "we *have* been considered somewhat capricious."

"Which is to say we don't know what she's planning," said Coileán, "but I doubt it's anything we'll like."

The queen nodded and pushed herself from the couch. "Very well. The trace failed, Toula?"

She nodded sullenly. "Not even a blip."

"Then maybe there's something helpful in the Archives files that Aiden has yet to unlock," she said, and sighed. "But until we find the missing wizards and Moyna, the Minor Arcanum and the Fringe need to evacuate. Coileán, mind if I use the gate in the bookcase?"

"Go for it," he told her. "Just move the vases first, please."

She did as he asked with a flick of her wrist, then widened the gate into the Fringe's outpost in Rigby, where the light was just beginning to fade toward the long summer evening. "Anyone home?" she called, poking her head into the next realm. "Hello? Badger?"

"Back in a second!" called a voice from the kitchen, and Kip popped out with a bag of tortilla chips and an open jar of salsa. "They went down the street to pick up pizza. Need me to call them?"

"If it's no trouble," she replied.

He nodded and pulled his phone from his pocket, then glanced through the gate and saw the rest of us watching. "You want to come over?"

Eleanor and Coileán accepted the invitation, but I hung back and watched him as he slouched against the counter, relaying the message. Kip was built like a smaller version of Frank—well, transformed Frank—a few inches above six feet and broad-shouldered. His complexion was golden-brown, the kind of color one might achieve after, say, a summer of surfing, but the ponytail falling halfway down his back was almost as red as Bee's curls. Though he was a bit younger than my parents, he looked about a decade their senior, the cost of living in the mortal realm. Once he'd put the phone aside, he picked up his snack again and headed into the den. "They're on their way. Chips?"

A few minutes later, the kitchen door opened, and Badger, Seamus, and Amy hurried in, their arms laden with pizza boxes and plastic bags of sides and pop. "What's the news?" Badger asked, dumping her burden on the table.

"In brief, all of you need to evacuate," said Eleanor, and quickly filled them in.

Badger frowned, deepening the wrinkles around her mouth and eyes, and ran a hand through her nearly white hair in thought. "I'll put out the call," she said after a moment. "The Fringe will listen. I make no promises with the Minor Arcanum, but the Joneses, at least, should be clever enough to get out of Dodge."

"And you four," said Coileán. "We're not having a repeat of Slim."

"*I'm* not going anywhere, and don't try to convince me

otherwise," she retorted. "Seamus—"

"Is staying with you," Seamus interrupted, wrapping his arm around her shoulders. "But the kids, now—"

"Nope," said Amy, slowly shaking her head. "Absolutely not."

Badger and Seamus traded looks with Kip, who came to Amy's side and gently raised her chin. "You're not safe here," he murmured, "especially if they're still looking for wands. Go on over. We'll be careful, sweetheart."

"I'm not leaving you," she insisted. "You're no match for a wizard."

"Neither are you."

"I'm the better shot," she countered.

"Agreed. But I'll shoot straighter if you're safe."

She reached up on her tiptoes and pulled his face toward hers. "Do you hear me, Kippit? I am *not leaving you.*"

"Amy," Eleanor tried, "this is—"

"Don't," she said firmly. "I don't care what's out there, I'm not leaving my husband. Forget it."

The elder Fringers exchanged glances, and then Seamus said, "What if the realm changed her mind? Could they both go?"

Eleanor grimaced. "She's stressed right now to begin with, especially if we're planning on an influx of wizards. If Kip crossed…"

"Or you could just ask her," I muttered, stepping away from the gate, then called, "Kura? Amy and Kip are coming over. Okay with that?"

A few seconds later, a shimmering mist appeared in front of the gate, and Kura's voice echoed in my head: *No.*

The others jumped, and I realized our conversation was public. "What happened to—"

Weak.

The king and queen stared at her, shocked. "How…did you just…" Coileán stuttered, then managed, "You *summoned* her? And she listened?"

But I turned my attention back to Kura, or at least the little she was able to manifest. "He's Fringe. What's the harm?"

He is kadalin, she replied. *Gray Lander.*

Given the late hour in Glastonbury, I was too tired to pretend I knew what she meant, but I didn't let that stop me. "Has Kip ever done anything to hurt you? Or anyone here? He's no more of a threat than my mom, right?"

I will not allow Nath's people in this realm, she said, growing more agitated. *Its safety is my responsibility, and—*

"Uh, excuse me," said Kip, approaching the gate. "Um…Kura, was it?"

It was difficult to say exactly what her amorphous mist was looking at, but I could have sworn it glared in his direction.

"We don't claim Nath," he continued, unbothered to find himself the focal point of Faerie's attention. "She considers us little more than beasts, so I am in no way working for her. I swear it."

"He's telling the truth," said Badger. "I've heard it from Nath herself. She doesn't consider the kadalin to be her people."

"Please," Kip continued, "it's not for me, I won't be any trouble to you, but Amy won't go…"

"You're being absolutely ridiculous," I told Kura. The mist flashed, and I felt her flicker of surprise and anger. "We're wasting time. Amy and Kip know how to help Aiden, and if there's anything in the Arcanum files that might tell us where the probationers and Moyna are hiding, they'll have a better chance of finding it if they work together here. Besides, I went to Glastonbury because you wanted me to," I told her, folding my arms. "And I want this in turn."

Impertinent.

"I'm trying to help you, and so is everyone else here. Be reasonable."

After a long, silent moment, I heard a sound in my

mind like the faintest of exhalations—a sigh of resignation—and the mist dissipated. I looked through the gate at Coileán and Eleanor and cocked my head in query. "That's a go, then?"

"You realize that when she's upset, she's literally our headache, yes?" he replied. "A nasty, nagging, unrelenting headache." He seemed to waver, but finally, he beckoned to Kip. "Come on, kid. Whatever happens, it's not your fault."

"I'll go first," Amy offered, grabbing one of the pizzas, then stepped through the gate and handed Bee the box. "See, nothing to it. It feels just like an intra-realm gate."

Kip nodded, then turned to Seamus and Badger as the king and queen crossed back. "You'll be okay?"

"We'll be fine, love," said Badger, giving him a quick hug. "If Aiden ever lets you get some rest, have him bring you to the Fringe settlement—the Stowes will take care of you. Yes?"

"And we'll pack your bags for you after dinner," Seamus offered. "Your kit, too, Amy."

"Thanks, but better let Badger do that—half my gear's steel," she replied, and held out her hand. "Whenever you're ready, Kip."

As he reached through the gate, I saw a telltale crackle of magic along his arm—a breaking spell, I realized, which fell apart as he stepped into Faerie. Suddenly, he was quite a bit taller, and that wasn't all.

"Holy hell," Bert cried from across the room, "he's a bloody centaur!"

Finding himself with an extra pair of legs, Kip stumbled on Coileán's rug, but Amy grabbed his other hand and held on while he recovered his balance. As he shook off his ruined tennis shoes, he stared glumly down at the remains of half his clothing. "Damn it, those were my favorites," he muttered, pawing at a ribbon of denim with one hoof.

"It's okay, sweetie," said Amy, releasing him, "you're all

right. Feel better?"

"Feels *weird*." He looked over his shoulder and flicked his tail. "Everything seems to be accounted for, but…" Frowning, he looked around the room and folded his arms self-consciously. "Uh…hate to be a bother, but could someone put that spell back together, please?"

"Oh, sure," said Toula, pushing up her sleeves, then stretched out her hand and mumbled under her breath. When the after-image of the magical flash cleared, Kip looked human again, restored jeans and all. "How's that?" she asked. "Did I miss anything?"

He patted his legs, tested his feet, then nodded. "No, that's great. Thanks, Toula."

But Amy seemed concerned by his quick transformation. "Kip, hon," she said, taking his hand again, "you don't have to. There isn't going to be a mass panic over here if you walk around unensorcelled."

He pointed to Bert, who still looked stunned. "Oh?"

"He's not from around here," said Toula. "Amy's right, you don't have to live with the bind."

"Understood," said Kip, looking down at Amy, "but I made my choice twenty years ago, and that's to be with you. Besides," he said, chuckling, "the sleeping arrangements would be really, *really* awkward otherwise."

She sighed. "*Kip.*"

"Nope." He swung her into his arms and noticed the pizza Bee was still holding, then bent Amy low enough to retrieve the box. "Okay, if someone could point us toward Aiden, we've got work to do."

"Follow me," Toula offered, and led them out of the room while Coileán shrunk the gate to its usual pinhole.

"Well, then," Bee muttered, brushing off her hands, "I think we've all learned something here today."

"The meaning of *kadalin*?" I asked.

"I was thinking more of the fact that we can't take Bert anywhere, but yeah, that, too." Heading toward my mom, she said, "Grand Magus, I'm more than willing to help with the evacuation, but if I'm not needed, may I borrow your guest bed again?"

Badger didn't mess around. Within two hours, she had worked through her phone trees for the Fringe and the Minor Arcanum, and she and Vivi Stowe, her coordinator counterpart in the settlement, had arranged pickup locations. All of the available Stowe brothers joined Toula, Bee, my parents, and me in helping Badger and Seamus get the necessary gates open quickly, and by nightfall, we'd filled the settlement's guesthouse and then some.

Bert, who'd been given a room in the guesthouse so that at least one Stowe could keep an eye on him, sat on the low wall at the edge of town and wearily watched the new arrivals pop over while Frank, tired and full of mutton, curled up a short distance away to wait for me. Near the end of the exodus, as I took a break, I heard Bert mutter, "How was I supposed to know?"

"I mean," said Sam, who'd plopped onto the brick beside him, "you *are* the grand magus, right?"

"But that doesn't make me omniscient! I'm supposed to be able to trust my people! How was I to know the probationers had swayed the welfare coordinators—"

"Dude, *enough*," Antony interrupted, and Bert twitched in surprise. "You screwed up. Own it, fix it, stop wallowing. Jeez," he said with a sigh, "no one feels sorry for you, okay?"

Frank rumbled low in his throat, and as Antony looked his way, he raised a front foot and curled his claws up tightly in invitation. Smiling, Antony fist-bumped him— well, fist-bumped his toe—then sank down against a tree and dozed until the last of the evacuees had crossed, when Dr. Stowe noticed him sleeping in the grass and half-dragged him to a bed.

CHAPTER 13

Amy had options as to where she could crash once Seamus delivered the promised luggage. Since a good chunk of the Fringe and nearly all of the Minor Arcanum used her wands, she would have been welcome in town, or if she had chosen to pull rank, Eleanor would have put her up for the time being—though a second-generation witch-blood, she was also Oberon's great-granddaughter. Instead, Aiden threw a couple of extra beds in his suite, and he, Vivi, Amy, and Kip slept in shifts, keeping three on the computers at all times. The password crackers had opened more files than the team had been able to parse to that point—Amy and Kip *did* have their computer business to keep them busy—and so they worked nonstop through the night and into Monday, digging in hopes of finding any clue as to the missing wizards' whereabouts.

After catching a few hours of sleep in the guesthouse, Antony asked me to bring him by to offer his help and apologize for not adequately hiding the pipeline he'd built out of Arcview, which had been shut down around the time that we went into the portrait storage rooms. "I'm a database guy," he explained, "and I've written a few apps. I did the best I could, but—"

"You did the best you could," said Aiden, offering him his hand. "Welcome aboard. If you need natural light, you've come to the wrong place."

While the five of them worked, sustained by a combination of catnaps and caffeine shots, the rest of us were left temporarily adrift. Mom and Dad had welcomed my friends, putting Bee and Daisy in the guestroom and Sam downstairs on the most comfortable couch, and all of us made up for lost sleep while we acclimated to the time shift. By Monday afternoon, we were well-fed and rested, and I called Dr. Stowe to ask about Bert. "He appears to be hiding," he told me. "We've left food outside his room, but he hasn't been out yet. Want to see if he's still alive?"

And so, I ventured into town and stopped by the guesthouse, which was still overflowing with newcomers. Robbie Stowe, an architect by trade, was putting the finishing touches on a second building to accommodate the influx, but while he worked, the evacuees milled about in the common areas and explored the settlement, taking in the Fringe's version of carless suburbia.

Dr. Stowe showed me to Bert's room and wished me luck, and I rapped on the door. "Bert! It's Ros!" I called. "You okay?"

After a moment of shuffling, I heard the lock turn, and Bert cracked the door open. The sliver of him that I could see looked like hell. "Any news?"

"May I come in?"

He stepped back and pulled the door aside, and I got a good look at him—dark-circled eyes, insomnia-puffed face, and a robe that looked like it'd been wallowed in. "You want coffee or something?" I offered, producing a mug from the ether. "Or there's food in the hall for you…"

Bert accepted the coffee and sat on his rumpled bed. "Not hungry, thanks."

"Have you touched base with Glastonbury?"

He nodded and drank deeply. "Rang Arnold this morning to let him know. He's covering for me, but he won't be able to hide the fact that I'm away for more than a few days, even if he's clever about it. Mum and Dad keep trying to reach me, but I'm not taking their calls right now." He sighed and closed his eyes. "Tell me there's good news."

"Not yet," I said, taking the chair opposite his narrow bed. "Aiden called a little while ago and said they have a few leads for someone to pursue. Nothing promising, but as long as there's a chance..." I shrugged. "Dad and a few of the Stowes are on recon, but Coileán and Eleanor insisted that anyone who's come from Glastonbury needs to stay here."

Bert stiffened and opened his eyes. "They can't hold me prisoner."

"They're not," I hastily explained. "They just don't want us running into more than we can handle in case any of the leads pan out. But look, these guys are pros, right?" I said, trying to sound chipper. "They'll figure out something."

"They should be keeping me apprised in the meantime."

"I'll pass that on," I replied, stifling the urge to laugh at him. With his pout and both hands wrapped around the mug, he looked like an overgrown toddler playing dress-up. "Not to be rude, but in all honesty, I think you're pretty far down the list of priorities right now."

"Whether they like it or not, I *am* the grand magus."

"And unless you know where to find the probationers, that doesn't mean much today." I hesitated, then suggested, "If you wanted to call out security, you know, maybe the assassin corps..."

Bert mulled it over while he sipped, but shook his head. "Can you tell me which of them I can trust? What's to say some of them haven't gone the way of the welfare coordinators?"

"Well, there *is* a way to find out." He looked at me strangely, and I explained, "Give someone like Val five minutes with them. Or Frank, even. Someone who's skilled enough at mental manipulation to get past whatever barriers they try to put up. I know Frank would do it if we asked him, and Val's *good*—"

"Oh, yes," Bert scoffed, "I can see that going over

beautifully. Exposing our security secrets to a hostile power—how quickly do you think the Council would hold a no-confidence vote on me, hmm? Especially if, God forbid, the probationers have sympathizers on the Council?"

"I think we both know the answer to that one," I murmured. Before Bert could protest, I held up a hand for silence. "Come on, man, Arnold doesn't trust half of them. All of those old aides who got their jobs only because their bosses were convicted—you really think they washed their hands of their own mentors?"

He looked green at the notion. "But to partner with *Moyna*...no one on the Council would be that stupid! She held Arc 1 under siege!"

I nodded. "Yep. And that time you had a werewolf attack in the silo? That was Mulligan and Moyna's doing. There's precedent."

Bert put his mug aside and rested his head in his hands. When the silence stretched uncomfortably between us, I said, "Uh...you okay, there?"

He looked up at me, his glasses smudged by his fingers and his eyes wet. "No one trained me for this. I don't know what to do, Ros. I haven't the first clue what I'm meant to be doing to fix this, and the Arcanum is my responsibility, and no one is telling me what to *do*."

I stood and shoved my hands into my pockets. "Wait it out for now. Let Arnold cover while you get your head on straight. And hey," I said, patting his shoulder, "this could be over tomorrow. The recon teams could find them any time now. Just hang on, Bert."

But the recon teams found nothing on Monday, and Tuesday was also a bust. The quintet working through the data dump pulled every possible place name they could find, and with an assist from a few of the Fringers and refugee wizards as to location landmarks, the scouts visited every conceivable hiding place, but they could find no trace of the missing. Badger even called Tanner Adler, prepared to negotiate a price, but the Company could offer nothing of use. The merrow were similarly flummoxed, though at least they were able to cross the Florida Keys off the list.

In the meantime, Mom and Toula hunkered down in Toula's palace apartment with every book of thaumaturgical theory the two of them could find, trying to put together a shield against the spell in the diary—or rather, what pieces of the spell they had to work with. Without the amplification and scaffolding ideas to dissect, they were left to guess how, exactly, Simon envisioned the spell coming together. They worked until their eyes blurred, and then Coileán, who had been delivering meals and checking on them, insisted that they nap before they dropped. Older faeries might get by with very little sleep, but Toula wasn't quite out of her fifties, and Mom was all too human. Besides, no matter how cool they tried to play it, there was no doubt that Coileán fretted over his headstrong live-in girlfriend.

By Wednesday, Toula was almost ready to give up. "The man was a genius, damn him," she muttered over breakfast in my parents' kitchen. "The only way I can see this working is with spellcraft and enchantment used in tandem, and if that's the case, there are just too many variables to work through. The confluences alone are enough to make me pull my hair out."

"How so?" Bee asked, refreshing her tea.

Toula raised her finger and began tracing a braid I recognized as a Bethune Stack—a triple channel that focused and amplified magic as it was forced along its path. "All stacks, no matter how good, have a limit. They're made of magic, after all, and when you try to run too strong a pulse down them, they break apart."

Bee nodded. "You're talking about the Ertz Limit?"

"Exactly." Catching the blank stares from Sam, Dad,

and Daisy, she reduced her diagram to a single channel, added a lightbulb on the top, then sent a continuous stream of white pulses up it. The bulb illuminated in time with the pulses, and Toula explained, "Channels are useful in spell construction because they keep activated magic contained and focused. Let's say I need something stronger." She twined another pair of channels around the first one in a stack, and the lightbulb flashed more brightly. "Basic Bethune. I feed all three channels simultaneously, and as the magic runs in close proximity to other active magic, the end result is amplified beyond what I put in to begin with. I can keep going," she continued, adding another four channels to the stack, and the blub blazed.

"Now, thickening a stack is one way to up the power. The other is to simply force more magic into the channels to begin with, like so." The pulses glowed more brightly now, and the bulb blazed like a miniature star. "But there's a catch. Overloading a spell breaks it, right? It's the easiest way to cut through a shield. And unless there are, for lack of a better term, flood channels built into the matrix to absorb some of that overload, the spell will fall apart once it reaches a certain point. That's the Ertz Limit. Observe." As the pulses running up her stack got brighter and brighter, the innermost channels began to glow red, then disintegrated, and the rest quickly followed in a chain reaction.

"Of course," said Toula, "the point of flood channels is to divert magic, so if I build those in, I'll have a nice little safeguard against overloading, but I'm not going to make my output any stronger past a certain point. Do you understand?"

Those at the table who hadn't suffered through a full Arcanum education—or worse, Toula's private tutelage—frowned but nodded along.

"So, what do I do to work around this?" she said, rebuilding her diagram with a careless wave. "I can add additional, independent stacks, like this"—another pair of them materialized around the lightbulb, and the glow intensified—"but eventually, I'm going to reach the Limit again. Remember what I said about magic in proximity to more magic?" Stacks manifested in a circle around the bulb, but as she activated them, their outermost channels began to glow red with failure, and soon the whole thing collapsed. "Too much, too close. And there, folks, is where we find the problem with spellcraft. You can use it to do incredibly complex things, but if you try to use it as a hammer, you can smash your own craft."

"So how does the Magus's protocol work, then?" Bee asked.

Toula reset her diagram, this time with a many-channeled stack that would overload immediately on use. "By shoring up the channels," she said as a neat yellow cylinder, followed by a chaotic green spiderweb, encircled the stack. "And by making a couple of important tweaks. The outer spell constantly rebuilds damaged channels," she explained, pointing to the cylinder. "But even that would overload once the stack failed—the magic would have to go *somewhere*. So what you could do, at least in theory, is add a protective layer of enchantment. Now, watch."

The stack glowed red at its core almost as quickly as she activated it, and the cylinder began to redden as the innermost channels were breached. But the extra power was then siphoned off into the enchantment around it, which glowed but held firm, letting the outer spell repair the channels as soon as they cracked.

"Enchantment is so strong because it's inherently flexible," said Toula. "It's a wilder sort of magic. Make the overflow network as large as you like—you can see that what's going up the stack is well beyond the Limit."

By then, I had to squint to look at the lightbulb. "So you get all the precision of a spell—"

"With all the force of an enchantment, yes," she replied. "And here's the neat bit: let's say you have a faerie who's old enough to know how to handle himself around spellcraft. Someone who *could* power a spell if his back was to a wall. I mean, he'd bitch the whole time," she muttered, "but trust me, it's doable."

"Yeah, but didn't that knock Robin out when he tried?" Dad asked.

"He was strong, but he didn't have any practice with it. Take someone much older, more accustomed to doing precision enchantment—"

"Like Coileán's wards?"

"Bingo, but someone older still. Someone who's *really* had time to experiment. Not only can he make the overflow network necessary to keep the spells intact, but he can power the stack as well…"

The pulses running up the stack changed from white to gold, and within seconds, the lightbulb exploded.

"And *that*," said Toula, "is fucking teamwork."

"The problem," said Mom, who'd been watching from the sink while she nursed a cup of coffee, "is that we don't have any clear idea of how they're actually constructing this spell. The Magus only gave vague directions—clear enough for a decent wizard to follow, but untested. They may have to rework this on the fly. And nothing in the diary talks about using enchantment to bolster the spell—I can't imagine that he would have contemplated going that route—but let's assume that Dad and his buddies are, because heaven knows none of them are strong enough to do this alone. We don't know the contours of the enchantments used, and so it's difficult to plan a defense."

"We need time to run simulations," said Toula. "To do tests. And I'm afraid we're just not going to have it."

I watched Toula's hybrid stack, which continued to shoot golden packets into the air until she dissolved it with a wave and reached for the pancakes.

Bert returned to Glastonbury that afternoon, though I tried to talk him out of it during my daily visit. "Grand

Magus Lowe has done all he can," he explained, freshening his three-day-old wardrobe with a muttered incantation. "This is my mess to fix, and I can't do it hiding here."

"Have you told the king and queen?" I asked.

But he just cleaned his glasses. "It's not their decision. Tell them I appreciate the hospitality, but I'm off," he said, then opened a gate into his office, where Arnold was waiting. "Do keep us informed, won't you?" he added on his way out.

I looked at Arnold, who shrugged and faintly shook his head while Bert's attention was elsewhere, and then I closed the gate behind him and went to the palace to deliver my report.

"The kid's an idiot," was Coileán's assessment, but he made no move to rise from his desk.

I gave his face quick consideration—Coileán had begun to look almost as haggard as Mom, Toula, and the tech team—and at the risk of causing offense, I pried. "Do you feel okay?"

He hesitated, then sighed and massaged his temples. "No," he muttered. "The realm's in distress, and she's letting us know, *loudly*. I haven't slept in days."

"Is there anything I can do?"

"No more than what's being done. Not unless you've got coordinates stashed somewhere," he said with a faint smile, but sobered immediately. "And on top of everything else, I once again get a chance to rationalize killing my own child, so, you know, I've had better weeks." He paused again, seemed to remember his audience, then waved me off. "Sorry, nothing for you to worry about, kid. Go home, don't give your parents anything else to fret over."

But I stayed where I was. "You don't have to *kill* her, do you? The cells here—"

"If I incarcerated her, it might well be until the end of time," Coileán interrupted. "Not to mention the number of Mab's people I've had stashed in there for decades already—no sense in giving them time to think about a jailbreak together. Besides, if Ellie gets a clear shot, Moyna's dead."

"You can't reason with her?"

"She's still slightly peeved about her husband's murder. I can't blame her, even if this is her niece we're talking about." He resumed his head massage and stared down at his blotter. "You're probably far too young for this, but have you ever looked back and found the pivot points? The spots where, if only you'd gone left instead of right, everything would be different now?"

"Sometimes."

He raised his face to mine, momentarily surprised, then seemed to slot the pieces together. "Ah. I remember Joey saying you still have nightmares."

"Not as often," I mumbled.

"You dream through all the ways it could have gone wrong, don't you?" I nodded, and an expression quite like sympathy flickered in his weary eyes. "And you will. Maybe for years. Maybe for the rest of your life. You were such a child…"

"I wasn't the only one," I reminded him. "Plenty of folks in town with nightmares, too."

"Mm. Ask Ellie about the Endicott twins sometime. They live with their grandmother, I believe. Still hate to be too close to fire, even candles. An entire generation of Fringers, traumatized in a thousand different ways," he said, slowly shaking his head. "Hunted, injured, orphaned…worse…"

My mind flashed to the rest home in the settlement, where many of Mulligan's hostages still lived, either catatonic or mad, and Coileán seemed to divine the direction of my thoughts. "I did some terrible things to Moyna," he murmured. "Necessary, I thought at the time. Still do. But I understand why she wants me dead."

"What about giving it time?" I asked. "Maybe you two could come to an understanding or—"

"This isn't the sort of difficulty that family therapy can

fix. I might as well ask you to sit down with James Mulligan and work through the sources of friction in your relationship. Throw your grandparents in there, too. Think you could find common ground? Maybe learn to respect each other's point of view?"

I snorted.

"Exactly. I can't see Moyna and me coming to peaceful terms, especially not if she's desperate enough to attack the damn realm, so that means I've at least tacitly agreed to kill her. More than tacitly, I suppose," he muttered as a half-full tumbler of whisky appeared on the desk. "I've been able to avoid this for a while, but we can't let her escape again. Once we find her, we'll have to move quickly. *Decisively*." He took a long sip, wincing as it went down. "Her mother died to save her, did you know that? Stepped between us. Moyna was about to take a shot at Meggy, and Meggy had no idea. I don't really think it would have mattered if she had," he mused, and drank again. "If I kill Moyna now…"

"Meggy's death's in vain?"

"It was always in vain," said Coileán. "But I may as well spit on her grave." He drained the tumbler and lowered it to the blotter, but his hand didn't release its grip on the glass. "Go home, Ros. Stay out of trouble. There's nothing you can do."

I didn't sleep well for the rest of the week. Dad looked more hopeless with every dead end, and Mom was little better than a zombie when Toula forced her back to the house for a few hours of rest every night. Bee, Daisy, Sam, and I tried to keep ourselves entertained and out from underfoot. I showed them around the settlement, and when we'd seen all there was to see, we raided my parents' closet of board games, but those only went so far. We all knew that as tense as we were, starting a long game of Monopoly would only end in tears, and possibly scorch marks.

Friday night, as I stared at the stars on my ceiling and tried to will myself to sleep, I heard someone rapping at my balcony door and sat up in bed. In the moonlight beyond the glass, Sam lifted a hand in greeting, and with a nod and a conspiratorial wink for me, Frank lumbered off behind him. Curious, I untangled myself from the blankets and let him in. "How did you—"

"Frank gave me a lift up a floor," Sam whispered. "I didn't want your parents to think I was sneaking around, and the stairs creak."

"But you *are* sneaking around."

"They don't know that," he replied with a quick grin. "Did I wake you?"

I shook my head and plopped onto the edge of the bed while Sam took in what little of his surroundings he could see. "Wow," he breathed, noticing the thousands of stars on the ceiling. "That's...intense. Did your parents paint that for you?"

"No. Kind of a 'welcome home' gift from Kura," I explained, and patted the comforter beside me. Sam took a seat and fell backward onto the mattress, the better to examine the expanse above us. "Couldn't sleep either, huh?"

"Not feeling it."

We lay side by side in comfortable silence for a few minutes, and I was about to lean over to see if Sam had nodded off when he murmured, "Wonder what Mama would think if she saw me now."

"I don't know. Sneaking into strange girls' bedrooms in the middle of the night?" I teased. "Buddying up to a giant lizard? Drinking *hot* tea? Horrors."

He chuckled briefly and tucked one hand beneath his head. "She'd be glad I'm not alone. It was always the two of us, and you saw how far away the neighbors were. I, uh...I never had many friends growing up. There was Mama and Miss Bonnie, and the Browns were nice, but I knew they thought I was weird. Guess they were right," he muttered. "Mama needed my help, especially when she was sick, so I didn't hang around school too often for clubs or sports and stuff..." He paused, then turned his head my way, and I could just make out the contours of his features as I felt his warm breath against my face. "You're the only real friend I've had until now."

I twined my fingers through his and squeezed. "It'll get better, Sam. I know it will."

"Assuming Moyna and your grandpa don't kill us all, you mean."

"That *is* the working assumption." I glanced at the illuminated ceiling and sighed. "Might just try to sleep. You want to stay here? I think your ride's wandered off."

"I think he's trying to be our wingman," he whispered. "He hasn't exactly been subtle."

"Dragons don't do subtle well," I agreed. "So, since Frank's obviously stranded you up here, want to crash at my place? It's only the polite thing to do."

He grinned and squeezed my hand, then released me and sat up. "Better take the floor. I don't want your folks to kill me in my sleep."

I passed him a pillow and spare blanket, and he stretched out on the thick rug beside me. "That can't be comfortable," I said.

"Beats camping."

Rolling over, I closed my eyes and tried to relax, but before I drifted off, I heard Sam murmur, "Are you scared, Ros?"

"Yeah," I admitted.

And after a long pause, he whispered, "Me, too."

At three-fifteen the next morning—according to my phone's clock, at least, as determining the precise hour in Faerie was always an exercise in guesstimation—I woke to the sound of Sam's ringtone, which, unfortunately, wailed like an emergency siren. He bolted awake and fumbled in his clothing until he found the offender, then answered the call with a mumbled, "Hello?" An instant later, he sat up and wiped the sleep from his eyes. "Miss Bonnie! Hi, how are... You what? Hang on, slow down, I didn't get that..." He listened for a moment, staring through the glass wall at the night beyond my room, then said, "Okay, hold up. I'm with Ros, we're in Faerie right now. Can you tell her what you just said, please?... Gotcha."

Seeing that I was awake and alert, Sam flipped on the phone's speaker and put it on the bed beside me. "She's listening, go ahead."

"You're in danger," said Bonnie, her voice slightly distorted and muffled. "I was calling to warn Sam, but you should hear this, too. In case you were thinking of coming over right now, *don't*."

"We're not going anywhere," I replied, holding his phone closer. "What's wrong?"

"The court's on the move," she replied. "I've been avoiding them ever since they returned from the Gray Lands, but they found me last night with a *summons*"—her tone was sharp was sarcasm—"from our apparent queen. Funny, I'd have thought she could do that without messengers, but what do I know?"

My heart raced. "Where are you? Where are *they*?"

"As to the first, I'm getting the hell away from them as we speak. Can you hear the engines?"

I realized that the odd sounds I was hearing on Bonnie's end came from a plane. "Are you safe in there?"

"For now. I'm going somewhere remote and hoping I'm more trouble than I'm worth. But as for your second question, they're mustering in the Bristol Channel. They've built a fleet and cloaked it, and they're staging now, calling as many of us in as they can find."

"Hang on," I said, hurrying to my desk, and threw open my computer. With a few clicks, I was looking at a map of the UK and its surrounding waterways. "They're going to attack Glastonbury?"

"That would be my first thought," said Bonnie. "I didn't know if Sam was still in this realm, but since you're both over there, stay put. If you know anyone in the Glastonbury installation, you might want to warn them to batten the hatches and get whatever shields they have up and running."

"Come over," said Sam, taking the phone from me. "No need to run to Timbuktu. Why don't you just jump over here?"

"Not without permission, sweetheart," she replied. "If your aunt or Coileán guarantees safe passage, then I'll think about it, but you should know that trespassing seldom ends well. Be safe, Sammy," she added, her voice softening. "And I'm so sorry about Audra's passing. I'd have been there for you, hon, but Moyna's been scouting for a while, and I didn't want to take a chance of leading the court to your doorstep."

"Thanks," he murmured, tightening his grip on the phone. "You be careful, now, okay? I'm going to get whatever clearance you need, and I'll call back."

By the time he hung up, I'd thrown on jeans and a jacket. "Come on," I said, shoving my shoes on, "we're going to Coileán."

"You think he'll let Miss Bonnie—"

"I don't know, but he needs to hear about the fleet off the coast. He'll forgive us if we wake—"

That was as far as I got before a flash, bright as an exploding sun, ripped apart the starlit sky outside my room. The ground began to tremble, and as I cried out and tumbled into Sam, I heard Kura's voice in my head—wordless, high, and screaming in pain. I held my hands over my ears, trying in vain to block out her shrieks, and when they finally faded, I realized I was hyperventilating on top of Sam on the rug.

"It's over, it's over," he soothed, holding me, then helped me sit up. "What they heck *was* that?"

"Kura," I said, dazed and wondering why I wasn't deaf. "Didn't you hear her?"

"Hear what?"

"Never mind. We've got to go." I picked myself off the floor and opened a gate into the hall outside Coileán's office, security protocol be damned. Hurrying through, I started pounding on the door and yelled, "Coileán! It's Ros! I know where Moyna is!" When that garnered no response, I jiggled the doorknob, found that it turned, and let myself in. "Uh…my lord? Coil—oh, *shit*," I muttered, and ran toward his desk.

The king was slumped over his blotter—at first glance, the logical result of his recent heavier-than-usual alcohol consumption. But his torso lay at an odd angle, nothing conducive to sleep, and one hand still rested atop his ear. He'd been trying to block the screaming, too, I deduced, and fearing the worst, I reached under his jaw to feel for a pulse.

That was how Val found me when he appeared seconds later. "Alive," I said before he could draw a dangerous conclusion about the cause of Coileán's unconsciousness. "He's out cold, but he's breathing."

Val pushed me aside and levitated him onto one of the couches, then sat on the coffee table and started patting at his face. "Coileán. *Coileán*," he insisted, "wake up, something's happened…"

It took him a moment, but the king's eyes finally fluttered. "Wha—" he mumbled, and groaned as he tried to sit up. "What…what was…"

"I don't know," said Val. "Something exploded in the sky, and the ground shook—"

"And Kura screamed," I interrupted, leaning over the back of the couch. "I'm not imagining that part, am I? Sam didn't hear anything…"

Val frowned. "Neither did I."

But Coileán looked up at me and nodded. "Loud and clear. *Too* loud and clear. I knew she could give me a headache, but I didn't realize she could knock me out," he said, and let Val pull him into a sitting position. "Ugh. At least she's gone quiet," he began, then froze and stared into space, stricken with a sudden realization. "Moon and stars, I can't hear her."

"That's a...bad thing?" Sam guessed.

"Bad. Very bad." He wobbled to his feet, bracing himself against Val's shoulder. "Feels like I've been hit by a train. Exhausted. *Weak.*"

Val's expression began to mirror Coileán's as he understood. "The power—"

"The boost is gone," he muttered. "I...I'm just me. Val, *I'm just me.*"

The captain gripped his arms before Coileán could panic. "Maybe the realm is gathering her strength. Surely this is temporary."

But the look on Coileán's face confirmed my fear. "She's not doing anything," I murmured, fighting my rising dread. "She's *gone.*"

The king and queen's saving grace was that no one, save the two of them, Aiden, and me, seemed to have heard Kura's exit. But that was the sole good news. Eleanor was as wobbly as Coileán, and even Aiden, who'd enjoyed only a small boost of the realm's power, felt hungover with its loss. While the three of them compared notes, Val and Nico plotted in the corner of Coileán's office, making arrangements to tighten security on their ailing lord and lady and to reinforce any enchantments currently drawing upon the monarchs' strength. It went without saying that if the courts got wind of the fact that their sovereigns had lost the extra power that allowed them to force the rest of Faerie into line, all hell would break loose. Sure, the two of them weren't *young*, but even Nico was six hundred years older than Coileán, and in a straight contest, Val could have wiped the floor with the lot of them that night—and he was by no means the eldest in the realm.

As the clock on the wall ticked toward dawn and Eleanor took Coileán up on his offer of scotch, I perched on a window ledge with Sam and racked my brain for a solution. Sam's arm had migrated around my shoulders, which I appreciated, but I was too distracted to truly enjoy our proximity.

Why *me*?

Of course Eleanor and Coileán had heard Kura in her agonizing moment of departure—that was a given. And since Aiden had been the beneficiary of her largesse, it made sense that he'd also be more tied to her than most. But what about me? In a weird sense, Kura had always been a bit like my faerie godmother, warping me to make sure that my mixed blood would be no impediment to my talent, opening gates into Faerie for me before I could be trusted to do so myself, and occasionally popping by with the odd piece of advice. I wouldn't call her a friend, exactly, but we had a relationship.

Maybe she'd panicked, I mused. She'd reached out to her default audience, and then, grasping at straws, she'd called to me instead of someone useful.

I broke from my reverie when a shadow fell across my lap, then looked up to find Val beside us. "Go home," he said softly. "There is nothing you can do now. Try to rest."

"What's the plan, then?" Sam asked. "Are they, uh…"

Val followed his gaze to the couches, then turned back to us and barely shook his head. "No change. Nico and I have this much, at least, under control. As for what comes next…" He offered a one-shouldered shrug. "Once we know what our opponents want, we can form a real plan. Until then, the plan is to wait—and to keep this quiet," he added, giving us a look that promised a world of hurt if we disobeyed.

I glanced out the window behind me, but there wasn't even a hint of morning, and with reluctance, I slid off my ledge. "You'll let me know if there's something I can do, right?" I asked Val.

He squeezed my shoulder in reply. "Rest. I'm sure Frank is wondering where you've gone—"

The crack of an opening gate echoed around the office, and the room turned toward the well-stocked bar and the rapidly widening hole in reality beside it. By the time it had opened sufficiently to allow a man passage, Nico and Val had their swords drawn and fire at the ready, and half a dozen guards were running into the room, shielding. Outclassed, I pulled Sam away from the gate and as far as I could go before the newcomer arrived—which, unfortunately, only meant behind Coileán's desk.

As the gate stabilized, a youthful blonde came striding into the office, a woman who would have been of average height were it not for the three-inch blood-red boots she wore beneath her black trousers. A red blouse completed the ensemble, and she'd carried the color scheme into her cosmetics, opting for dark, overly winged eyeliner and vampiric lips that smirked as her pale blue eyes lighted on the king.

While the guards clustered around Coileán and Eleanor, the rest of the woman's party filed into the room—a variety of men and women at first, all certainly fae, and then faces I knew from my nightmares: the remaining Mulligans, Antony's aunt, Silas's and Lyle's parents...

My grandparents. Older, grayer in Grandpa's case, still bottle-blonde in Grandma's. Both, like the rest of the Arcanum contingent, wore the tactical black of the assassin corps.

And then, bringing up the rear in a well-pressed blue robe and wingtips, came Bert.

The red-booted blonde waited until the last of them had come through, then planted her hands on her hips and turned toward the wall of guards. "Hello, Coileán," she said, the picture of mocking triumph. "Miss me?"

"Ros," Sam hissed in my ear, "who the hell is that, and

what's Bert doing?"

The longer I looked at the crowd, the more I felt as though I'd been sucker-punched, but I couldn't pull myself away. "Those would be some of the missing wizards," I murmured, counting and recounting them. "I'm pretty sure that's Moyna. And Bert's played us for fools."

CHAPTER 14

A ring of fireballs materialized in the guards' hands, but Moyna waggled a finger and *tsk*ed. "You don't want to do that," she said, even as her own apparent guards took up positions near her. "You see, if anything happens to me, the realm dies."

"Hold," Val muttered, but before he could give the next order, Coileán pushed through the line and showed her his empty hands.

"What have you done?" he asked with forced calm.

"Isn't it obvious?" she replied, smiling. "Quite a boom on the other side. I assume it was at least noticeable over here, but...well," she said, shrugging, "I would have thought you'd noticed *something* by now."

He didn't break eye contact with her. "What did you do to the realm?"

"Took her on a little vacation. She hasn't been out in so long, my friends and I thought she was overdue. Don't worry, she's perfectly safe...for the moment."

"You're playing with fire," he said through gritted teeth. "If something happens to her—"

"I'm well aware," she interrupted, crossing her arms, and glanced at Grandpa. "Magus Carver has informed me of the risks in great detail. If she's killed, if she's away for too long..." She smiled again. "Curtains, yes?"

By then, Eleanor had shoved her way to the front as well. "And that will hurt you as much as it hurts us, you stupid cow! You can't mean to—"

"Relax, Ellie. She'll be just fine." Moyna's smile

hardened. "You see, I know the two of you won't let anything happen to your little pet."

"She's not a *pet*—" Coileán began, but Moyna lifted her hand to silence him.

"Semantics. I know she's important to you, so you'll do this my way. Of course, if I'm wrong, well, what's my loss? I've been denied my birthright all this time, and my associates here were bound," she said, gesturing toward the wizards. "You know I can't abide that, Coileán. At least *they* were allowed to keep their minds intact, unlike some of us."

"Moyna," he tried, "I was wrong. I'm sorry."

"I don't care. But as I was saying, we've all been denied power—if you lose it, too, we're no worse off than we were."

Flabbergasted, he sputtered for a response, but Eleanor stepped into the breach. "Your terms, then, for her safe return?"

"So glad you asked," Moyna replied. "Nice to see at least one of you has a grain of sense. You did back the wrong horse, Ellie, but maybe we can work together after all—with the necessary concessions, of course."

As the rest of the room watched, Moyna slipped through her party to Coileán's bar, where she helped herself to a tumbler of aged rum. "Smooth," she announced, closing her eyes as it went down. "I think I'll enjoy that bottle."

"Your *terms*," Eleanor snapped.

"Patience, old girl. This is thirsty work," she retorted, and carried the glass with her back to the head of her pack. "My terms are simple. Coileán will surrender, abdicate in my favor, and leave Faerie. If he's a good boy, I'll bring your little friend back. If he declines, I'll kill her myself."

Eleanor turned to Coileán, who seemed oddly unbothered by Moyna's declaration. "You know as well as I do that abdication may not be possible," he told his daughter. "It's up to the realm. It's never *been* done. So even if I stroll off into the sunset, you may not get the court."

Her little smile didn't waiver. "If abdication doesn't work, I know of an alternative that will." She sipped her drink again, eyes twinkling. "It's so *nice* being an only child."

He sighed and spread his hands. "Moyna, I made mistakes. I thought I was doing the right thing, giving you a fresh start—"

She coughed into her rum, then dropped the tumbler onto the stone floor, sending shards of glass and splashes of alcohol in all directions. "A *fresh start?*" she cried. "You murdered my mother, you stole my *soul* from me, and you left me with your whore, bound and powerless! In what delusion of yours is that a fresh start?" She took three long strides across the room, and with the help of her boots, she could almost look him dead in the eye as she glowered. "I'm going to enjoy this, Coileán. Every second of it. Maybe it won't stop those lovely nightmares you've given me—you know, the ones where Mother screams as that sword burns its way into her back? And don't try to tell me that it wasn't your fault, Ironhand—you might not have held the hilt, but I know it was your plan."

"It wasn't, actually," he murmured. "I was prepared to surrender—anything to save you and Meggy. But she set your uncle on fire. Kind of forced my hand, there."

"Rationalize it however you like—it doesn't matter to me." She stepped back and held out her palm as another tumbler appeared, then took a test sip. "Close. I'm getting the hang of this, you know. I'm sure it'll be much simpler once I'm queen."

"Trust me," Eleanor muttered, "*nothing* is simple about being queen."

"We'll see," Moyna replied with a grin, then cocked her glass toward Coileán in mock salute. "And I'll even give you a parting gift. I'll return tomorrow at dawn for your decision. Take the day. Decide what's truly important to you, Coileán." She paused, and her smile slid into a smirk. "Settle your affairs."

Without another word, the invaders retreated through their gate, and Val slammed it closed behind them. "My lord," he began, turning to Coileán, but the king shook his head and sank onto a couch.

"Aiden?" he muttered, and waited until my uncle hurried near. "You know who to call."

Sam and I weren't exactly part of the king and queen's inner emergency circle—honestly, most of them looked at us like we weren't even adults—but since no one insisted that we leave, we lingered in the office as it filled and new furniture appeared to accommodate the crowd.

Whatever phone tree Aiden had set up resulted in an odd mix: Toula, naturally, and my parents, plus Vivi, Dr. Stowe and Poppy, Slim, Mr. Galloway, Father Paul, and Kuni, the piq permanent envoy. The gate in the bookcase had been widened to let Badger and Seamus in on the discussion, and to my surprise, Aiden left a phone on speaker in the middle of the table—whatever differences the courts and the Company had, someone still thought Tanner needed to be looped in. Seemingly half of the combined guards ringed the walls of the office, but Val and Nico clustered close to the center, along with their seconds. I didn't know Nico's, but I recognized Mina, one of Coileán's few remaining nieces.

"Your intel is good," said Tanner's phone-distorted voice. "We got visual confirmation ten minutes ago. They're still off the coast near Glastonbury."

Slim frowned. "I would have thought they'd glamour up…"

"Oh, they did. We got within the perimeter. Three ships, currently anchored and connected to each other. No idea of the personnel—that's going to take a little more work to get someone on board—but my agent counted three dozen of them on deck."

"Thank your agent for us," said Eleanor, leaning closer to the phone. "And add it to our tab, I suppose."

Tanner snorted. "Moyna's bad news for us, too, so this is on the house. I'll be back if I get anything useful in time," he added, and ended the call.

With Tanner out, the conversation segued from English into Fae. "All right," Eleanor said, going to her feet, "thoughts. I don't care how ridiculous. How do we defeat them?"

For a long, drawn moment, the room was silent but for the ticking of the wall clock.

"Just an idea," said Father Paul, "but since we know where they are, why don't you go after them now? Or wait for darkness, hit them then?"

"There's the slight problem of the realm to consider," Val explained. "We can't take a chance of bringing her to harm."

"What about the merrow?" Dad suggested. "Are there any that far north?"

"Probably," Coileán muttered, nursing a well-laced cup of coffee.

"Okay, so we wait for the Company to figure out the numbers, maybe find our hostage, then send the merrow after them with...I don't know, chainsaws or whatever."

Aiden's eyebrow rose. "*Chainsaws?*"

"Spitballing, here. Harpoons. Sea mines. Something to blow holes in the ships and take out the survivors."

"That would be suicide," said Nico, shaking his head. "They're defenseless against magic, and Grivam isn't going to send his people to their deaths unless he's desperate."

Mr. Galloway raised a finger. "We could pull Moyna over by herself with one of those summoning thingies. I mean, it worked on you, Colin."

"Yeah, but I wasn't hiding," the king replied.

"Summoners only work if the target is exposed," Toula told Mr. Galloway. "Whatever spell she has on her that's blocking traces and such will block a summoner, too…" She paused as a thought hit, then added in a rush, "But Moyna came across the border, so all spells on her broke, and if we act quickly—"

"Doubtful," Mom interrupted, shaking her head. "If Dad's hidden her this long, he's not going to be sloppy now."

"There's still a chance," she retorted, rising, and headed for the hallway. "I'll be in my apartment."

When the door slammed behind her, Coileán looked at Val, who barely nodded. "Can't you feel it?" the captain murmured. "She's terrified."

"Just making sure I wasn't projecting," said Coileán, and sighed as he rubbed his head. "Unless Toula's able to drag Moyna over with a summoner and let us set up our own hostage situation, we don't have a viable plan. Even that one might fail, depending on how fond of her the shadow court is." He grimaced as he pressed on his temples. "The bottom line is that the realm must be protected at all costs. That's not negotiable. If we lose her, we lose Faerie, we lose all magic in…what, a few weeks?"

"Probably," said Eleanor. "And Nath will certainly find out before then."

"So that's it for the mortal realm, too." He sat up straight and looked around the circle. "We can't risk that. Unless we stumble onto a miracle between now and tomorrow morning, I won't call Moyna's bluff. Let her have the court—I'm not worth that loss."

"Come on, Coileán," Aiden protested, "let's not be hasty about this. Even if the realm lets you abdicate, you know Moyna will turn around and kill you."

"I'm well aware," he replied, and looked at Eleanor. "Which is why I'm asking you to protect the Fringe settlement. God only knows what she'd do to them, especially if Mulligan's people are whispering in her ear. Move them, hide them, whatever it takes, but—"

"Of course," she murmured, and squeezed his hand.

"We'll get an evacuation order out within the hour," Vivi offered, and her brother nodded emphatically. "Kids and anyone who can afford to lose the years should probably get out. I hate to move the Minor Arcanum again—I mean, we *just* got them situated—"

"They're safer now in the other realm," said Poppy. "And they have homes to return to. Give me the phone," she said, beckoning toward the coffee table, "let me talk to Adler. If he's feeling generous, maybe he'll open a safehouse for the Fringe kids."

Dr. Stowe watched as Slim passed her the phone, then quietly said, "It's a good idea, sweetie, but do you think you're the best person to negotiate with him?"

She arched a brow in challenge. "Remind me, dear, which of us has a Company pedigree?"

"I'm just saying—"

"He fired me. I still speak his language," she retorted, and followed the path Toula had blazed to make the call in another room. "If I don't get any traction with him, my next call is to Mom and Dad, because I'm sure as hell not leaving Malcolm here to square off with Moyna."

Dr. Stowe frowned at the pronouncement. "You think they'd shelter him?"

"*I* may be the black sheep of the Kane clan, Rufe," said Poppy, walking backward, "but if the last, oh, two decades of unanswered messages are any indication, they'll take him with open arms. And before you get any ideas, he's *twelve*, and there's no way I'm letting him stay here."

"Evacuate him," Eleanor interjected before Dr. Stowe could reply. "Absolutely. And anyone else who will go."

"Now," said Coileán, pointing to Aiden, Dad, and Val, "I have one last job for you, if you'll take it."

"Coileán," Aiden tried again, but was silenced with an upraised hand.

"Once the realm is safe...once Moyna has the court," he continued, looking each in the eye, "I'm asking you to eliminate her. Do whatever it takes. You probably won't be able to get to her immediately, but you all know how effective a sword and a good nail gun can be."

"You're talking suicide!" Aiden sputtered.

"Not for you." He grabbed Aiden's wrist and held his gaze. "The realm gave you a king's power before. You know how to wield it. When you have the opportunity, *take the court*. Lead it again."

"But—"

"I have far more faith in you than I do in her," said Coileán. "And once Moyna's out, you're the natural heir. You can do this, Aiden."

Struggling for words, he looked down at his brother's hand on his arm, then back at Coileán, and finally said, "They won't follow me again, I'm not you—"

"*Good*. And they will follow you," he replied, cutting his eyes to Val. "You'll have help, I hope."

Val's head bobbed silently, but Aiden didn't give up. "You don't have to do this," he tried. "*Don't* do this. Coileán…"

Aiden's voice petered out as Coileán stood, then pulled him to his feet and hugged him tightly. "I love you, little brother," he murmured. "And I'm counting on you to follow through with the plan."

"It's a shit plan," Aiden replied.

"Best I've got right now." Coileán pulled back and gripped Aiden's shoulders. "But we've got the day, and I'm all ears."

The ticking clock was less of a help than a mockery, however. Sam and I stayed close, doing what little we could to assist the Archives review team and occasionally drifting toward Coileán's office to listen for updates, but there were no flashes of brilliance, no friendly deities descending from the rafters. The only good news was that the Company proved willing to lend a hand to the refugees, and over the course of the afternoon, the Stowe brothers saw to it that all children and the newcomers were evacuated to one of the Company's facilities high in the Rocky Mountains. Last to go was Malcolm Stowe, but unlike the others, he was sent to meet his grandparents, who had been forcibly retired from the Company years before with the rest of the lupine shifters. Vivi, who had seen her young nephew off, returned to Aiden's suite with the full report.

"The Kanes cried," she said, settling in for her shift. "*All* of them. Poppy's parents fussed over Mal, they fussed over Poppy through the gate, they fussed *at* Rufe for cradle robbing before deciding they were happier as grandparents, and then they fussed at him to keep her safe." She shook her head as she logged in. "That's one way to meet your in-laws, I guess."

The afternoon brought no progress, and our pilfered files were no help. By nightfall, Antony had agreed to join the rest of us at my parents' place—there was imagined security, if not safety, in numbers, and we hadn't been thrown out of Faerie yet—and so I headed for Coileán's office to let him know, on the off chance that he'd come looking for us that night. But as I rounded the corner, I heard his muffled voice through the cracked door to a sitting room, and then Toula's reply came through loud and clear: "There's another possibility, I just need time—"

"You need to go to safety," said Coileán as I shamelessly pressed my eye to the gap. "Badger and Seamus will give you a bed, you know that."

"I am *not* leaving you." Her voice sounded thicker than normal, and I didn't think I'd imagined the hitch I'd heard in it. "This isn't over. We're not giving up, we've got the night—"

Coileán cut her off with a long kiss, and Toula gave as good as she got. When they parted, he brushed her bangs from her face and gave her a sad smile. "Let it go, Glinda. I want you safe."

"Not your call, Gramps."

It was Toula who leaned in first that time, and with no less urgency. As they separated again, they continued to hold each other in the candlelit room, neither speaking for the space of half a dozen slow breaths. When Toula spoke again, her voice was low. "I'm coming with you."

"What do you mean?"

"I mean that I'm going to assume the realm will let you step down and Moyna will let you go unharmed, and I'm leaving with you. Someone needs to watch your back, and it's not like she's going to let me keep my apartment here."

"Toula—"

She put a finger to his lips. "Don't. I'll pack my things, and I'll plan to be in a hotel with you tomorrow night. Once our brothers have taken care of business on their end, you'll be safe again."

"Toula," Coileán murmured, "you have to—"

"And if I'm wrong," she continued over his protestations, fighting angry tears, "then I'll kill the little bitch myself, for you and Megs both. Took out a queen once, and I'll do it again if I have to."

"I know." He pulled her against his chest and sighed into her hair. "If this goes wrong, you'll have a place with Ellie. She promised." Toula said nothing, and Coileán rubbed her back. "Don't cry over me. I've had better than eight centuries—that's far more years than I should have had, all things considered," he said with a slight chuckle.

"But I've only had you for fifteen of those years," she mumbled, "and I'm not ready to end this just yet."

"Nor am I." He hesitated, then added, "But if it's ended for us tomorrow…I'm grateful for what we've had."

I slipped away then before I could see more, in part to give them their privacy, but also because the sight of tears on Toula's face scared me more than I cared to admit.

When I got home, I found our crew in the barn, sitting glumly on hay bales near Frank and picking at dinner. "Your parents are packing," said Bee, handing me a covered plate. "They're going into the backcountry with

Aiden to start working on a counterstrike."

"Already?" I asked, lifting the makeshift cloche. Gran's fried chicken steamed beside a mound of mashed potatoes and gravy—comfort food if I'd ever seen it—but it couldn't tempt my stomach, and I put the plate aside. "What about us?"

"They tried to make us evacuate, but I'm not going anywhere."

"Likewise," said Daisy. "The Fringers who didn't leave are being moved into the queen's mansion tonight. Bee and I are going to help guard them. Antony, you'd better come, too," she said, and I saw his shoulders tense before she added, "I'm sure it wouldn't hurt to have another wand at the door."

"Same goes for you two," said Bee, nodding to Sam and me. "How about it, Sam, party at your aunt's place?"

"Sounds like fun," he replied with a snort. "Ros, you in?"

But I shook my head. "They're going to need bodies in the front lines tomorrow, and even if I can't take on the shadow court by myself, I can make the wizards' lives difficult."

Want help?

"Thanks, bud," I said, patting Frank's leg. "And if they're stupid enough to keep a gate open, we may even have sufficient dark magic inflow for a barbeque."

Or I could just eat them raw. I don't mind.

Whatever small appetite I might have had disappeared with *that* thought, and I plopped onto a bale with the others. "So, who's planning to sleep tonight?"

Antony pointed to the far end of the barn, where Rego and Zafira were tangled up in a post-dinner nap, snoring like an avalanche. "Depends on whether anyone has access to earplugs."

Bee muttered until several pairs of orange foam bits appeared in her palm. "Here," she said, passing a set to Antony. "Try to sleep. Whatever happens, tomorrow should be a long day."

Though the house was still and empty, no one wanted to be alone that night, and so we made camp in the barn, pulling cots from the ether and blocking out the draconic cacophony as necessary. Having long since grown numb to it, I bedded down closest to Frank's head and let his snorts and rumbles lull me to sleep. Still, even his nightly noises weren't enough to deafen me to the shrill chiming of my phone when it went off in the wee hours, and I almost fell off my cot in my rush to locate the source of the sound before I remembered what was still in my pocket. Picking the sleep from my eyes, I opened the line and mumbled, "Hello?"

"I can't talk long," said a familiar voice in a rushed whisper, "so listen, yeah?"

"Bert," I growled, swinging my legs over the side of the cot and going to my feet. "You fucking little weasel—"

"*Listen*," he insisted. "They've got my mum and dad. I'm playing along to save their lives, that's all. I'm not working with them!"

"Right, sure. Going to sell me a bridge next?"

He huffed in frustration. "Seriously, I have five minutes, tops. This spell is a pain to hold together, and if they find out I've rung you, I'm dead. Please listen, Ros."

I wanted nothing more than to curse him with every bit of profanity in my vocabulary, but the edge of fear in his voice suggested he might just be telling the truth. "Talk," I muttered.

Bert didn't waste time with pleasantries. "Moyna's got a little fleet, and we're off the coast—"

"Bristol Channel, yeah."

"You've heard, then. I'm on the flagship. There's maybe three hundred here, faeries and wizards both. My parents are being held in the brig until this is over."

"So you're helping them. Just like the Harrisons."

"I'm trying to sabotage them, if you'll let me finish," he snapped. "By the time I got home, they'd taken my parents. I sent word to Grand Magus Lowe to keep him apprised of the situation before I met my *escort*." The word dripped with sarcasm. "My job is to step aside and name Russell Mulligan my successor once the situation in Faerie is sorted."

With at least one life on the line, Bert's phrasing could have been better, but I let it slide. "That's going to go over well."

"Not as well as you're envisioning, I'm sure. Pardoning the probationers and making them magi again are two very different matters. But if Russell walks in with Moyna at his back, who's going to stand in their way?"

"All part and parcel of the backscratching, I take it?" I asked.

"From what I've gathered. Grace Mulligan hid Moyna's court using your grandfather's techniques, and once they realized the possibilities in the Magus's diary, they pulled together this plan. The wizards do the necessary casting, the faeries power the enterprise, and once Moyna's settled, she'll back Russell. Or so she says."

I could almost see the tiny smile in his voice. "You've heard otherwise?"

"After my first night in the guesthouse, that Rufus fellow offered me the local tongue. I've been playing dumb around the ship, so I've probably overheard more than I was intended to hear. Let's just say that the court's assessment of Russell as a magus worthy of respect leaves much to be desired."

"You think Moyna will backstab him?" I pressed. It wasn't much in the way of good news, but that night, I was ready to grasp at anything.

"Maybe. I can't imagine she'll have any further need of his support once she's crowned, or whatever it is you people do." Bert hesitated, then said, "Before you ask, I can't attack Moyna. She's protected, I'm outclassed by her security, and if something should happen to the hostage…"

His voice faded, and hate it though I did, he had a valid point. "How is she?"

"I can't get close to her. She's in the brig, too, but she's well guarded. I'm sorry, Ros, I truly am, but I can't—"

"I know," I said curtly, cutting his apology short. "Be careful over there."

"You, too." He paused again, longer that time, then asked, "Is there a plan? They're not just conceding, are they?" I gave no reply, and Bert sighed. "Don't trust me, do you?"

"Or your spellcraft."

"Touché. You know, I didn't get this job for my good looks…oh, shit, someone's coming," he muttered, and the line went dead.

Surrounded by snoring dragons and my fitfully sleeping friends, I looked at the silent phone, considering who needed to hear of Bert's call first. Coileán, of course…but remembering my last glimpse of him and Toula that afternoon, I stayed my finger. There was no telling what he was doing that night, and nothing Bert had said was so earth-shattering that it warranted disturbing him. My parents were already out with Aiden, making preparations for Moyna's predicted takeover, which left only one choice.

Five minutes later, having picked the hay from my hair, I pounded on Val's door and waited, hoping I wasn't waking him. I had only a few seconds to fret before he opened the door and let a glowing orb float overhead, illuminating the night-dark hallway of the guards' quarters. His eyes were troubled but alert, and something told me he hadn't touched his bed. "Ros?" he asked.

"Bert called. May I—"

He stepped back from the threshold and ushered me inside, and when the door was latched behind us, I recounted my recent conversation. When I finished, Val perched on the edge of his desk and folded his arms. "It's not much good news," he said, "and it won't help Coileán.

But if Moyna is foolish enough to break faith with her Arcanum supporters, then perhaps there's hope for the mortal realm yet. With Eleanor's help, together..." His shoulders slumped. "But that's a question for another day. What are your plans for the morning?"

"Frank and I will be there," I replied, leaning against the wall. "And Sam. Bee, Daisy, and Antony are going over to Eleanor's to guard the remaining Fringe."

"Mm. And assuming no one has a flash of brilliance between now and sunrise, what do you plan to do once Moyna takes the court? You can't stay here," he said as I struggled for an answer. "Your parents and Aiden can take care of themselves in the wilds for now, and your grandparents will be somewhat safe with the Fringe, I trust, but you're young enough to flee. Take the others and hide in the mortal realm for now. Go to Rigby," he suggested. "Seamus and Badger may not have all the answers, but they've played this game. If nothing else, there's safety in numbers."

"If you're trying to get me out before this goes down—"

"No. I'm not fighting another lost cause tonight," he said as he walked across the office for his sword belt. "But before Moyna begins any planned purging, I want you out of this realm, child."

As he tightened the belt, he pulled the leather-wrapped hilt of the sword a few inches free of its scabbard, and I frowned at the silvery glint of steel instead of his customary bronze. "What are you doing with—"

"Desperate times," he muttered, putting the blade back in place. "Your father has quite a collection." Satisfied with his backup weapon, he threw on a gray cloak against the predawn wind and beckoned for me to follow him out. "I'm going to Eleanor's for a quick inspection," he explained as we walked through the quiet palace. "Nico and the best of their guards will be with the queen, and if they want reinforcements from ours, I need to know now.

The girls and Antony are there already?"

"No, sleeping in the barn," I replied, half-jogging to keep up with his quick steps. "Should I wake them?"

Val paused beside a window, considered the starlit sky, then nodded. "The sooner everyone is in position, the better I'll feel. Wake them, please."

I wondered why he didn't just open a gate to the mansion until I realized he was directing us toward the kitchen. "Here," he said, thrusting a whole loaf of Astrid's secret-recipe honey wheat into my arms. "Breakfast. Share this with the others...and this," he added, pulling jars of her preserves from one of the pantry cabinets. "You need to eat."

"Val—"

"I will meet you back here," he said, squeezing my shoulder, "though if you wanted to please me, the lot of you would be well on your way to Virginia by the time Moyna arrives."

"Sorry," I murmured, meeting his stare. "Not yet. And hey, I might be useful—I mean, I've had a pretty decent coach," I said, trying to smile.

His grip tightened briefly in acknowledgement. "It's been my pleasure. But I can't give you the years and the strength you'd need to hold your own against her best. Stay well back from the front line and keep your shield ready."

He opened a gate in the middle of the kitchen, but I stopped him before he could depart. "Will you serve her?" I blurted. "Moyna?"

His answer was immediate. "No. Nor will most of the guards."

"But if she's leading Mab's court—"

"*That* is not Mab's court," he said, silencing me. "That court is broken and scattered. She's nothing but a rebel at the head of a band of rebels, and any claim she makes to Mab's throne is utterly baseless. Besides, I made my choice," he continued, snagging another unguarded loaf from the breadbox. "Even if she were Mab herself, that's not my court."

"What if it were?" I countered, rushing to get the words out as inspiration struck. "If you took the throne, they'd have to listen to you, and you could call this off—"

"It doesn't work like that," he said, and my heart sank. "The realm gives power to Coileán and Eleanor because she recognizes those courts. She refuses to acknowledge Mab's, so even if I wanted it, which I do *not*, I wouldn't have the power to force compliance. And seeing as no one has any extra power at the moment, this is all a moot point. I'm sorry," he murmured, and turned again to go. "Wake the others. Morning will be here sooner than I'd like."

CHAPTER 15

By the time the first pink rays of dawn blazed over the horizon, our battle lines were drawn. Eleanor had sent the entire Stowe clan to the mansion to fatten the defensive ranks guarding the vulnerable Fringers inside, many of whom were too weak to do more than attempt to shield. But though they were magically deficient, most had at least competency with a weapon or two, and so the innermost rooms of the mansion bristled with swords and guns. After much persuasion, Toula had agreed to join them. It was obvious that she didn't want to leave Coileán, but he, Eleanor, and Val eventually coaxed her into putting distance between herself and Moyna. Val seemed relieved to see her go, but Coileán stared at the place where her gate had been for a few seconds after it sealed, and I wondered if he had seen his last of her.

My parents and Aiden had checked in with Val by phone shortly before daybreak from their mountain camp. The dragons had made it out there safely—all but Frank, who remained with me—and ringed their cabin, a first line of defense for the counter-strike team. Val and Nico knew the way to them, and if the morning went as badly as we feared it might, Val would be on his way to the cabin to plot before Moyna knew he was gone...or so we hoped.

As for me, though I'd promised my parents that I'd run from Faerie if the situation turned dire, I continued to wait and hold out hope for a stroke of brilliance. While the guards shuffled on the palace lawn, I perched at the base of Frank's neck with Sam, whom I'd been unable to persuade to join the rest of our pack at the mansion. Sure, Sam was fairly useless as faeries went, but I felt better with his arm snaked around my waist—and despite my nerves, part of me insisted that if we survived the morning, I wasn't going to wait for Sam to make the first move. A louder part of me chastised my libido for interrupting at a time like that, but I couldn't help myself—I was scared and taut as a drawn bow, and Sam's warm presence at my back was a comfort.

We held our positions as the light cycled through orange, then yellow, and finally, as the morning fully dawned across the palace, a massive gate ripped open by the doors, and Moyna marched through with a score of her followers. She'd chosen a strange dress for the occasion, a black number heavy on the leather that ended above her knees in the front and trailed behind her in a yard-long shadow-like train, and the wind and rising sun turned her pale hair into a blazing white corona. She took her time crossing the lawn to greet us, her dark lips curved into a satisfied smirk, and I gripped my saddle horn so hard that my knuckles bleached. All thoughts of Sam were forgotten as my brain shouted a new mantra: *do something think of something stop her do something.*

In my distress, I felt Frank's mind connect with mine, and then a sudden wave of calm broke over me. It certainly wasn't my emotion, and it didn't last more than a moment, but I patted his neck in thanks for the effort.

When she was well within hailing range, Moyna pointed at Eleanor and laughed. "Glad you could join us, Ellie," she called. "Wanted to see what a real queen looks like?"

Arms folded across her sensible blue twinset, Eleanor stood stiffly beside Coileán, ignoring the bait.

But Moyna was undaunted by her silence. "We'll have such fun, we girls," she continued, never breaking her stride. "Perhaps we can even come to an understanding. It's not too late to join me," she added, spreading her hands. "Late is better than never. I'm sure even you can see that."

"Go to hell," said Eleanor, enunciating without raising her voice.

Moyna laughed again and shook her head as if she were witnessing the antics of a surly child. "Still sore over your doddering little boyfriend? I did you a favor. What good is an old mortal, anyway?"

Coileán stepped between them before Eleanor could explode. "Where is she?"

"Perfectly safe."

"Show me."

She paused a few feet from the pair, then sighed and motioned over her shoulder. The edges of the gate began to shimmer, and I watched as it drifted toward them, giving them a clear view of what awaited on the other side. Soon, even I could see Moyna's prize—and there was no mistaking Kura.

She wasn't glowing anymore, and though she looked more solid than I'd ever seen her, she seemed smaller, frailer, a bird too weak to fly. Her blonde hair, usually styled in flowing waves, fell around her thin shoulders like a dirty mop. Given the stiffness of its clumps, I guessed that someone had given Kura an unwanted bath with a bucket of seawater. She wore a stained gray sleeveless smock that left her legs and bare feet exposed, and I saw hints of discoloration on her face and limbs—bruises, almost certainly. I was too far away to get a clear view of the spell binding her, but she stood tantalizingly close to the gate. One step across would be all it would take to break her bonds.

Unfortunately, her captors had taken precautions. Beyond binding her wrists and ankles with ropes, a group of wizards kept her pinned in the center of a ring of steel swords that closed around her once Coileán and Eleanor had an opportunity to see that she was still alive.

Moyna turned away from the gate and shrugged. "As I said, perfectly safe. Now, Ironhand, have you given any consideration to my terms?"

I couldn't see the look on Coileán's face, but his voice remained strong. "I have."

"And?"

"You swear by all you hold dear that you will break the spell on the realm and restore her if I abdicate?"

Her smirk shifted toward a triumphant smile. "I swear it by my life…and my throne," she added, looking more pleased by the second. "So—do we have a deal?"

I held my breath, willing Coileán to say anything but *yes*…

…and in an instant, the world around me went black.

I gasped and flailed until I recognized the void and my lone companion: Kura, unbound but still disheveled, her bruises even more pronounced with our sudden proximity. "We don't have much time," she said, taking my hand to steady me. "This is the space between instants, Ros. I cannot hold us here indefinitely, not in my current condition."

Overjoyed and awash with relief, I threw my arms around her, and she winced as I squeezed. "Oh—sorry," I said, withdrawing. "You're hurt, I didn't—"

"Never mind that," she replied, absently rubbing her arms.

"How are we even here? You're still bound, aren't you?"

"Unfortunately," she said, but allowed herself a small smile. "Simon Magus was a clever man, but he was not omniscient, and he never tested his theory. The bind is close to total, but not *quite* complete, and since I'm standing very near a gate, here we are. But this is all I can do," she added, dashing my hopes before they could get far off the ground. "I can't break the spell with my own power."

"How can I help?"

Despite her stated time crunch, Kura hesitated. "Moyna cannot be allowed to rule. She would tear apart the peace Eleanor and Coileán have forged, force the courts back into war, throw Faerie into chaos…this can't happen."

"You won't power her up, then?"

She sighed. "I have…obligations…that I must consider. Should Coileán die, the throne is Moyna's by right."

"But if she kills him to get it—"

"That does not matter. Not for the terms of my agreement, I mean," she allowed. "But it is *imperative* that she be stopped."

"*How?* We're out of ideas. If we attack them, they'll kill you, and then that's it for…no?" I asked, seeing her head swivel. "I don't understand, if something happens to you—"

"Again," said Kura, "your sources know much, but their knowledge is imperfect. How do you suppose I gained this position?"

The question left me at a loss. Kura seldom spoke of her past, and when she did, her answers had always been vague. "I don't know," I admitted.

"Long ago, when I was about your age and the world was much younger, the border between Faerie and the Gray Lands began to thin. There were wars on both sides, magic and dark magic flung about with abandon, and the skin began to tear," she explained. "Gates opened overnight, hundreds of them, and the Gray Landers brought their conflict to us. It took everything the realm could give to heal the breaches, and she pushed herself too far. She knew me as I know you, and as she died, she called to me." Seeing my confusion, Kura said, "I can pass this position to another. Someone on the proper side of the gate, for example. But the recipient must be willing—I cannot force it onto a successor."

My breath caught in my throat as I realized the

ramifications of what Kura was telling me. "You mean—"

She took my hands and looked up into my eyes. "I can't save Faerie by myself. Will you do this? Become the new vessel?"

"I...I mean..." I stammered, "I don't know how, I don't know *anything* about—"

"I will be there to guide you," she murmured. "In part, at least. Just as my predecessors remain with me." She glanced to her right as the darkness around us cracked, exposing a sliver of seeming daylight beyond our frozen moment. "We're out of time. Will you, Ros?"

My mind whirled, but the crack was widening, and I knew it was then or never. "I will," I told Kura, squeezing her delicate hands. "What do I need to do?"

Her smile spoke of mingled relief and sadness. "You will know," she replied as the void shattered around us.

Coileán's mouth opened to answer Moyna's question, but before he could utter the first syllable, I caught a flash of motion through the gate, then felt an agonizing pain in my stomach like stabbing fire.

Be brave, whispered Kura's voice, and in that split-second of connection, I knew what she had done. Though her captors had bound her ankles, they had left her enough slack in the hobbling rope to take small steps—which was all she had needed to thrust herself upon one of the blades around her. As the steel impaled her, it burned everything it touched, and Kura shrieked in torment.

I knew she had died when a tsunami of power crashed into me, over me, instantaneously rending me into a million pieces. I tried to gasp for air with disintegrating lungs and somehow managed to scream as the last of me flared like a dying star.

And then all was chaos.

Reality crumbled, a crude wall that had been holding back the overwhelming simultaneity of *everything*, and I found myself—or something that had once been myself—at the center of a swirling maelstrom of sight and sound and smell and touch and taste and knowing and being, a sensory mountain of glitter tossed into the air and falling in front of a strobe light from which I struggled to pull coherent meaning. I was nowhere and everywhere in the realm, and as I began to recognize places and faces among the millions of impressions flooding my mind, I clung to them, seeking an anchor in the storm.

There were Mom and Dad, holding hands across a table in their mountain cabin. Aiden stood at the window, eyes closed and forehead pressed to the glass, mouthing words like bottled messages tossed into the sea. Lailu, queen of the piq, a black-haired little woman barely taller than Dad's hand whose purple glow matched the deep violet in her wings, paced across the far end of the table, while Kuni and a dozen of his fellows flitted around the outside of the cabin doing perimeter sweeps, occasionally lighting on the dragons' heads when their wings tired.

There was Bee, standing in Eleanor's massive foyer with her wand clenched in her fist. Daisy and Antony, neither of them strong fighters, had been stationed close to the Fringe, but Bee had insisted that she could take a spot in the first line. She was scared—terror thrummed through her like an electric current, making her muscles tense and her jaw tremble—but she clenched her teeth and tried to put on a brave front. To one side of her stood Ned, eldest of the Stowe brothers, and to the other, Adela, one of Eleanor's guards. Both were similarly afraid, but they hid it better, the benefit of age and practice. Though they thought Bee was massively foolish, they respected her decision to do her part. Still, the two had reached an unspoken agreement to pinch forward and push her behind them in case of engagement.

Then I found Frank, swinging his neck wildly and mentally shouting my name. He couldn't hear me—I'd vanished like the flame of a snuffed candle, a sudden black hole in his overlay of the minds around him—and he was desperately trying to locate me. Poor Sam clung to the saddle, attempting to keep his seat on the panicking dragon, and called for me as well. One moment, he had been holding me, and after my sudden screaming flare, he'd been left empty-handed and seeing spots from the afterglow.

Beyond them, I viewed the commotion through the gate—the wizards calling out and trying to revive Kura, the faeries around them shoving through to see what had happened. Moyna's entourage had turned back toward the gate at the uproar, and even she looked aside, annoyed at the interruption to her long-awaited moment of triumph.

But that wasn't all I saw. Coileán and Eleanor were staring in horror at the scene on the other side of the gate…and the longer I looked at them, the more clearly the bonds came into focus, darkened filaments that seemed to stretch from the core of my shattered being into each of them.

Dry channels awaiting the flood.

I opened the dam.

The bonds blazed, and the king and queen stumbled with the jolt of returning power as it plowed into them. As they regained their balance, they looked at each other in alarm, saw that the other was glowing white, and began to smile with the first stirrings of hope.

There was another bond, I saw, a smaller one leading to Aiden. I activated it, and his eyes flew open wide with the shock as his power swelled. "Faerie's back," he said, turning to my parents and Lailu. "I can feel her, the boost is there again…"

But I couldn't linger. A fourth bond had caught my eye, one as thick as Coileán's and Eleanor's…and yes, there was Val on the other end, coiled like a spring and trying to make quick sense of the shouting from the far side of the gate.

I'm sorry, I thought, hoping he could hear me, then set

the bond alight.

Unprepared for the surge, Val stiffened with the impact, then cried out and fell to his knees as his body grappled with the all-engulfing influx of power. "Captain!" Mina yelled, running to catch him before he could hurt himself, but as the telltale white corona flared around him, she came to a sudden halt and held the rest of the guards back.

Distracted by the wizards' ministrations to Kura's corpse, Moyna didn't see Coileán raise his hand, and she jumped in alarm when he sealed the gate behind her, cutting her and her fellows off from the ship and their reinforcements. "No," he growled, "we do *not* have a deal. And you're not running away this time, little girl."

A blast of enchantment plucked her off the ground and held her squirming in the air, arms pinned to her sides and feet kicking for purchase. "Help me!" she shrieked at her followers. "Get him, kill him!"

But the old faeries around her had their eyes on another target. Panting but still glowing, Val staggered to his feet and stared down the line of invaders until Moyna's captain stepped forward and whispered, "Valerius?"

He nodded. "Kiet."

Flabbergasted, he stuttered, "You...but you..."

Val glanced at his luminous arm, then back at Kiet. "Mab never cared to claim me."

Moyna's forces looked at each other, and I felt their tumult of emotions: the yearning to go home, the hope for Moyna's success, the anticipation of a battle...and then the confusion of finding their king, a legitimate heir, standing *right there*.

Kiet reached his decision first and sank to the grass. "My lord."

The others quickly followed suit, and Val, looking supremely uncomfortable with the situation, muttered, "Stand down," then headed straight for Moyna, who continued to scream in vain for her allies to help her.

When he reached her side, he looked back at Coileán and Eleanor in query. Eleanor nodded, and Coileán, after a long moment's pause, did likewise and closed his eyes. With one smooth motion, Val pulled his sword free, then sliced it straight across Moyna's neck, almost decapitating her. He dissolved the enchantment that had held her aloft, and she fell like a broken doll, her seared neck smoking from the steel.

I wanted to stay with them, but I couldn't hold on any longer. Exhausted and overwhelmed, I released my focus and allowed myself to float, feeling everything and nothing.

I couldn't find myself.

The thought would have been worrying, had my mind been coherent enough to understand worry. Instead, it had fractured into all-seeing shards, and what was left of me was, more or less, trapped at the center of a universe of stimuli, absorbing without processing. Occasionally, I caught flashes of impressions that I almost recognized: Frank morosely scanning the sky, Mom sobbing in Dad's arms, the brief moment of loss as Coileán and Eleanor slipped across the border, the satisfaction as they returned. In time, I began to pick up on Kura's memories, which had intertwined with mine like vines clinging to a tree. I saw ages unfold before me, wars and parties and beddings and murders flickering into view as a jumble of instants. Letting myself reach back farther, I saw what Kura had never wished to discuss: a half-fae man, a mortal woman, his score of other children with power their child would never be able to match, and the helpful, meddling realm, molding the girl before she drew her first breath, walking beside her as she grew, watching with pride as she made friends and took lovers, then reaching out to her in her agonizing last moments and thrusting the weight of the realm upon her.

As she had done to me. Now I was lost, drowning in the memories of millennia, of beings who had lived and died centuries before my birth, and I couldn't seem to remember where they left off and I began. No matter. I was the realm, all-seeing, all-hearing, nowhere and everywhere...

And then, like a searchlight in a midnight fog, I heard Val call my name. "Ros," he said, and paused to listen. "Roslyn. Talk to me."

Finally, I had found an island in the endless sea, but though I struggled to reach him, Val never came into focus. *I can't find you!* I cried. *Where are you? Val!*

His tone remained calm, though I could feel his excitement at our contact. "Concentrate on my voice," he replied, deep and steady. "Come to me, Ros. I'm here."

I tried again, over and over—for hours, I would later understand—but I could never quite lock onto him. *I can't,* I said, wanting to sob with frustration and lacking eyes to do so. *Don't leave me here, I can't find you...*

"I'm not leaving you," he said, though he sounded tired. "Let me sleep for a few minutes, little one. Rest. We'll try again shortly."

Val!

"I am not abandoning you. Trust me."

And I did, though now that I saw how much of myself was still scattered, I feared I would never be able to escape the sensory hell into which I'd fallen. But Val's word was his bond, and soon enough, I heard him call me again—a little groggy, perhaps, but there.

It took hours for me to find the familiar stone walls of the guards' quarters, and then, ever so slowly, I was able to will myself forward, now down the hallway, now through Val's door, and then, finally, I saw him sitting in his chair with his eyes closed and the lights low, breathing slowly as his mind probed for mine.

Val, I thought like a sigh, overcome with relief, and latched on to him.

His dark eyes opened as I made contact, and he looked around the office as if expecting me to have appeared. "Hello, Ros," he said, and smiled wearily. "Welcome back."

But my strength was already failing me. *I can't hold it!* I cried as I felt myself slipping away again. *Val, I can't—*

"Catch your breath," he replied, my unflappable coach once more. "Again, now."

I knew the routine all too well. Val had spent a decade pushing me to my limits, then nudging me just beyond them, forcing me to grow and hone my skills. And if I'd learned anything under his tutelage, it was that Val never let my exhaustion get in the way of his lesson plans. Falling back into habit, I caught myself before I could spin away, then forced myself to concentrate, always aiming for him.

Val didn't sleep that night. Shortly before dawn the next morning, I managed to pull myself together and hold on to him for a minute, straining the new muscles I was still developing. *How did you know where to find me?* I asked. *With everything else that was going on...*

He flashed a brief, weary smile. "We saw Kura die, and suddenly, you were missing. The pieces were not difficult to put together."

Frank is upset. I haven't tried to reach him—

"Frank can take care of himself for now. Don't worry about him or anyone else," he said, rubbing his forehead. "You need to master yourself first."

I'm trying.

"I know. And you're slipping again."

Sorry.

"Don't be sorry. Rest," he ordered. "I'll do the same, and we'll resume later in the morning."

By early evening, it was becoming easier for me to lock on a target and keep my focus in one place, and Val began to pry. "What's it like being Faerie?" he asked, crossing his legs and addressing the empty room as if I were standing in front of him.

Overwhelming, I thought, lacking a better term. *There's so much information constantly coming in, old and new, and just sorting it takes all I have. I'm not even treading water yet.*

"What can I do to help you?"

No more than you're doing now. I paused to cobble together an explanation that made sense and settled for, *There's a group mind, sort of. Bits and pieces of Kura and the ones who came before. They're trying to help me—they keep nudging me toward the surface, if you will—but holding on to myself takes work, and I don't understand everything.*

"There's no rush, child," he soothed. "I'm not going anywhere, and I won't leave you."

What about the Arcanum? The probationers? Moyna's people? I should know, but I can't find what I'm looking for, I thought, frustrated at my failure.

"Patience," said Val. "Those who came with Moyna are enjoying the hospitality of Coileán's cells for the time being. Some of their fellows have been incarcerated there since the last attempted invasion—I'm sure they have much to discuss," he muttered. "As for the Arcanum, Eleanor and Coileán sent word to Arnold as soon as the threat here was neutralized, and they took a significant force across later in the morning to take out Moyna's fleet. The faeries were brought here for safekeeping, and the wizards were returned to Arcanum custody."

My grandparents?

"Alive. Put your mind at ease—Arnold will not be hasty."

He allowed me to rest after that while he ate a quick dinner, and within the hour, we were back at it, Val sitting and waiting, sometimes calling to me as my homing beacon, and me trying to find my way to him more quickly and hold on longer. Through practice, I began to draw myself back together—and then, shortly after midnight, I finally materialized in Val's office. It was barely a blip, just long enough for me to throw my arms around his neck and whisper my thanks, but it was a start.

All throughout that long, tiring Friday, Val encouraged me to appear again and again, at first doing whatever he could to keep me focused, and then, once I'd started to get cocky, doing all in his power to distract me. I started to remember what physicality felt like, and though it was exhausting to keep a body together, I was able to sit on his desk by nightfall and play catch with a rubber stress ball he kept in the drawer, even if I glowed as I did so.

"Your parents have been apprised of your progress," he said, tossing me the ball from across the room. "It's my understanding that they've told Bee as well."

Before I could answer him, I realized that none of this was news to me—I'd known about their conversations, but I hadn't paid attention to them while I struggled to process the rest of the realm, a task akin to trying to sip daintily from a firehose on full blast. "Bee's been with Frank for the last days. I appreciate it," I said, lobbing the ball back to him.

He caught it and immediately threw it underhand my way. "Sam's been asking about you, too, you know."

At the mention of his name, I felt myself becoming flustered, and I only recognized that I'd started to disappear again when Val called me back and chuckled at my embarrassment. "You're entitled to like him," he said as I picked the ball off the floor. "He has feelings for you, doesn't he?"

"He does," I replied, unable to be anything but cognizant of his state of mind. As long as Sam was within the realm's borders, his thoughts were more than open to me—they were constantly being broadcast, along with everyone else's. Only then was I beginning to learn to take in the information and pick through the important bits.

"Then may I suggest you enjoy each other's company?" said Val, catching my toss and returning it.

"Yes, in all of my free time," I muttered, and changed the subject. "Make this easy for me. How, exactly, did you find me?"

My throw went wide, but he caught it all the same. "I felt you in here," he explained, tapping the side of his head. "So did the king and queen. How did Eleanor put it...yes, like a drunk moth bumping around a flame. I think that's fairly accurate."

"They sent you after me?"

"No, I told them I would do it. They've been occupied, and I thought I had a decent chance of getting your attention," he said with a little smirk. "Seems to have worked. They've come down to ask about you. Coileán brings food as though I'm an invalid."

Val hesitated and squeezed the ball, but though I knew exactly what was on his mind, I did the polite thing and let him wrestle it out on his own.

"Ros," he began after a long pause, "when Moyna came through and Kura died...something happened to me."

"I did it."

He sighed and continued to pump the stress ball. "I was afraid of that. You know how I feel about—"

"This isn't up for discussion."

Val jerked, startled from his thoughts, and stared at me. "What do you—"

"Kura should have done that twenty-four years ago when Mab died. It *pained* her not to—that deal she arranged with the original Three actually caused her physical pain when she broke it."

"*Mab* broke it," he protested.

"There was still her court to consider. When Mab was gone, the power should have immediately flowed to you so as to keep the court together and out of trouble. You were her heir for *ages*, did you know that?"

"But I don't want it!" he cried, throwing the ball against the wall. "You know I don't! I've never sought it, this isn't—"

"You have a duty," I interrupted. "And like it or not, you're the heir. Someone has to step up," I pressed on before he could cut in. "How long was Coileán planning to keep Mab's people incarcerated? I mean, he's had some of them in there for decades!"

"That isn't my concern."

"They need a leader, Val. You know as well as I do that we're not going to see an end to the shadow court until Mab's is restored. Let them come home. Take charge."

He jerked a finger toward the ball, which flew back into his hand for another agitated ricochet off the stone. "Even if I wanted to, they wouldn't follow me."

"Oh, really? Did you see what happened right before you killed Moyna?"

"They were surprised. I've been attached to this court since I was twenty-three, and they know it. Why would they ever accept me?"

"Because you're the best option available to them," I murmured, scooping up and tossing him the ball. "Because they saw you and had *hope*. Moon and stars, Val, they just want to come home. Stop fighting me, take the court, and restore order. Anyway, you're good at bossing people around—this is just more of the same. And you kept Coileán's court afloat during Aiden's regency. I have faith."

He glowered at the stress ball, then lifted his eyes to meet my gaze. "I don't want this, Ros," he muttered, but I heard the shadow of defeat in his voice.

"Yeah, well," I replied as I began to fade with exhaustion, "this wasn't exactly the career move I'd envisioned, either."

That earned a faint snort, and Val continued to stare at the place where I'd been even after I disappeared. "You're impossible, my lady."

I'm right.

"And what's Coileán going to say about this?" he tried. "You expect him to be pleased?"

It's not his decision. Sleep on it, Val.

"Impossible," he grumbled, but after a few minutes, he

put the ball back in his desk and collapsed into bed. I waited the moment or two it took for him to fall asleep, then let myself spread thin again and, metaphorically speaking, took a deep breath.

All right, I thought to the waiting group mind. *I'm ready. Show me everything.*

CHAPTER 16

Several days of constant work with me had taken their toll on Val, and he slept deeply through the night. By the time he rose the next morning, I was able to direct my focus toward him without latching on, allowing me to observe while still taking note of the rest of the realm. Adapting to omniscience had a steep learning curve, and I was still adjusting to the strangeness of processing multiple streams of information simultaneously—like sitting in a security control room and paying careful attention to dozens of camera feeds at once, only magnified a billionfold. Still, I followed Val as he made himself presentable, ate a solitary breakfast he produced from thin air, then strapped on his customary bronze blade and went upstairs to find Coileán. He rapped twice on the office door and waited until it opened remotely, then let himself in and closed it behind him.

"Glad to see you've come out of hiding," said Coileán, abandoning the stack of papers on his desk. "Coffee?"

"If you're having it," Val replied, and took a seat on one of the couches as Coileán passed him a mug. "She's progressed well."

"Yes, I can feel it." He took a sip, stalling, then murmured, "Can you?"

"I think we both know the answer to that."

Coileán grinned, then stood again and headed for his bar. "The coffee's missing something, don't you agree?"

Val waited until he returned with a bottle of Jameson and poured a generous splash into both mugs. "I tried to make her reconsider. She won't."

"Smart kid. And whatever you've been doing, it's worked," he added before taste-testing his beverage. "It's starting to feel more like Faerie did before."

"I wouldn't know," Val replied, shrugging.

"The presence is always there in the back of your mind. It's weird as hell, but you grow accustomed to it, and unless she's letting you know that she's displeased, it doesn't hurt." He drank again, then frowned. "Well, that's not quite accurate. If she gets overly excited, it's like someone's shouting in your ears. But most of the time, it's much like this," he said, tapping his temple.

Val downed half his spiked coffee in two long gulps. "Honestly, I'm not sure how I feel about the idea of *Ros* taking up residence in my head."

"Don't think we have a choice," Coileán replied. "It could be worse."

"Yes, but…"

Coileán watched him struggle, then said, "She's young, I know."

"She's a *child*."

"Well, technically…" He chuckled at the look Val shot him. "We'll make the best of it, yes?"

"I suppose so." Val finished his drink, then returned the mug to atoms and folded his hands in his lap. "And in light of recent events, I, uh…I must tender my resignation."

"Good. You're calling your court, then?"

"As you said, I don't think we have a choice," he muttered.

Coileán gave Val a moment to stew while he sipped his coffee, then said, "It's for the best. I mean, as much as I'm going to miss having you here to keep the guards in line, we need a third court again. At least let me clean out my cells, won't you?"

Val sighed and rubbed his face. "This will be a disaster."

"Oh, the position is definitely a pain in the ass," Coileán agreed cheerily, "but at least you have colleagues who can commiserate." With that, he pulled his phone from his pocket, flipped it open, and called Eleanor, who was in the middle of breakfast. "Could you stop by?" he asked. "Val's here."

I watched Eleanor push aside her plate and rise from the table. "Is he..."

"Yeah."

"On my way."

The gate opened seconds later, and she hurried through, beaming. "You're doing it?" she asked Val. "Is that what I'm hearing?"

He nodded, though he looked decidedly glummer than either Eleanor or Coileán. "And this pleases you, I take it?"

"If it means we can put the bloody shadow court to rest, then yes, absolutely," she replied, plopping onto the couch beside him, then noticed the bottle of whiskey on the table and poured a glass. "Here," she said, handing it to Val as she poured a second one for herself. "You'll need this."

"I got him started," said Coileán, tilting his mug. "The morning's young yet."

"And I've never known you to turn down alcohol," she said, producing a glass for him as well, then raised hers and clinked it against the others. "Cheers, lads."

Val threw his back, squinted at the burn, then put his glass on the table and turned to Coileán. "One request, if I may."

"What's that?"

"Let me be the one to tell the guards. I've served with some of them longer than you've been alive, and this...*news*...needs to come from me."

"That seems only fair," said Coileán, and smirked into his whiskey. "You're not going to try to poach, are you?"

"Your court, your guards," Val replied, pushing himself from the couch. "And knowing them as well as I do, if I may make a suggestion…"

"Please."

"Put Mina in charge in my stead. I trust her judgment, and the others will follow her. And seeing as she's your niece, I wouldn't be concerned about defection," he added. "Now, if you'll excuse me, I have a meeting to call."

He was almost to the door when Eleanor asked, "Does Toula know?"

Val stopped and looked her way. "I've said nothing to her for days, but…"

"There *has* been a rumor going around," she admitted. "I would think she's more than aware by now."

Coileán put his glass aside and rose. "And speaking of whom…"

Finally, Val cracked a smile at Coileán's sudden anxiety. "What my sister does with her personal life is not my decision, and she would be the first to remind me if I forgot."

"Thank you," he said, and dipped his head.

"It's only the truth, Coileán," he replied with a slight shrug. "But know that if you break her heart, I *will* kill you."

Eleanor snorted and made a cup of tea. "*Please*, boys. I'd trust that Toula can take care of herself without your tender assistance by now."

Having long cultivated a bad habit of listening to conversations I wasn't intended to hear, I felt only the slightest pang of guilt in silently attending the guards' meeting that afternoon before I recalled that I had no choice but to overhear it. Whether I consciously paid attention to any particular facet of Faerie was irrelevant in the long run, as the larger part of me that was now the realm soaked up everything and stored it away for use as needed. Millennia of minutiae were available to me with instant recall—I could, if I chose, describe what every sentient being in the realm had been thinking at any given instant in Faerie's existence—and the magnitude and scope of my trove were dizzying.

Still, I did feel the teeniest bit like an interloper as I surveyed the modified dungeon room where the guards had been holding their group meetings for centuries. Several rows of wooden chairs arced in front of a short platform, behind which was mounted a copy of the duty roster kept in Val's office, which updated as he changed the assignments. A table against one wall held the usual refreshments, which had slowly entered the menu as new guards came on board: a jug of wine, a tapped cask of small beer, a carafe of fruit juice, and the newest addition, a pot of coffee that never drained to its dregs.

Val lurked by the wall farthest from the beverage table as his fellows filed in and made themselves comfortable, taking chairs in configurations long ago set in stone and chatting with their neighbors. He was anxious, I knew, reluctant to make an announcement that felt so much like betrayal to him. These were the men and women with whom he'd trained and fought—they looked to him as their reliable leader. How was he supposed to walk away from the history they shared? Beneath his nerves was an undercurrent of deep sadness, and for an instant, I thought about giving him the choice to leave the third court leaderless. I didn't think he would take it—Val knew I was right—but I didn't want to give him the opportunity to back out.

As the last of the guards closed the door and hurried to his seat, Val took a deep breath, then stepped onto the platform and tried to discreetly wipe the sweat from his palms as the room quieted. "Good afternoon," he began when the murmurs had stilled. "I apologize for the sudden notice, especially to the night shift." His eyes fell on the cluster of guards holding coffee cups, who grinned wearily in acknowledgement. "This won't be an extended meeting."

Mina, his longtime second, sat in the front row and studied him, paying careful attention to the tension in his face, the way he nervously licked his lip when he paused. She suspected, but she held her peace.

"I don't know how much you have heard," Val continued, "and I'm sorry for not giving you a fuller report before now, but I've been occupied. In brief, Lady Roslyn is in control of the realm. She..." He hesitated and swallowed hard. "She has decided to honor the agreement her predecessor made with the Three. In its entirety."

The muttering resumed, and Val locked eyes with Mina, who nodded encouragement.

He lifted a hand for quiet, and the volume dropped again. "I may be mistaken, but I don't believe that my maternity is a secret to anyone here. Correct?" He waited as the guards nodded back at him, then sighed as he faced the inevitable. "Strange as it sounds, especially to me, I am Mab's heir. And as the new regime insists, I...I will call my court in the morning."

He almost tripped over the words, which felt foreign and nonsensical on his tongue, and he waited, holding his breath, to see how his comrades would react.

No one moved until Mina rose and folded her arms. "If you think you're quitting that easily, Captain, you've lost your mind," she said, and raised a teasing eyebrow.

Taken aback by her unexpected declaration, Val frowned and cocked his head. "Oh?"

"You can do whatever you like in the morning," she explained, "but tonight, we drink, and you're going to be there. And I don't want any argument, old boy," she added as his mouth opened. "If you're retiring, then we're sending you off properly, and that's that."

One by one, the rest of the guards began to clap and whistle, and Val, reddening, saluted Mina. "If you insist, my lady."

"Oh, I do," she replied, and smiled back at him. "My lord."

Mina could have given Daisy a masterclass in organizational prowess, and she didn't limit the sendoff to the current guards. Within the hour, anyone in the realm who had suffered the misfortune of training under Val had an invitation to the night's revels, including my uncle and my father. Aiden made plans to be there without hesitation, but Dad balked when Mina showed up on my parents' doorstep. "Please send my regards," he told her, "but this isn't a good time. Helen—"

"Needs to leave the house," said Mina. "As do you, little cousin."

"We've lost our daughter," Dad snapped. "Neither of us is really in a festive mood right now."

The look on Mina's face, a blank expression with eyebrows slightly raised in challenge, was one she had cribbed from Val and put to excellent use over the years. "You're speaking as if she's *dead*."

"She might as well be! Have you seen her anywhere?" he demanded, sweeping one arm across the porch.

Mina glanced over his shoulder into the house. "Joey—"

"We should have made her evacuate. *I* should have made her leave."

"*Joey*."

Dad groaned and covered his face. "God, I should have been there. I could have—"

"Damn it, Joey, turn around!"

By then, I'd managed to materialize and lock into my physical form—and just in time, as the moment Dad laid eyes on me, he gasped and grabbed me tightly enough to squeeze the air from my lungs. *I'm sorry I couldn't come sooner*, I told him, unable to get breath enough to speak in his embrace. *Val's been helping me get to this point.*

When Dad finally loosened his death grip and took a step back, his face was red and wet, and his jaw quivered in spite of his best efforts to control himself. "I'm okay," I said, and hugged him again, feeling the wash of his mingled guilt, grief, and now relief.

"I'm so sorry, baby," he mumbled into my hair. "We shouldn't have let you—"

"Kura and I did what we needed to do," I interrupted, and gave him a little smile. "Come on, didn't you and Mom want me to get a job someday?"

The answer he was trying to formulate never happened, as Mom, who by then had crept from the solitude of their bedroom to see what the shouting was about downstairs, noticed me glowing in the foyer and screamed. I met her as she raced down and once again held on as a parent hugged me toward blackout conditions. After a few seconds, however, the strain became too great, and I let myself disappear. Mom cried out, finding herself with nothing in her arms but empty air, but I quickly pulled myself together and hugged her from behind. "Still getting the hang of this," I said as she turned to embrace me again. "Corporeality is *not* my current default."

By then, she was crying too hard to speak to me, but I recognized in her the emotions I'd felt in Dad. "I'm okay, really," I told her as she soaked my shoulder. "I'm here. Not exactly going anywhere, so that's one less thing to worry about, right?"

Mom raised her head and gave me a look that asked how I could possibly joke at a time like that.

"I promise I'm okay. Still getting my head on straight, but…I'll be all right. And stop blaming Coileán, he had nothing to do with this."

Her eyes widened. "How did you—"

"I am literally everywhere in this realm. I *am* the realm. Surprising me for my birthday just got a hell of a lot more challenging," I said, grinning. "But yeah, I know it's been a rough week for you, and I'm sorry it's taken me this long, but…*wow*, it's a lot to take in, and there are no training wheels." Glancing down at myself to be sure I was still intact, I muttered, "And I'm kind of glowy, so that's something else to deal with, but one thing at a time."

"Honey, I don't care what you look like, I'm just thrilled to have you home," said Mom, crushing my ribs again. "Let me get some fresh sheets on your bed, and Frank—"

"I can't stay." Mom stiffened, perplexed, and I said, "Holding my body together takes a lot of work. It's exhausting, really. It'll get easier, I'm sure of it, but right now, I'm pushing my limits, and I don't think I actually sleep anymore…"

Mom reached up and cupped my face in her hands. "You listen to me, Roslyn," she said in her low, Mom's-giving-orders voice. "There will be sheets on that bed. I don't care if you never use them, but you're going to have them. Got it?"

I slipped from her grasp and kissed her cheek. "Got it. Dad…"

"You know where to find us," he said, and wrapped his arm around Mom. "And if you don't visit, your mother is going to be *very* upset."

"Just Mom?" I teased, then pointed to Mina, who had watched our reunion from the threshold. "Seriously, go party. Those guys are *pros*."

"You've got an invitation as well," Mina told me. "I mean, I assumed you'd be somewhere around, but there is a formal invite, too."

"I'll do my best," I replied, and felt myself begin to fade. "Mom, Dad…"

I fell apart before I could finish, but Dad smiled sadly at the spot where I'd been and tightened his grip on Mom. "Love you, too, baby girl."

The party, held in the palace dungeon for optimal noise muffling, was a smashing success. Almost everyone who had put in time with Val showed up to drink and commiserate about old injuries, and even Coileán wandered down that night to toast him and formally announce that he'd accepted his resignation. "Now, I'm not saying you have to move out immediately," he said, refilling empty glasses with bourbon, "but bear in mind that I am *not* loaning you my throne room. Might need to throw something together, eh? And the new captain might want your quarters," he added, cocking his thumb toward Mina, who beamed with pleasure as her fellows cheered.

I couldn't manifest for more than a few minutes of the party, but I withstood a barrage of back-thumping from the guards and drank a few sips of tequila, the first food or drink I'd had in nearly a week. I simply didn't need it, and the alcohol had zero effect on me, but I wasn't about to decline when Val put a tumbler in my hand. Mom seemed less unhappy that time after I disappeared, and for the rest of the night, Aiden made a concerted effort to keep her glass full and her mind distracted. She knew what he was up to, but she played along.

The festivities lasted until nearly midnight, when only Val, Mina, and Toula remained in the tidied room. Mina begged off to sleep, having her work cut out for her the next day, and when she had taken her leave, Toula looked at her brother, folded her arms, and asked, "So...want to build a house or something?"

I followed them north into the deep woods, far beyond Coileán's palace and the piq territory, and into a pleasantly green pasture in the mountains. As Toula watched, Val obliterated part of the western peaks that ringed the high valley, giving them a clear view of the sea. "Nice," she remarked. "Going to pitch a tent?"

He snorted and muttered, "Step back," then closed his eyes, spread his hands over the grass, and exhaled.

Wall by wall, a magnificent villa emerged from thin air. It wasn't a purely Classical design, I mused, studying it as it coalesced. Though it favored breezeways and enclosed gardens, it was built on a different floorplan, with separate wings branching off from each of the four corners of the massive central courtyard. Leading his approving sister through the villa, Val tweaked dimensions and windows and roof pitch, then turned his attention to decoration. The walls he kept a neutral white, at least for the evening, but he covered the floors in lavish, colorful geometric mosaics, and he set the ceiling mosaics in motion to reflect the sky above.

Two of the wings had a view to the ocean, and Val selected one for himself, putting together a bedroom and an adjoining office, both with retractable doors to let in the breeze. After a moment's consideration, he put a smaller office adjacent to his for the undetermined captain of his theoretical guard. Experience, after all, was an excellent teacher.

With his living quarters appointed, he headed into the courtyard at the heart of the villa and studied the untouched grass. I knew Val didn't favor a proper throne room—it wasn't his style—but as a concession to the necessities of his position, he tiled the courtyard, ringed it with a lovely ornamental garden, then folded a marble throne into the end nearest his office. As a final touch, he tossed a thick green cushion onto the throne, then stepped back, took it all in, and turned to Toula. "You know you're welcome to an apartment here, too."

She grinned and patted his arm. "If things go south, I'll be by."

"Very well. But just in case, why don't you fix that to your liking?" he suggested, pointing to the other wing with western exposure. "Surely you're not insinuating that I'll never see you again just because I'm moving out of the palace."

Toula chuckled and took another look at the gardens. "It's really lovely, Val. Just remember that you're going to need a kitchen somewhere."

"There are two other wings."

"And storage."

"Understood."

"And a place to house your guards."

He sighed and swept his arm around the garden. "Plenty of room to expand, and I'll deal with it once I survive the morning. Is there anything critical that I've forgotten?"

"Critical?" Toula echoed, looked into the nearest pool of the elaborate fountain complex Val had spread throughout the villa, then shook her head and held her palm above the rippling water. "No, not *critical*."

He looked down at her handiwork, an animated mosaic of multicolored fish that lazed and darted through the fountains. "Nice touch."

"Yeah? You like it?"

He kissed her forehead and grinned. "Will you come tomorrow?"

"Do you want me there?" she asked, smiling back at him. "Arcanum interloper and all?"

"Whatever else you may be, you are my sister," he replied, "and I would love to have at least one person there who doesn't want me dead."

"Tough crowd, huh?"

"Coileán is releasing his prisoners to my custody, so perhaps that will help, but overall…"

Toula linked her arm around his and steered him toward the throne. "You're not going to get anywhere by catastrophizing in the middle of the night. But while we're here, you might as well give that a test drive," she said, pointing to the cushion. "Make sure it's thick enough. If you meant to do some sort of big production about taking the throne tomorrow, I'll just act impressed when you do it for real."

"Ha," he muttered, and took a seat.

She stepped back and examined the final result. "Suits you."

"Hardly."

"Give it time. And if it makes it any easier, just know there's no way in hell I'm calling you 'my lord,' so at least one thing remains constant."

Val stood, fluffed the cushion ever so slightly, then smirked at his sister. "Truly, Glinda, I would expect nothing less from you."

"Hey. *Hey*, now," she snapped as he headed out of the courtyard, "only Coileán gets away with that crap."

"Mm."

"Seriously, have you even seen that movie?" she called. As Val began whistling "We're Off to See the Wizard," she grunted and scowled her annoyance at the heavens, then hurried after her brother.

Val might not have been completely on board with his new job, but he didn't waste time. Sunrise found him on the throne once again, staring out at the empty courtyard as the first rays crested the roof…and went straight into his eyes. He imagined shades into place, cloth draperies spanning the courtyard at regular intervals to create patches of shadow, then drummed his fingers on the armrests and muttered, "Ready?"

Let's do it, I replied. *Keep it simple.*

He bowed his head, formulating the message he wished to send, and I caught it and sent it exploding across the realm and through the open gates, seeking out the scattered members of the court whom I somehow already knew by heart and searching for others of their bloodlines.

Come home. Your king commands it.

I alerted Coileán and Eleanor as well—Coileán, at least, would need to give the okay before his prisoners were transferred, and I thought it only fitting to keep them apprised of what was going on to the north. And as the members of the wayward court began to wake to the summons across the realms, I caught a glimpse of Toula opening her eyes in bed beside Coileán, blinking in the shaded darkness, and muttering, "Oh, *hell* no, I'm not getting up yet."

"I thought you told him you'd come," Coileán

mumbled, tugging on the blankets to straighten what they'd tangled in the night.

"Yeah," she said, snuggling back against him, "but I didn't specify when."

Before long, the first of the exiles crossed the border, and I guided them into the mountains to the villa. Some were taken aback—Mab, like Titania, had favored more imposing stone fortresses—but soon enough, as they wandered the corridors and followed the fountains into the courtyard, they began to relax. Val spoke with each, set up chairs and benches and tables of food and drink as the crowd swelled, and was beginning to find his rhythm when Eleanor and Coileán arrived at the head of a pack of guards.

I felt the tension in the courtyard spike—the court expected a trap, and not without reason—but the king and queen quickly stated that they'd only stopped by to pay their respects and deliver the prisoners. Val accompanied them outside, noted the ring of mixed guards around the former invaders, and nodded to Mina and Nico, who created an opening. Stepping into the breach, he quietly addressed his people and offered a choice: fealty or death. Within a minute, the captives were kneeling, and Val motioned for them to rise. "You're home," he told them, and pointed to the bustling villa. "Be welcome."

As they hurried past him to reunite with the rest of the court, Val caught Kiet's shoulder and held him back. "A word?" he asked.

Moyna's former captain nodded. "My lord."

Val led him into his office—he'd left the external doors open to let in the breeze—and showed him to a pair of couches that looked suspiciously like Coileán's, albeit in a lighter leather. "What remains of Mab's guard?" he asked once the two were seated.

Kiet began to count on his fingers. "Myself, two of the boys who were in training at the expulsion, and another two born in the Gray Lands."

"You served Moyna in her stead?"

"And Geheret before her. I serve the court," Kiet replied, "which is why I abandoned Moyna on the field last week."

"Will you serve me?"

He straightened, surprised at the request—he had gone into the office anticipating censure. "Your pardon, my lord, I—"

"You heard me," said Val. "I'm beginning with nothing, Kiet. No guard, no staff, and a court that knows quite well where my loyalties have lain until now. This is uncomfortable for all of us."

"Agreed," he muttered. "Following your sister would have been difficult enough, but…"

"I'm no one's favorite, I understand that. But I need a team I can trust. You're trained and experienced, and if my memory is accurate, you're also half-blooded. Yes?"

Kiet nodded. "That suddenly counts in my favor?"

"To me, it does." Val sat back and crossed his legs. "I've worked with full and half. The full-blooded are useful when they're angry and pointed in the right direction. The half fae are the ones I can count on to be rational the rest of the time. I need a captain with whom I can reason. Someone who knows this court well enough to select and train a new guard."

He mulled that over, then regarded Val with faint suspicion. "Why would you trust me? You know what I've done."

"As you said, for the good of the court. Coileán trusted me," he said, then paused, and I heard the question in his mind: *Am I crazy?*

Nope.

"And I'm willing to trust you," he concluded. "If you're interested."

With that, Kiet slid from the couch and knelt again. "Yes, my lord."

"Rise," said Val, and smiled. "Back to the courtyard.

Eat and drink as you like—we'll begin this afternoon."

By the time they returned, the crowd had grown even further, fed by a steady trickle of exiles who'd run from the Gray Lands and been hiding from the rest of the court. They kept to themselves—I recognized Bonnie among their number—but Val made the rounds to speak with them and to tell off a younger faerie who had tried to harass them. Finally, he took his throne, raised his hand for quiet, and looked out over the sea of faces, some weary, some wary, many hopeful. "Welcome home," he said, his amplified voice echoing across the courtyard and the surrounding valley. "I am Valerius. Some of you know me, many do not. This we can rectify, but let's address the most pressing issues first."

He stood, the better to see over the throng. "Some of you abandoned Mab after her expulsion. Some followed her into the Gray Lands. Some served Geheret. And some of you, out of desperation or simple foolishness, followed Moyna across the border. Some more than once." He paused, letting the echo subside, then said, "Today, we start afresh. Put aside your old grievances with each other. If you can't forget them, then don't act on them. There is ample land here—build your homes, be at peace, and don't go past our southern border without my *express* permission. I will make clear where the boundary runs. Is that understood?"

The court murmured assent and nodded.

"And you are to stay away from the mortal realm," he continued. "I anticipate sufficient conflict among you here without having to track you down across two realms." A few of his audience chuckled, and Val shrugged. "In time, perhaps. For now…" He flicked his wrist, and a projection of his claimed territory, taken straight from Dad and Aiden's maps, appeared above the heads of the crowd. "I've taken the liberty of dividing this," he said as an overlay appeared on the map. "In a few minutes, you may draw lots and choose your homesteads. But before we begin, I need to know if there are any among you who refuse my authority."

Kiet was the first to take a knee, and the others quickly followed—well, all but Toula, who stood by herself behind a column and watched the proceedings. Val looked down at his court, folded his arms, and smiled. "Good. Enjoy yourselves," he said as they began to rise. "We'll see to the land shortly. Seamus, may I speak with you?"

His nephew, who had been awkwardly hanging out in a corner of the courtyard, hurried toward him, and Val ushered him into his office. "What I just said does not apply to you," he reassured him, gripping Seamus's shoulder. "I don't want Badger to kill me in my sleep."

Seamus grinned, relieved. "Glad to hear it, because that was going to be a tricky conversation."

"You're as much Fringe as anything, and though you're welcome here, I understand if you'd prefer to stay with your wife," Val replied, then gestured toward a carafe of red wine on the sideboard. "Thirsty?"

"Just a sip. I've been off it for weeks."

Val looked at him strangely. "Whatever for?"

"Don't laugh."

"With a warning like that, I make no guarantees," said Val, heading for the wine. "Why the abstinence?"

"Well, ehm…there's a charity marathon in Rigby a fortnight from last Saturday, and Badger got it in her head that marathoning is on her bucket list, and I said I'd do it with her, so…I told you not to laugh," he muttered.

Chuckling, Val poured a small glass for Seamus and a larger one for himself. "How far is this race, again?"

"Twenty-six-point-two miles. It's to raise money for a new public library. We've been training since March, and—"

"And you couldn't just give the library the funds and be done with it? You pay them for the privilege of running twenty-six miles?"

"Point two," Seamus mumbled, and downed his wine

in one gulp. "It matters in August. Anyway, we've cut out alcohol of late, and except for the occasional weekend pizza or Chinese, we've been eating well. Badger's blood pressure has dropped," he added, "so that's a bonus."

"Granted," said Val, "but after the last week..."

He shrugged it off and put the empty glass on the sideboard. "Getting the kids back across the border was nothing, the Company has been remarkably cooperative, and Eleanor and Coileán brought the heavy guns to the boat fight. I mean, yeah, I got to punch a few wizards, but Arnold had them in hand quickly enough."

Val leaned against the wall and sipped his wine. "You'll forgive me if I'm behind on the news. Is Arnold heading the Arcanum again?"

"For now. The kid who was doing it got caught up with the probationers and Moyna, so if I've got my sources straight, he's more or less on house arrest until the Council decides what's to be done with the lot of them."

"Didn't Arnold just resign that position?"

"Yeah, he's not thrilled to be back at the helm," said Seamus. "But what else could they do? Try to entice Helen over? Offer Badger the job?" He paused, then nodded toward the inner door. "Sounds like no one's dead yet, but do you think you should get back and supervise?"

"Probably," Val replied, and polished off his glass. "I saw Toula in the back in case of rioting, but I'd rather not leave that on her shoulders."

By noon, Val's court had begun construction on their new dwellings, Val had cleaned up the leavings of the morning's affair, and he and Kiet were deep in discussion about logistics over lunch. Confident that I wasn't going to be needed, I turned my attention to more personal matters.

Antony, Bee, and Daisy had already been recalled to Glastonbury to assist Arnold, but Sam, bless him, had done his best over the last week to keep Frank occupied. I felt terrible for leaving Frank without so much as a word—we'd been partners since the day he'd hatched, and I knew he was worried sick—but after the previous day's manifestations, I'd needed time to gather my strength. When I focused on them, I found then inside the barn, Frank curled around Sam, who sat on a hay bale with a chess board, trying to teach him to play. Sam was forced to move the pieces for the both of them, seeing as Frank's claws were far too large to make the delicate adjustments to the board, but Frank was paying close attention to Sam's quick lecture about the importance of saving the queen until I appeared at the barn door. Feeling me once again, Frank raised his head in alarm, noticed me, then knocked over both the board and poor Sam in his rush to my side.

"I am *so* sorry it's taken this long, bud," I told him as he rubbed his head against me, nearly pushing me off my feet. "Are you okay?"

The thought he sent me was almost pure emotion, which would have been difficult for me to parse a week before but now, somehow, made sense. He'd been desperate to find me, then despondent when he learned what had happened. Mine was the voice he'd heard when everyone else's had gone silent, the one mind he'd always been able to reach, and suddenly, he'd been cut off. He'd panicked, he'd fretted, he'd stress-eaten several dozen sheep, but that hadn't helped. But now I was back, and everything was fine again, the void was filled...

"I can't stay," I told him, standing on tiptoe to rub the spot between his eyes. "Not like this. But even if you can't hear me, I can always hear you. I'm not leaving you, Frank. We're still partners, yeah?"

Yeah, he replied, but the thought was colored by disappointment. *I guess there's no chance of us going back to Glastonbury, is there?*

"I can't. Doesn't mean you're stuck here, but I can't manifest like this across the border. Tethered to this realm, you know?" Giving him a pat, I turned to find Sam standing close by, well away from Frank's twitching tail. "Hey, Sam," I began, starting toward him, then remembered I was glowing and paused. "Uh…how's it going?" I asked as my stomach knotted.

"Better now," he said, and hugged me.

I luxuriated in the feeling of his rough cotton shirt against my cheek. "Thanks for staying with Frank. I thought you might have wanted to go back to Arc 2 with the others."

"Not yet. Things are messy over there right now, so I thought I'd stick around here, figure myself out. Got a room at Aunt Ellie's, and she said she'd line up someone to work with me. At least Val's too busy to volunteer," he added, and faked a shudder.

I raised my head from his shoulder, and he brushed a clump of hair out of my eyes with two fingers. "It's really good to see you again," he said softly.

"You, too," I replied, then hesitated, knowing what I needed to say and hating that I had to say it. "Sam…about, um…us."

"Yep?"

I took a deep breath, though, strictly speaking, my corporeal form didn't require air. "You've got a lot on your plate, and I'm, uh…complicated…so if all of this is too much, I understand."

He frowned in bemusement. "All of what?"

"Me. I can't manifest all the time, I glow when I do, and I know what you're about to say—"

"Then why bother asking?" he interrupted, and kissed me.

Yes, part of me knew it was coming, but I'd been trying to ignore it in order to give Sam the courtesy of a semi-normal conversation, and so the shock of his lips on mine surprised me too much to keep myself together. I vanished, leaving Sam with his arms encircling empty air and his mouth pressed against nothing. He stumbled as he adjusted to my sudden departure, then looked around and laughed. "Aw, come on, am I *that* bad at it?"

Not at all, I replied, then rematerialized behind him, turned him around, and pulled him toward me.

I allowed myself then to open to his thoughts and was rewarded with a wave of pleasure and need, all shaded by a cast of performance anxiety. As I reveled in my own sensory impressions, I received a simultaneous dose of his—the warmth of my skin, the softness of my hair, the taste of my mouth—and lost myself in the moment, willing it to last. But Sam eventually came up for air, and from the look on his face, I'd managed to share with him at least a fraction of what I'd experienced.

"Wow," he whispered, breathing heavily. "That's...*wow*."

Though I was growing tired, I was loath to let Sam go. "Should we try again? Make sure it wasn't a fluke?"

Frank, who had wandered off to the sheep pen in the interim, snorted at our attempts at flirtation and tossed a bleating ewe into his mouth. *Mate already, will you?*

Sam arched an eyebrow, then cocked his head toward the door from the barn into my parents' kitchen. "You know, I could be mistaken, but I think we have the house to ourselves right now."

I felt myself smile. "Yeah, Mom and Dad are out for a bit."

"If we're quiet and close the door, keep the lights out..."

"They're not due back for a while," I replied, wrapping my arms around his neck. "And it doesn't matter if you turn the lights off. You do realize that sex in the dark is entirely impossible with me, right? I am my own nightlight."

"Mm. Then it's probably a good thing that I don't mind this view," he said, and kissed me again. "Any chance I might see more of it?"

"Maybe, if I can hold this body together..."

Sam bent and scooped me into his arms. "I'm in no rush, honey. How long did you say we have?"

"Well, they're in town, and Pop's grilling. Could be hours." All too conscious of our mutually intensifying need, I grinned and batted my eyes. "You feeling lucky, cowboy?"

"Yes, *ma'am*," he said as the door opened wide. "Frank, you're on guard."

Yeehaw, Frank thought dryly, and rolled his eyes as I slammed the door shut.

When one of Eleanor's aides showed Val into her private dining room that night, she and Coileán were already waiting at the table with champagne. "You wanted to discuss something?" Val asked, taking an available chair.

"That was a ruse," she replied, handing him a fizzing flute. "To surviving your first day on the job. And should you need to get anything off your chest, you have an audience."

Val took the drink with gratitude. "Moon and stars," he muttered before sipping, and the others traded knowing looks. "They're arguing *already*. They're back, no one is in a cell—*yet*—and they've already found reason to quarrel."

"Par for the course," said Coileán, sliding him the bottle. "Do you have a staff?"

"A captain and a possible cook, but those are the only overtures I've made," he replied, swirling his champagne. "I don't know them well enough to choose the best people, and besides that, the court's smaller than either of yours."

"They *have* had a difficult millennium," said Eleanor.

Bonnie, I thought, and appeared near the table. "Sam's old neighbor, Bonnie. She's tough, she's organized, and since she's never tried to invade Faerie, she might make a good chief of staff."

"Appreciated," he replied, and gestured to a chair.

"You can't help it, can you?"

I slid into the seat and shrugged. "It's apparently my job to be nosy, so here we are."

"Help yourself, dear," Eleanor said as she pulled the champagne back my way. "Though I admit I'm somewhat surprised to see you tonight. Your predecessor seldom chose to pop by in the flesh."

"Still working out the kinks," I said, producing a flute from the ether. "Anyway, since this is the first time the Three have been together as such in ages…"

They looked at each other, and Coileán lifted his glass. "To keeping the peace."

"Hear, hear," Eleanor muttered, and drank. When she put her glass back on the table, an odd smile played on her lips. "And how is Sam doing, Ros?"

"Fine," I began, then paid attention to more than my immediate concern of maintaining corporeality and realized what I had been ignoring. I was the voice in the back of their heads—whenever they were in the realm, the Three would feel my presence because of our strong connection, and I could most easily focus on them. They could feel it when I was displeased or agitated or excited…

Or…

"*Shit*," I mumbled into my hands. My manifestation didn't need to blush, but my mind was stuck on the idea that this was the correct response to humiliation, and I could feel my cheeks growing warm under my palms.

"What did you do?" Coileán asked, and Eleanor sent the others a quick mental snapshot explaining the situation.

"Oh. *Oh*," laughed Val, "so *that* was what that feeling was this afternoon. I'd wondered what was happening."

"Can I just curl up and die now, please?" I muttered as I replayed my afternoon with Sam from their perspective. Everything had been calm, and then, from out of nowhere, had come a cresting wave of bliss…

But Eleanor gently pulled my hands from my face and

smiled. "Come, now, it's only fair. I imagine you've seen your share of private moments already, haven't you?"

In truth, I had trillions of such moments in my larger memory, and when the group mind had shown me the repository, I had almost immediately—and inadvertently—stumbled upon my own conception. "I try not to think about it," I replied, and filled my glass. So what if the alcohol wouldn't affect me? A girl—or a realm—could always pretend.

CHAPTER 17

Three days later, shortly after Val had a long talk with Bonnie about how she planned to entertain herself and whether she might consider a stint in his employ, Toula rapped on his office door and let herself in. "Got a minute?"

"As many as you need," he replied, hastily putting his stress ball back into his desk. "How are you?"

"Honestly?" She closed the door and flopped onto one of his couches. "Kind of nervous, not going to lie."

"About what?" he asked, rising from his chair to join her. "Has Coileán—"

"*No*, we're fine," she interrupted with a look of reproach. "It's, uh…it's the Arcanum."

Val perched on the armrest and looked at her upside-down face. "What about it?"

"Arnold called. They're going to choose a new grand magus in the morning."

He moved to the couch opposite hers as she sat up. "Arnold is returning to retirement, is he?"

"He's done his time," Toula replied, "and he blames himself for mishandling the probationers, so he told me he wouldn't take it if they asked."

"And the boy? They cleared him of treason, yes?"

She nodded. "Yeah, Bert's off the hook, but he's tainted now, and the powers that be think he's toothless. Fine academic, and he'll probably make a decent teacher, but he's not grand magus material." Propping her feet on the coffee table, she leaned back into the cushion and pressed the heels of her hands against her eyes. "In a way, it's reassuring to see how many of the magi have come out against the Mulligan crew, but there's still plenty of housecleaning to be done on the Council, and the new grand magus is going to have to pull the prisoners out of the dungeon *someday* and deal with them."

"Or he could leave them to rot—I wouldn't mind," said Val. "Who's your pick, then? Do any names rise to the top?"

"Actually, I was thinking of taking a stab at it."

Val paused, caught off guard, then began to nod. "That might work. The Arcanum won't regain stability without change...and pulling in someone from beyond the Council snake pit could move it in the right direction."

She uncovered her eyes and blinked to focus on him. "You're not opposed?"

"No. You're an incredibly talented wizard—"

"Witch-blood. Part of the problem."

"Whatever you wish to call yourself, I'm confident that you could out-cast the Council, probably all at once, and isn't that the primary consideration for the job?"

"One of them," she replied, "and since there's no clear succession, it might be the only one that matters. There's a provision way back in the rules, but I won't bore you."

"You seldom bore me, little sister." Val studied her for a moment, then asked, "Is this what you want?"

"I think so," she replied after a long pause. "Yes. I think I know the Arcanum well enough to be of use."

"And I imagine that our relations with Glastonbury might be somewhat less strained if you were at the helm."

"Quite possibly," she said, and grinned.

"Well, you'll have no opposition from me." Val hesitated, then asked, "Have you spoken of this to Coileán?"

Toula made a face. "Not yet. I wanted to get your take on it first."

"Why?" He laughed, surprised. "You don't need my

permission."

"Not even going to try to play your ace?" she teased. "What's the fun of being king if you can't boss people around?"

But Val smiled and shook his head. "Not you. Never you." Seeing her puzzlement, he reached across the table and took her hands. "You're the closest family I have left, Toula. I love you, and I respect you, and this isn't a matter in which I have any right to order you about. If you're determined to run the Arcanum, then you'll have my support—not as your king, but as your brother. End of discussion." He gave her hands a squeeze before releasing them. "You really should mention this to Coileán, though."

"I will," she said, and sighed. "Thought I might talk to Ellie first."

"Stalling?"

Toula didn't deny it, nor could she.

Eleanor proved to be similarly surprised and supportive when Toula stopped by, but she raised the same question, which only deepened Toula's unease. Finally, having avoided the conversation as long as she could with the rest of the Three, Toula went to Coileán's office that afternoon and stood by the door, wrestling with the knot in her stomach, as she told him what she had in mind. "It's something I really want," she said, avoiding his wide eyes. "And I think I could be good for the Arcanum. I'd already have an open line of communication with the courts," she added, laughing weakly. "Make it easier for you in case of emergency."

Coileán took a moment to flounder in his swirling thoughts, then managed, "I see the perks, but would you be safe there?"

"I can shield pretty well. Decent at warding, too, you know."

Neither spoke of the real issue on their minds, and I watched in frustration as they continued to mumble around the elephant in the room. Finally, growing impatient with their conversation, I appeared and folded my arms with a huff. "*Seriously*, folks. You both know how to make gates, and the wards around the castle are off most of the time. She's not trying to end things with you," I told Coileán, "and he's just scared that you're going to end up like Mom," I said, turning to Toula. "There. Talk about it. You don't have to break up just because Toula wants a new gig."

They stared at me, neither speaking, until Toula mumbled, "Uh…hello to you, too."

Coileán gave me a long, hard look. "The effort is appreciated," he said quietly, "but you and I are going to have a talk about pretending that we all still have privacy, okay?"

"Fine, but you know I'm right."

"As am I," he retorted, and looked at Toula. "The last time there was a grand magus with ties to Faerie, she was the target of a coup. Do you really think this is wise?"

"Wise? Maybe not," she replied, "but I may be the best chance the Arcanum has for recovery. I'm stronger than Carver, I'm older than she was, and I'm not afraid to make heads roll. I *am* a Pavli," she added with a smirk. "And yeah, I fully expect some pushback, but this might be our best chance to deal with the problems that Mulligan brought to the fore. Keep the Arcanum on an even keel while working to make it a partner in the larger magical community instead of a problem. I'm not afraid to try."

"I think you're underestimating what it will take to turn the Arcanum around," he said. "And I don't want you to become a martyr to that cause."

"You're right to be scared, Coileán," I interjected. "The Arcanum's issues run deep. But Toula's right, too—she's better suited for the job than my mother was. I think it's worth a try—and that's the realm's view, not Ros's." Seeing his face work, I added, "You know, there's no way of getting around her ties to Val, but there's no reason to go trumpeting *your* relationship from the rafters in Glastonbury. It doesn't need to be public knowledge that you two are an item. Might be safer that way."

They looked at each other, both anxious and uncertain, and Toula cupped her hand against Coileán's cheek. "I love you. This doesn't change anything."

He covered her hand with his own and closed his eyes. "If something happened to you…"

"You and Val would burn the castle to the ground," she murmured. "Ellie would join in. And the Council will damn well know it." She glanced at me and nodded. "Okay, Ros, this is the part where you go away and we pretend you're not watching."

"Go find Sam," Coileán added as I began to fade.

"Yeah, yeah, you're welcome," I muttered, and took my leave.

Though I could see beyond the gates into the mortal realm, my influence there was drastically reduced, and pressing myself too far past a gate was wearying. Still, I didn't want to miss the Council meeting, and so I hitched a ride with Val, who hadn't been a king long enough to recognize the strangeness of my continued presence in his mind once he crossed the border. Sure, it was sneaky, but it wasn't as if he could have stopped me, had he known.

He and Toula entered Arnold's office through a gate the former grand magus had opened. "You're sure about this?" Arnold asked as Toula straightened her black suit.

"Fairly," she replied, and tugged her jacket into place. "Okay, let's go crash the Council."

The magi seated around the conference table barely glanced up when Arnold entered, but they jumped in shock when Toula and Val followed him in and closed the door. "Good morning," said Toula as Arnold took his seat. "You're choosing a grand magus, correct?"

"That was the plan," said a magus with a strong

German accent, "and why are you—"

"I invoke the Ivanovich Rule," she said, planting her palms on the table.

A few of the magi seemed perplexed by her declaration, and Arnold came to the rescue. "The Ivanovich Rule provides that in cases of uncertain succession, when there is no clear candidate to serve as grand magus, any wizard may challenge the other potential candidates in single combat. The one left standing gets the job."

"And it's only been used twice, once for Grand Magus Ivanovich himself," said the Australian head of Arc 7, vehemently shaking her head. "It's barely more than a footnote—"

"Because the succession has been generally clear until now. A candidate has almost always arisen eventually. But we don't have the luxury of time to wait for someone to come of age," said Arnold. "If Ms. Pavli wants to try, I won't stand against it."

The magi muttered among themselves, and finally, the German spoke again. "Ms. Pavli's...*talent*...is no secret," he said, tapping his pen against the table. "Allowing her to enter combat when she has enchantment at her disposal—"

"I'll limit myself to spellcraft," Toula interrupted. "If that suits. Are you challenging me?"

"No, because you are unqualified," he retorted. "A witch-blood—"

"There is no rule preventing a witch-blood from acquiring magushood. Believe me, I was as surprised as you are, but it seems the issue has never come up." She leaned into the table and smiled. "There's never been a mongrel like me, you see. So come on, kids, who's first?"

"Oh, right, you plan to fight," snapped the Australian, "and if anyone bests you, big brother is there to lend a hand, yeah?" She jabbed her finger toward Val, who leaned against the bookcase, silently watching with his arms crossed. "Why not just throw the chain to the courts and let them squabble over it, if we're going this route?"

At that, Val quietly said, "I claim no authority over my sister. What she does, she does, and I will not insult her by offering to fight her battles for her. With that said, if she should win today, and if any harm of the type that befell Helen Carver should subsequently come to her, then there would be hell to pay."

"Threatening us already?" said an Italian.

"I don't make threats," Val replied.

"A proposition for you," Toula interjected, drawing the table's attention back to her. "If no one wants to fight me, then bring me aboard on a trial basis. Should someone more qualified come up, I'll step aside."

A thin woman at the far end of the table, the American head of Arc 1, began to laugh in disbelief. "Do you honestly think that anyone here is going to stand back and let Grand Magus *Pavli* happen? Get real. I think we all know what happened the last time a Pavli—"

"My father was far from perfect," she said, her voice clear and firm. "I'm not going to stand here and defend his actions. But Missy Harrison told me the truth about him: he was trying to get justice for someone he believed the Arcanum had wronged. The wizards he killed were assassins in training…and if the corps then was anything like the corps has been in the last twenty years, maybe he did us a favor. In any case," she continued, staring at the magi one by one, "Apollonios didn't raise me. The Arcanum did. I was fostered by six different families of seemingly reputable wizards, some of whom even managed to look past my surname from time to time. So if there is something in me with which you find fault, don't blame my father. Don't blame my mother, either—I only met her in the last few minutes of her life, and she wasn't at all pleased with me by the end. If there's something wrong with me, let the blame fall to the Arcanum, because I am nothing if not a product of your kind mercies."

As the table sat in silence, Arnold cleared his throat and

rose. "Does anyone accept Ms. Pavli's challenge, then? Any other contenders for the office?" When no one spoke, he said, "Very well. We vote. Toula, if you would, please step outside."

She and Val headed into the hallway, and he patted her back as they waited for the outcome. Ten long minutes later, Arnold emerged and gave her a tight smile. "Grand Magus, the Council asks that you rejoin the meeting."

"I'll wait," Val whispered, settling onto a bench, and Toula, smiling in quiet satisfaction, followed Arnold back into the Council's meeting room.

She was willing to make concessions. At the Council's request, Toula agreed to keep the news of her appointment quiet for a few days so that the magi could decide how best to inform the rest of the Arcanum that their new leader was a witch-blooded Pavli. Still, when the meeting concluded, Arnold took Toula upstairs to the larger offices, including Bert's, and asked her to choose one. She selected an empty suite with a lovely view of the town, and Arnold watched as she began redecorating, adding an accent wall and turning the tops of the arched windows to stained glass. "Have I forgotten anything critical?" she asked Val, who was testing her new couch.

"Guards."

"Ha. Anything furniture-related, I mean."

"It looks lovely," said Arnold, admiring her oriental rug. "I'll have a computer and telephone set up before you move in." He gave her a once-over, then remarked, "You know, you and I were in the same year."

"Were we?" asked Toula, adding cushions to the window seats.

"I'm only about a month your junior. Sorry I didn't know you back then."

I studied the two of them: Toula, eternally a dark-haired young woman who seemed barely older than me, and Arnold, a gray-haired man with glasses who looked every day of his nearly six decades.

"I was wondering," said Arnold, "if you planned to do this with glamour."

Toula glanced up from her decorating, found him waiting with his hands in his robe pockets, and shook her head. "Nope. I spent too many years trying to impress the Arcanum—now they can deal with me."

"Understood, but it's obvious you've not aged."

"So?" She added a last throw pillow and dusted off her hands. "I'm witch-blooded. I'm also the best damn wizard in this realm or any other, and if anyone would like to prove me wrong, my offer stands." She paused, but Arnold had no rebuttal, and she smiled as she came around her desk. "Now, be honest with me. How much blowback is there going to be if I invite my brother to my ceremony?"

In the end, Val filled Toula's office with flowers but opted to stay away. "The last time this happened, it was Aiden watching Helen, and I'm not one to tempt fate," he explained. "You look lovely, by the way."

She'd chosen a dark suit and a deep blue robe that brought out her eyes, and her hair lacked its customary colorful accents. "Kind of feels like I'm playing dress-up," she said, grinning as she did a quick twirl. "Who'd have ever thought *I'd* need a robe?"

Val lifted her necklace, a large sapphire in a simple gold setting, and nodding approvingly. "Your own design?"

"A gift."

"I wonder who the giver could have been," he replied, rolling his eyes, then kissed her cheek. "Go on, be amazing. I'm here if you need me."

The Arcanum hadn't put on a full ceremony for an incoming grand magus in years. Since Toula had never been through a magus ceremony, however, the Council gave her the all-out production that Friday evening, an hour-long affair of speeches—even one from Bert—

followed by a reception that lasted half the night, which I caught in snippets of her memory on her next trip back. As Glastonbury was almost half a day ahead of Faerie that night, Toula remained in her new apartment in the castle to begin to acclimate to the time, but she made sure to call Val and Coileán before turning in to reassure them both that she was alive and well. "I'll be over next weekend," she promised Coileán before hanging up. "Assuming magic as we know it doesn't end in the interim."

Saturday morning was sunny and uneventful in Faerie—I couldn't see the point in throwing a miserably warm or wet summer day into the mix—and I watched as the Three went about their business. Eleanor took a hot bath with a bottomless cup of tea. Coileán surprised Dad and Aiden outside the barn with a bag of doughnuts before they could embark on another day of their endless mapping project. Val, meanwhile, had opted for an early start with the growing stack of complaints from his court, each of them received or transcribed by Bonnie and delivered in a string-tied bundle with breakfast. He was refilling his espresso cup when his phone rang, and seeing the name on the ID, he smiled as he opened the line. "Do you have any feet left, or did you wear them down to the bone in service of the library?"

"We didn't finish," said Seamus, sounding decidedly less jovial than his uncle. "Badger's had a heart attack."

"*What?*"

"A heart attack," he repeated, picking up speed. "She's stable, but she's in hospital in Virginia Beach. They're talking about airlifting her to Richmond or Charlottesville, there's better cardiologists there—"

"Slow down," said Val. "They're treating her?"

"They're running tests. I had no idea this was coming, she's been healthy, we've been doing everything right—"

"Seamus, listen to me. Are you listening?"

"Yeah," he mumbled, though he sounded like he was on the verge of flying into a fresh panic.

"I'll come by tonight to see if I can be of help," Val told him. "After hours, when we're unlikely to be disturbed. Send me a picture of the room and let me know when to come."

A moment later, the phone beeped with the requested information. *13:30 here*, Seamus noted. *Come after 20. Will update if moved.*

Val was impatient for the rest of the morning, keeping to himself and periodically checking his silent phone. By midafternoon, it was finally safe to go, but then Kiet stopped by with a report of fighting in the mountains—a skirmish between one of Mab's devotees and a half faerie who'd fled her court for the remotest parts of Canada until finally settling in Vancouver. Val followed him to the scene, rounded up the bloodied combatants, resisted his rising urge to throw them both into the sea, and informed them in a quiet tone that cautioned of a storm coming behind it that this was their one warning. Leaving Kiet to ascertain that they went home without further violence, Val hurried back to his office, studied the photograph Seamus had sent, then opened a gate into Badger's hospital room.

I watched from the far side as he padded around the dark space, letting the light from his office guide his steps. The first thing he came across was the spare bed, on which Seamus, heavily glamoured as usual and still wearing his dirty race clothes, was sleeping. Someone had left one of the rails down, and Seamus, having covered the metal with a sheet, had collapsed into an exhausted nap. A partial curtain separated the two beds, and I heard Badger uncertainly ask, "Hello? Someone there?"

She sounded weak and raspy but very much alive, which gave me a bit of relief.

Val pulled back the curtain and took in the situation: Badger tucked beneath a beige blanket and cheap white sheet, dressed in a hospital gown and halfway propped on pillows as she read on her phone. She looked cleaner than

Seamus—someone had washed the sweat off of her, at least—but her face was bare, her white hair was limp and mussed from the bed, and her left arm was connected to an IV pole by a length of tubing and medical tape. The gown was low and loose enough to show the network of sensors taped to her chest, which fed into a beeping cardiac monitor.

"Hiya," she said, giving Val a little wave, then joked, "Don't let Nath find out—I'm in no position for a fight right now."

"How do you feel?" he asked, sliding between her bed and the window.

"Eh." Badger offered a one-shouldered shrug and pointed to the monitor. "Heart's back at it, so I could be worse. Plenty of paramedics at the race, and they got me on a clotbuster before I had much damage. Ran a catheter through, but they didn't have to put a stent in, and I'm not going to need a bypass, so that's good news. Really, I'm fortunate. They'll turn me out in a day or two."

Much of that, I realized, was worse than Greek to Val, who seemed unconvinced by Badger's tired optimism. "You don't have a healing spell in place," he chided.

"Because of all this lovely, very expensive equipment," she explained. "I'll throw together something once I'm discharged, but I'd hate to ruin the nice doctors' toys."

She put the phone down, and he took her free hand, carefully avoiding the metal railing. "You could have died. You realize that, don't you?"

"Wasn't lost on me. Unfortunately, the ticker's not as young as it used to be. Nor is the rest of me," she said with a chuckle. "But they'll give me medication, and I'll take care with my diet, be better about seeing a GP…"

"Hannah," he murmured as her voice trailed off, "it's time. Your fight is over."

"Really?" she countered. "Has someone told Nath, then?"

"You know you can't hold her back forever. There's

help now. Toula's in as grand magus—"

"*Toula?*"

"Took office last night in Glastonbury. And if—when," he allowed—"Nath makes an attempt on this realm again, we will be there to stop her. I swear it. But you've done more than your duty, and the invitation stands."

With Badger still in the mortal realm, I couldn't see into her mind, but her contemplative frown told me she was mulling the offer over. As she thought about it, Val said, "It is your choice. I understand if you choose not to—if you wish to live your span and die, that's your right."

"I'm not in love with the notion," she replied, "but...are you religious, Val?"

It was his turn to frown into space as he pondered. "Not particularly," he said after a moment, "but it would not surprise me if I were wrong."

"Never been much of a churchgoer, myself," said Badger. "Mama was—Texan, you know—and she was convinced there was something beyond all of this, but I've never been certain. I mean, I like the idea of seeing them again someday, but..."

"Not yet?" Val offered.

"No. And...you know, Seamie, I...I don't want to lose him again. This is where I've been needed, doing what I've been doing, but I..." She struggled with her thoughts, then confessed, "I'm scared. I really am. You go about life, and everything's all right, no one's coming to kill you, and then...*wham*. You wake up with a needle in your arm and electrodes all over your chest, and you make yourself face the fact that you're not getting any younger and you're falling apart." Badger waited as Val sat at the foot of her bed, then told him, "I'm sixty-eight. No cancer yet, no diabetes, blood pressure's under control—I've been fortunate thus far. Still have at least most of my faculties," she added with a quick grin. "But I peaked a long time ago, and it's only going to get worse, and I…honestly, I'm fucking terrified," she confessed. "Maybe I'll feel better about it once I'm out of here, but waking up in hospital does tend to make one confront one's own mortality."

While they had been talking, Seamus had begun to stir, and he hurriedly slid off his bed and joined them. "Sorry, I must have fallen asleep," he said as Val motioned him closer. "Still stable. Looking good, but the cardiologist wants another check in the morning." Glancing back and forth between their faces, he asked, "Did I miss something?"

"I was reminding Badger that the invitation stands," said Val. "And given her current condition, this might be the time to revisit it." He lifted his hand as Seamus began to protest and spoke over him. "This isn't about coercing you out of this realm, nephew. I respect your choice to stay. But I also respect what Badger has done. The Fringe here can carry on without you," he said, turning to her again. "And Amy and Kip have decided to stay in the settlement, have they not? You've fought as hard as they have, if not harder, but you've done all you can to protect this realm. Pass the torch to someone else."

Badger considered it a moment longer, looking from Val and Seamus to the open gate near the wall, then nodded curtly. "Once I start pulling things off, we won't have long. There's an alarm. I'll need someone's help."

Val smiled and moved out of the way, and Seamus slipped as close to the steel implements surrounding his wife as he dared. "IV first, love, the cardiac monitor's the bigger problem. Do you want me to—"

"Just give me your hand," she said, and gripped him to distract herself while she ripped off the tape and pulled the needle from her arm. Freed from the IV pole, she fumbled with the bed railing until it dropped, then swung her legs over the side and waited until she was steady and the tempo of the beeps returned to its previous rhythm. "Seamie?"

"Right here," he said, rubbing her shoulders through her thin sleeves.

Badger looked up at him and bit her lip. "Are you certain? We don't have to go if you're happy in—"

"I couldn't care less where we are as long as you're happy and healthy," he insisted. "And I'll go back to Rigby and pack. Let's patch you up, get you healing, and take it from there, eh?" He tapped one of the adhesive patches on her chest and smiled. "Pick or rip?"

"Get it over with," she replied, and helped him free her from the machine, which began to wail with the lost signal. Wobbling with as much dignity as she could muster barefoot and in a backless gown, Badger let Seamus help her through the gate, and Val closed it behind them just as the duty nurse ran in with a crash cart.

Safe in Val's office, Seamus half-carried Badger to a couch and made her comfortable. "If you'd work up the healing enchantment, Val, I'd be grateful," he said, fussing with the pillows. "You've got the advantage on me..." Noticing that his hand suddenly looked forty years younger, Seamus realized that his glamour had dropped and cringed. "Sorry, Badge, forgot about the border. I'll fix my face—"

"Wait," said Val, perching on the coffee table beside them. As he quickly crafted the necessary enchantment around her, he murmured, "I can't give you true youth...can I?" he asked, glancing at the ceiling as if he expected to find me hiding in the puffy clouds of the mosaic.

No. I can't even do that, I told him.

"I thought not. But that doesn't mean I can't give you the *appearance* of it, if you'd prefer," he continued, looking at Badger. "Make you match again, but in the other direction."

She glanced at Seamus, then back at Val. "How vain am I going to seem if I take you up on that?"

"Not at all," he said, and grinned. After a quick

rummage through Seamus's memory for reference images, he created a second enchantment around her, then produced a hand mirror and passed it her way. "Close? Anything you'd like to change?"

Badger took one look at her smoothed cheeks and darkened hair, against which her white stripe once again stood out prominently, and laughed in disbelief. "You're kind," she said, still staring at the glass, "but I've never looked this good."

"I beg to differ," said Seamus, smiling almost shyly as he took her hand. "That's how you've always looked to me."

"Then you need glasses," she retorted, but smiled back at him.

"The two of you can dispute this as long as you like, then tell me what to change," said Val, rising from the table. "Why don't you stay with me for a few days? Give the enchantment time to work, then decide whether you want to move to the settlement or build around here."

"We don't want to impose," Badger began, but Val waved it aside.

"Toula's not using her wing, I have a decent cook, and the breeze can't hurt," he said, gesturing toward the western doors.

"Not a bad view," said Seamus, rubbing his chin. "Where are we, anyway? I don't recognize those mountains…"

"I'll show you the maps later," he replied, and produced a bathrobe for Badger as Seamus helped her back to her feet. "Go explore once she's feeling herself again." He helped her to dress and opened the office door, revealing one of the many fountains and a glimpse of the distant courtyard. "I think you've earned a vacation, don't you?"

With Badger on the mend, the Fringe settlement at peace,

and the courts as calm as they ever were, I began to relax into my new normal, testing my limits and grappling with my abilities. Manifestation grew easier, if still tiring, with practice, and Sam was patience incarnate with me. He'd been hard at work as well with one of Eleanor's aides, and without a crisis to distract him, Sam proved to be a quick study. I knew he still missed his mother terribly—he couldn't hide that from me if he'd tried—but keeping him busy helped the long grieving process. In the meantime, the spark that had ignited between us was beginning to flare into something more, and I gave myself permission to go for it and…well…be happy.

There was just one problem.

Though Frank was more at ease with my altered state and had no reservations about letting Sam get close, he was still miserable. I tried not to pry at first, but soon enough, I couldn't help myself. He was lost—unmoored, adrift, and bored. In his dreams, he frequently returned to Glastonbury, and he woke unsettled, grappling with a loss he couldn't quite describe. I wanted to help him, but I couldn't take him back, and I didn't know how to help my morose partner find meaning in a life largely spent in the barn. Sure, it suited his siblings well enough, but Frank wanted more than Dad or I could give him.

As promised, a week after taking office, Toula sneaked back to Faerie to visit her brother and her boyfriend, but to my surprise, she didn't come alone. "Ros?" she called as she crossed into Val's office. "I'm bringing a friend. Don't be difficult, okay?"

What sort of friend?

She twitched as she heard me in her head. "Arcanum. He won't be here long."

Fine.

I monitored all of the realm's gates simultaneously, but it always felt different when wizards came through—not bad, but noticeable. Still, Toula's new friend looked decidedly unwizardly. He was maybe five and a half feet tall and chubby, a short man in cargo pants and loafers with a salt-and-peppered blond ponytail down to his shoulder blades. His shirt was a tent-like Hawaiian number, bright orange flowers atop a background of curling waves. The only feature that didn't fit his apparent slacker persona were his eyes: light blue, inquisitive, and partially obscured by round glasses that darkened when he stepped into a sunny patch.

Val regarded him with the same suspicion I did, but he nodded and closed the gate. "And you are..."

"This is Ted Girard," said Toula as her companion took in his spacious surroundings. "I told him he could meet Frank."

That gave me pause, and Val, sensing my disquiet, pressed her. "For what purpose?"

"Just a chat," said Ted, smiling nervously. "Maybe a proposition, if he's interested. If, uh...if that's all right, my lord?"

Val nodded. "If he'll see you. I wouldn't try to force a dragon to do anything he was disinclined to do, were I you. Friendly warning."

"Good point," Ted muttered, and looked to Toula, who hurried him out through an intra-realm gate with a mouthed *Thank you* to her brother.

The gate opened next door to the barn, and while Toula led Ted to the house to let my parents know they were there, I appeared by Frank and nudged him awake from his late-afternoon nap. "Someone's here to see you, bud," I told him as he blinked groggily at me. "Toula's comfortable with him, so maybe don't eat him right away, huh?"

He grunted and stretched his wings, and by the time Toula and Ted emerged, he was curled up in the sun, waiting. Toula headed for him without hesitation, but Ted held back for a few seconds before grinning like a kid and hurrying after her.

"Frank," she said once Ted had caught up, "this is Ted

Girard from Glastonbury."

"Well, not originally," Ted babbled as he studied Frank. "By way of Toronto and a stint in Montana until last year. My *goodness*, Mr. White, you're magnificent."

Frank snorted, amused. *You've heard of me?*

"Mostly from Antony Copeland, but Grand Magus Lowe filled in some details. I mean, you think you have some idea of how big a dragon is, and then you realize how much you've lowballed." Frank's amusement was broadcast that time, and Ted stepped back a pace and rubbed his neck. "Sorry. I'm being rude, aren't I? I'd shake your hand, but I'm pretty sure you'd crush me."

How do you know Antony?

"IT," he explained. "I was the guy who found the Archives breach—Antony hid it pretty well, but he's got a lot to learn. Smart kid. I talked him into working with me."

"Ted's more than just IT," said Toula. "He has an archaeology background."

"I was doing fieldwork when Mulligan recalled everyone," he muttered. "Can't do much digging from the silo, so I spent a lot of time with computers and the Archives. I couldn't convince Mulligan to let me do much in the way of upgrading their systems, but Lowe and Wold were warming up to the idea. Anyway, after seeing how much trouble that damn diary caused, the new boss here"—he jabbed his thumb toward Toula—"is letting me put together a team."

A team? Frank echoed, cocking his head. *What sort?*

"I'm looking for square pegs," said Ted. Sensing Frank's confusion, he clarified, "World's full of round holes. I'm after the square pegs that don't fit just right. The people with unique skillsets. Basically, the plan is to systematically comb the Archives for mentions of possible lost artifacts—books, scrolls, magic weaponry, what have you—separate the myths from the real deal, and try to track down the missing items. Won't be easy, might not work, but I think it's worth a try if we can prevent another diary incident." He paused and shoved his hands into the topmost of his pants' many pockets. "I was wondering if you might be interested."

He was—I could feel it in his thoughts—but Frank was cautious. *I'm not qualified for anything like that.*

"Sure, you are. She says you're a quick learner," he replied, nodding to Toula, "and if nothing else, you're a mind reader with a built-in flamethrower, and that's nothing to sneeze at."

That's…true, Frank allowed.

"Antony says you're all right. Like I said, he's joined up, and I've got a couple of other prospects on the horizon, but we're in early days yet. Now, the only consideration is that we'd have to get you into a form that could fit inside the castle—"

Not a problem.

"Really? Great!" Ted beamed. "Well, you think it over and get back with me, eh? No rush. But if you're interested, let me know."

Frank continued to stare at the place their gate had been long after it closed, and I whispered, *If you don't go, you're crazy.* His thoughts began to cloud—a touch of separation anxiety, worry about me, fear of being on his own in a castle full of wizards—and I rushed to soothe him. *I'll be fine, bud, and I'll always be here. If it'll make you happy, go see what they have to offer.*

He stood and stretched. *I'll think about it.*

Good. In the meantime… I materialized in my usual spot at the back of his neck and gave him a pat. "Want to go for a flight for old times' sake? You and me?"

Frank looked back and flashed his razor teeth. *I can carry one more. Call him.*

Soon enough, Sam was climbing aboard, and Frank laughed to himself at Sam's nervousness. *I'm not going to drop you*, he protested as Sam situated himself in the sweet spot.

"It's not you I'm worried about," he replied. "I never

learned to ride, remember? Horses hate me."

You may not have noticed, but I'm not a horse.

"Smartass," he muttered, sliding my old helmet into place. "Okay, how does this—"

The rest of his question turned into a scream as Frank ran and leapt for the sky, but by the time he leveled out, Sam was laughing through his terror. I closed my eyes, wrapped my arms around his waist, and enjoyed the familiar sensations of flight—the motion of Frank's body, the thump and crack of his wings, the wind and sun in my face. As he circled, giving Sam time to acclimate, I let my consciousness spread to take in the entirety of the realm— *my* realm, my second self. Far in the distance, farther than Dad or I had ever flown, were the undefined edges of Faerie, places ripe for creation, lands yet unborn that waited to flow from me.

The great western sea would have another shore, I decided, and made it so.

I opened my eyes again and gave Frank a pat. *Come on,* I said, speaking to both of them, *aim for the sun. I have so much I want to show you.*

ACKNOWLEDGEMENTS

Hello again, dear reader, and thank you for coming along on this ride. I hope you've enjoyed—it's not over yet!

My thanks go to the wonderful Novel Chicks for their friendship and feedback. Adam Domby continues to make these books better, and I'm grateful for his input.

And yes, here's to you, Mom and Dad.

ABOUT THE AUTHOR

When not writing fiction, Ash Fitzsimmons is an appellate attorney and an unrepentant car singer.

Find her online:
www.ashfitzsimmons.com